WINGS OVER VALLETTA

a&b

WINGS OVER VALLETTA

TRACY COOK

Allison & Busby Limited
11 Wardour Mews
London W1F 8AN
allisonandbusby.com

First published in Great Britain by Allison & Busby in 2026.

A CIP catalogue record for this book is available from
the British Library.

First Edition

ISBN 978-0-7490-3329-3

By choosing this product, you help take care of the world's forests.
Learn more: www.fsc.org.

Printed and bound in Great Britain by Clays Ltd. Elcograf S.p.A

EU GPSR Authorised Representative
LOGOS EUROPE, 9 rue Nicolas Poussin, 17000, LA ROCHELLE, France
E-mail: Contact@logoseurope.eu

For Jonathan, always

Chapter One

16th January 1941

'How many bombers do the Italians have?'

Michael Fortini grinned from under his shock of dark hair, tomato from lunch still on his top lip.

Kitty turned from writing *Chapter Three* on the blackboard, chalk poised in her hand. Dust floated in the sunlight streaming through the tall classroom windows, an unusually warm day for January. She bit her lip trying to stop herself laughing. Heavens, he must be the cheekiest eleven-year-old in the whole of Valletta, God love him, but the fact she didn't want to stop his endless questions – it had been 'When will Malta get Spitfires?' two minutes ago, as if *she* knew – showed just how much she wasn't cut out for teaching. Especially Dickens. She couldn't believe she was still here, really, four years on. After all, joining the Britannia School had been yet another of Father's bloody ideas to 'cheer her up', after they arrived on the island.

Michael threw a paper plane, RAF roundels neatly drawn on the wings, across the room and tilted back, so his gas mask fell off the chair and thumped to the ground. The children giggled.

'*Ghoxrin miljun*,' called out Giuseppe.

'English, please.' Kitty smiled at the little boy crammed into a sweater that was far too small for him.

'Twenty million.' He grinned round at the children. 'At least that's how many shillings Michael would pay for a *ħobża biż-żejt*.'

They all laughed. Everyone knew how Michael loved his tomato panne. Kitty smiled. Let them laugh. After all, outside these walls there was so much to cry about, what with the island besieged and the Italians bombing them. At least Father's jewel of the fleet, HMS *Illustrious*, had made it to safety. The whole of Valletta had gone down to Grand Harbour to cheer as tugs pulled the listing, damaged aircraft carrier in. One day of joy at least.

Miss Lavigne, Adela, must have been having the same thoughts, as across the corridor, she was thumping the piano and singing a rousing chorus of 'Happy Days Are Here Again'. That nightclub voice of hers was wasted on the little ones, but still, it was a wonder that old dragon, Miss Mazelli, hadn't swept in to stop her.

As the laughter quieted, Kitty waved a copy of the novel.

'Class, let's get back to Pip—'

The high-pitched wail of the air raid siren drowned out her words.

Even after all these months, that whine still made Kitty's stomach drop, the hairs on the back of her neck prickle. The children jumped up.

'Hurry, children. Go to the shelter,' Kitty cried, as they grabbed their gas masks and scrambled into the corridor.

'Not again.' Adela rolled her big eyes at Kitty. She led a small child in each hand, herding the rest before her towards the arched front doors.

'Father warned me they might come after *Illustrious* today.'

'*Zut alors.*' Fear shone in Adela's dark eyes as she glanced down at the small, frightened children. 'Let's hope it's over quickly, then.'

'Yes. You go first.' Kitty held the front door open, glancing behind her to check all the children had left her classroom. 'I'll give you a hand with them when everyone's out. They get so upset.'

Kitty ushered her class out onto the narrow, stepped street and glanced up at the tall old houses with their covered wooden balconies, brightly painted in dark greens, sky blues and beetroot reds. Washing strung between the windows flapped in the breeze. How could this familiar old street be dangerous?

But already overhead, engines droned and the *rat-a-tat* of anti-aircraft guns firing echoed from the old stone bastions round Grand Harbour.

'Hurry, hurry,' Kitty called as the children ran ahead, gas masks banging against their legs. They bounded like the milk goats up the steep limestone steps of St John Street, joining the people streaming into the sandbagged shelter on the corner. Opposite, Mr Zejtun slammed the shutter down on his bakery and hurried up the steps.

Crump, crump, crump. Explosions echoed and smoke and the smell of cordite, sharp like nail polish, filled the air. The aircraft drone grew louder.

Kitty glanced down the far end of the street to the blue sea, sparkling in the sunshine. Across the water, in the dockyards on the far side of Grand Harbour, staccato guns fired from the decks of the huge aircraft carrier. Above it, a trail of black and white puffs of smoke was stitched across the sky, where rows of black crosses roared. A bomb whistled as it fell, exploding in a deafening boom. Kitty clapped her hands to her ears. A huge fountain of water blew up over the ship.

'They *are* after *Illustrious*!' Kitty shouted.

God, was Father over there today?

'*Malajr*! *Malajr*!' Stout Miss Mazelli bustled past with the older children. 'Quick!'

'Hurry, *chérie*,' Adela called as she struggled with two little ones up the shallow stone steps, her voice almost lost over the boom of the guns.

Crikey, even in the middle of an air raid, Adela still exuded Parisian chic, juggling her handbag, her legs wobbling in pale blue heels. But little Carmela Cortis trailed behind, bless her, struggling to hold both her mask and her teddy.

Kitty swept her up in her arms.

The little girl's chubby legs clung round her waist, one soft arm gripping tight round her neck, the other clutching the bear. Kitty's heart squeezed. How she adored this little girl. Alice would be the same age as her now.

Carmela pressed her soft curls against Kitty's cheek and Kitty breathed in her sweet smell of warm skin and Pears soap. Would Alice smell like this now?

Kitty checked in her pocket for the little photograph wallet, her talisman. Still there, still safe.

Stop it, stop it. Focus on the children.

'It's alright, sweetheart, I've got you. Not far now.' She hurried up the steps, passing Mr Manduca, who dropped a crate of tomatoes and ran, not caring where they rolled.

The noise was deafening. Another huge explosion, too close, rattled the windows in the buildings. Kitty startled. Carmela cried out, dropped the teddy. They watched, as if in slow motion, as the golden-furred bear tumbled down the steps. He landed ten yards away, face down, outside a café, caught by the leg of a table. An abandoned coffee cup still steamed on top.

'Teddy!' screamed Carmela, her hand a starfish reaching for him.

'Leave it, Kitty!' Adela shouted up ahead.

'My teddy. Teddy!' Carmela's distraught eyes burnt into Kitty's.

An echo of another look, years before, when she'd let another little girl down. Kitty blinked.

She had a choice this time.

Quick as a flash she raced up to Adela.

'Take her!' she yelled, thrusting Carmela into Adela's arms.

'No, Kitty!'

A split-second look passed between them, Adela's dark eyes aghast.

Kitty turned and ran back down the steps. Huge shadows swooped across the sunlit street. She glanced up. Aircraft like birds of prey with strange bent gull wings blocked out the blue sky. She froze. Arrow shapes of five, dozens of them, wave after wave.

What the hell was going on? She'd never seen so many aircraft before. She pressed her hands to her ears, the roar of so many engines making her very insides vibrate.

Hot metal shrapnel whizzed past her shoulder. She shrieked, jumped aside, as it clattered, still smoking, on the step beside her. Her heart slammed against her ribs. Shrapnel drummed like hail on the steps near the bear. She screamed.

The shrill whistle of a bomb dropping. She flinched, ducking. Christ, was it overhead? Please God, not here, not now.

She dashed down the last few steps, cursing her too-tight T-bar shoes, and grabbed the bear. Sweat slicked her back. Too close, the bomb exploded. A deafening crash, louder than thunder, the rumbling of tumbling masonry, shattering glass. The ground shook like an earthquake. A shower of thick dust poured on her head and shoulders. Choking smoke filled her lungs and she staggered, coughing. She glanced up, terrified the houses might collapse.

Up ahead, the Air Raid Precaution warden at the shelter frantically blew his whistle.

It was then she heard it. A chilling, high-pitched scream that drilled into her ears and her soul. She glanced back at Grand Harbour, swathed in thick grey smoke, as a plane dropped in a steep dive like an arrow, aiming for *Illustrious*'s deck. She watched, mesmerised, as at the very last second, the plane released its bomb and pulled right up. The boom of an explosion echoed across the harbour and a fountain of water, taller than the ship, sprayed up.

She took a sharp breath.

Stukas.

She'd seen them on the Gaumont News at The Majestic.

Her heart pounded.

Christ, was this the Nazis?

She turned, fixed her eyes on the shelter door and raced back up the street.

'*Chérie*, are you alright?' Adela pulled her into a tight hug. '*Mon Dieu*! Are you hurt?'

'I'm fine, really.'

But Kitty trembled. What had she been thinking? She handed

the bear to Carmela, whose eyes lit up with joy as she buried her face in its fur. Kitty sank onto the bench. She brushed the dust off her pale green cardigan and did her best to throw a reassuring smile at the children who stared up at her in the gloom, their eyes wide with fear.

'You could have been killed!' Adela whispered. In the candlelight, the whites of her eyes glittered in her face. She gestured at Carmela, cuddling the teddy. 'And for a toy?'

'I had to.'

Their eyes met.

'I know, *chérie*.'

Loss washed over Kitty, triggered, as it so often was, when she least expected it, by the cry of a newborn, a mother kissing a small child, a little girl playing hopscotch. The worst thing was that over the years she had grown used to missing her, but that was not the same thing as getting over it, as Mother and Father thought she had.

Adela smiled and shook her head. 'You're an idiot.' She nudged Kitty with her shoulder. 'But a brave idiot.'

Kitty squeezed Adela's hand, grateful she understood. The only person who did, really. The only person she had ever confided in about Alice. And Adela had been a complete brick about it, hadn't judged her, like the rest of the world had, this determined young woman who'd fled to Fez with five francs, a Josephine Baker songbook and a dream.

Kitty had trusted her from the day they'd met in the school staff lavatory, as Adela changed into a slinky red dress and heels that should have had Miss Mazelli firing her on the spot. '*Chérie*, can you zip me up?' Adela had asked her, as if people changed into evening dresses every day after teaching at school.

Kitty, stunned, had obliged. 'I'm singing at The Star tonight, but don't tell anyone.' And Adela had winked and climbed out of the window to escape through the alleyway.

She'd brought colour and life back into Kitty's grey world back then. Still did.

An explosion rocked the tunnel, cut deep into the limestone rock. They instinctively ducked and covered their heads. Dirt and grit showered from the ceiling, catching in Kitty's hair, filling her nostrils.

God, would she ever get used to this?

She glanced round the mattresses and outstretched legs, people crammed on benches and folding chairs in the low-ceilinged shelter. The musty air was thick with the odour of damp wool, bodies and fear. Here and there, candles and oil lamps flickered from niches in the walls, illuminating pinned-up pictures of the Blessed Virgin. An old woman in a headscarf, fingers busy on her worn rosary beads, muttered a prayer. No one was playing cards or knitting, like they usually did. Everyone sat stiff, tense, silent.

Boom, boom, boom.

Explosions thundered above. Such relentless ferocity – it was like nothing she'd heard before. The shelter filled with smoke. Kitty coughed, her throat sore from the caustic dust, and helped the children pull on their gas masks.

Michael rocked, his arms round his knees.

'Will my Omm be alright?'

'Sweetheart, of course she will. She'll be in a shelter with your little sister.'

God, Kitty hoped her own mother had gone to a shelter too. She usually sat through air raids in her favourite wing-backed armchair in the drawing room. 'That little Fascist Mussolini isn't going to drive me underground,' she always said, unswerving as ever. Please let her have gone.

Even the older children with Miss Mazelli were trying hard not to cry, shutting their eyes or pressing their hands to their ears.

Carmela sucked her thumb, tears trickling down her cheeks, and Kitty pulled her onto her lap.

'Me want Omm.'

'I know, poppet.' Kitty stroked her hair. 'It's alright, you're safe here.'

She kissed the top of Carmela's velvet dark hair as Carmela's rosebud mouth whispered to Ted. But it was her lashes, long and dark, fluttering on her pale cheeks, that reminded her of another set of lashes on baby cheeks. Kitty shut her eyes.

Where was Alice now? Also huddled and scared, perhaps in some London Underground station? Her chest tightened. Would someone be taking good care of her?

As if she could read her thoughts, Adela leant across and took her hand. '*Chérie*, she will be alright.' Her gentle brown eyes stared deep into Kitty's. 'And you – you must forgive yourself.'

A lump filled Kitty's throat. She blinked and looked away.

A deafening crash shook the walls. Carmela whimpered and Kitty held her tight. Dust poured from the rough-hewn ceiling.

'*Mon Dieu*, will the roof hold?' Adela stared up at it, terrified. 'There'll be nothing left of Valletta.'

'Holy Mother of God.' An old man in a knitted waistcoat jumped to his feet. 'What the hell's going on? The Italians usually only send one or two planes to bomb us.'

'This isn't the Italians.' The ARP warden by the shelter door stepped forward, straightening his tin hat. 'It's Hitler. He's finally sent the bloody Luftwaffe here.'

No one spoke.

Fear settled like a dense fog. They all knew what had happened when the Germans invaded Europe last year. The Nazi swastika flying over Paris . . .

Kitty's heart thudded. Were they to be invaded? Was she going to die here, on this island? Never know anything about her daughter? Not even know if she was alive?

She had to find her.

But only Father knew. Only Father knew where he had taken her all those years ago, and he had never told Kitty. It was in the child's best interests, he'd said. And lost and scared, back then, she'd believed him. Hadn't believed she deserved to be a mother.

Guilt stabbed at her insides.

Well, no more.

Kitty straightened her shoulders, filled with a sudden energy. She wasn't beaten down as she had been five years ago. She was thirty-two and wiser now.

She had to get home and speak to Father. Make him tell her where Alice had been taken.

Then she would find her daughter.

Chapter Two

As soon as the flat whine of the all-clear sounded and the children had been collected, Kitty set off up the street for home. Thick swirls of soot hung like confetti in the air. Dust rose in clouds over a mound of limestone rubble, where a house had collapsed further up the street. Glass and blackened shrapnel lay scattered up and down the steps.

At the bottom of the street, Grand Harbour lay under a pall of grey smoke as thick as fog. She could just make out *Illustrious*'s turrets poking through. Not sunk, thank goodness.

She hurried on as people, soldiers and ARP wardens ran past her, crying out, shouting instructions, blowing whistles. The bells of ambulances and fire engines rang out in every direction. One woman stood sobbing, holding a bloodied handkerchief to her head. Another man shouted curses, shaking his hand at the sky.

As she turned into Old Bakery Street, her way was blocked by a mountain of rubble two storeys high. Part of a room was left clinging to the wall – just a kitchen sink, its ruffled curtain flapping in the breeze. A headscarfed woman wailed as she tore at the mound of stones with her bare hands.

Kitty pressed herself against the wall as soldiers from the 2nd Devonshire's rushed up the narrow street with stretchers and shovels. As she set off and turned the corner, she crashed into someone hurrying in the opposite direction. She reeled, spinning back into the wall.

'Watch out!' a man's voice shouted.

The flash of a leather briefcase skating into the road, horse's hooves approaching, the blue-grey blur of an RAF officer as he dived to snatch the briefcase up. A flutter of photographs spilling across the road, the clop and rattle of a gharry trotting by, the driver yelling, '*Oqghod attent!*'

'I'm so sorry,' said Kitty, rubbing her throbbing shoulder. 'Are you alright?'

She glanced at the dishevelled figure, a tall RAF pilot, his face hidden by his peaked cap and the upturned collar of his flying jacket as he bent to retrieve the photographs that fluttered down the cobbled street in the breeze. His sheepskin flying boots were muddied, as if he'd just run off the airfield.

'I'm fine. Dammit, I'm late enough with these as it is,' he said, turning away and chasing the photographs.

'It's my fault. Here, let me give you a hand.' Kitty, her eye caught by the large black and white aerial images, knelt to pick up the photograph near her feet.

'No, it's alright. Just leave them,' he called, snatching at another. But it was lifted by the wind and skittered down the street.

'Honestly, it's the least I can do,' she called over her shoulder. 'So sorry. I didn't mean to crash into you. Is your briefcase alright?'

'It's fine,' he said, pushing a photograph into it. 'Survived a stream of bullets at seven thousand feet, so a horse's hooves are child's play in comparison.'

She smiled and glanced at him, hearing the amusement in his voice, even though his back was turned to her.

'Are you alright?' he added, glancing over as an afterthought. 'I didn't mean to crash into you either. Rushing too much.'

'Yes, fine,' she said, but her attention was caught by the photograph she'd picked up.

It was still sticky with fluid. Recently developed, then. She breathed in its chemical smell and, for a second, with a tug in her chest, was taken back to the bathroom in her Bloomsbury flat, the strings of pegged photographs drying over the bath. But this photograph was intriguing. Clearly an enemy airfield. Where was it? She peered more closely at it. The shot had been taken from a great height, and showed tiny crosses laid out in row after row.

She breathed in sharply.

'My God. Stukas. There's hundreds of them.' She glanced over at him, where he was brushing dust off a picture, still turned away from her. 'Did you take these?'

'Yes, unfortunately. And they've just given us a right pasting, haven't they. Damn air raid's made me late.'

As he held up a photograph she glimpsed his left hand. The back was red and scarred, the skin wrinkled, his fingers curved and stiff. It had been badly burnt, and recently, by the look of it.

He came over and squatted near her to pick up the last few pictures, and she glanced at him curiously. His face was in side profile beside her, his expression intelligent, determined, his jaw firm with a dimple in the middle, his eyelashes dark against his clean-shaven cheek. Handsome.

An almost forgotten tingle of excitement shot through her, one she hadn't felt in years. For a second, she had the strange sensation of already knowing him, as if from some other life. He smelt of fresh air and warm uniform serge, a tang of engine oil.

But when he turned his face to her and smiled, her breath caught in her throat.

The other side of his face had been entirely burnt.

Purple scarred skin, puckered and shining, ran across his forehead, down his right cheek and neck and disappeared into his collar. His right eyebrow was missing, his eye pulled down by the drooping hood of his eyelid. The right corner of his mouth was puckered and taut.

For a moment, his eyes stared into hers, appraising, kind. It was as if a feeling passed between them, of recognition, of understanding.

A wave of empathy washed through her. He was so badly injured, poor man; he must have been in a terrible air crash, yet he only looked about her age.

And he was still flying.

His cheeks flushed and he looked away, jamming his cap even lower over his forehead, so the peak partially hid the scarring.

'Righto, thanks,' he said stiffly. 'I can take it from here.'

He was clearly embarrassed and looked like he wished he were a million miles away.

Heat rose up Kitty's face and her cheeks burnt. God, had she stared? She hadn't meant to stare. To hide her confusion, she picked up another photograph. An aerial shot of ships in a harbour.

'Sharp focus,' she said to break the awkward moment, but the admiration in her voice was genuine. 'Not easy from that height, I'm sure.'

He glanced at her, surprised. 'You're a photographer?'

Kitty nodded, handing him the photographs. 'Yes. I had a studio in—'

'Actually, they're top secret,' he cut across her, his face flushing pink. He took the photographs and shuffled them into the pile in his hand. 'Don't tell anyone or I'll have to kill you.'

'What?' She looked at him, startled.

His hooded eye and the drooping mouth twitched. Crikey, he was trying to wink.

'Ha, I see,' she smiled. 'Of course not.'

They both got to their feet.

'Seriously, though, they are actually top secret.' His blue-grey eyes gazed at her intently as he tucked them in the briefcase. 'Please, don't mention what you've seen to anyone.'

'No, no. Of course not.'

'Righto. Well, thank you for your help.'

He stared at her for a moment, his eyes taking her in, noticing the dirty smudges on her cardigan, the dust on her knees, and she suddenly felt embarrassed at the state she must look. He smiled, his face softening, and touched the peak of his cap in mock salute.

'Sorry to have caused you all this bother. Must dash. Got to get these to RAF HQ.'

Kitty stood gazing after him as he hurried away down the street, wanting to know a lot more about the photographs and wondering who, exactly, this pilot was.

* * *

'Mother. Mother.'

Kitty's voice echoed in the high-ceilinged hall as she burst through the double doors of their grace and favour villa in Old Theatre Street. Oil paintings, of brocaded Royal Navy grandees, stared down at her, their gilt frames askew. One lay on the floor, the canvas ripped. Her foot crunched on broken glass. She glanced up. Crystal droplets had been shaken off the huge chandelier that dominated the hall. Her heart thudded. At least the windows hadn't blown out.

'Mother? Are you alright?'

Silence.

Kitty glanced in the baroque gilt mirror by the front door and her harassed face, red from running and smudged with soot, stared back at her. Her hair was tangled and full of dust – God, what must that pilot have thought of her? – and she pulled at her honey-brown shoulder-length curls, trying to smooth them into place. Her hazel eyes glittered with agitation and her mouth was too pale, the Tangee lipstick she'd applied that morning long since faded. She pressed her lips together to hide that little gap she so hated between her front teeth.

Kitty hurried into the drawing room and glanced at Mother's favourite wing-tipped armchair. Empty. Mother must have gone to the shelter. A miracle. Kitty leant against a pillar, panting with relief.

A spluttering cough from another room made her turn.

'Katherine? Is that you?'

'Mother!'

Kitty hurried into the dining room next door and glanced round. There was no one there, just the long polished table and *bizzilla* lace table runner, now covered with plaster dust, where Kitty, glancing up, could see the ceiling had cracked. A three-armed candlestick holder had fallen over and lay beached like a silver tall-ship, candles like toppled masts. Where on earth was she? Was she hurt?

'Give me a hand up, would you? My hip . . .'

Goodness, she was under the dining table. Kitty pushed a chair aside and ducked underneath.

'Are you alright? You should've gone to the shelter. I've been so worried about you.'

Lydia's white face glared back, her violet-grey eyes scrunched in her face like tiny pebbles. Her pinched blue lips gave her away. She looked ill.

'Yes, well. That nasty little man Mussolini seems to have outdone himself today.' She coughed and a spasm ran through her whole body. 'Thought I'd better take some precautions.'

'It's not Mussolini. It's the Germans. Seems they've joined the war against Malta.'

'The Nazis!' Mother pulled a lace handkerchief out from under the gold chain of her watch strap and pressed it to her cheek. 'Goodness. We're for it now.'

Kitty pictured the Stukas she'd just seen in those photographs and swallowed.

'Are you sure you're alright, Mother?'

'I'm fine,' her voice was crisp, 'and stop calling me Mother.'

This again. Now? God, she was incorrigible. Hard to like, never mind love, but even as the thought flashed across Kitty's mind, she guiltily pushed it away. But calling her 'Lydia' still grated, even after all these years, even though Kitty had long ago left Willow End to set up her own photography studio in London. What kind of mother didn't want to be called Mother?

Mummy.

She shut her eyes a moment. She would have loved to have been called that, even for a day or two. They'd called her 'Miss Campbell' in the maternity home, saying 'Miss' in such disapproving tones it was as if they were actually saying 'you're a disgrace' each time. A lump like a stone formed in her throat.

She pictured the aproned mothers who had just tearfully fallen on their children at school, covering them with kisses. Their warm gratitude to her and Adela for keeping their children safe. Michael's mother had patted her cheeks; Mrs Cortis had pulled her to her ample bosom and hugged her tight, murmuring '*Grazzi, grazzi*' into her ear.

Kitty took a deep breath, forcing her voice to stay calm. 'Let me help you up.'

She reached for Lydia's small white hand, cold and bony like a bird's claw, the waft of her violet water strong. With difficulty, Kitty pulled her up, one arm round Lydia's thin back, and heaved her across the Turkish rug, Lydia taking care not to ladder her silk stockings or catch her long string of pearls on the carved edge of the table leg. Lydia's chest heaved under her tussore silk blouse and she spasmed with coughing again.

'Here, sit down.' Kitty tugged round a tall-backed mahogany chair, but Mother, *Lydia* – she mentally rolled her eyes – swatted her away.

'Stop fussing, Kitty.'

Kitty took a deep breath. It was just Lydia. She couldn't give support or accept it. Never had done. And yet Kitty had left Willow End, come to Malta, to help look after her. 'What with her heart condition and the warm climate, it'll help lift you out of your melancholy,' Father had said. And she'd agreed.

What else could she have done, after Alice had gone? Life had been meaningless.

Kitty bit back the retort on the tip of her tongue and patted her hand. 'Let me get your tablets.'

'I don't want any wretched pills.' Lydia's eyes were pink and watering. 'They upset my stomach.' She frowned as she re-pinned the normally neat greying hair that had tumbled down. 'Did they hit *Illustrious*?'

'I'm not sure, there was so much smoke.' Kitty didn't mention the fires burning among the steeples and domes of the Three Cities by the dockyards across Grand Harbour. She didn't want to bring on another of Lydia's coughing fits. 'I could only see her turrets—'

A knock rapped at the front door. Lydia's brow creased.

Kitty turned, her footsteps tapping on the marble as she crossed the hall and opened the door.

Two naval officers stood to attention in full white dress uniform, peaked caps and gilt buttons glinting in the sun. One was young and fresh-faced, the other more senior with steel-grey hair and a severe expression.

'Miss Campbell?' The younger of the two saluted, his gaze fixed at a point above Kitty's right shoulder. 'Lieutenant Mills. Is Mrs Campbell here?'

The senior officer wouldn't meet her eye.

She knew then.

All the air squeezed out of her body.

Kitty was only half aware of Lydia joining her at the door, the rustle of her blouse as her hand went to her throat, her intake of breath.

'It's Ronald, isn't it?'

'Just tell us,' Kitty whispered. Her heart hammered in her chest.

The senior officer saluted, and in unison, they removed their caps and tucked them under their arms.

'Ma'am. We've come straight from the dockyards,' the senior officer said, his face filling with compassion. 'I'm sorry to have to tell you that Vice-Admiral Campbell passed away this afternoon. The air raid . . .'

Kitty clutched the door jamb, her legs giving way beneath her.

His words burbled on, but she couldn't follow them as they buzzed in her ears. Dead? Father couldn't be dead. He just couldn't be . . . Bright lights flashed at the edges of her vision, her head swam and the road seemed to tip and sway. Above the roaring in her ears, Kitty heard Lydia say in a crisp voice, 'At least we won't have to stay on this godforsaken island any longer.'

But as blackness closed in, one thought reverberated in her mind.

How would she find Alice now?

Chapter Three

A week later, Lydia and Kitty waited on the high-ceilinged landing of Admiralty House, an old palace built by the Knights of St John, admiring the grand sweep of the marble staircase in front of them. Rows of former admirals glared unsmiling from the walls, while down the corridor, tall windows threw rectangles of sunlight between the pillars. Just the sort of place Father would have wanted his will read, Kitty thought, mentally rolling her eyes.

'I just want to get this over with.' Lydia's fingers drummed the top of her bag, her face pale under her black velvet hat.

Kitty glanced at her. She was nervous too. Kitty's own stomach was roiling as much as it had on that dreadful boat crossing over from Sicily all those years ago. Her fingernails dug into her palm. After all, this was it. Her last chance to find out something about Alice.

Would Father have left her some sort of letter or file with information about Alice in his will? She needed something, some clue, to help her find out where she had been taken.

Naval officers in white gold-buttoned uniforms scurried past them, and now and then a door would open, phones would ring, and voices barked things like 'When will HMS *Warspite* arrive?' or 'Has the convoy left Alexandria yet?'

Kitty watched them, longing to be involved, longing to be able to do something, to make a difference to the war effort. She thought about the photographs that pilot had dropped in the street the other day. If only she could help in some way.

Everything was changing now the Nazi bombings had started. It was like the London Blitz, air raids happening several times a day, forcing everyone to run to the nearest shelter. The streets were filled with a sea of khaki, army jeeps and families fleeing Valletta to stay with relatives in the countryside. They'd had to push through the crowds to get here today – old men, mothers with little children, people pushing carts or prams piled high with saucepans, jars of oil or sacks of flour, all heading towards the arched main gate of Valletta. Miss Mazelli had even warned all the teachers that the school may have to close.

'It'll be a miracle if we get through the whole will.' Lydia interrupted her thoughts, peeling off her black gloves and folding them over the handbag on her lap. 'I expect Jerry will disrupt us with their busy schedule.'

Kitty patted her arm. 'Don't worry. I spotted the shelter on the way in.'

At least Lydia was agreeing to go to them now. Kitty had carried down two folding chairs, some blankets and pillows and made them a snug little corner, so they could sleep at night. Every day she left a basket packed with a thermos of tea, a torch and Lydia's knitting by the door, so they could grab it as they ran for the shelter.

Kitty glanced at her. Lydia's long-sleeved black crêpe dress was the only indication she was in mourning. She hadn't cried a single tear at the funeral the other day, a hasty gathering of senior officers in the Royal Naval Cemetery across the bay from Valletta, as the Last Post played.

But then Kitty had never really seen a display of affection between her parents, a fact that had only occurred to her once she had fallen madly in love with Dexter. There'd just been a chilly civility that permeated the whole household, an aching loneliness at the silent dinner table, which back then she had barely understood. Gosh, no wonder she had spent so many years yearning for a sister.

Kitty had felt numb when Father died, but as his coffin was lowered, choking tears had risen in her throat. She loved him, perhaps, but she couldn't forgive him. Not for what he had done. Anger settled like burning coals in her chest.

'And then when the will's settled, I want to leave.' Lydia brushed her skirt down as if she could brush all memory of Malta away.

'Leave?' Kitty sat up. 'You know we can't leave! The Nazis bomb every ship they can. They've mined the sea.' She patted Lydia's hand. 'We'll be safe in the shelters. They can't get us there.'

At that moment, the heavy door beside them creaked open and they were beckoned inside.

'In addition to the vice-admiral's collection of seafaring oil paintings, Mrs Campbell, he also bequeaths you his other personal items.' Lieutenant Commander Jennings leant across the large mahogany desk, his small eyes almost invisible behind heavy purple pouches and the thick wire-rimmed glasses that clung to his ears.

'That's to say, all his medals, including the Distinguished Service Order from Gallipoli, 1915, the King George V Silver Jubilee Medal and his Fears dress watch.'

In lawyerly fashion, he held a sheaf of thick cream paper in his pudgy hands, nails clipped so short red lines showed at the blunt rim. Although upside down, Kitty could see each page crested with the Royal Navy emblem and the flourish of Father's initials at the bottom. She could picture him signing, dipping his favourite gold-trimmed fountain pen in ink, sucking his pipe, brow wrinkled in concentration.

Lydia sat, straight-backed and still. The room was airless, tall shutters pulled against the sudden warmth of the late January day. Kitty sat, her fists clenched, almost nauseous with expectation.

'And to you, Miss Katherine Campbell.' Lieutenant Commander Jennings glanced up at her.

Kitty stiffened.

Now. Now she'd find out. Sweat bloomed on her back.

'He leaves the silver-framed photograph of himself, and I quote, "the first photograph my dear girl ever took of me. I wish her to know my pride and love for her has no bounds."'

Hot tears pricked at the back of her eyes. He remembered. He did know how much that photograph had meant to her. She'd taken it on that first Box Brownie she had begged for when she was thirteen. Why had he never said anything like that to her when he was alive? These were his first kind words in years. Ever since he returned home after the Great War, he'd been so cold. Shushed her when she ran into rooms, shouted out of the French windows for her to be quiet when she played with Rufus in the garden. Frowned if she giggled at the dinner table.

'He's also left you his sketches of ships in Deal Harbour, his gold Hunter watch and his collection of non-naval books.'

Her pulse quickened. 'Is there anything else?'

'Anything else?' Lieutenant Commander Jennings looked puzzled. He glanced down at the paperwork.

'I mean a letter, perhaps. A document?'

He shuffled a few pages and looked up. 'Not that I'm aware of. Were you expecting something?'

Kitty took a deep breath. 'Some information about a matter that happened in 1936.'

Lydia looked up sharply. 'Not this again, Katherine. Surely we've left all that . . .' she fluttered her hand, 'unfortunate business in the past.'

'I haven't.' Kitty clenched her jaw. 'I need to know where she was taken.'

'I've told you before, I don't know.' Lydia pursed her lips and clasped her hands tightly over her handbag. 'You know Ronald dealt with the whole matter.'

Lieutenant Commander Jennings looked from Kitty to Lydia, a confused expression on his face. 'To which matter are we alluding?'

'A private matter.' Kitty's voice was quiet. 'About, um, a child.' *My child.* 'Placed with adoptive parents in 1936.'

'Ah.' He cleared his throat and his already pink whisky-flushed cheeks turned purple. 'I see.' He rifled through a few more folders in painful silence and pushed his glasses up his nose. 'No. There is no document pertaining to a matter of that nature.'

'I'm not surprised. It was all settled back then.' Lydia's voice was less sharp now. 'It's better for her that way, Katherine. You know that.'

'How could he?' Water brimmed in her eyes. Her heart banged against her ribs. 'I thought if it was the last thing on earth he could do, he would tell me where she is.'

Her voice hung in the silence.

Lieutenant Commander Jennings ran his finger round his collar and glanced from Kitty to Lydia, clearly embarrassed. 'Perhaps this information may be among his personal papers.'

Kitty looked up, hope surging through her. 'His personal papers? Where are they?'

'I'm sure your father's office will see they are delivered to you.'

'Thank you. Thank you so much.' Kitty sank back into her chair. Of course. Father was so organised, it would surely be among his papers somewhere. Relief flooded through her.

'Now. There's a rather delicate matter we must come to.' He frowned, looking uncomfortable, as he steepled his fingers together. 'It concerns the house.'

'The house?' Lydia breathed in sharply. 'Good God. Of course. The Navy will want us out. And at a time like this.' She pulled her folded handkerchief from under her wristwatch strap and dabbed her mouth.

'Mother, don't worry.' Kitty patted her arm. She wasn't that bothered about Old Theatre Street; it had never felt like a proper home, even though they'd been there four years. Too echoey and grand, all crystal chandeliers and dining tables for twenty. Not like the battered comfort of Willow End. 'I can find us somewhere else . . .'

Lieutenant Commander Jennings looked at Lydia, his fingers drumming on his leather-bound blotter. 'Actually, it wasn't that house I meant.'

'Sorry?'

'It's the other house. The one in England.'

'Willow End?' Kitty's voice was sharp.

'Willow End. Yes.' Sweat beaded on his forehead. 'It's the assets, you see. The vice-admiral wants them divided. Vice-Admiral Campbell has left half of his fortune to another beneficiary.'

There was a moment of silence. The ormolu clock on the high marble mantelpiece behind them ticked. Kitty's heart thudded.

'Another beneficiary? What on earth do you mean?'

'The money is to go to an account here in Malta. To "Someone I know well and trust implicitly", he writes here.'

There was a stunned silence.

'What?' said Kitty.

'In Malta?' Lydia's voice was high. The blood drained from her face.

'Lydia, breathe.' Kitty took her hand and rubbed it. 'Mother, breathe.' She turned to Jennings. 'Who on earth does the account belong to?'

'Under the terms of the will, I'm not allowed to divulge that information.'

'What? Why would Father do that? Who the hell would he give it to?'

Lydia stared at the floor, her eyes glazed, her face ashen.

Jennings steepled his fingers together. 'Often in these cases it may be a charitable cause he wishes to support, a colleague he wishes to reward, or he may feel, how shall I put it? Indebted to someone for some deed.'

'Indebted?' echoed Kitty, her voice high and disbelieving.

'So looking at your assets, I'm afraid it will mean selling Willow End.'

'Sell Willow End? No. Absolutely not.'

A wave of anger rushed through her. How could Father do this to them?

Willow End was her childhood home, the only thing about her childhood that had been warm and nurturing, where she'd baked shortbread in the kitchen with Mrs Maltby, spent winter afternoons by the fire drinking cocoa, where she had taken her first photographs of Rufus rolling in the stream.

But then another more terrible thought struck her. Suppose the details about Alice's adoption were not in his papers here, but stored in the attic at Willow End? After all, they'd stowed so many other things when they had hastily packed before they left in 1936. They'd never expected war to break out. Never expected to stay in Malta this long. If the details about Alice were there, they would be lost for ever . . .

Suddenly the room was stifling, the air thick and suffocating. Kitty couldn't breathe.

Lieutenant Commander Jennings shook his head. 'His wish is clear. Half of these assets must go to this other beneficiary's account. You must make arrangements to sell Willow End. As soon as you can.'

Chapter Four

'I can't believe he's making us sell it!'

Kitty paced up and down Adela's airy living room, in front of the tall windows that overlooked Grand Harbour. She sank down in the cane chair, exhausted at telling Adela the whole story, and gazed out across the harbour. It was always worth the climb to Adela's sixth-floor flat in this elegant old building for the prize of this spectacular view.

For a moment her eyes roved across the water sparkling in the evening sun, to the imposing limestone walls that lined the harbour on both sides. Nearest on the left were the Crusader bastions of St John's and St James' Cavaliers and the colonnaded terrace of the Upper Barrakka Gardens.

Across the water, three long islands protruded into the harbour like fingers, the stone walls of Fort Ricasoli and Fort St Angelo commanding the waterfront. By the docks, a destroyer was being repaired. Kitty took a sharp breath.

'*Illustrious* has gone!' She turned to Adela, sitting at her old Singer sewing machine, its gold-flowered etching glinting in the honeyed light. 'They've managed to repair her. She's got away!'

'Mmm, must've slid out in the middle of the night. Wasn't

there when I opened the blackouts this morning.' Adela removed a pin from between her teeth. 'But I'm so sorry for you, *chérie*. What he's done is shocking. Who do you think he's left it to?'

'I haven't the least bloody idea. And that's the problem. I need to find out who they are. Talk to them about not making us sell Willow End.' Kitty sat down and released a long breath. 'What terrifies me most is that he might have left all the information about Alice there. Then I'll never find out where she is.'

'I'm so sorry.' Adela's dark eyes shone with sympathy. She pulled the thread from the needle and bit it off. She was stitching a sea of silver satin that rippled across the little gate-legged table, while the sweet melody of Josephine Baker singing 'J'ai Deux Amours' filled the room from the old gramophone on the side table. On the wall behind her were pinned a patchwork of black and white magazine pictures of the singer and of Charlie Parker puffing into his saxophone. 'But surely he can't make you do this?'

'Of course he can. He's a man, isn't he?' They exchanged glances. 'It's his money.'

'Of course it is.' Adela rolled her eyes. 'Oh, *chérie*. I know how much finding Alice means to you.'

'Lydia won't discuss it. Says she doesn't want to talk about it "ever again".'

'Hmm.' Adela glanced at Kitty, hesitating. 'I don't know much of British men, but if he was French, he would be leaving his money to his mistress.'

'Adela!' Kitty looked at her aghast. 'Good grief no, not Father. Far too proper. You know what he was like. Far too much a stickler for everything shipshape and Bristol fashion.'

'True.' Adela stood, holding the fabric up to her shoulders. 'What do you think?'

'Darling, it's ravishing.'

The silver dress draped across Adela's slim body, shining against her black-skinned limbs, illuminating the whites of her eyes and the sheen of the oil on her black short-cropped bob. On anyone else the haircut would have looked old-fashioned, but on Adela it looked chic and modern.

'I've asked Giorgio for more sets at The Star, now school's closing.' Adela sat down and pushed a seam back under the foot of the needle. 'I'll be singing every evening except Mondays.'

'That's exciting.' Kitty smiled at her. 'Yes, I've been thinking I'd like to help the war effort, join the ARP or something,' she added, although her stomach tightened at the thought of not seeing Carmela any more. 'But is anyone still going to clubs with all this bombing?'

'*Bien sûr.*' Adela's pencilled eyebrows shot up. 'You've no idea how many soldiers, sailors and airmen want to forget their troubles. *Les danses, les boîtes.* Strait Street's bars are packed every night. *Alors*, you must come.' She flashed her white teeth and turned back to her sewing. 'But do you know anything about this person?'

'No, absolutely bloody nothing. Father wanted it kept secret.' Kitty sipped the mint tea Adela had put on the cane table for her. A listing frigate was approaching the dockyards now. 'That's what's so awful. How the hell could he give away our family home? How can he care so little about us?'

Adela stopped sewing and looked up at her. 'I'm sure he cared for you.'

'It doesn't feel like it. It's never felt like it . . .' Kitty's voice trailed away. Tears pricked at the back of her eyes.

'You ask me about families? What do I know?' Adela turned the handle and sewed a seam, her hand deft as she manoeuvred the fabric. '*La mauvaise fille* who ran away to sing cabaret.'

Kitty smiled weakly. 'Don't you miss them?'

'Of course.'

Adela reached for a Marich cigarette and lit up, her polished crimson nails glossy as she held it to her mouth. 'We were close, my brothers and I, Jean-Paul and Louis.' She released a stream of smoke. 'All fighting over who could steal the croissants off the counter without Maman noticing in our *boulangerie*. They would take me fishing on the Seine. My older brother, Jean-Paul, taught me to drive our delivery van when I was twelve. He even turned a blind eye when I was older, when he knew I was taking it to Montmartre to sing in a bar at night.'

Kitty smiled. 'I'd have loved to have had brothers or sisters.'

'Anyway, I've found my new family now, at the club.' Adela fingered the silver fabric, her eyes defiant. She took a drag at her cigarette. 'Singing is all I've ever wanted to do.'

'That's how I felt about photography.' Kitty's voice was quiet.

She understood what Adela meant completely. It was as if there was a connection between them, no matter that their lives had been so different, an understanding of pain or loss – she couldn't explain it really. Or maybe they just instinctively recognised the spark in one another, the passion for having something more in a woman's life, in a world that didn't want you to have it.

'I know you were a successful photographer,' Adela eyed her, hesitating, 'but I've never seen you take a photograph.'

Kitty's chest tightened.

'I just can't. Not any more.'

'Why not?' Adela's voice was gentle.

A rush of memories assailed Kitty. How proud she'd been to make it in London society, to work for the magazines she'd so long admired, the glamour of the photo shoots. It all seemed a lifetime ago.

It *was* a lifetime ago.

She thought of her precious Rolleiflex Automat camera in its leather case, buried in a trunk in the attic at Willow End. The anticipation in loading the film, adjusting the lens, perfecting the light. The excitement she'd felt at making someone seen, revealing a truth in someone's expression, telling their story in a perfect image.

Maybe, she realised now, because she'd spent so many years feeling unseen herself.

Her fingers reached for the photograph in her pocket, her thumb stroking the soft leather folder. She had never shown her baby's picture to anyone. Never shared this part of her soul.

It was the only image of Alice that she had.

She thought back to the day she had taken it, barely able to focus as tears streamed down her cheeks, fingers shaking on the lens, breasts throbbing with milk as she heaved herself out of bed. Alice sleeping, perfect in her yellow waffle blanket, tiny arms up by her head, cheeks sucking as she slept.

She passed the photograph to Adela.

'It's the last photograph I took. I haven't taken one since.' Kitty's voice cracked.

She stared across Grand Harbour, her eyes blurring. She heard the rustle as Adela put down her cigarette and opened the wallet, knew by heart the black and white picture Adela saw.

The fan of dark eyelashes on the soft swell of milky cheeks, her baby's rosebud-plump mouth, the stretch of tiny fingers above the blanket.

'Alice,' Adela gasped. 'She's adorable.'

'She'd be nearly five now. And I don't know what she looks like . . .'

'Oh, *chérie*.'

'If I die in this war, my child will grow up knowing I gave her up. Abandoned her. And I'm not going to let that happen. I have to find her.'

'Oh, Kitty.' Adela placed the image carefully on the little table and pulled Kitty into her arms. 'My darling.'

Adela held her, the sweet smell of her Guerlain perfume and coconut hair oil comforting.

Eventually Kitty pulled away, wiped the tears from her face.

'I have to find this person. Stop them selling the house. We can't sell it, we just can't.'

'Then don't. You know important people, at Admiralty House, yes?' Adela released a fierce stream of smoke as if it could blow away all objections. 'Find out who this person is and come to some arrangement with them. There's always a way.'

Kitty stared at her.

'Oh my goodness, you're right.' She shook her head. 'I don't know what's happened to me. I've lost all my fight.'

Christ, she had lost herself when she lost Alice.

She was like a faded photograph left forgotten on a dusty shelf. Where was the Kitty Campbell who had left Willow End and gone to London with a portfolio of photographs under her arm, pitched up to see the editors of *Woman's Own* and *Picture Post*; the Kitty Campbell who had talked her way into bigger commissions, photographed stars like Margaret Lockwood and Norman Hartnell? How had she lost her way so badly?

She thought back to the bathroom in the Bloomsbury flat, the glittering evenings, dizzy on excitement and anticipation, putting lipstick on while Violet smoked Players and lounged in the bath, taking care not to dislodge Kitty's photographs strung on lines across the tiny room. Dexter picking her up in the Lady Luck, chrome gleaming from every handle, and whisking her off for yet another night of dancing.

'I know what you have lost, *chérie*,' Adela said, meaningfully. 'But think. Someone in the Navy must know more about this.'

Kitty shifted in the cane chair.

'Lieutenant Westfield, Father's adjutant. Of course! He worked with Father every day. He must know something . . .'

She jumped up and pulled Adela into a hug.

'Darling, what would I do without you.'

Chapter Five

A few days later Kitty took a blue-and-yellow-painted *dgħajsa* across Grand Harbour. Lieutenant Westfield had agreed to see her, even if it would feel strange, now, going into Father's office in the dockyards.

The boatman stood, pushing the oars like a gondola into the azure water behind her. She sat on the narrow wooden bench, the wind ruffling her hair, her bag clutched on her lap. Small waves slapped the prow of the wooden boat as they pulled further out and Kitty trailed her fingers in the cold water.

It was only when they were halfway across, when she could see straight down the harbour to the boom defences and out to sea, that she realised how vulnerable they were. Grand Harbour looked so much wider from down here. Since *Illustrious* left, the Luftwaffe had been quieter for a couple of days, but if the sirens went off now, and bombers swooped in over the harbour, what would they do? They would be sitting ducks. She shivered. The imposing Knights of St John bastions loomed high above them, sandbagged anti-aircraft gun emplacements pointed at the sky, poised for attack.

She glanced up at the signals station on top of the Auberge

de Castille, the HQ for Military Command, a former palace of the Knights of Castille and Portugal, praying the signals of a red flag for bombers, or red and white for fighters, would not appear and the wail of the air alert would not echo round the harbour.

As they pulled closer to the dockyards, the clang of hammering and squeak of pulleys grew louder and more reassuring. The boatman helped her up onto the stone steps carved into the harbour wall and she stared up at the grey destroyer, HMS *Diamond*, sailors stripped to the waist riveting holes in her sides. It was so hard now for ships to reach Malta and when they did, they were bombed to pieces.

Would they be strong enough to defeat the Nazis? England was standing alone in northern Europe against them; cities at home were being bombed. And now that the Germans had joined the Fascist Italians fighting here in the Mediterranean, the Luftwaffe seemed even stronger.

She shivered and walked towards the old Royal Navy offices, frowning at the portico of pillars and tall arched windows now buried under stacks of sandbags.

'I'm sorry for your loss.' Lieutenant Westfield smiled at her uneasily across the desk, the gold stripes on his cuffs glinting in the sunshine that poured through the windows. 'A terrible shock to us all.'

He waved at the blank space above the marble fireplace, the paint lighter than the rest of the wall, where Father's portrait had already been taken down. 'Apologies. It's just these things are now more rushed than usual . . .'

Kitty nodded, her confidence ebbing away, her gaze fixed on

this blond-haired man, of whom she'd had such high hopes. As she'd been shown into Father's outer office, she'd winced at the gilt sign on the door within, 'Vice-Admiral Campbell' already changed to 'Vice-Admiral Morgan'. Crikey, already she and Lydia were history, irritations to be dealt with, swept aside by the winds of war.

She eyed the insipid young man, his weak chin disappearing into his collar. She had worn her favourite cornflower-blue dress with the puffed sleeves, hoping to charm him, remembering the few times he had come home with Father for early evening drinks. Now he looked more nervous than charmed, his pale eyes gazing at her from under pale eyebrows. Honestly, did he think she was going to break into pieces like a porcelain doll, or start crying?

Lieutenant Westfield fidgeted in his chair. 'He was a good man, your father. Strict but fair. I enjoyed working for him.'

It was strange hearing this assessment of Father. A good man? Was he? She didn't think so.

A memory flashed of that bitter November day in the living room, when he had sealed her fate. She'd been six months pregnant by then, showing badly and disgraced in the eyes of the world, and she'd had no choice but to flee home to Willow End.

Her life had fallen apart. Dexter, her beloved Dexter, couldn't have run faster once she told him about his baby. And even Elizabeth, editor at *Woman's Life* magazine, forward-thinking enough to employ a female photographer, had said she could no longer give her any commissions. An unmarried mother was beyond society's pale, apparently. Oh, she'd tried everywhere, written notes all over town, no longer daring to show up in person, to all the editors who for the previous five years had been keen to give her photography commissions. But word seemed to have spread. It left her unable to afford the flat she rented with Violet Denby.

Her heart had broken completely when Violet posted her a clipping from the 'Social Diary' pages of the *Daily Post*. A photograph of Dexter, in black tie at The Savoy, their favourite restaurant, but with his arm round a glowing woman in a silk bias-cut dress and pearls. The caption underneath read *Dexter Bullington Esq.,* Architects' Review *editor and British Motor Sports Winner, 1934, accompanied by his beautiful wife, Mrs Vanessa Bullington*. A bitter way to find out that the man she had loved for over three years had married.

She had given up then.

And stuck back at Willow End, she had sat on the low sofa while Father towered over her, pacing in front of the fire, hands behind his back, a disappointed headmaster in front of a troubled pupil. Never mind that she was an adult of twenty-six by then. Allowed to vote, but not to have a baby on her own.

He hadn't been able to meet her eye.

'Your mother and I think it's best if you stay with Aunt Polly in Suffolk, until the, erm, end. You know how people talk. I have my position to think of . . .'

He had looked away, embarrassed, stared out of the window, where the garden rolled down the slope, the line of willows at the bottom dipping green tendrils into the stream.

'The *child*,' he frowned, distaste at saying the word crossing his face, 'should have a proper home. A mother and a father. This . . .' he gestured at her stomach, 'is not right.'

'I want to look after the baby.'

He had wheeled round. 'How, Kitty? How? You've no idea

how hard people will make this for you. You'll be shunned, the child teased, humiliated. And who would marry you now? How will you support yourself?'

She had hung her head. The last few weeks had shown her what he said was true.

'No,' he had said. 'It's better for the child, for you too, if we make arrangements. A nice home. A proper family, a mother and father. The best thing you can do for this child is to release her.'

His words had swum in her ears. *Release her.* Release her, like she was a sick puppy? But what choice did she have? And worn down, alone, she had let her go.

She had let her go.

A good man. Lieutenant Westfield's words rang now in her ears.

A good man? She clenched her jaw, ran her thumb along the smooth leather of the photograph wallet in her pocket. She blinked at Lieutenant Westfield, trying to stop her feelings showing on her face. Her silence flustered him and he shifted on his chair.

'How can I help you?'

Kitty pulled herself back to the present and cleared her throat. 'I was wondering about Father's personal things.'

'Ah yes. We found various items.'

'Really?' Kitty sat up. Had he found something about Alice? Her breathing quickened. 'Are there papers? Private papers, I mean?'

A small shrug. 'The secretary cleared his desk.' He made a note and looked up. 'I'll see they're sent to you and your mother.'

'Thank you.'

The disinterested look on his face suggested he hadn't found anything out of the ordinary. Or maybe he hadn't looked. Hope rose in her chest. She'd have to wait and see for herself. But did he know anything else?

'I also wanted to ask you about Father's will. The unusual bequest . . .'

'I can't discuss that, Miss Campbell.' He straightened the blotter on his desk. 'It's a confidential document.'

His eyes dropped from hers and a pink flush crept up his pale cheeks.

Of course he knew. It had probably spread like wildfire, whispers in corners, everyone knowing. Well, good. Maybe that could work to her advantage.

She smiled at him. 'You worked closely with him. You must have seen many highly confidential documents cross his desk.'

'Indeed, but none that I'm able to share with you, I'm afraid.' He opened his hands in a gesture of apology.

'Lieutenant Westfield, I need your help. Please. You must have heard we have to sell our home—'

'I would love to help you. Really, I would, Miss Campbell.'

For a moment, his eyes filled with compassion as he stared at her, but then a shutter came down and he looked away towards the open window. A chilly breeze blew in and the clatter of chains echoed as an anchor dropped.

'Please. He trusted you a great deal. You must know something.'

He breathed out uncomfortably. 'The details lie entirely with the lawyers. I can't comment.'

'You spent so much time working with him, Lieutenant.' Kitty's voice was persuasive. 'He shared so much with you. He didn't expect to die so soon. You know that. He was making provision for years away . . .'

'I-I . . .' Lieutenant Westfield stammered, his cheeks suffused with red. 'We don't know that.' He ran a hand through his wiry hair. 'But you should take heart that it was someone he knew well and trusted implicitly.'

She breathed in. *Someone he knew well and trusted implicitly.* That phrase again.

'You know, don't you?' Kitty looked him in the eye.

'Not at all, I couldn't possibly . . .' He fiddled awkwardly with the pen lid, his eyes fixed on the desk. His Adam's apple bobbed above his collar and tie. 'You must understand these were your father's highly personal matters. Where he went on a Wednesday night was his business.'

'He was at his club, wasn't he?' Kitty said, puzzled.

He blinked at her, panic flashing across his face, before he broke eye contact and stared down at his desk. Pink rose up his neck and cheeks.

It was as if he had thrown a bucket of cold water over her. She took a sharp breath in.

'Ah. I see.' Understanding washed over her, chilling her to her core. 'So he wasn't spending time with the other officers.' That's what he'd told them when he stayed away each Wednesday night. Her mind reeled. 'No, no, of course he wasn't.'

It was as if a fog had lifted from a view of something that had been right in front of her all the time. A wave of dizziness ran through her. She gripped the bag on her lap as if it were a life raft in a tossing sea. Father had made fools of them. Her and Lydia. Utter fools.

'Do you know who it is?'

'I-I couldn't possibly . . .' Lieutenant Westfield's eyes remained fixed on the desk, his forehead beading.

He knew.

Her heart speeded up.

'Please, tell me.'

'I, erm,' he ran a hand through his hair, so it stood on end, 'I'm sorry. This is most inappropriate.'

'Please.' Kitty looked up at him, her eyes as desperate as she could make them. 'Who is she?'

'You would do well, madam, not to ask too many questions, or you may not like the answers.' Flustered, he rose to his feet. 'I'm sorry. I can't help you.' He gestured to the door. 'HMS *Gloucester* is due in any minute.'

She picked up her handbag, rose to her feet.

'Thank you for seeing me today.' Her voice was cold. She didn't shake his hand.

'I'm sorry not to be able to help.' He stepped towards the door and opened it, his rattled eyes fixed over her shoulder. 'I wish you and your mother well, Miss Campbell. Good day.'

She walked away down the long, echoing marble corridor in a daze, her pulse thundering in her ears, her chest so tight she could hardly breathe. Brisk naval officers carrying clipboards swerved round her, frowning, and from open doors came the clack of typewriters and the jangle of telephones ringing, and voices she barely registered asking about ship repairs and minesweepers. She stopped in front of a noticeboard to collect her thoughts.

A picture of Lydia in her armchair at home knitting sweaters for bombed-out children rose in her mind. He couldn't have been seeing another woman. Not Father. That felt like a betrayal not just of Lydia, but her too.

Adela was right. It clearly was a . . . *mistress*. The word tasted sour in her mouth. How tawdry. How disappointing. What a thing to find out when they were at war. Her eye wondered distractedly over the notices of Navy regulations and lists of appointments.

How could he? The bastard. Christ, how little did he think of them?

But that phrase echoed in her head again. What was it? *Someone he knew well and trusted implicitly.* That lawyer Jennings had said it at the will reading too.

Then it hit her. How could she forget? That day, when Father had told her to give up her baby, she had looked at him, her eyes filling with tears, and asked how anyone else could ever be good enough to care for her child.

And he had turned away from her, looked out of the window, his hands behind his back, and had promised it would be *someone he knew well and trusted implicitly.* She was sure of it. That phrase that day had been scorched into her mind because she had wanted to scream back that no one, no matter how well he knew them or trusted them, *no one else* would ever be good enough to care for her child.

She leant back against the wall. Did this mean that this, this *person* – she mentally spat the word – was connected to Alice in some way? Could they know something about where she was? Her stomach tightened.

She had to find her. She had to.

She stepped forward, wanting to get out of the place as fast as she could. As she approached the corridor leading to the entrance, a door opened ahead and a tall man came out. He was clutching a folder and a smart leather briefcase, and he caught her eye because of the grey-blue of his RAF uniform, a contrast to the dark blue of the naval officers.

He turned and said back through the doorway to whoever was inside, 'Absolutely, sir. Glad to be of help.'

Her heart lurched.

She recognised that voice. A jolt of excitement fired through her.

It was him, she was sure of it.

The pilot she'd crashed into with the photographs.

Chapter Six

She stopped in her tracks. He shut the door and glanced down the corridor, and his eyes brightened in surprise as he saw her. He grasped for the cap under his arm and in the juggle of cap, folder and briefcase, he dropped the folder. A couple of photographs scattered out onto the floor.

'Dammit!'

She hurried towards him as he dropped to his knees, hastily scooping the photographs back into the folder. He got to his feet, a look of embarrassment sweeping across his face, flooding the ridged surface of his scarred skin a mottled purple. As she walked up to him, he put the cap on, so the peak covered the scarred side of his face, and turned towards her, so she could only see the unscarred side.

'It's you again.' She smiled at him. Her heart thudded in her chest.

'Ah,' he said, awkwardly. 'The woman who ran into me.' He smiled and his mouth pulled tight and lopsided. 'We must stop meeting like this.'

'That's not very gentlemanly. I helped you pick up all your photographs.'

He laughed and she took in again that intelligent gleam in his eyes, the determined set of his mouth, the dimple in the square of his chin. Her stomach contracted. He had been so good-looking.

'Thank you, you did indeed.' He flashed her a rueful look. 'Good Lord, you must think I spend my whole time dropping things. I don't, of course – except, it seems, when I see you.'

She laughed, her cheeks flushing hot, in spite of herself. 'At least this time it's not my fault.'

'Not at all.' He threw her a lopsided smile of even white teeth, so the scarred skin at the corner of his mouth tightened and pulled his burnt eyelid down. His RAF battle tunic brought out the colour of his steel-blue eyes. They were like the colour of the sea on a stormy day. 'Look, I'm glad to see you again. I feel I owe you an apology for the other day. I rushed off. Should've checked you were alright, walked you home or something.'

'Honestly, no apology necessary.' Kitty forced herself to tear her gaze away from his. Her stomach seemed to be doing tiny flips of its own accord. 'I'm perfectly able to walk home on my own. And anyway, it was my fault.'

'Not at all.' He held out his good hand and smiled. 'Sorry, I should have done this last time. Flying Officer Bill Hamilton of 69 Photographic Reconnaissance Squadron, at your service.'

His handshake was warm and firm.

Kitty smiled. 'Kitty Campbell.'

Her eye caught on a small photograph lying on the marble and she bent to pick it up. It was a fogged scene, hard to identify it was so faint, possibly a harbour with a ghostly outline of a battleship.

'Here.' She passed it to him. 'Looks like this one didn't have long enough in the developing fluid.'

He glanced at her, his eyes thoughtful. 'Ah yes. You said you were a photographer.'

He'd remembered. Her heart beat a little faster.

'Was. Years ago. I had a studio, back in London.' Heat rose up her neck. 'Not now.'

'No?' He gazed at her curiously.

'Too busy, no time.' She glanced away up the corridor and released an embarrassed laugh. 'No camera.'

'Don't you miss it?'

'Not really.' But as she said it, Kitty knew she was lying. She shifted her feet.

As his warm eyes appraised her, Kitty could see that he guessed there was more to it, but he had the sensitivity not to ask any more.

'Well, you're right. We are struggling with all the developing.' He pushed the photograph into the briefcase with the others.

'Why?'

'We're flying so many reconnaissance missions we can barely keep up with all the film we use. My batman developed these. No surprise they aren't works of art.'

'That's terrible, after all you must have gone through to take them.'

'Yes, well, we're all stretched right now,' he shrugged. 'Anyway, you don't want to hear about our problems.' He ground the toe of his flying boot into the marble and glanced through the open front doors. 'Look, I've got a few minutes before I have to get back to the airfield. Don't suppose you've got time for a coffee?'

He looked at her, a hopeful child asking for an ice cream.

'I'd love to,' Kitty said, her heart fluttering.

As they left and walked down the shattered ruins of the street, she was acutely aware of his physical presence beside her, the smell of his serge jacket and his Lifebuoy soap.

They turned into a small square of bombed houses, where soldiers from the Royal West Kent's were clearing rubble from damaged walls. A blue-painted hardware shop, Agius Stores, remained standing, a *Tools for hire* sign swinging from a nail. Just then, the smell of coffee hit her nostrils and across the square, she spotted a couple of chairs and a small table perched outside a door. A hand-scrawled sign read *Best coffee in the Three Cities.*

'You've got to admire the guts of the Maltese,' Bill smiled and led her to the table.

As they sat, Bill nodded to the sapper near them, trying to repair the pipe that leaked away down the street. She ordered a mint tea and Bill even ordered *imqaret*, a real treat now. The breeze ruffled her dress and the sun warmed her face as she bit into the date pastry, revelling in its cinnamon-spiced sweetness. Between the gaps in the building, the blue water of Grand Harbour glittered.

'So,' Bill sipped his coffee, his eyes amused, 'what's brought you to the naval dockyards today? Trying to find out more war secrets?'

Kitty laughed. He had a hint of an accent in his voice. Birmingham maybe? Although she didn't really want to talk about it, she was surprised to find herself explaining about Father's death and his mysterious bequest to a stranger. He was a good listener, sympathetic, encouraging, and she found him easy to talk to – although of course, she didn't tell him anything about the mistress. Or Alice. Far too private.

'So your father was Vice-Admiral Campbell?' he interrupted, his eyes widening. He ran a finger under his collar. 'Crikey. I thought you were a photographer . . .' A shadow of nervousness flitted across his face.

Goodness, was he intimidated by her background? But he had a medal, with purple and white diagonal stripes, sewn under the wings on his RAF jacket. She noticed he kept his scarred hand in his trouser pocket, his cap tilted low over his forehead, trying to hide the scarring, and she wished for his sake that he didn't feel that way. He was good company, quite sweet actually. It must have been a terrible accident; he had nothing to be ashamed of.

'So what do you do now?' he asked.

'I'm teaching, but the school's closing. I want to do something to help the war effort.'

'Really?' He looked at her, hesitating. 'RAF Headquarters are looking for civilians. Admin, support, what have you, if you're interested. Although you might think it's a bit beneath you, of course,' he offered, with an apologetic smile.

'Not at all.' Kitty looked up, surprised. Just because she was a vice-admiral's daughter didn't mean she was above an honest day's work, for goodness' sake.

'They also want plotters.' He glanced at her, uncertain. 'Back home the WAAFs do it. Now there are so many raids, they haven't got enough staff.'

'Plotters?' Kitty leant forward, her interest piqued. 'What on earth are they?'

'They monitor our and the enemy's aircraft positions as we

fly. Help the commander work out our attack strategy.' He looked at her hopefully.

'Gosh, that sounds extraordinary.' Kitty sat bolt upright in her chair, a buzz in her stomach. 'You're sure they want civilians?'

'Maltese or British.' He smiled, those steel-blue eyes shining. 'Yes, I'd like to think of you down there, guiding me home. I could put in a good word . . .'

'Really? That would be simply marvellous.'

'Pop into RAF HQ. Top of Scots Street. See what you think. Say I sent you.'

'Thank you, Bill. I will.'

At that moment the air raid siren wailed.

'Damn,' said Bill.

They leapt to their feet, glancing round for the nearest shelter.

'Christ, not again,' said Kitty, her throat tightening.

'I've got to get back to the airfield,' yelled Bill above the whining howl, snatching up his bag. He gestured to the shelter across the square. 'You'll be alright?'

She nodded and he ran off. But as Kitty hurried through the sandbagged doorway, she suddenly realised, with a sinking feeling in her stomach, that they hadn't arranged to meet again.

As the single tone of the all-clear wailed, Kitty emerged from the shelter and looked round hopefully for Bill, but he was nowhere to be seen. Soldiers ran past carrying spades, dark smoke clouded up into the sky and she could hear the distant clang of fire engine bells.

Shaken – it had been another heavy air raid – she crossed Grand Harbour and caught the lift back up to the Upper

Barrakka Gardens, relieved to be back across the open water. As she walked up Britannia Street, soldiers shovelled fallen rubble aside and stacked sandbags against windowsills, and on every street, the Royal Engineers were digging under houses to extend cellars, to build more shelters. Posters hastily pasted onto bombed-out buildings warned them to remember their gas masks, or hurry to the shelter when the *twissija ta' attakk mill-ajru*, or air raid warning, sounded.

She hurried past an old man perched on an ambulance tailgate, wrapped in a blanket, a bloodied bandage wrapped round his head. A tear trickled through the white dust on his cheek and she shivered, wondering who he had lost. She was glad to arrive at Scots Street and hurried up the steps straight into RAF HQ.

'My condolences for your loss,' said the dark-haired Maltese woman sitting opposite her, who had introduced herself as Irene Johnson, captain of something called D Watch. She glanced at the application Kitty had just filled out and looked at her curiously. 'But with the vice-admiral as your father, I would have thought you'd apply to the Navy.'

Kitty hesitated, caught on a back foot. She seemed to be in some sort of impromptu interview, and not one she had prepared for. But to be fair, the captain was right – it had been odd to enter a doorway headed with RAF insignia, to see information signs topped with RAF eagles, the grey-blue of the uniformed officers passing her in the corridor. But she'd had her fill of Navy semi-truths lately.

'I do know more than my fair share about ships.' Kitty smiled at Mrs Johnson, playing for time.

Mrs Johnson – Captain Johnson? – wasn't in uniform and didn't look like a 'captain' at all, more like a ballet dancer, really. Kitty eyed her. She was fortyish, petite, almost lost behind the enormous metal desk under the tall window, but she held her neck like a swan, shoulders down under her crisply ironed blouse, her hair in a tight bun. A silver-framed photograph of two young men in army uniform – maybe her sons? – grinned up at her. Kitty liked the look of this woman, brisk, efficient, and suddenly wanted to be honest with her.

'But I want to help fight against the Nazis. Help the war effort, help people, make a real difference to their lives. Especially now,' Kitty continued, gesturing to the window, where outside soldiers were shovelling blown-up masonry.

'Good.' Mrs Johnson sat back and observed her shrewdly. 'This is extremely important, tracking enemy aircraft movements. And given the dramatic increase in Nazi attacks, we really need to improve how we do it. In Britain it's carried out by the WAAFs, but we need to recruit more plotters urgently, so we're having to rely on civilians. Afterall, the Luftwaffe sent over more than five hundred aircraft to bomb *Illustrious* . . .'

Kitty's eyes widened to hear such numbers.

'And we need to extend our systems so we can manage such big attacks.' Mrs Johnson steepled her fingers together and looked Kitty in the eye. 'You'd be working at the very nerve centre of our aerial defences at Fighter Command. It's where we plan our most secret war strategy and operations against the enemy.'

Kitty nodded, excitement bubbling in her belly.

Mrs Johnson narrowed her eyes at Kitty. 'How did you hear about this?'

'Flying Officer Bill Hamilton suggested I apply.'

Mrs Johnson raised an eyebrow. 'Did he now? Photographic Reconnaissance? A dangerous game. He doesn't suffer fools gladly.'

'Right.' Kitty nodded, storing away this nugget about Bill like a squirrel hoarding a nut.

Mrs Johnson glanced at Kitty's application again.

'I see you were a photographer. Good. I like a woman who has gumption.' She tapped her pen on her desk, approval in her eyes. 'The shifts are intense and not for the faint-hearted. We work round the clock, night and day, on a five-watch system with five or more women on each watch. And we expect you here on time, whether there's an air raid on or not.'

The hairs on Kitty's arms rose. This sounded important, like she could make a real difference. She hadn't felt like this in years, not since she'd sat at an editor's desk and been handed a commission for a challenging photography shoot. 'Not a problem.'

'You will need to be resilient and resourceful, but it sounds, Miss Campbell, like you have those qualities.' A glimmer of a smile. 'I have high standards for my watches and am a stickler for punctuality.'

Kitty nodded. 'You can rely on me.'

'Excellent.' She sat back and eyed Kitty. 'Men expect us women to let them down. I like to prove them wrong.'

'Me too.' Kitty smiled back, warming to this captain. 'And thank you. I really want the job.'

'Good. I'll discuss your application with my commanding officer.' Mrs Johnson closed her folder and looked at Kitty.

'I fear the war is only just beginning for us, Miss Campbell.

Here in Malta, every civilian is on the frontline. It's our job to help them keep their nerve. Strength and courage will serve us all well if we are to win the fight. We expect everyone to do their bit to defend the island.'

Chapter Seven

For the first time ever when the school bell rang, Michael Fortini didn't race like a shot to the door. Instead, he remained in his chair, with the other two children still left in class, drawing Spitfires; they all longed to see one, but there were none yet in Malta. When he wrote *To Miss Campbell* on his picture, a lump formed in Kitty's throat.

'Will my brothers be alright?' Michael asked as he presented her with his drawing.

She had heard Malta's Governor William Dobbie announce on the Rediffusion, the island's cable radio system, that conscription was to be introduced, and Kitty had already seen lines of young men – boys, really – marching off to be issued with uniforms and start parade training at a nearby school. Kitty bent down and looked into his sad, drawn face.

'They will be proud to defend their country.'

'Will we ever see you again?'

'Heavens, of course,' Kitty said, faking cheeriness. 'I'll come and see how you're doing,' she winked. 'Make sure you're still reading Dickens!'

Michael screwed up his face in horror and she laughed,

but she welled up as he flung his arms round her and held her tight.

Her chest tightened as she thought of saying goodbye to Carmela. Her touchstone. Carmela's family ran a greengrocer's shop nearby, so she was still coming to school. Kitty had come in even more since the interview last week to help with reading in kindergarten, but really to spend more time with the little girl. It had been upsetting to see how much rushing to the air raid shelters distressed them all, no matter how much she tried to distract them with songs and games. But still, how could she bear to say goodbye to her?

At lunchtime Miss Mazelli gathered the staff together to thank them over a small glass of *bajtra*, the local prickly pear liqueur. They crammed into her gloomy office, the sunlight obscured by sandbags piled up on the windowsill.

Miss Mazelli looked weary, hunched behind her desk, her tweedy bosom resting on the blotter in front of her, greying hair tightly pulled back into a bun. She motioned to Adela to shut the door and clasped her hands in front of her.

'I'm sorry we have to close, after so long teaching children on the island.'

A murmur of sympathy broke out among the half-dozen teachers squashed into the room.

'But what with Mr Debono and Mr Sammut joining the Royal Malta Artillery . . .' she continued.

Kitty glanced at the two jacketed teachers leaning against the stationery cupboard.

'And now with food rationing, it's difficult for us to continue.' Miss Mazelli made the sign of the cross. 'Mary, Mother of God, we may be invaded any day.'

Mr Sammut ran an ink-stained hand through his Brylcreemed hair. 'If there's anything left to invade after the Nazis have pulverised us,' he said bitterly.

Miss Mazelli fingered the crucifix at her neck. 'God help us through this siege.' She straightened the ruler on her desk. 'Twenty-five years I've run this school. If only they'd left the fighting to the Italians, they were so much easier on us . . . You know, my mother still lives in Sicily.' She shook her head. 'She's only sixty miles away, but it might as well be sixty thousand.' Miss Mazelli's voice trailed away and she looked up at them, her eyes pink and moist.

Kitty nodded. How hard it must be for her to have family in Italy; what a conflict of loyalties that must bring for so many Maltese. How close the Maltese ties with Italy were – they'd only changed the second-language street signs in Valletta from Italian to English two years before the war started.

Miss Mazelli's toast as she raised her glass was as defiant as the hammer she claimed she kept by her pillow.

'We may be closing the school, but we Maltese will never be defeated by the Nazis,' she cried stoutly.

Kitty's eyes filled as they all raised their glasses.

'To Malta.'

Later, in the staffroom, Kitty went to make a cup of tea and found Adela staring blankly at a pile of sheet music on her lap. Her eyes were red.

'Darling, are you alright?'

Adela nodded, not speaking.

'I know it's sad,' Kitty crouched down and put her arm round her, 'and awful for the children.'

'It's not just that,' Adela said, her voice quiet. 'School closing makes it so real. The Nazis are getting closer . . .'

Kitty took her hand. 'I know—'

'No. No, you don't.' Tears beaded in Adela's dark brown eyes as she snatched her hand away. 'Look at me. I can't hide. To the Nazis, I'm "non-Aryan".' She spat the words.

'Oh, Adela!'

'Those disgusting Nazi Race Laws they introduced against Jews apply to me too. That's why I left Europe. Back in '36.' She trembled, her eyes staring into Kitty's, glistening with fear. 'I had to get out. Get as far away as I could from their disgusting ideology.'

'I'm so sorry.' Kitty's eyes filled. 'I hadn't thought . . .'

Adela pulled out a cigarette, her hand trembling so she could barely light it. She looked at Kitty.

'You know, if the Germans invade, I'll be rounded up.'

'What?' Fear jolted up Kitty's spine.

Adela breathed out a stream of smoke. 'My brother, Jean-Paul, joined the French Army before war broke out. A Black regiment. When the Nazis occupied Paris, they took the white soldiers prisoner, but they shot the Black soldiers.' Her voice broke. 'Hundreds of them,' she whispered, 'massacred. Including Jean-Paul.'

'Oh my God.' Kitty went cold.

'Louis told me, in that last letter I had from him, after he'd escaped from Paris. He was in Marseille, trying to get a boat to North Africa.' She shook her head. 'I don't know if he got away.'

'I'm so sorry.'

'But the Germans are coming here now. You heard what Miss Mazelli said.' Adela closed her eyes.

'We won't let the Germans invade. Look at what Churchill said. We'll fight them with everything we've got.'

Adela looked up, a glimmer of hope in her eyes. 'You think we can defeat them?'

'We defeated them in the Battle of Britain last summer,' Kitty said with more bravado than she really felt. Her mind went to the photograph Bill had taken of the rows of Stukas, and her stomach tightened. 'But we can all try and do something to help.'

'You're right.' Adela stubbed out her cigarette and her face calmed. 'Actually, I've signed up to drive ambulances in the daytime, before I sing at The Star. Thought it would be good to actually do something.'

'You'll be good at that,' Kitty said, remembering the injured old man she'd seen.

'I do a two-month nursing diploma first, of course, but I don't think the driving will be so different from Jean-Louis's truck.' She sighed and pushed her sheet music into her bag. 'I guess we just have to make the best of things.'

Outside in the corridor, a child ran by roaring loudly, pretending to be an aeroplane. The two women exchanged glances, smiling.

'I'm going to miss this. The children . . .' Kitty went to the door. 'Quietly please, Gianni. School's not quite finished yet.'

The roar stopped and light footsteps disappeared down the corridor. Kitty picked up a used teacup and rinsed it in the sink in the corner.

'What about you?' said Adela. 'Any idea what you might do?'

'Actually, I ran into that pilot I told you about. Ended up having an interview at RAF HQ.'

'The pilot, eh?' Adela's eyes danced up at her as she pulled her compact out of her bag and checked her face. 'Of course you'll get the job, *chérie*. They'll be lucky to have you.' Adela glanced at her, suddenly remembering. 'But tell me. What did that lieutenant say?'

'You were right.' Kitty glanced towards the door, checking no one was passing. 'Father did have a . . .' she lowered her voice, 'mistress.'

'*Chérie*, I'm so sorry. I didn't want to be right about this.' Adela's eyes shone with sympathy. 'Can you meet her?'

'No. He wouldn't tell me her name, so I've no idea who she is. But I'm determined to find her. Goodness knows how, though.'

'Did he tell you anything about her?'

'He barely admitted she existed, so I haven't got much to go on.'

'*Alors*, that's not very helpful. I'm so sorry.' Adela glanced at her, before putting on her crimson lipstick. 'Look, you need cheering up. We both do. Come to The Star next week. I'm starting my new set. Frank's coming, said he'll bring his aircrew.'

'That sounds fun. And I'd love to see your show,' Kitty smiled. 'So, who's Frank?'

Adela arched a painted eyebrow at her, her brown eyes brightening.

'You know.' She nudged Kitty with her elbow. 'I told you. I met him at The Monico last week. He's a sweetheart. Let's face it, we all need some consolation in this damn war.'

At the end of the afternoon as the final bell clanged, the children left the classroom and Kitty stood outside on the stepped street, to say a final farewell. The children were subdued and even Miss

Mazelli wasn't barking instructions about wearing hats and straightening ties as she normally would.

Kitty knelt down and pressed her cheek against Carmela's, breathed in her sweet smell for the last time. She had asked Adela to sew a cloth doll, with dark curls of wool for hair, a soft velvet face and a pale green cotton pinafore dress, like Carmela's own. Adela had come up trumps, scouring the shelves of Mr Gatt's tiny haberdasher's shop on Old Mint Street. Kitty pulled the doll from her bag and gave it to Carmela.

Her violet eyes widened with delight.

'Dolly wearing dress like me.' Carmela kissed the little face and hugged her to her chest.

Kitty's throat closed. Her eyes filled. She stood up and for a moment the pavement blurred. What was she going to do without her? Just seeing Carmela, knowing her smell, the way she still sucked her thumb, watching her play, somehow kept Alice more alive, more real for her. Kitty shut her eyes. What was happening to Alice? Was she being pulled out of school, evacuated from her home, sent to live with strangers?

Suddenly warm arms were around her, and Mrs Cortis pulled her close, crushing her against her generously bosomed apron. Hot breath in her ear.

'*Grazzi, grazzi ħafna.* My little girl, she talks about you so much. You always take such great care of her.'

Mrs Cortis pulled away and lifted a cloth-covered basket filled to the brim.

'A small gift to thank you for all you have done.' She pushed the basket into Kitty's arms and turned up the corner, revealing oranges, artichokes and broad beans. She put her finger to her lips. 'Don't say anything or everyone will want some.'

Kitty welled up, smiling at the kindness of this tired-looking, stout woman. 'Thank you so much. I'll miss Carmela very much.'

'She will miss you too. But you must come and see us.'

'I'd love to.'

Mrs Cortis smiled at her, her small eyes shrewd. 'One day you will find such happiness with one of your own.'

Kitty knelt to give Carmela a final cuddle. Then they walked down the street, turned the corner and were gone.

That evening when she got home, she found a letter waiting for her on the silver tray in the hallway. She snatched it up and ripped it open.

Air Officer Commanding Atkinson was delighted to offer her the job as civilian aircraft plotter. Her heart raced. She was to report to Military HQ at Lascaris, 9 a.m. sharp next Monday.

Precise and bossy, but that must be the military way. That would take some getting used to. A handwritten note scrawled underneath, presumably from Mrs Johnson, the captain of D Watch, instructed her to bring her gas mask and tin hat. It also gave her instructions on how to find the secret hidden entrance to Fighter Command.

Kitty hugged it to her chest. She couldn't wait to start.

Chapter Eight

With Mrs Johnson's words *whether there's an air raid on or not* ringing in her ears, Kitty arrived early in the Upper Barrakka Gardens, leaving plenty of time to find the hidden entrance. She walked past the fountain through the tall arched colonnades and leant over the ornate iron railing above the saluting battery. She checked her watch again. Quarter to. The glass face glinted in the morning rays and she lifted her own face to the early February warmth. Nerves flooded her stomach. She wasn't sure what to expect. No uniform, clearly, so she had decided to follow Mrs Johnson's lead, and wore a cream blouse with wide lapels and an inoffensive moss-green skirt that she hoped would fit in.

A seagull cawed overhead. Kitty stared across the dazzling water of Grand Harbour, a destroyer and a frigate moored up. Far out to sea, the white condensation trails of a dogfight circled and looped, like embroidery across the blue sky. She hadn't wanted to come to Valletta after Alice was born, but it was amazing how this place, with its churches, convents and auberges at every turn, had got under her skin. She loved the creamy stone, the heat, the dust. How every street led down to the sea, how warm and welcoming the people were. Even if it was being ravaged by war.

She walked to the Bofors anti-aircraft gun emplacement, trained over the harbour. Two soldiers from the Royal Malta Artillery lolled, smoking, against the walls of sandbags; another whistled as he adjusted something on the gun.

'Fancy a gasper, love?' a sergeant called.

She smiled her *no thanks* and hurried off to find the entrance.

'Welcome to Fighter Command, Katherine.'

'Please, call me Kitty. And thank you for the directions. I wouldn't have found the place without them.'

'Yes, we're one of the best-kept secrets of the war down here,' Mrs Johnson smiled as she led her into a small reception area, 'and we want to keep it that way. And please, call me Irene.' She gestured round her at the drab paintwork of the windowless room. 'This is the nerve centre of Malta's defence. Since the Nazis started bombing us, we're gradually moving all Army, Navy, RAF and Military Intelligence to be based here at Lascaris. Much safer, so deep in these old Crusader tunnels. And hopefully no one would ever guess they're here.'

She stood as Kitty remembered her, shoulders back, neck tall, and her hands folded together in front.

'Now the good news is that you'll be joining my D Watch. It's been a busy morning so far, first raid at six-forty, you may have heard the alert earlier.'

Kitty nodded.

'Yes, a formation of Junkers and Messerschmitts dropping bombs over a minesweeper near Filfla,' Irene continued. 'Best we head down to the Operations Room and get you started.

But first you need to take the Oath. Please, follow me.'

'The Oath?'

Irene turned to her. 'Of secrecy. You'll find out a lot of top-secret military information here about war strategy, military planning and so on. You must never breathe a word to anyone about what you hear or see here in the course of your duty.'

'Of course,' Kitty nodded, her skin tingling. 'But honestly, I don't need an oath. I'd never tell anyone what I heard here.'

As Kitty put her hand on the Bible and read the typed words Irene put in front of her, she couldn't think of a single reason she really needed to take it. She'd never betray her country. Of course she wouldn't.

Kitty's eyes widened as they descended deep down through a complex of dimly lit passageways and tunnels that Irene said ran under the huge Crusader bastions. Navy and Army officers hurried past carrying files. Kitty kept her eyes glued on Irene's neat bun gliding along like a gazelle in front of her, wondering how on earth she'd ever find her way about, as Irene pointed out side rooms for Gunnery Liaison, where they ran the ack-ack guns positioned all over the island, the Interceptor and Cipher Room, where they decoded messages picked up from enemy shipping or aircraft, the Filter Room, which received air raid warnings from spotter stations positioned across the island, as well as from radar. Not to mention Signals traffic, Military Intelligence, Combined Operations and a stream of other baffling names she couldn't keep track of.

They passed a briefing room full of officers and women civilians lined up in rows. A senior RAF officer at the back of the room pointed to various aerial reconnaissance photographs, smoke coiling from a cigarette pinched between his finger and thumb as he talked.

'That's the air officer commanding, the AOC, Andrew Atkinson,' Irene smiled at Kitty. 'We call him "Ash", for obvious reasons. He's doing Morning Prayers.'

'Right.' Kitty must have looked confused, as Irene raised an eyebrow.

'Not actual prayers, of course. The all-service daily briefing on what's going on, troop movements, shipping convoys, aircraft deliveries, communiques from the War Office in London and so on. You can attend if you're on morning shift.'

'Right.'

Kitty was so busy staring through the doorway that she almost knocked an overalled engineer off his ladder.

'Watch out,' he called, with a wink, snatching a piece of ventilation tubing that threatened to fall. 'You want to keep breathing, don't you?'

'Sorry.' Kitty's cheeks burnt.

'You alright?' Irene eyed her calmly. 'We've only just moved in and they're still extending lighting and whatnot in the tunnels. You'll get used to it down here.'

They walked through more sunless corridors.

'Of course, you're joining us at a critical time for Malta. And for Britain too. We're sitting alone in the middle of the Mediterranean, as Axis power expands around us.'

Kitty nodded, trying to keep up with her. They stopped in front of a map of the Mediterranean and Irene tapped the tiny images of Malta and Gozo.

'Malta is the jewel of the Mediterranean. From Grand Harbour, the entire sea can be dominated by warships.'

Irene stared at Kitty. 'Whoever controls Malta controls the Mediterranean and beyond, with access to the Suez Canal and through to India and so on. If we are defeated, Britain will be left to stand entirely alone against the enemy in Europe.'

The hairs lifted on the back of Kitty's neck. Of course, she followed the newsreels at The Regent, and broadcasts from the BBC in London on the Rediffusion – but somehow, hearing it from this tiny woman so far below the ground in this sunless secret bunker, she understood the precariousness of their situation, of the island, of their lives, as never before.

Her fingers felt for the wallet in her pocket, and for a moment she drew comfort from knowing that her baby's photograph was there.

'And this,' Irene whispered over her shoulder as she pushed open a heavy door, 'is where you'll be working – Number 8 Sector Operations Room. The best-kept secret in the Mediterranean.'

'Hostiles approaching from the north.'

Kitty startled as her headset crackled to life. A woman's calm voice sounded in her ears.

'Twelve Messerschmitts at Angels twelve. Approaching N for Nuts.'

Angels twelve. That meant the enemy fighters were flying at a height of 12,000 feet. Kitty jumped forward to adjust the details on an arrow-shaped block and with her wooden rod, pushed the marker representing the enemy aircraft into position onto the plotting table. It was crucial she got it right; the fighters depended on knowing exactly where the enemy were.

The whole table was covered by a gridded map of Malta

extending to the coastline of Sicily and Italy. All Kitty could remember was N for Nuts was Malta, H for Harry was Sicily. The six plotters marked up red, yellow and blue arrows on wooden blocks, according to their instructions from the Filter Room, and pushed them onto the table.

Another big attack was coming.

An icy shiver ran down her spine. Up above, the siren would be wailing, and people all over the island would be running for shelters. She hoped Lydia and Adela were doing the same. She felt with her foot for the basket under the table containing her helmet and gas mask. Just in case. They were so removed down here in this bunker, like a secret world. Bombs could be falling, guns firing, but they were so deep underground that not a vibration, not a crumb of dust fell from the ceiling.

Irene stood on her tiptoes, to chalk the 'aircraft out' on the board with the grace of a dancer. Kitty could see Stallion Blue Two was out, somewhere over Italy. Stallion, Irene had told her, as she knew Flying Officer Bill Hamilton, was the code name for 69 Squadron's reconnaissance planes.

Was it Bill's?

Her stomach fluttered.

She didn't know his call sign – hadn't even known he had one. Didn't dare ask now. Irene had lectured her about keeping her personal life out of work, but she had been thinking about him since meeting him again the other day, remembering those shrewd grey-blue eyes staring into hers when she'd said she didn't miss photography. It was as if he saw something in her that even she had forgotten existed.

Irene had been a complete brick showing her round, explaining in a whisper as raids went on how Fighter Control worked. Kitty glanced at her now, glad she had been put in her D Watch. She caught Kitty's eye.

'Everything alright? I know it's a lot to take in at first. Just remember, accuracy is key.'

'Of course.' Kitty nodded. Her armpits bloomed with sweat.

Irene must have seen the flicker of uncertainty flash across her face, as she glanced across the table. 'Rita'll help you.'

Rita, a stocky, jolly-looking Maltese plotter, with dark wild curls barely constrained by her headphones, glanced up and threw Kitty a quick smile.

'You'll soon get the hang of things. No heels, though.' She stuck out a sensible brown lace-up shoe and winked. 'It's the aching feet you don't get used to. No good if you want to go out dancing later with your beau.'

Kitty smiled at her. She was younger, but Kitty liked her hearty tone straightaway. But would she get used to it all? Kitty rolled her shoulders, her blouse sticking to her back. There was so much complicated jargon and so many code names for the squadrons, the heavy headset made her ears sore, and she kept jumping every time she heard a voice in her ears from the women in the Filter Room giving her aircraft positions.

The Filter Room received information about aircraft, whether hostile or friendly, how many of them and their height, from the radar and observer points all over the island. They passed them to Kitty and the other plotters, who repeated them to the senior controller through the microphone on their headsets that curved to their chins. The plotters then marked them on the table.

Tension hung as thick as the fog of cigarette smoke in the room. Hushed concentration fell, as every man and woman focused on the map on the huge plotting table. Raised above them, running along one side of the room on a balcony they called the Shelf, senior officers had a good view looking down to plan the attack. Now they barked instructions down telephones as they assessed the enemy's position and decided which squadron to use.

The AOC, 'Ash' Atkinson, was up there – an energetic-looking man with an unruly moustache, and a cigarette pinched tight between thumb and forefinger. His fingers drummed constantly as he hung over the balcony, eyes fixed on the plots. He snatched up the receiver and barked into it.

'Come in, Ta'Qali airfield, this is Ash. Scramble Pinto Red Squadron.' The tannoy above them crackled into life, reverberating with his words. 'Repeat, Scramble Pinto Red Squadron.'

Kitty knew now that at Ta'Qali airfield, Hurricanes from 249 Squadron, code-named Pinto, would be taking off, preparing for battle. Rita marked their plot and moved them onto the table. Through her headset, Kitty received the new position for the Hostiles she was tracking.

'Twelve Messerschmitts incoming, at Angels twelve. Headed south,' Kitty called into her microphone and inched her plot across the table.

'Pinto Red Squadron, climb to fifteen thousand feet,' Ash ordered. 'Get above the Hostiles, Douggie.'

'Pinto Red One here.' Douggie the squadron leader's voice, thick with a Scottish accent, burst through the static over the roar of his engine, the radio in his plane broadcast through the speaker. 'Heading up to fifteen thousand feet.'

Kitty jolted. She hadn't realised she would hear the voices

of men literally going into battle. Her heart speeded up.

'Bandits at Angels twelve, approaching south. Target Valletta,' Kitty said into her microphone. She pushed the Hostiles plot forward as the Filter Room confirmed their position.

Douggie's voice crackled into life, shouting anxiously over the tannoy again. 'Pinto Red Five, where are you? I can't see you. Stick to me like glue.'

'This is Red Five, coming in on your right side. Over.'

Christ, the Red Five pilot's voice sounded so high and young. He was just a boy. Kitty swallowed.

Inch by inch Kitty and Rita pushed the plots for the Hostiles and 249 Squadron across the map, following the positions they were given through their headsets, until the aircraft met in the same square.

'I see them! Bandits at three o'clock!' Douggie shouted. 'Tally ho, tally ho!'

'Go get 'em, Douggie.' Ash's voice was calm, commanding.

The battle had begun.

The loud throttle of an engine, urgent yells, the staccato of gunfire. Then the radio cut out.

Silence fell across the room. The plotters exchanged glances, faces drawn in anxious frowns. It was over to the pilots now.

Kitty shut her eyes, her heart racing. High above them men were firing at fighter planes, swooping over Grand Harbour, fighting for their lives. Fighting for all their lives. All they could do was wait. Long seconds ticked by. Everyone held their breath.

Eventually, the tannoy crackled back into life, Douggie shouting.

'Pinto Red Five's bought it. He's going down. Going down!'

Loud static. The high whine of a diving plane. 'Bale out, man! Come on, bale out!'

Kitty's knuckles were white on her cue as she strained to hear. More engine roar.

'Can't see a parachute. No parachute!' Douggie shouted, alarm in his voice. Then the radio cut out again and the tannoy fell silent.

The room seemed to hold its breath. A Hurricane pilot was crash-diving into the sea right now and there was nothing anyone could do.

Seconds later, the Filter Room confirmed the information no one wanted to hear.

'Pinto Red Five, plot faded.' Rita repeated the words into her mic.

His plane had crashed into the sea and his plot had disappeared from the radar.

That poor young pilot.

'Christ,' Ash said, up on the Shelf. He ran his hand through his hair. 'That's Kenny, the new pilot officer.' He stubbed his cigarette out hard in the ashtray. 'He's only been in Malta five weeks.'

Shaking, Kitty forced herself to concentrate on the voice in her ears, giving her new enemy aircraft positions.

'Hostiles turning, headed north-east,' Kitty called. They were headed back to Sicily.

The attack had ended.

She pushed their plot off the map as they left Malta. Ash gave orders for Pinto Squadron to return to Ta'Qali and the 'Raiders passed' was called.

The tension in the room dropped; the plotters set down

their cues and murmured round the table. Up on the Shelf, Ash lit another cigarette.

Irene stepped forward and called up to him. 'Ash, this is Katherine Campbell, our new plotter. Vice-Admiral Campbell's daughter.'

Ash's eyebrows shot up. 'Ah, good man. A great loss to us all.' He blew out a stream of smoke while he appraised her from above. 'Welcome aboard, Campbell.'

He bounded down the short flight of steps two at a time and thrust his hand out at her. His grip was strong, his expression energetic. 'I'm sure you'll settle in just fine.'

'Thank you.' She swallowed.

'Bad show this morning. Don't like losing one of ours.' He frowned, glancing at the board. 'Just Stallion Blue Two to come in now.'

It was over an hour later when Kitty picked up the reconnaissance plane returning and inched its plot across the grids towards Malta. Was it Bill's?

'Stallion Blue Two approaching south-west at Angels ten,' she called. She held her breath, hoping no enemy aircraft would appear.

Ash's voice boomed over the speaker. 'Calling Stallion Blue Two. All safe and sound, over?'

'Bit of a hot reception, but we're in one piece, over.'

It was him. Bill's steady, cheerful voice. He was back. Kitty released a long breath. Thank God.

'Good show. Welcome home. Over.'

'See you at the debrief. Over.'

So this was what Bill had meant the other day when he'd

said he liked to think she would be watching over him. She longed to tell him she understood, now.

She hadn't imagined just how close the contact would be with the moment of battle, how unreal it would feel to plot aircraft in the sky like chess pieces, only with no power over the outcome whatsoever. How intimate it was to hear the tension in the pilot's voices as they fought for their lives, to hear what could be their last words, and yet often not even know who they were.

How it would bring her to confronting the line between life and death and the moment in which it turned, every day.

She realised that her hand was jammed in her pocket, her fingers running over and over the little photograph wallet. It frightened her then, to understand just how far away she was from finding Alice.

Chapter Nine

The following evening Kitty sipped a Gin and It, glad she was tucked at a tiny table at the back of the club, huddled beside a fusty-smelling red velvet curtain. At least no one was likely to talk to her here. She squeezed her sequinned evening bag on her lap, one Dexter had given her a million years ago. The Star was hot and dark, filled with a haze of cigarette smoke, the musty smell of beer and the cheering shouts and stamps of soldiers, sailors and airmen all crammed together, the shaded lights reflected in the mirrors that lined both sides of the room.

All eyes were fixed on Adela, slinky in the silver sheath, singing her heart out into the microphone on the small glittering stage. Kitty tingled to the tips of her fingers as Adela's powerful, melodic voice soared up to the rafters. She had never seen her sing like this before.

Adela delivered a spellbinding series of songs, one minute crooning as if the microphone were her lover, the next minute belting out bigger songs as if she had a full orchestra behind her and was on stage at The Palladium. Instead, she was jammed in between an upright piano, where a chubby man in a bow-tie and bowler hat thumped the ivories with pudgy fingers, and a balloon-cheeked saxophonist, his stomach straining against the buttons of his too-tight suit as he fingered the glinting keys. As she sang 'Night and Day', Adela caught sight of her across the room and winked.

Kitty grinned back. The music washed over her and a bubbling feeling fizzed in her stomach, a reminder of the carefree excitement she used to feel on nights out with Dexter, when he'd arrive clutching a bottle of champagne and wind up the gramophone before they went out dancing at the Gargoyle. Her shoulders dropped, her foot tapped and she felt lighter, freer, than she had in ages – and for a moment, thoughts of war drifted away. She smoothed her emerald silk dress, realising with a shock that she had never been to a club in Malta. Now she was here she felt comfortable, despite the thin straps over her shoulders that Lydia had earlier so irritatingly disapproved of, raising her eyebrow as Kitty checked her reflection in the hall mirror and saying, 'Cover yourself up with a wrap.'

It was as if Kitty had buried herself.

Well, no more.

Adela's powerful high voice rose to a crescendo as she finished 'It's a Lovely Day Tomorrow' and the place erupted with loud cheers, stamping and whistling, the audience throwing up khaki caps and white sailor hats so they spun like plates in the red light. Kitty clapped until her palms ached, delighted her friend was so popular.

Minutes later, Adela pushed her way through the crowded room, beaming from ear to ear.

'Adela, you were brilliant.' Kitty hugged her, shouting above the roar of chatter. 'Just breathtaking.' Up on stage another girl was beginning a gypsy routine, stamping and banging a tambourine.

Adela took her arm and led her over to a group of airmen who leapt into action, making introductions, pulling up chairs, offering drinks and cigarettes until they were all squashed round a small table, a candle flickering in the middle.

'To the stunner who sang the best set of the night.' Frank's grin split his face under his ginger moustache, his tie loose under his RAF jacket. He raised his glass. 'Chaps, isn't she bloody terrific!' His pale eyes twinkled as his large hand grabbed Adela round her silver shimmering waist.

Kitty scrambled to raise her glass with the others as he swept Adela into a big kiss.

'Frank, *chéri*, enough!' Adela laughed, as he pretended to swoon away.

Frank's ginger-lashed eyes stayed fixed on Adela's face as he gazed at her adoringly, and Kitty felt a stab of envy. It was a long time since Dexter, or anyone, had looked at her like that. Everyone laughed uproariously and Kitty sipped her gin and leant forward to join their conversation. They were ragging about some pilot in their group, a chap called Bingo, who'd just come back from a flight to Alexandria that day laden with cigarettes and whisky.

Behind them in the dark, glimpsed through the throng, she could just make out a pilot, the peak of his cap covering his face, pushing his way through the crowd to their table from the bar. He clutched a bottle to his chest, glasses grasped in his other hand, and something about the stiff curve of that hand, the taut skin, the rigid fingers holding the bottle made her heart lurch in her chest.

Bill.

Heat rose through her body.

He didn't notice her at first, thumped the glasses onto the table, unscrewed the bottle and poured the whisky at chest height, moving the waterfall of golden liquid seamlessly across one glass to another, pouring a neat inch of whisky in each.

'Direct hit! About time, Bingo,' laughed Frank, raising his glass.

'For once your aim's straight, mate,' called Tubby, the other flyer. 'Makes a change.'

'Idiots.' He pretended to cuff Frank with his scarred hand. As he looked up, his gaze fell on Kitty.

'Kitty!'

Surprise flashed in his eyes, his hand jolted and the whisky pattered like a stream onto the marble tabletop, before he snatched the bottle up. 'What are you doing here?'

Whisky pooled across the table, dripping down her leg, and, distracted, she dashed at it with her hand.

'God, I'm sorry.' Bingo dropped to his knees and fished out an oil-stained handkerchief from his uniform jacket. 'Didn't mean to give you a shower.'

'Oh, don't worry, it's nothing,' she said, flustered, as he dabbed at her leg. His fingernails were rimmed with oil and she caught the whiff of aircraft gasoline above the whisky. He must have come straight from the airfield. He looked up at her from under his cap, his scarred skin softened in the dark. Those kind grey-blue eyes looked straight into hers.

'Christ, we really must stop meeting like this . . .'

The intensity of his gaze left her surprisingly hot. She tore her eyes away from his and grabbed the handkerchief, embarrassed at his inept handling of her silk-covered legs.

'Here, let me.' She dabbed at the stain. 'Honestly, it's nothing. Really.'

The flying officers cracked jokes about bailing out while you had the chance and nine lives, and despite her mood she found herself smiling at their boyish humour.

'What *are* you doing, Bill?' Frank asked. 'Adela, Bill's in his cups again . . .'

'I'm most certainly not in my cups.' Bill rose to his feet and made an extravagant bow. 'I'm sorry. Let me pour you a drink to apologise for your unexpected shower.'

'God, don't let him have the bottle again.' Frank poured her a fresh drink.

Bill laughed, his mouth tightening in that lopsided pull of skin, and Kitty was glad when he pulled up a chair next to her. Understanding what he did, the danger he was in, hearing his voice on the R/T as he flew back from a mission had created a bond, an intimacy she was longing to share with him. He'd been careful to draw up his chair on her right, she noticed, probably so she couldn't see his scar. She remembered how he had tried to hide his hand at the café and felt a wave of protectiveness towards him.

'Kitty, what a lovely surprise. Chaps, this is the lovely Katherine Campbell I was telling you about.' He winked at her, the eyelid pulling shut, that spasm across his taut skin again.

But her insides warmed at the fact he had been talking about her. She caught Adela's smiling eye.

'And these two clowns are our navigator, Frank Jeffreys,' Bill went on, 'he of the famous ear-splitting whistle. You can hear it as far away as Tobruk.'

Frank pursed his lips, but the others shouted, 'Not now, Frank!'

'And Rear Gunner Tubby Maclaine.'

Tubby was anything but, a tall scarecrow of a man, with a thin face to match and legs that seemed too long to fold under the table, so that his knees banged the top.

'So you fly together?' Kitty asked, biting her lip at the stupid question. Goodness, she was out of practice at socialising.

'For our sins,' laughed Tubby. 'Bingo here's in charge. Allegedly.'

Bill tossed a Cisk beer mat at him. 'As if there's any corralling you two idiots.' He swigged his whisky and eyed Kitty over the glass. 'I'm really glad to see you, actually. So sorry I had to run off the other day. You were alright, though?'

'Oh, fine.' She smiled at him, her insides glowing. The evening had taken on a whole new meaning. The roar of chatter, the clink of glasses, the snap of castanets seemed to melt away and for a moment it was just Bill and her. 'I'm really glad to see you too.'

'Really?'

Their eyes met.

Heat rose in her cheeks. 'I wanted to thank you for telling me about the plotter job.'

Bill's eyes lit up. 'Have you applied?'

'I've started actually.' She touched his arm lightly and her fingertips tingled at the warmth of his body through his uniform jacket. 'Had my first day yesterday.'

Bill's eyes widened. 'So you were there when I . . .'

'Yes, Stallion Blue Two, you landed beautifully.'

He laughed. 'That's great news. You'll be excellent. And Lord knows how much we need you.' His eyes softened as he smiled at her. 'So now you're one of us!'

He raised his glass and waved it at the group. 'Come on, boys, time to celebrate. Kitty here has come on board with us at HQ. She'll be in the Ops Room flying us in from now on.'

Frank and Tubby looked up at her, a new respect in their eyes. 'Good for you,' said Frank.

'Best behaviour required now, lads,' laughed Tubby, raising his glass. 'None of your swearing, Frank, when Bill lands her like an old crate.'

Bill laughed and raised his glass. 'To Kitty, our new recruit.' They roared her name and chinked glasses.

When the congratulations died down and chatter started up, Kitty turned back to Bill. He leant forward in his chair, his appraising eyes on hers. His shirt-sleeved arm radiated warmth right next to hers, bare in her silk dress; the smell of him, a mix of soap and engine oil already pleasantly familiar.

'You know, I can't tell you how reassuring it'll be when we're up at ten thousand feet,' his fingers toyed with a beer mat as he glanced at her sideways, his eyes shining, 'knowing you're there.'

Kitty felt breathless, her chest filled with lightness. She'd been thinking for a few days about what she could do to thank Bill, but now the moment was here to actually suggest it, her mouth went dry and her stomach seemed to be filled with a meadow full of very busy butterflies. She took a deep breath.

'Actually, I'd like to do something to thank you.'

He stared back at her quizzically.

'I was thinking about how you said you were struggling to get all the developing done. Why don't I come over and develop some rolls for you?'

'You don't need to do that.'

'I'd like to, honestly,' her voice was earnest, 'I want to help. I understand now how terribly important reconnaissance photographs are. How vital for planning missions.'

'Really? Well, Fighter Command keep asking us to do more and 69 Squadron are certainly stretched . . .' His eyes gleamed as he ran a finger round his glass, thinking. 'I'll clear it with the Brass, but I'm sure it'll be alright now you're one of us.'

'Marvellous.'

'How about I pick you up and show you round Luqa first? Then we can work through some film together.'

A warm feeling of anticipation bubbled up inside her and suddenly, for the first time in years, she couldn't wait to get back into a darkroom.

Chapter Ten

Sixteen raiders down, another probable eight damaged, screamed the headlines on the news-stands as Kitty hurried through the quiet streets to the Porta Reale, the grand arched gate of Valletta, to meet Bill. Some good news at last. It had been a tiring first couple of weeks at Fighter Command, topped off by a heavy raid last night, noisy and frightening. Exhausted, she and Lydia had given up on trying to get back to bed and stayed in the shelter all night.

But Kitty hummed as she walked in the late-February sunshine. She was looking forward to seeing Bill, had surprised herself by fussing over which lipstick, which blouse to wear this morning, the flower-sprigged one or the pink with the piping? She'd chosen the pink. And what was really putting a spring in her step was the idea of getting stuck in with some film. All made doubly rewarding of course, as it would really help 69 Squadron out and she knew now how much Ash relied on their intelligence.

She passed through one of the two main stone arches and smiled when she saw Bill waiting for her. He stood by the RAF motorbike, smoking, dressed in his flying jacket, a leather helmet with goggles pushed high on his forehead so it hid some of his scar. His face lit up when he saw her, the lopsided scarred smile lifting his drooping eye, a shadow of relief flickering across his face.

Had he worried she might not come? An unexpected wave of warmth filled her.

'Thanks so much for picking me up. There are so few buses now what with the petrol rationing, it would have taken me all morning to get to you. It's really kind of you.'

'My pleasure entirely.' He threw down the cigarette and gestured to the motorbike. 'Sure you're alright with this? I'll drive carefully.' He winked at her.

She laughed. 'I'm looking forward to it.'

She had always wanted to ride a motorcycle and her insides bubbled with excitement. She was pleased she'd worn trousers today, much to Lydia's disapproval. 'Watch those flying boys. I hear pilots are the worst,' Lydia had tutted as she left the house earlier. 'We don't want any more unpleasant surprises.' Kitty had to really work at biting her tongue as she left the house.

Bill handed her the spare leather helmet and a pair of goggles. 'Let's go and see Betty.' He ground his cigarette out with his foot. 'Hop on.'

'Betty?' She strapped on her helmet.

'My plane.' He grinned as he sat astride the bike and pulled his goggles down. 'Now we just need Jerry to give us some peace and quiet today.'

She pulled on the goggles, tucked her hair under the helmet and climbed on behind him.

'Hold on to me,' he yelled over his shoulder. She put her arms round his waist and pressed against him, suddenly aware of the solid warmth of him against her chest and momentarily embarrassed at the intimacy. He revved the engine and they set off in a cloud of dust.

The ride was as thrilling and noisy as the drives in Lady Luck with Dexter used to be and she clung to Bill, her hands tight on his waist, her cheek hot against the collar of his flying jacket, hair whipping in her face. She soon got used to the sensation of swaying with his body as he roared into the flat patchwork fields of the countryside, turning left and right, as they speeded down winding lanes lined with stone walls. She was acutely aware of his body moving against hers, his back firm against her chest, the muscles of his stomach rippling under her hands as he leant from one side to another. She breathed in, and the smell of him and the serge of his uniform filled her nostrils.

After a few minutes they came to a stop. Prickly pear cacti, yellow jonquils and pink anemones nodded by a wire fence; a lizard darted on the stones. Bill cut the engine and the sound of birds tweeting and the rush of the breeze filled her ears. She dismounted, moving away from his body, suddenly awkward at his physical closeness.

'Welcome to Luqa airfield.' Bill waved his hand at the long runway that stretched into the green of the island, the blue sea glittering far in the distance. Behind them the battlements of the ancient city of Mdina shimmered against the sky. 'You've probably already heard a lot about it.'

She nodded, gazing as a steamroller busily smoothed bomb craters on the runway, and a canvas windsock flopped limp. Here and there hangars, huts and barrack blocks were dotted round the airfield, and at regular intervals round the perimeter the sandbagged emplacements of ack-ack guns pointed, poised for attack. A handful of biplanes and several large twin-engined bombers faced the runway, the white, red and blue of the wing roundels shining in the sun, a clutch of deckchairs around them. The loud sound of hammering echoed across the field as groundcrew clambered over the fuselages.

He pointed proudly to the nearest plane.

'Betty. Welcome to 69 Squadron.'

A table with a chess set and two chairs stood beside it.

'Good to see the game's still standing. I was about to checkmate Frank yesterday,' he laughed. 'Betty's a Martin 167 Maryland, all the RAF could spare after the Battle of Britain last autumn, but she's not so bad. A real thoroughbred, built as a bomber, but the boys have refitted her for photo reconnaissance. We shoot through her bomb-bay.'

'Really?' Kitty nodded, trying to imagine operating a camera in a jolting plane, hanging out over the void of sky on the floor. Her stomach knotted. 'Crikey, I don't know how you manage to take pictures.'

'Well, she's pretty fast and manoeuvrable,' he smiled. 'We've got four machine guns on the wings, and forward and rear-facing guns.' He pointed them out. 'That's why I need Tubby and Frank. Frank navigates and is front gun, Tubby is wireless in that turret halfway along the fuselage.'

Seeing where Bill and Frank sat made it all seem very real. Kitty shivered despite the heat of the day. Her eye ran along the plane's metal body and she was shocked to see it looked pretty shot up, a hunk of metal missing from the wing, the cockpit glass shattered.

'But she's so badly damaged.'

'Bit of excitement over Tripoli yesterday.' He smiled ruefully. 'She did whistle a bit where the wind got in on the way home, but the lads'll soon get her patched up again. We flew in nice and low, got some pretty decent photographs of Nazi ships. The photographs help us keep track of them and where they're headed, so Military Intelligence can plan how to attack them.'

He talked on about the difficulties of photographing through thick cloud, how low they sometimes had to fly. His eyes lit up as he spoke, his voice confident and calm, and he took on a self-assuredness Kitty hadn't seen in him before.

She shut her eyes for a second, trying to imagine what it must be like to be flying and be shot at, the courage you would need to dive down right into the fire of anti-aircraft guns to take photographs. Christ, they were brave. She suddenly understood how his crew would trust him, believe in his judgement, and how he would always do his best to bring them home.

'Why do they call you Bingo?'

He turned to her, a sheepish look on his face. 'I shot down three fighters in my first week. Lucky fluke, really.'

'I'm sure it wasn't.'

He laughed. 'Anyway, I'd rather you called me Bill.' He fished in the breast pocket of his jacket and pulled out a bullet. It glinted in the sunshine.

Kitty's eyes widened.

'I call it my lucky charm. Came in straight through the cockpit, whistled through my collar and lodged in the webbing on the other side of the plane.'

'Your collar?' Kitty stared at the bullet. How could he stand it, day after day, knowing he might get hurt again? 'But can't you fly another plane? One that isn't shot up?'

'There are no other planes.' He put the bullet back in his pocket. 'That's the thing. We just can't get them to Malta fast enough. Nor ammo, nor fuel. For one thing, Churchill needs them to fight the Nazis in the Atlantic, and for another, Jerry pretty much controls the Mediterranean.'

'And do their best to sink our convoys,' said Kitty, thinking of *Illustrious*.

'And it's not just us – the boys over at Ta'Qali airfield desperately need more fighter Hurricanes too. Anything else and they can't catch up with the bloody German Messerschmitts. They're too fast. We've had a few Hurricanes delivered this month, but they're shot down faster than we can get our hands on them.' He smiled wryly at her. 'Sorry. You don't want a lecture about lack of war supplies.'

'No, it's helpful to understand what's going on.' She put her hand on his arm.

Their eyes met for a moment and heat flooded her cheeks. Then she turned and made for the motorbike.

'Come on, let's get cracking. We can at least get your films developed today. Take a bit of pressure off.'

Kitty pored over the developing tray, her tongs swirling the paper floating in the liquid. Row upon row of tiny black crosses were literally appearing on the paper, like dots of ink rising on blotting paper.

'There are just hundreds of them. Literally hundreds.' She shivered, remembering the high-pitched scream their sirens had made as they dived vertically into attack. Her stomach churned and it wasn't because of the distinctive vinegar-like smells of the chemicals.

'Every airfield in Sicily is bristling with them,' Bill shook his head, 'and we've photographed more in Tripoli. They think Rommel's going to start an offensive to push us right back across North Africa to Egypt.'

'And they're all focused on one thing. Capturing Malta.' Kitty stared down at the lines of Stukas. 'And it's just you and the fighters at Ta'Qali standing between them.'

'Don't forget the artillery lads,' Bill protested, as he pulled up one of the rolls of negative and held it to the red-light bulb, 'they're doing us proud.'

The airfield's small darkroom was in a Nissen hut behind the NAAFI, a home-strung affair of a tabletop with containers of developing and fixing fluid, and a curtain of blackout felt stopping light from the door. A cat's cradle of lines of string ran back and forth along the length of the tiny room, with ribbons of negatives that they'd spent the morning developing now pegged up drying, and rows of photographs that reminded Kitty of how she'd strung the children's paintings at school. Only these were no innocent images. Every single one contained the threat of death, devastation and destruction to their tiny island.

Her stomach fizzed at the feel of Bill's body working so closely beside her, the way his bicep flexed in his RAF shirtsleeves as he shook the chemicals together; how his shirt buttons pulled across his chest as he held up the film; the easy, confident way he assessed the negatives as he held them up to check them. The red light of the darkroom highlighted the ridges and ripples of the scarred skin running down his face and for a moment she longed to reach up and touch the tautness of his tight skin.

She shook herself. Focus, Kitty.

She glanced at her watch, checking the timing, judged the photograph was ready and tweezered it out of the developing fluid. She slid it into the next tray to stop the image developing any further, before lifting it out and sliding it into the fixer in the final tray, to set the image.

Goosebumps rose at the rediscovery of the forgotten spellbinding magic, the way images appeared like ghosts emerging through a fog. For a moment she was taken back to the last time she had created this magic, remembering the fan of eyelashes, the rosebud lips, the tiny hands that had appeared, all those years ago in the bathroom at Willow End. The photograph of her baby. The only piece of her she still had. Her heart squeezed.

'Yes!' Bill exclaimed, his voice triumphant.

Kitty dragged herself back to the present.

Bill was running a roll of negatives through his fingers, squinting at each image until he found the one he was looking for.

'Yes! This is it. The urgent one I really need to do,' he said excitedly. 'The one that shows that fourth battleship sailing just off Messina. We flew back at first light this morning to check. Circled the enemy flotilla, re-counting all the cruisers and destroyers accompanying them as well.' He picked up the scissors, cut a row of images and peered at them under the enlarger. 'Bingo.'

He exposed the print onto the paper and looked up at Kitty. 'I knew I'd seen that fourth battleship yesterday, but the Brass's intelligence sources are convinced there's only three, so they thought I'd miscounted.'

'So you're right.' Kitty removed the Stuka photograph from

the fixer and dipped it into a tray of water to wash the chemicals off. The neat lines of bombers covering the airfield showed up clearly now.

'Yup. I'd counted them yesterday, but that extra battleship didn't show up on the negatives, as there was too much cloud cover.' He frowned, counting. 'I must get this over to them urgently. The Navy need to know before they plan their attack.'

'Hand it over, then.' She refilled the developer tray. 'We'd better run off the print.'

His fingers brushed hers as he passed her the exposed paper, sending a current through her body. Her hand throbbed with heat where he'd touched her and the tweezers trembled as she slid the paper into the developing tray. She stared at the paper, hoping he hadn't noticed.

'I must say, this makes a change,' he smiled at her gratefully, 'having someone who knows what they're doing.'

'I'm a bit rusty.' She looked up at him and their eyes met.

'You don't seem it.' His gaze was earnest. 'So, what about you? What did you used to photograph?'

She stiffened. The sharp smells of the familiar chemicals, the smooth touch of the film, the exotic world created by the red light was thrilling and her senses tingled at being immersed in it all again. It was as if rediscovering the joy of the process was like a return to herself, a return home, bringing her back to life . . .

But Bill's question brought everything rushing back. Her old life. The bathroom in Bloomsbury. Dexter. Alice.

She hesitated, poked the print in the liquid.

'Oh, nothing as important as this.' Her voice was stiff.

She didn't want to talk about her past. About her beautiful daughter. Not here. Not now. It was fused into some private place in her soul that she had to bury away, just to get through each day. She stepped away from the table and feigned interest in one of the pegged-up photographs.

'The focus is so sharp, from so high up,' she babbled, trying to distract him. 'I don't know how you do it.'

'Thanks.' He leant back against the table. 'But seriously, what did you like photographing?'

She couldn't look at him.

'Oh, you know. People mainly.'

There was a silence and he nodded encouragingly, so she felt obliged to say more.

'Fashion designers, aristocracy, actors.' She didn't mention the buildings for Dexter's *Architectural Review*, rattled on about women's magazines so he couldn't probe, like a fish flapping on a hook. 'But I always preferred photographing real people, doing ordinary things.' She brightened as memories flared, of girls in hats laughing on London streets, the housewife on her knees scrubbing her front step, the old lady newspaper seller on the corner of the Underground.

'So why did you stop?'

She froze, her fingertips on the photograph. Stared at him, blinking, a butterfly pinned to a board. Her hand fluttered to her baby's photograph in her pocket.

She broke eye contact.

'I was ill and . . . Father's job brought us here.'

She turned away from him. There was a moment of silence.

'Anyway, I don't have my camera here,' she said, forcing a false cheeriness in her voice, desperate to change the subject. She picked up the tweezers and pushed at the photographic paper in the tray.

'That would make it rather difficult.'

His eyes were full of compassion. He knew she wasn't telling him everything. Once again, she had the sensation that he understood her pain.

The silence was broken by the high-pitched wail of the air raid siren, deafening as the speaker was just over the door of the Nissen hut. Immediately came the sounds of running feet, people shouting, artillery guns bursting into life.

'Damn.' Bill cocked his head, listening. The heavy drone of engines in the distance. 'Bombers. Lots of them.'

They both glanced at the paper in the developing tray. The four ships were appearing like silhouettes in a mist. Kitty checked her watch. For a moment she thought of the women in the Ops Room. They would be receiving instructions about these aircraft right now, setting up the plots, moving into action. She lifted the print and slid it into the fixer.

The roar grew louder.

The ack-ack guns fired nearby. The red-light bulb swayed overhead, throwing eerie shadows. Glass beakers rattled together on the shelves, the liquid in the developing trays swilled back and forth like a series of tidal waves, the pegged-up ribbons of film swayed like seaweed in rough water.

Kitty's insides vibrated and she grabbed the edge of the counter to steady herself.

'Christ,' Bill yelled, grabbing his flying jacket and helmet. 'I've got to get Betty off the ground, before she's hit.'

'Go, go!'

'The print—' Bill glanced at the tray.

'I'll do it. Just go!'

'No, leave it,' Bill shouted, running for the door. 'Come on!'

An ear-splitting explosion made them duck. The table legs jumped off the floorboards, brown chemical bottles smashed to the ground and the blackout curtains pinned at the door billowed.

'Hurry,' Bill yelled, his hand on the door.

'I'll be right behind you!'

'Promise me you'll leave?' he shouted.

'Yes, just go!'

With a last desperate glance back, he pushed through the blackouts and disappeared.

Kitty turned back to the table.

A series of piercing whistles and bombs exploded one after the other, *boom, boom, boom*, so close her ears were muffled as if she were underwater. Her heart raced, but her mind was clear. She'd get the print. Her hands were clammy as she agitated it in the fixer. Checked her watch.

Just one more minute. That was all she needed. Just one more bloody minute.

Overhead the scream of a Stuka shrieked, growing louder as it dived. The hairs on the back of her neck stood on end and she dived under the table. Christ, was this it? She glanced up, terrified the Stuka was about to appear through the corrugated metal roof.

Thirty seconds. Thirty seconds more, please God, please.

All she had to do was wash the print. Focus, Kitty, focus. She could do this.

She leapt up, the shrieking whine rattling her brain against her skull, and tipped the fixer away. She gritted her teeth, her shoulders stiff, and poured water over the print.

Come on, come on, just get it washed. Christ, it wasn't enough, but it would have to do.

She snatched up the photograph, burst out of the hut and sprinted for the shelter across a patch of grass. The rattle of bullets, the roar of ack-ack guns, the crash as bomb after bomb exploded, rang in her ears.

Black smoke drifted like fog, cordite acrid in her mouth. Burning shrapnel rained down around her. She glanced across the airfield. Fires blazed on the runway, from the NAAFI, the dispersal hut, the barracks. Dark shadows swooped across the ground as wave after wave of bombers flew overhead.

How could Bill get Betty up in this?

She ran across the grass as fast as she could, but tripped, hit the ground with a *whumph*, bit her tongue. Christ, no. She wasn't going to die like this, not now. She was up in a second, stumbling, knees throbbing, the photograph crushed to her chest. She threw herself into the shelter as a blast pushed at her back, a ball of fire leapt into the sky and the darkroom exploded.

Chapter Eleven

The ammo lorry driver she'd hitched a lift with after the raid dropped Kitty off by the Porta Reale. She ran down Kingsway, clutching the print to her chest, praying Bill was still alive. She elbowed her way through streams of people emerging from shelters, hurried across Castille Square to St Peter and Paul Bastion and down the long flight of steps into Fighter Command. Kitty strode through the corridors, relieved to be back in familiar surroundings so deep underground, and burst through the door of the Operations Room.

Tension hit her.

The clock below the gallery ticked loudly, the familiar low hum of the ventilation too loud. The pallid, drained faces of B Watch looked up at her. Kitty paused, panting for breath. She caught Jean's eye, but the leader of B Watch didn't smile back. What they must have heard through their headsets.

A single Hostile plot was on the table, the click of the plotter's rod echoing as it was pushed over the square for Luqa. An enemy reconnaissance plane most likely, returned to photograph the damage. Up on the Shelf, Ash leant forward, making notes, a curl of smoke wreathing his head.

'Kitty! What are you doing here?' Irene stepped forward. She was dressed in a blue silk suit, white gloves on her hands, two strings of pearls at her neck, a grey cross on her forehead.

It was their day off. She must have hurried here straight from Ash Wednesday Mass, Kitty thought distantly.

'Are you alright?' Irene eyed Kitty with concern.

Kitty realised what a mess she must look. There were grass stains on her trousers. Dirt had stuck to the large developing fluid stains on her pink blouse. Her hands were smutted with mud and black marks from the burnt photograph, and her hair must be so tangled.

'I've just come from Luqa.'

'Luqa?' Irene echoed loudly. The girls on B Watch looked up at her.

Ash's head whipped up.

'Did you say Luqa? Christ.' He bounded down and crossed the Operations Room in three steps.

'It was terrible. The sky was full of Stukas. Wave after wave of them. They've bombed everything.' Kitty's voice wavered. 'So many planes on fire. Hardly a hangar or mess building left.'

Ash and Irene stared at her, their eyes wide.

'Why were you there?' Irene asked.

'I was helping Flying Officer Bill Hamilton develop photographs. Then the raid started. He had to get his Maryland in the air. I stayed behind to develop this.'

'What, under fire?' Irene looked startled.

Kitty nodded and held out the print to Ash. 'He urgently wanted to get it to you and the naval commanding officer. It's the enemy convoy off Messina, first thing this morning.'

Ash took the photograph, narrowing his eyes at it. He released a low whistle.

'Bloody marvellous. There *were* four battleships. Bingo was right.' He looked back up at Kitty. 'Good work, Campbell. Look, this is highly confidential information. I need to let the admiral know immediately, so the Navy can plan their attack strategy.' He glanced round the room. 'So where is Bingo?'

Sweat pooled under her arms. 'I don't know if he got airborne . . .'

'Yup, so an attack by one hundred enemy aircraft, you say? Christ.' Ash rubbed his hand over his forehead and frowned as he listened to the information on the other end of the telephone, but to Kitty his voice was muffled, as if he were down the far end of a tunnel, a whine deafening in her ears.

'And we had what, just eight Hurricanes in the air?' Ash continued. 'Jesus.'

Kitty and Irene exchanged glances on the other side of his desk. They were so outnumbered.

Kitty thought of Bill, hurrying out of the darkroom. No wonder he'd been desperate to get his Maryland airborne. He had to. Kitty twisted her hands in her lap, acid churning in her stomach, frantic to know what had happened to him. Dear God, please let him be alright, please.

Ash had returned from his discussion with the admiral and thanked her again for getting the photograph to them, and she had debriefed him on what she'd seen. Now, as he confirmed facts with the controller at Luqa, she closed her eyes, trying to push away the images that kept replaying in her mind, the sticks of bombs falling like rain, the booming guns, the explosions.

She distracted herself by gazing round the tiny office, with its old wooden desk and metal army chairs, surprised by the sawn-off shell cartridge case Ash tapped his cigarette over.

'So we shot down eight enemy planes, damaged nine more? Bloody good show.' He jotted in his notebook and took a drag on his cigarette. 'And how many planes have we lost?'

Kitty dug her nails into her palm. She leant forward, trying to hear the voice down the phone, desperate to snatch the receiver, yell, 'Is Bill alive?' But he was just one of so many pilots. She saw every day how they came and went. Was it wise to care about someone in the midst of war? She closed her eyes. Nothing had really happened between them, but somehow Kitty knew that didn't matter, that somehow it was already too late . . .

'Four Hurricanes lost? And six Wellingtons burnt on the ground, with seven more damaged? Jesus Christ.' Ash closed his eyes, rubbed his forehead. 'We don't have enough of the bloody things as it is . . . yes . . . and one Maryland?'

A Maryland?

Kitty's stomach plummeted like a falling bomb. Please don't let it be Bill.

'Right . . . right . . . I see.' Ash eyed her, his pen moving across the paper as he talked on. Kitty leant forward, her heart pounding, straining to make out the upside-down squiggles.

He slammed the receiver down.

'Bill? Is he alright?'

Ash glanced at her, fumbling in his jacket pocket for a Lucky Strike. 'Landed half an hour ago, apparently.'

She slumped back in her chair, her heart pounding with relief.

Ash lit up and tossed the match into the ashtray. 'Bloody murder out there. Six artillery chaps killed, fourteen civilians injured. And three-quarters of the houses destroyed in Luqa village.'

'Christ,' Kitty whispered.

'It's as bad as that first raid on *Illustrious*,' said Irene.

'The Luftwaffe have certainly thrown everything at it.' Ash released a long stream of smoke. He drummed his fingers on his desk. 'Malta may be what Churchill calls "an unsinkable aircraft carrier", but we're outnumbered five to one in planes, ships and submarines. London have got to get more supplies to us. More planes, more ships, more fuel, more ammo.'

Kitty shivered. She wasn't used to hearing senior officers talk so frankly. Knowing the truth of what was really going on.

'We must keep the pressure up on the War Office in London,' Irene said calmly. She folded her narrow hands in her lap. 'And we must keep fighting. We won't let Malta fall.'

Kitty looked at Irene with renewed respect. Irene's British husband had been sent with his regiment to India and her two sons were fighting with the Royal Malta Artillery, but she had such strength. Her words bolstered Kitty and she sat up straighter.

For the first time she understood they were all cogs in the great machine of this war, but that a small piece of information could make a huge difference to its outcome. She was glad she'd stayed behind to save the intelligence photograph. She would do everything she could to fight for Malta.

'Damn right,' said Ash. He smoothed his moustache. 'Our wireless interceptors picked up a top-secret message last week on German radio. Apparently Nazi High Command think they can take Malta in a fortnight.' He stubbed his cigarette out. 'It seems we're looking down the barrel of a German invasion.'

Kitty and Irene exchanged anxious glances.

Kitty went cold. Her pulse speeded up. Time was running out. She was still no further forward in finding her daughter. She had to find out who that woman was. And soon.

Chapter Twelve

Later that evening, Kitty was in her bedroom pulling on her dressing gown, when the air raid siren went off. She stiffened. Not again. There were so many raids every night now. She went out onto the marble-floored landing, where the wail of the siren echoed louder, and knocked on Lydia's bedroom door.

There was no reply.

'Lydia?'

Muffled sobs came back. Christ, was Lydia crying? She'd never seen Lydia cry before.

Kitty pushed open the door. Lydia, her dressing gown undone, grey hair unbrushed, stood by the mantelpiece, shivering. Her face was red and contorted, her eyes puffy. She looked up at Kitty.

'I can't do this any more. I just can't,' whispered Lydia. The heavy throttle of engines droned in the distance. She pressed her hands to her ears. 'Make it stop. Please, make it stop.'

'Oh, Lydia, darling.' Kitty rushed to put her arms round her, her heart in her mouth. Goodness, Lydia was panicking. She had to calm her down. 'It's alright. We'll go to the shelter.'

'No, no,' Lydia moaned.

'We'll be safe there.'

Kitty tried to reassure her as she steered Lydia to the bedroom door. The throb of aircraft engines was growing louder and the windows rattled behind the shutters.

Her heart raced. No matter how many air raids she went through, it didn't get any easier.

'Let's get to the shelter. It won't be so loud there.'

By the time they got down the stairs to the front door, the boom of the guns round Grand Harbour was deafening. Kitty picked up the basket she kept there and glanced at Lydia. A fine sheen of sweat glistened on her white face. Kitty hoped it wasn't her heart and checked the basket for her tablets, reassured they were there. She opened the door and chilly night air rushed in, the bang of ack-ack guns loud.

'Come on, darling – just a few steps further and you'll be safe. You can do it.'

The roar of guns and the heavy throb of bombers thundered in her ears as they walked the few yards up the street. In seconds, Kitty led Lydia into the shelter.

Although she had found a regular nook for them and done her best to make it homely, the shelter was too crowded, too warm, the walls beading with moisture. The smell of sweat and fear filled her nostrils. People crowded in, coughing, murmuring, praying. Some slept, stretched out on blankets as best they could.

Lydia seemed calmer now and Kitty set out the board, hoping to distract her with a game of draughts. Kitty poured a cup of tea from the thermos and passed it to her.

'Here. It'll make you feel better.'

Lydia took a sip, staring vacantly at the board.

'I'm going to Aunt Polly's in Alexandria.'

'What?'

'I can't stand this, Kitty. Sitting in shelters, waiting for bombs to drop. Waiting for the Germans to invade at any minute.' She shook her head. 'They'll bomb us until they win. My nerves can't take it.'

'But Lydia, you can't leave.' Oh dear, fear was muddling her. Kitty took her hand and rubbed her papery skin. 'There are no ships. It wouldn't be safe.'

'You think it's safe to stay?' Lydia pulled her hand away. 'I've written to Admiral Cunningham. He always respected your father. Asked him to get us on the first ship out of here.'

'Us?'

The clear thought that she didn't want to leave, wouldn't leave even if she could, dropped into Kitty's mind like a stone into a pond.

'I can't leave Malta, these people.' Kitty gestured round the shelter. 'They need me. We all need to fight. For God's sake, Lydia.' She stared at her, hardly able to believe she was having to spell this out. 'If we lose Malta, we lose the Mediterranean and probably the whole damn war. I can't leave.'

'Are you mad? Your father dragged us halfway round the world to this godforsaken rock.' Lydia's eyes filled. 'He always did what he wanted.' She swallowed back the tears and lifted her chin. 'There's no longer any reason for us to stay.'

'And I can't let Father give half of Willow End to a stranger. I have to find out who it is.'

And I have to find out where Alice has been taken – but Kitty didn't say the words out loud. Couldn't bear Lydia to dismiss her baby, again.

'I've told you. It doesn't matter who it is.' Lydia reached into her dressing gown pocket and pulled out a thin blue air letter. 'I've written to Dentons in Deal, instructing them to sell Willow End.'

'What? No!' Kitty sprang to her feet and snatched the envelope out of her hand. 'You can't do that.'

She unfolded the letter, her mother's instructions clear. To put the house up for sale, all contents included.

Her chest constricted.

All contents included.

The stuff in the attic.

'Jennings said it could take months to settle the will. We don't need to rush into this.' Kitty folded up the letter. 'We need more time—'

'Why?'

'To fight this, of course. To find a way to keep Willow End. Mother, please.' She stared at Lydia, the letter trembling between her fingers. She hadn't had enough time to find Father's mistress, needed to try harder. Lydia couldn't do this. 'Don't send it. Please. Let me have more time.'

Lydia gazed at her and shook her head. 'I don't know what miracle you think you're going to work, Kitty. We've got to sell the house and I'd rather just get on with it.'

'No. Please, Lydia. Don't do this.'

'There's no point in delaying.' She took the letter and replaced it in her pocket. 'Oh, and I forgot.'

Lydia's lips tightened.

'The Navy sent your father's things. They're in the drawing room.'

* * *

Dawn had barely cracked across the sky, the all-clear still whining, as Kitty banged her way back into the house and ran across the hall to Father's study. She pushed open the heavy door, hairs prickling at the back of her neck, and surveyed the room.

The shutters were closed, the room dark. Father's favourite portrait of Churchill stared down at her, the walls either side lined with navigation manuals and atlases, leather-bound collections of etchings of clippers from across the centuries. She had rarely been invited in here and it felt wrong, a violation of his privacy, to enter. His smell filled the room: tobacco from his favourite pipe, the wax cream he used to smooth his hair, the cologne he dabbed on his sharp-shaved chin every morning. She half expected him to appear at the door and bark, 'What do you think you're doing in here?'

She switched on the low lamp on his desk and light shimmered on the silver filigree of his pen holder. The whisky bottle on a table in the corner glowed a soft amber.

But most important of all was the large tea-chest by the desk, stamped *Property of the Royal Navy*, covered with a singed packing blanket. It was all they had left, they said. A fire in a storeroom . . .

Her mouth went dry.

She sat in his heavy teak chair and hesitated a moment. She'd checked his desk a few weeks ago, after the meeting with that lawyer, Jennings, and all she'd found was a spare tin of Marich's tobacco and a packet of pipe-cleaners nestling among a well-thumbed copy of *The Cheltenham Square Murder*. But of course. He wouldn't have kept confidential files lying around at home. He would have kept them safe at work.

Wouldn't he?

She eyed the tea-chest, blackened across one corner, presumably by the fire, goosebumps lifting on her arms. She knelt down on the rug and pulled aside the blanket.

On top lay his peaked cap, dark serge neatly brushed, gold piping and gold emblem at the peak shining. She stroked the flat top, her palms clammy, and smells of cordite and smoke wafted up. Her stomach clenched. Had it been taken off him after they recovered his body? Next his Navy identity card, faded and well worn, his stern face staring up at her, giving nothing away, in the tiny photograph.

She pulled out a sheaf of papers embossed with the Royal Navy logo at the top – copies of letters he'd signed recently. She put them aside and fumbled deeper in the chest, her fingertips brushing something hard. His pipe, the wood at the mouthpiece ground and chewed. A lump formed in her throat. She pictured him, that old habit he had, pipe in mouth – how between sucks at the pipe, he rolled his tongue, clicked his teeth and moved the pipe from one cheek to another. She placed the pipe down carefully.

Next was a stack of yellowing, curled naval reports and documents on ship movements. She lifted them out and dumped them on the Turkish carpet, and a cloud of dust flew up. A stack of manila folders. She scooped them up, leafed through each one, hoping, praying for one marked *For the attention of Katherine Campbell,* or *Adoption,* or even just *March 1936.*

But the folders were filled with pages of close-typed memos about dull admin matters. As she flicked through one after the other, her hands shook. Surely he'd left the information for her somewhere. But where the bloody hell was it?

Fallen to the bottom, half hidden by copies of a ship's manual, was a sliver of black leather. She reached in and pulled it out.

Father's wallet.

She hesitated, turning it over in her hand. There would be nothing in here about Alice. He would never have wanted her to search it. She put it down.

This was hopeless.

Frustration punched like a fist in her belly. How dare he. How dare he die without telling her how she could find her daughter. She picked up a handful of folders and threw them across the room, so they scattered, pages fluttering and splaying against the bookcase.

She gazed at the wallet, a wave of hot anger burning up her chest and neck. Why should she care for his wishes when he had not given a whit for hers. When he had not cared a fig about what she wanted when it came to the most important thing in the world.

She snatched up the wallet and tipped it up. A shilling or two dropped out and rolled across the rug. She pulled open the red-silk-lined sections and pulled out a pound note and a receipt for his favourite marmalade from the Wembley Store on Kingsway.

Nothing else. As she went to put it down, her turquoise ring, an heirloom from Grandmother, snagged on a tiny thread of red silk. As she held it up to the light to pull the thread from the clasps, she noticed a tiny flap on the side of the wallet.

She pushed her finger in and touched a piece of card. She eased it out and a tiny sepia photograph with fraying edges dropped to the floor. It was faded, worn with being held, the indentation of a thumbprint at the bottom. On the back was written *Senglea Photographic Studios, 1919.*

She picked it up, expecting to see Lydia. But the kind face of a young woman, her eyes filled with tenderness, dark hair pulled back, a silver filigree cross on the lace collar at her throat, smiled back.

Chapter Thirteen

'*Sacrebleu*! It's got to be her, hasn't it?' Adela held the small photograph up to the tasselled gold lampshade in her tiny hallway. 'The mistress?'

Kitty nodded, leaning against the door frame, puffed after the six flights of steps.

'I have to say, she's beautiful.' Adela peered at the photo. 'Lovely eyes.'

'Maybe,' Kitty huffed, thinking of Lydia's tired, puffy eyes.

'It's so worn. You can almost see his thumbprint. He's been looking at it for years.'

'I know.' Although it was a few days since she had found the photograph, Kitty still felt nauseous picturing Father in his study.

'Gosh.' Adela smoothed the curled edges with her thumb. 'To think he left half your home to her.'

'He's not a bloody romantic hero, Adela.' Kitty snatched the photograph back. Adela was being far too rosy-eyed about this. 'It's a huge betrayal.'

'I know, *chérie*, of course. Sorry.' Adela hesitated. 'But this is good luck finding this, no? It might help you find her.'

'I don't think it's going to be that easy . . .'

Kitty sneezed as she put the photograph back in her bag. She glanced round the apartment. A sharp smell irritated her nostrils. 'Gosh, what's that dreadful stink?'

Adela rolled her eyes. 'Iodine. It clings like bad perfume, no matter how much I wash my uniform.'

Adela, still in her crimson dress from the club, gestured through the bathroom door to the nurse's overall and apron dripping on a hanger over the bath. Kitty stared at her uniform, so different from her club dresses, fascinated by this new incarnation of her friend, the incongruousness of her roles. But they were all having to become someone different to who they were before the war.

Adela smiled. 'I know, it doesn't seem real, *non*? Me nursing!'

'How's it going?' said Kitty as they walked into the living room.

'All I do is bandage grazes from people tripping over rubble, or cuts from broken glass. Mostly I lance boils,' Adela said darkly as she pulled the pink gin out of the sideboard. 'Just another four weeks and we should start being trained on the ambulances, thank goodness. That's the best bit.'

She clinked the glasses onto the Bakelite tray and whirled round smiling. 'But I have other good news! Frank told me that two Free French airmen have arrived on Malta. They escaped from Tunisia, in North Africa.'

Kitty stared at her questioningly, not quite following.

Adela shook her head impatiently, her dark eyes shining. 'Remember? Louis might have managed to get a boat there, if he left Marseille. It's part of Vichy France.'

'Ahh.'

'Don't you see? The airmen might have met him. Who knows?' She clapped her hands together with glee. 'I've asked

Frank to invite them to the club one night, so I can talk to them. Find out if they might have met someone like Louis.'

'That's such good news. But is it likely?'

'There can't be that many Black soldiers there, just escaped from Paris. Just to know he's alive would be . . .' Adela put her hands to her cheeks, her eyes beaming, '*magnifique*!'

'It would be marvellous, darling.'

'Come on, then. Let's take the drinks up on the roof and you can tell me all about this photograph. I can't stand this casualty smell a minute longer.'

Adela picked up the tray with a flourish and led the way upstairs.

Up on the roof, they slumped into two deckchairs, an upside-down crate the table between them. Kitty gazed out across the dark expanse of Grand Harbour. The night air was cool, the bastions rimed with pewter highlights, the sea shimmering, glossed in silver moonlight. Far away at the harbour mouth searchlights weaved, their narrow beams cutting through the dark sky in a never-ending dance. Now and then, orange tracer fire flashed in the darkness, and distant planes cut through the light and disappeared, a dogfight in progress far out to sea. They had settled for running six flights down to the shelter only if they heard the heavy hum of bombers.

It was after curfew, so Kitty was staying the night. She had arranged for Lydia to have a break from the worst of the bombing, staying with Phyllis Enright up at the quieter end of the island at St Paul's Bay. Phyllis's husband, a navy commander, had collected Lydia that afternoon and Kitty was relishing a snatched evening with Adela. They had already raised their glasses to the Free French airmen and were now discussing the photograph.

Adela held it close to her face, illuminating it briefly with the flickering flame of her lighter in the dark.

'So she's the one who is "someone he . . ." – what was it?'

'"Someone he knew well and trusted implicitly." That's what Father said when he took—' Kitty stopped, unable to say Alice's name out loud, 'my baby. And it's the same phrase that lawyer used about the person Willow End was left to.'

'Sounds promising.' Adela eyed her over her glass.

'It's all I've got.'

'At least you know what she looks like now.'

'Well, what she looked like twenty years ago.' Kitty ran her finger round her glass. 'I've still no idea who she is. And Lydia's desperate to sell Willow End. If I don't find her soon, it'll be too late.'

'Could you advertise? Put her picture in the *Times of Malta* or something, say you wish to speak to her?'

'I don't think she'd come forward, would she? If he's kept her secret all these years?'

'Someone else might recognise her.'

'Unless she looks completely different now . . .'

'Who knows?' Adela shrugged, putting the photograph down. 'It wouldn't hurt to try.'

'You know, you're right.' Kitty sat up. 'I've got nothing to lose. And frankly, I haven't got much else to go on. It could be my last chance to find her.'

A full moon came out from behind a cloud and bathed the terrace in a silver lustre, a sheen on the small photograph on the crate.

'To think your father has been seeing her all these years.'

'We don't know that,' Kitty bristled. She pulled her cardigan round her and crossed her arms. 'Not for sure.'

Adela eyed her sympathetically. 'It's most likely, *non*?' she said gently. 'I would like to believe a great love like that is possible.' Her voice was wistful. 'Wouldn't you?'

Kitty glanced at her. While she didn't like what Father had done, she didn't want to spoil Adela's dreams. She adored her for having them. But frankly, a great love?

It was a fantasy.

She thought back to Dexter, the glamorous dinners at The Savoy, the passionate nights in soft beds at The Ritz. His lips on her body, his whisper in her ear of promises for their future, the comfort of his gentle words. How she had loved him. She'd been so young, so naïve.

How when she'd finally realised she was pregnant, she couldn't quite believe it herself at first, she'd been so careful to use the Volpar gel – but the alarm on his face when she had told him. Fear, if she was honest. His eyes had flicked from side to side as if he just wanted to make his escape right there and then from the table.

The bitter memory still stung. For a moment her glass trembled in her hand.

'I'm not sure it exists.'

'Of course it does.' Adela sighed. She sipped her drink. 'I will find love, one day. And so will you.'

'I'm sure you will, darling. You're so brave and strong.' Kitty shook her head. 'But I've had my chance.'

How could she have ever agreed to give her baby away? She didn't deserve love, ever again. She never had. She rubbed away the drop of condensation that trickled down her glass, swallowing down hot tears that suddenly welled up.

'No.' Adela took her hand. 'You deserve love too.'

Kitty nodded dumbly and a tear rolled down her cheek. She was a fool to think anything would come of her feelings for Bill. She hadn't even seen him since Luqa was bombed. She stared out at the searchlights, blinking, waiting for the blur to settle.

In the far distance came the staccato of AA guns, stitches of light across the sky.

Adela picked up the photograph again. 'Have you shown this to Lydia?'

'Of course not. She'd be devastated. Anyway, she can't wait to be evacuated.'

'Really?' Adela sat up straight. 'You're not going too, are you?'

'God, no.'

'Thank goodness.' Adela sat back. 'Then come and live with me.'

'Really?'

'Margaretta is moving to a place in Pietà in a few weeks, so you can have her room.'

'I'd love that.' Kitty beamed at her. 'Thank you.'

Chapter Fourteen

On her way into work the next morning, Kitty stopped off at the *Times of Malta* offices in St Paul's Street and placed an advertisement headlined *Searching for this Person*. She handed over the shillings and the photograph, planning to collect it later in the week, before heading into Fighter Command.

She slipped into the back of the Briefing Room and took a seat as Ash strode in to start Morning Prayers. As he outlined the day's news, she scanned the backs of the heads lined up in front of her. Was Bill here? She hadn't seen his call sign up in the Ops Room flying in or out of Malta for a few days, which was odd. But there appeared to be no sign of him here either. What did that mean? Where was he?

She shifted in her seat, unsettled, and turned her attention back to Ash in time to hear him give the good news that a convoy carrying eleven Hurricanes was expected from Gibraltar. Everyone applauded and she joined in, her cheeks hot as she hoped no one could tell she hadn't been listening properly.

As everyone got up to go, she hung back to check Bill definitely wasn't there. Ash came out last, shuffling papers into his briefcase. His eyes brightened when he saw her.

'Ah, Campbell. Just the person.'

'Sir?'

'Yes, I just wanted to let you know.' He glanced at the crowd milling away down the corridor, gestured her to follow him back into the Briefing Room and shut the door.

'Those four battleships – the photograph you developed?' He smoothed his moustache. 'The Navy carried out a top-secret torpedo attack on the enemy convoy yesterday evening. *Illustrious* and *Warspite* were involved, apparently.'

She nodded, recognising both ships. 'How did it go?'

'Apparently early reports are a cruiser was hit and a destroyer damaged. We're not releasing the information until Reconnaissance have had a chance to confirm all the details today, so keep it under your hat. Just wanted you to know, after your sterling work. Apparently knowing about that fourth ship made all the difference to their attack strategy.'

Kitty nodded, her heart thudding. 'Thank you for telling me.'

Ash turned to leave the room. 'Good work, Campbell. Keep it up.'

Kitty watched him stride away down the corridor, before she headed down to the Operations Room smiling from ear to ear.

'Pinto Red Three, Pinto Red Four heading back to base. Descending to Angels six,' said Kitty into her mic. Her heartbeat slowed as she moved the plots representing the two Hurricanes she had been tracking, while they turned to fly back towards Ta'Qali.

Enemy planes had been buzzing round the submarine base at Manoel Island and the two Hurricanes had been scrambled from Ta'Qali. There'd been quite a long dogfight but their fighter planes had escaped unscathed, which was a relief. Pinto Three had excitedly called that he had hit one of the Me 109s, although both enemy fighters had turned away, and Rita was now tracking them, inching their plot away to Sicily and off the map. Hopefully one was damaged, at least.

Kitty rolled her shoulders and glanced round. All morning the six women of D Watch had had their eyes on the table, concentrating hard on the messages coming through their headsets, their movements quick and accurate as they pushed plots forward, constantly calling aircraft positions. There had been a never-ending procession of Hostiles. A bombing attack by ten Junkers and five Me 109 fighters on the naval airbase at Hal Far, then a raid that indiscriminately dropped dozens of parachute mines over Valletta.

Up on the Shelf, Ash frowned as he smoked his way through one cigarette after another. Beside him the other officers had barked instructions down the phone to the airfields or gunnery officers, everyone poised for the next raid. It could start without warning at any minute.

But for a moment, the table was empty.

'Well done, ladies,' Irene called. 'Looks like we've got a minute.'

Kitty and the other plotters propped their rods against the table, keeping them within fingertip's grasp, and chatted quietly. Behind her the door squeaked open and there was a cough.

Kitty looked round and nearly tripped over her cue.

Bill stood there, his flying jacket hanging open. Why she was surprised she wasn't sure, as she'd been hoping all morning she'd see him.

He snatched off his RAF cap and smoothed his hair, glancing

round the room for her. When he saw her, his face lit up.

'Kitty,' he said, his eyes shining. 'Is this a good time for a quick word?'

She glanced over at Irene, embarrassed to feel her cheeks grow hot.

Irene's eyes flitted from Kitty to Bill and she smiled. 'Two minutes.'

Kitty took off her headset and went out into the corridor. Bill was waiting for her further down the passageway, his peaked cap tucked under his arm.

'Thank God you're alright.' His beaming eyes fixed on hers.

'Thank God *you're* alright,' she replied. 'I didn't know what happened to you . . .'

They babbled, their voices loud, talking over each other, their relief at seeing one another palpable. They stood so close she could feel his warm breath on her cheek. She longed to touch him, to pull him into her arms, but he stood stiffly, both of them all too aware of where they were.

'Thank you so much for getting that photograph here. Ash told me. I can't believe you stayed and finished it.' He stared into her eyes, his good eyebrow raised so the scarred skin pulled his face taut. 'I'd never have left if I thought you weren't going straight to the shelter. You risked your life—'

'It was worth it, though, wasn't it?'

'You could have been killed.'

'So could you.'

'Touché,' he laughed, his face relaxing, the scar wrinkling into ridges and hooding over his right eye. 'I'm sorry I haven't been in touch. Lot of flying over North Africa. Only got back this morning.'

'I was worried about you.' Kitty longed to take his hand, but an RAF officer was walking towards them down the corridor.

Bill looked away until the officer passed them and turned a corner, then reached out with his good hand and squeezed hers. Their eyes met.

A jolt of heat fired through Kitty's body.

'Look, I owe you a huge thank you. So might you be free this weekend for a picnic?' He looked into her eyes, his face hopeful. 'We could visit Mdina, go for a walk at Dingli Cliffs? Think we could both do with a change of scenery.'

It was ages since she'd visited the ancient walled city of Mdina or been for a walk along the cliffs. Not since Italy had declared war last summer. And who knew, the way things were going, how much longer they'd be able to visit them at all? Suddenly, the idea of fresh air, countryside and open views sounded too good to turn down.

The air raid alert sounded through the loudspeaker above their heads and they exchanged frustrated glances.

'I'd better get back.' She gestured behind her. 'But I'd love to.'

He caught her fingers and held them until she pulled away, smiling as she ran back to the Operations Room.

Chapter Fifteen

The bike roared to a stop beside the old stone bridge and Kitty reluctantly removed her arms from Bill's middle. This time she hadn't felt awkward pressed against his back, enjoying leaning into his firm warmth, and had laughed as they raced past the fields along stone-walled roads, the wind whipping her hair.

'You alright back there?' Bill cut the engine and smiled back at her. 'I tried to take the corners gently.'

'That was thrilling.'

She climbed off the bike, pulling off her goggles and helmet, and screwed her eyes up at the tall baroque stone city gate. She put her hand to her brow against the dazzle as she admired its ornately decorated pillars, the sun bouncing off the cream stone walls that stretched away on either side. A donkey pulling a cart and a couple of soldiers hurried through the central arch.

It felt calmer here out in the country and she stared across the bright green blanket of the island, stippled with the yellow, red and pink wildflowers of early March. Beyond, Valletta shimmered in the distance, cobalt sea bright behind it, and here and there small villages dotted the landscape, church spires and domes glinting in the sunshine.

A cry of *'Meraq frisk ghall-bejgh'* – 'Fresh juice for sale' – pulled her back to the leather-skinned old man in a straw hat selling prickly pears and oranges, under the pink froth of a Judas tree's blossom. A small cart laden with goat's milk churns rattled past.

A *Times of Malta* newspaper billboard caught her eye – *Enemy cruiser hit and destroyer damaged in major attack on convoy* – and she hurried to the stand to buy a copy. She handed over a sixpence and stood in the hot sun transfixed, reading the details about the attack out at sea near Sicily.

'Ah yes,' Bill said, joining her and glancing over her shoulder. 'Jolly good show, thanks to you. The Brass are delighted.'

'And to you. You saw the four battleships in the first place.'

'Mmm. I flew over them yesterday actually on their way back to Sicily, to photograph the damage.'

'You actually saw them? How were they?'

'The cruiser was listing and in a bad way, and the destroyer had damage to a propeller.'

'Excellent news!'

He looked at her intently. 'I'd say we're a pretty good team.'

She grinned and hit him playfully with the newspaper. 'Come on, let's get out of this hot sun.'

They walked across the bridge, through the highly decorated arch, under the Grand Master's coat of arms and into the shaded narrow streets of the Silent City. It was as if they had stepped back in time. Tall medieval walls loomed over them, dotted here and there with wrought-iron lamps and imposing double doorways that gave nothing away, but led into hidden palaces beyond.

They strolled through hushed streets to the wide cobbled square and stared up at the huge baroque towers and central cross of St Paul's Cathedral, which soared into the blue sky. It looked like it had been transplanted from Florence, except now it was sandbagged to the hilt and a military jeep was parked at a jaunty angle outside.

'Do you want to go inside?'

She shook her head. 'The last time I was here was with Father, for some official service he made us come to,' she shuddered. 'We always had to look the part. You know, "the vice-admiral and his happy family", but we weren't. We never were.'

'That must have been hard.'

'Turns out he had a . . .' The word still stuck in her throat. 'A mistress.' She eyed him. 'That's who he's left half of everything to. That's why we have to sell Willow End.'

His one eyebrow shot up in his head. 'Good God. A man of his standing?'

She rifled in her handbag and pulled out the small photograph. 'Turns out he's been seeing her for years.'

He examined the photograph and looked up, shocked. 'But this was taken in 1919.'

'He was hospitalised here during the Great War.'

'Bloody hell, that's not on.' He shook his head. 'No wonder you're so keen to find her. What a dreadful thing of him to do.'

'A cruel thing.' But she was surprised, and if she was honest, gratified, at the level of disapproval in his voice.

He handed it back and she tucked it away in her bag. They walked on through the winding streets and found a spot by the city walls, in the shade of a fig tree. She told him what little she knew about the affair and selling Willow End, but found she couldn't quite tell him the real reason she wanted to find the mistress.

She felt for the little photograph folder of her baby in her pocket. She wasn't sure she could share her yet.

Later, on the clifftops at Dingli, Bill spread out a blanket and unwrapped a picnic of bread, tomatoes and hard-boiled eggs that he'd bought from the makeshift NAAFI, and they toasted his thanks to her with a nip of whisky he'd brought in his saddlebag.

Afterwards, they walked in comfortable silence along the rocky cliff path, admiring the expanse of sea sparkling beside them. It stretched away all around them to the horizon. Above, in the clear azure sky, the occasional puff of white cloud drifted, and from the foot of the cliffs came the rhythmic pounding of waves as they crashed onto the rocks. At the edges of the path, spring flowers swayed in the wind, releasing their scents of pink-purple thyme, the yellow flowers of fennel and white caper as their legs brushed them.

'Thank you for bringing me here again. I'd forgotten how beautiful it was,' said Kitty. The cool breeze ruffled her hair. 'Even though you can see the radar just up the path there.' She gestured to the huge metal structures topped with what looked like a giant golf ball, like a strange version of a child's Meccano kit, partially hidden by bushes and fenced off behind a mesh of barbed wire.

'Beautiful in their own way,' smiled Bill.

'True,' laughed Kitty. 'What would we do without them?' They walked on across the wild open clifftops. 'It's hard to believe we're surrounded by the enemy when you see all this.'

'I know. To think Tripoli's just over there.' Bill squinted into the afternoon sun, staring across the sea. The wind lifted his hair, blowing it off the scar on his forehead no matter how many times he tried to smooth it back down. 'And Alexandria's that way, eight hundred miles east.'

'That's where Mother wants to go.'

'She won't be able to now.' He shook his head. 'Not if Rommel has his way.'

Kitty looked out to the horizon. 'Do you think the Germans will invade?'

He didn't answer, just picked up a stone and threw it over the cliff edge with a strong cricketer's arm. It hurtled through the air and disappeared into the waves below.

'Not if we can bloody help it.' He glanced at her, smiling, but the smile didn't reach his eyes.

They walked on, side by side, and her body filled with heat as her arm bumped against his. Hard, muscular, warm. She wanted to take his hand and glanced up at him, wondering if he'd noticed too, but he looked straight ahead, lost in his own thoughts.

He was on the right side of her, his profile turned so she couldn't see the scar running down the other side of his face, and she got another glimpse of how he would have looked, before. Determined, intelligent, energetic. The kind of man who wouldn't let a problem defeat him. Firm jaw, full lips, a faint shadow of stubble that he must have to battle to control now it no longer grew on the other side, where his face had burnt. Taller than her, he'd slowed his pace to match hers.

'You know, if you need anything, I can always buy it on a refuel stop while I'm over there, or in Greece. Soap? Fry's chocolate?'

'Oh, soap please! And lipstick. My last one was blown up in my handbag in the darkroom.'

'Well, I owe you one, then.'

She wheeled round, an idea striking her. 'Might you be able to buy children's toys?'

'Toys?' He stopped and gazed at her, puzzled.

'For the children I visit, from school. There's nothing to buy here now, with all the rationing.'

She had visited Michael and his family that week, taken him a sketchbook and a box of fresh pencils, knowing how he loved to draw aeroplanes – although he'd been most delighted with an aircraft-spotting chart she'd cadged off her ARP warden. Now Michael's brothers had been conscripted, he was working in the family bakery and he'd been thrilled to show her how the till worked when she bought some cheese *pastizzi*.

'I'm seeing another little girl, Carmela.' Her voice cracked as she said her name, picturing her rosy cheeks, her happy violet eyes. She cleared her throat. 'Next week. I'd love to take her a game or something.'

For a moment she closed her eyes, hoping someone somewhere was giving Alice little treats too.

'I wasn't expecting a children's shopping list, but you're on,' Bill laughed. 'If I stop in Egypt, I'll see what I can get.' He gave her a sideways glance. 'The lads'll give me hell, of course.'

'Thank you.' She took his arm and squeezed it. Their eyes met.

He turned and pulled her into his arms, staring into her eyes.

'I've never met anyone like you, Katherine Campbell.' He leant down and kissed her gently.

She kissed him back, his lips melding into hers. After a few moments, she pulled away.

'And I've never met anyone like you.' She hesitated for a

moment and her gaze wandered to the scar on his forehead. 'May I ask?' She bit her lip.

He put his hand up and touched his scar, the tender skin pinking in the sun. 'About this?'

'Sorry, that's rude of me.' She looked away, her cheeks burning. She'd embarrassed him, embarrassed herself. It was none of her business.

'No, no. I'd rather you asked. I mean, you can't miss it. Now I'm no longer the best-looking bloke in the room.'

She smiled, but inside her heart twisted. She understood all too well the hiding of such deep pain. Could he sense that in her too?

He stared out to sea.

'I've always wanted to fly. As a boy I used to hang about the local airfield, clean the hangars, make pilots tea, anything I could do to be round a plane. 'Course, we didn't have money for lessons. Dad ran a grocer's. Hamilton and Son's Fine Provisions.'

He glanced at her, a flicker of nervousness flashing across his face.

Goodness, he thought she would think less of him because his father ran a shop. Kitty nodded encouragingly, forced herself not to react, kept her eyes fixed on his.

'I was doomed to work in the family shop. Oh, I applied to the RAF, over and over, but they turned me down.' He kicked a pebble into the scrub. 'Seems they didn't like grammar school boys back then.' He glanced at her again out of the corner of his eye and his cheeks flushed.

Their rejection of him had clearly stung.

'I'm sorry.' Her voice was quiet.

'When war threatened, they let me in. Got my pilot officer

wings that summer and was packed off to join my squadron.' He touched his scarred cheek. 'It was in the Battle of France, last summer—'

She put a hand on his arm. 'Honestly, you don't have to tell me.'

'No, it's fine. One night we'd dropped our bombs and were heading home over Normandy. Jerry appeared out of nowhere . . .' His voice trailed away. 'They took our engines out.'

He stopped walking and turned to her.

'We were in a dive. Fire everywhere . . .' His eyes shut as he remembered. 'The cockpit shield jammed.' His voice cracked and he looked away, his Adam's apple working in his throat.

Kitty shut her eyes, trying to imagine an aircraft dropping in darkness, flames licking, the terror of being trapped . . .

'I bailed out over the Channel. Got Mackie, my navigator, out too.' His voice was too bright. Too forced.

A boom like thunder reverberated as a large wave smashed against the cliff hundreds of feet below them. Kitty stared out at the lines of white-topped waves running across the surface of the sea towards them and shivered. She couldn't imagine how terrifying it must have been. Tears pricked at the back of her eyes. She longed to reach out and cup his poor damaged cheek in her palm, but his jaw was set, his gaze unblinking as he stared at the horizon.

'Is that why you won this?' She gestured to the small line of purple and white diagonal stripes sewn over his battle shirt pocket, under his flying wings. She knew how rarely it was awarded.

'The Distinguished Flying Cross?' He nodded. 'I'd gone in low on a key military bridge. A direct hit.' He cleared his throat and turned his head. 'You don't want to hear about this.' He threw her a small smile. 'Anyway, after a dozen operations, they retrained me and packed me off to Malta. And here I am.'

She stood on her toes and kissed him, wishing she could kiss his pain away, knowing that she never could, just as his kisses couldn't take away hers.

After a moment, she tucked her arm in his and squeezed it. A quiet acceptance hung between them – just the wind blowing, the rustling of bushes on the clifftop.

For a moment she longed to tell him about Alice, why she was really so desperate to find this woman. Longed to tell him her truth, as he had told her his.

But in the distance a hum, like a distant colony of bees, built into a low rumble and then a roar. Planes approaching.

'Not again,' said Kitty.

They squinted towards the horizon, hands steepled over their foreheads, until they could make out slivers of glinting aluminium which as they drew nearer became formations of dark crosses, until they seemed to fill the whole sky.

'Junkers 87s and 88s.' Bill let out a low whistle. 'Christ, let's hope they're not after the radar.' He grabbed her hand. 'Run!'

The air raid warning wailed as they ran down the path towards Bill's bike. Behind them came the *crump, crump* of anti-aircraft guns and puffs of black smoke dotted the sky, then the *rat-a-tat* of distant machine guns opening fire. As they ran the roar grew louder, until it was a deafening thunder and her very insides seemed to vibrate. Rows of dark gull-like shadows passed over the sea and then rose up the cliff edges until giant in size, darkening the ground around them. They threw themselves under a rocky overhang by the cliff path.

The growl and roar of engines grew intense, stabbing Kitty's eardrums. Her heart raced; blood pulsed in her veins. As the ground shook under her, smoke filled her mouth and grit crunched between her teeth. Her breathing came too fast, until she couldn't breathe, she couldn't breathe. Kitty huddled, her body trembling, eyes screwed shut, hands over her ears, frantic to shut it all out.

It seemed to take a lifetime for the bombers to pass overhead, blocking out the sun, filling the air around them with choking dust.

But as she lay beside Bill's warm firm body, the serge of his tunic against her cheek, the smell of his sweat in her nostrils, all she could think about was his strong arms wrapped around her and the thudding of her heart so close to his.

Chapter Sixteen

A few days later, Kitty arrived home from Fighter Command laden with packages. Bill had done her proud with children's toys. She had gone in this morning to find a large package tied with string under their wooden pigeonholes. She had unwrapped it to find a low aerial photograph of a camel train and Bedouins, their shadows long across a sand dune. A warm thrill had run through her. He was thinking of her. She'd turned it over, hoping for a message. On the back was scrawled, *Dinner, Saturday night?*

She had laughed out loud and hadn't stopped smiling as she pulled out the other items. Soap wrapped in sheets of Arabic newspaper, silk stockings – *silk!* – and he had found a tasselled fez and a snake charmer's pipe, which she knew Michael would love. For Carmela he had sent a small wooden camel on wheels and a skipping rope. The gifts were perfect.

As she took off her coat, the melodic strains of the BBC Symphony Orchestra drifted out from the Rediffusion speaker and into the hall, coupled with the rhythmic clicks of Lydia's knitting needles. Kitty put her head round the drawing room door. Lydia sat in her favourite wing-backed armchair, balls of wool at her feet.

'They say we're to expect more night raids.' Lydia didn't look up as the needles flashed in her hands.

'I know.'

Lydia finished a row, set the sock in her lap and looked up. 'There's a letter for you.' She pursed her lips. 'A Żebbuġ postmark.'

'Oh?'

Kitty turned back to the hall and her eye fell on the stiff cream envelope propped against the mirror. She didn't recognise the handwriting. She seized it up and opened it.

A thick sheet of paper fell out, covered in looping blue ink. The letter was brief.

Dear Katherine (if I may address you that way),
I was so pleased to see your advertisement searching for me
in the Times.

Her heart speeded up.

It was her. The mistress. Kitty gripped the letter . . .

Since Ronald's death I have thought often about whether I
should write to you. I did not know if you knew about me,
or if hearing from me would cause you pain.

Kitty grunted.

This I never wished to do, so I'll keep this brief. Ronald's
lawyers have informed me that Willow End is to be sold.
Before you do something you may regret, I would urgently

*like to discuss this matter, and others, with you, so please
may I ask if we can arrange to meet?*

*In particular, I have news that I am sure will be of
<u>extreme importance</u> to you. Please write to me at the
address above.*

Yours most sincerely,
Maria Montebello

Kitty sank into a chair, the paper trembling in her hand.

'Who's it from?' Lydia called from the drawing room.

Kitty's throat closed.

'Oh, no one.' She hoped Lydia didn't notice the waver in
her voice.

Maria Montebello.

So that was the woman's name.

She had found her.

Revulsion coiled in her stomach like writhing snakes. Now
that she had, Kitty had never wanted to meet someone less in
her life.

'She's written to me. Father's . . .' Kitty still couldn't bear to say
the word 'mistress'.

Bill stopped in his tracks and the toys rattled in the haversack
he'd slung on his shoulder. 'Really? Gosh, what a surprise. And
after all that lawyer's cloak-and-dagger nonsense.'

'I know.' Kitty tucked her arm in his as they walked down
the steps of St Ursula Street, heading for Carmela's family
greengrocer's.

Kitty had invited him to come with her to give the toys to
the children. They had just been to Michael's and the little boy

had been beside himself with excitement, not only at the fez but at having a real live RAF pilot at his house for tea.

'That's excellent news. You can talk to her about Willow End.'

'Mmm, I suppose so. But it's made me feel uncomfortable. I don't know if I actually want to see her.' She looked at him, not sure how to explain how she felt. 'That letter, I don't know. It brought it home that she really exists. That Father had an actual life with her . . . It's all the lies. The deceit, you know? It went on for so many years. I mean, what kind of *hussy*,' she spat the word, 'must she be?'

Bill's eyes widened and he glanced at her, surprised. 'I see what you mean . . .' he said, not sounding like he did at all.

'Sorry,' she mumbled, her cheeks flushing, casting a sideways look at him, hoping she hadn't put him off. 'I just mean it's horrible for me to think about them. Together, you know . . .'

They arrived at the shop door. She took his hand and squeezed it. 'Anyway, enough about that. Come and meet Carmela.'

The bell jangled as they stepped inside, the smell of muddy vegetables and sweet fruit hitting her nostrils. Mrs Cortis, in her flower-sprigged apron and turban, welcomed them both with warm open arms and led them upstairs to the tiny flat.

Kitty's heart tugged as she glimpsed Carmela, listless on the floor with a pile of pick-up sticks. Her face was pale and drawn; dark circles ringed her violet eyes as she stared dully at the game.

But her eyes lit up at the sight of the camel and once Bill had sorted out a wonky wheel, she charged up and down the hallway, giggling as she pulled it behind her.

'He can runded so fast! And look! His head nods! And he smileded at me.'

'How is she?' Kitty asked quietly in the kitchen, helping Mrs Cortis with the tea things.

Mrs Cortis put a plate of *kannoli tal-irkotta* on the *bizzilla* lace tablecloth and sat down, her brow furrowed. Worry filled her dark brown eyes as they watched Carmela playing.

'When the air raid siren went off last night, she sat up in bed and was sick.' She shook her head. 'Even in the shelter, I can't soothe her.'

Kitty's chest tightened. She squeezed Mrs Cortis's hand. 'I'm so sorry.'

'She's forgetting her English. She misses school.' Mrs Cortis wiped a crumb off the lace. 'And you, of course.'

Carmela came running into the kitchen and climbed into Kitty's lap. She wrapped her chubby arms round Kitty's neck and pressed her soft cheek next to Kitty's. Bill came and sat down, and Kitty's cheeks warmed as she felt his caring eyes on them both.

'Thank you, Miss Campbell. I love him so much. He's called Carmelo the Camel and he's the bestest camel in Malta.'

'Is he, sweetheart?' Kitty laughed, pulling her close. 'I'm glad you like him.'

As she read Carmela a story, she stroked her soft velvet hair, breathing in her smell of Pears soap and apples. She glanced at Carmela's dark shining eyes, dancing with joy now, ringed with that fan of dark lashes that reminded her of that other precious set, all those years ago. She shut her eyes a moment, squeezed Carmela tight. How she'd missed this little girl.

Mrs Cortis eyed her. 'We're closing the shop. I wanted

to stay, be somewhere people could buy fresh food here in Valletta,' she threw up her hands, 'but it's too much. I must get her out into the countryside.'

'Have you family you can stay with?'

'My sister-in-law has a farm, so we're going to stay with her.' Mrs Cortis nodded at Carmela. 'You know, I would do anything to protect her.'

Later, her words rang in Kitty's ears as she walked home with Bill.

I would do anything to protect her.

Was Alice becoming silent and withdrawn as bombs fell around her? Was someone doing everything they could to protect *her*? And the most painful thought of all.

She had never held her own little girl in her lap.

Her fingers trembled on her baby's photograph in her pocket.

I would do anything to protect her.

She knew what she had to do. That evening she wrote to Maria, arranging to meet her.

Chapter Seventeen

On her next day off, she borrowed a bicycle from Adela and cycled out of Valletta, the sun warm on her face. As she pedalled out into the flat countryside, sprinkled with the butter-yellow heads of crown daisies and golden sprays of mimosa flowers, it was a relief to get away from the shattered ruins of the city.

But her insides clenched at the idea of confronting this Maria Montebello.

Kitty was dragging a dark secret about Father's life into the light, and she wasn't sure she wanted to do it. Her hands tightened on the handlebars, and she pumped hard on the pedals as she passed patchwork fields, lined with stone walls and filled with aubergines and tomatoes. As she cycled through Hamrun and Qormi, her back grew wet with sweat, her breathing fast, but it wasn't because of the hot March sun.

She would have to tread carefully. *Someone I know well and trust implicitly.* Father's words rang in her ears. Who was this woman? And most importantly, would she have answers about her daughter?

As Kitty approached the little town, she slowed her pace, wanting to catch her breath. Fields gave way to houses, their doors brightly painted in dark reds, greens and sky blues. Bright geraniums fluttered outside arched doorways and on balconies as she pedalled through the streets, and she was surprised they were not too badly bombed. For a moment her heart lifted, remembering life on the island before the war.

Her wheels jolted over the stones and she slowed down, as the voice of a priest giving the Litany grew louder in her ears. She stopped, leant her bicycle against an olive tree and glanced at her watch. She was early. Ahead of her an elaborately carved baroque church with two tall towers dominated the wide cobbled square, sandbagged around the front steps and walls. The bakery and café were shuttered; a distant waft of fried garlic hung in the air. Old men, women and children lined the narrow street on her left, heads bowed in prayer. The priest's voice was as rich as the pour of communion wine and the crowd's murmured responses mingled like a well-rehearsed choir. Families stood outside each house in what was evidently their Sunday best. Little girls in dresses and fraying hair ribbons, young boys buttoned in too-tight jackets, women in faded dresses stood praying. She had heard some villages had prayers in the street, tired of rushing into shelters when the air raid sirens wailed.

She scanned the women's faces, hoping to spot Maria. Would she have changed much since the photo was taken? Would she even recognise her? Sweat bloomed under her pale blue shirt dress.

The priest, in a long black cassock, chanted in Latin as he walked down the street, swinging a silver incense ball. Musky frankincense drifted in the air and caught at the back of her throat.

'. . . *Holy Mary, Mother of God, pray for us sinners . . .*' People chanted to the end of the response and, in unison, a hundred hands made the sign of the cross on their chests.

A black and white cat licked itself in a patch of sunlight.

There was a moment's silence, just the rattle of swaying palm tree fronds, as if they were bowing in prayer too. The tranquillity of this moment was like another world after the destruction in Valletta, and Kitty felt humbled by how this tight community seemed so united in their belief in God. Suddenly this didn't seem the right day for anger, or recriminations.

The hushed silence broke, children tore away from doorsteps and women turned to chatter to neighbours. The priest walked towards her.

'*Int barrani hawn*. You are a stranger here.' It was a statement, not a question.

Kitty pulled the letter out of her handbag and pointed to the address at the top. '*Iva*. I'm trying to find—'

'Ahh.' His bushy eyebrows shot up to his black square biretta. 'I see.'

His gaze appraised her, his look knowing, as if he recognised who she was. She looked away, feeling suddenly uncomfortable.

'Maria Montebello. This street.' He pointed at the narrow one with the bakery on the corner. 'Fifth on the left. Green front door.'

She followed his instructions and her heart raced as she found the stone house. She raised her clenched hand to the door. The knocker, a brass anchor and chain – of course it would be – gleamed in the sunshine. Christ, Father was written all over this house and she hadn't even got inside yet.

She took a deep breath. How many times had he stood

outside this door? She hesitated a moment, not wanting to knock, not wanting to walk through into the secrets that lay beyond.

But as she hesitated, the corner of Alice's photograph wallet jabbed her thigh through her dress. Focus. She had to focus on what she was here for.

She knocked and from inside came the scuffle of steps. Kitty's mouth went dry. What to say? Where to begin?

The door opened and a short, sturdy woman in her fifties stood on the doorstep, wiping flour-covered hands on the apron tied at her waist. She was like a more wrinkled version of the photograph, her dark hair pinned up, only with grey dusting her temples, and with that same capable face that looked like she could take all that life threw at her. At her neck the silver filigree crucifix, the same one as in the photograph, sparkled in the sun. She put her hands on her cheeks and broke into a broad smile.

'Katherine! At last! How I have longed to meet you!'

She had? Kitty stared at her, dazed.

'Katherine, I am Maria.' She stepped forward and pulled her into a hug.

For a moment Kitty couldn't breathe. Her arms hung limp by her sides, then she pulled away. How dare Maria hug her like that? She didn't even know her. Kitty stepped back and glared at her.

'Kitty, may I call you Kitty? I feel I know you so well.' Maria's gentle eyes beamed with joy.

'Call me Katherine.' Kitty's voice was harsh and for a moment, Maria looked stricken.

She clapped her hands to her cheeks, her face clouding.

'I'm sorry. This must be a big shock for you.' She stepped aside at the door and gestured for Kitty to enter. 'Please, forgive me. Come in, come in.'

'Thank you,' Kitty muttered, her heart banging against her ribs. She just wanted to get this over with.

She took a deep breath and stepped through the door.

Chapter Eighteen

Kitty sat down on the sofa and was so busy looking round the room that she barely noticed Maria picking up a photograph from the dresser top and sliding it into a drawer, as she bustled away to make tea.

The room smelt of warm dust and baking. It felt airy, with a vaulted arch and wooden beams along the ceiling. The old stone-block walls shone a warm cream colour in the sunshine falling through the tall window, and cushioned chairs were pulled up on a rug to the stone fireplace. So this was where Father had spent so much of his time. She didn't know what she had expected – some dark, formal place. But this? This was charming. Cosy, homely.

Her hands trembled on her bag.

A wooden dresser dominated the wall by the stairs, *bizzilla* lace on top and a medical kit with a red cross and a white cap on one side. Was Maria a nurse? Is that how she'd met Father? Silver filigree picture frames jostled for space and Kitty's eye snagged on a photograph of Father, pipe between his teeth. Her chest tightened.

Kitty glanced round, searching for more clues of Father's betrayal.

In a basket near the armchair was the lace frame and dozens of needles and thread to stitch the complicated design for a cushion. On the table beside it was a silver filigree box. Kitty stiffened, guessing what was inside. She flipped open the lid and the smell of tobacco filled the room. She slammed it shut as images of Maria and Father smoking his pipe, sitting companionably together in the evening – all those Wednesday nights – filled her mind.

'You must excuse me.' Maria brought in a tray of tea things and set it down. She rubbed her hands on her apron and a fine cloud of dust danced in the air. 'I've been making *pastizzi*.'

Father's favourite. Kitty swallowed.

'You're taller than I imagined.' Maria stood back, her face kindly, scrutinising her. 'But I can see Ronald in the set of your chin.'

Kitty didn't reply. She didn't want to talk about him. She needed time to digest all that she was beginning to understand. Needed to reframe her own life through this new lens.

'I was so pleased to see your advertisement. To know you were looking for me. Such a relief, after all these years. I've heard so much about you, your whole life.' Maria smiled, her eyes dancing. 'Would you like tea? I always kept some for . . .' She broke off as she poured.

It would be Earl Grey. Of course it would.

A rattle at the back door in the kitchen and a young woman in a simple cotton dress clattered into the room, rolling a metal canister. Her dark brown hair curled loose around her flushed face as she kicked the canister with scuffed brown lace-up shoes.

'There wasn't enough kerosene on the cart for everyone

today, Omm. Mr Zammit wanted you to have his ration, though. Said you'd looked after him so well last time he was sick . . .' Her voice trailed off as she saw Kitty and she broke into a big smile. 'Katherine! It's so nice to meet you at last.'

Kitty stared at her. Who was this?

The girl's eyes flitted anxiously to Maria's, then back to Kitty.

Maria cleared her throat. 'Katherine, this is Ċensa, my daughter. Your half-sister.'

Kitty blinked.

For a moment, the words did not register. The world seemed to slow. Her mind reeled. Kitty quivered, like a highly strung bow that had been plucked too hard, staring at the girl.

Half-sister. Half-sister.

The words reverberated without making sense.

Kitty's mind splintered in a thousand directions.

Father and Maria had created a family together. A life, a home. One she and Lydia had known nothing about. Her breath was crushed out of her as, in a moment, she reassessed her whole life's story. Years of her childhood unravelled before her: all those long absences when he was away overseas, his coldness towards her when he returned, the stiff silences round the dinner table every night. Of course – it was because he'd been posted here.

With her.

'Father has another child?' Her voice broke. 'Another daughter?'

Kitty had been trying so hard not to think about Father's affair, how long it had been going on, how many years of lies he must have told. But now here was living proof of how long his betrayal had been. A lifetime.

Her lifetime.

'I've wanted to meet you for so long,' Ċensa smiled. 'I've always longed for a sister.'

'You have?' said Kitty, distantly. Her breathing was coming in shallow gasps. Her whole childhood she had longed for a sister too, and she'd had one the whole bloody time. The irony of it. She would have laughed, if the urge to cry hadn't been stronger.

Kitty eyed the girl. Early twenties, an apron over her print dress; a fresh, open, gentle face, no make-up. Disjointed thoughts floated: she doesn't even look like me; her hair's too dark, her eyes too brown, her face too round. But then Ċensa smiled shyly and Kitty's insides clenched. She had the same small gap between her front teeth.

Acid burnt at the back of her throat. Her hand shook and she tipped up the saucer as she banged the cup down. Tea sloshed over the edge. She couldn't deal with this right now. She must keep focused. Just find out what she needed to know.

'About Willow End—'

'Katherine, I never wanted him to leave your home to me.' Maria smiled sadly at her. 'I was surprised when the lawyer's letter came. I knew nothing about his will.'

'We have to sell Willow End. To give you half the money.'

'No, truly, I don't need your money.' Maria gazed at her steadily. 'I don't want you to lose your home. I have everything I need right here. At first, after Ronald passed . . .' Her voice trailed away. 'I didn't know what to do for the best. Whether to contact you or not. I wasn't sure if you knew anything about me.'

'No. We didn't,' Kitty said through gritted teeth.

'You didn't?' Maria's eyes widened and her hands flew to her cheeks. She and Ċensa exchanged surprised glances. 'When we saw your advert, we thought he must have told you about me. Oh my goodness, I'm so sorry, Katherine.' Her voice wavered, her eyes full of compassion. 'This must be such a shock. I didn't realise . . .'

'We never meant to hurt you.' Ċensa's voice was timid, her eyes shining with concern.

Tears pricked at the back of Kitty's eyes. 'I just found your photograph in Father's wallet.'

Maria gasped. 'Oh my goodness.' Her eyes filled. 'Katherine, I'm so sorry.'

'How painful for you to find out like that.' Ċensa looked stricken too. She pulled a handkerchief from her apron and passed it to Kitty. Tiny forget-me-nots were embroidered round its border.

Kitty nodded mutely, swallowing back the tears.

There was a moment of silence.

'Look, about the house – I'll write to the lawyers, tell them I don't want it,' said Maria, eager to make amends. She squeezed Kitty's hand. 'Please, rest assured, Willow End is yours.'

'Really?' Kitty dabbed her eyes, her voice hopeful. 'You would do that?'

'I'll write the letter today. I mean it. You can keep your home. I understand how much it means to you.'

'Thank you.' Kitty's shoulders dropped, and she slumped back in her chair. The worst of it was that Maria and Ċensa seemed quite sweet, kind even, and in spite of herself, Kitty was finding herself warming to them. Dammit. Damn Father. 'Thank you.'

But her fingers felt for the photograph in her pocket and she sat up. A tingle ran through her. Now. Maybe now she'd find out what she'd been longing to know for the last five years.

'There's one more thing I need to ask you—'

'About your baby?' Maria said quietly.

Kitty took a sharp breath. Every nerve in her body strung taut.

She knew. She knew about her daughter.

'It's what I wanted to tell you.' Maria sat forward, her eyes earnest. 'What I've been desperate to tell you. Did you know I called at your house after Ronald passed—'

'You came to the house?' Kitty's head whipped up. 'When?'

'A few weeks ago. Lydia wouldn't talk to me. Turned me away—'

'What?'

'There's something you should know. That your father didn't tell you.'

'What is it?' A chill spiralled through Kitty's veins.

Maria twisted her apron and closed her eyes for a moment, as if summoning the courage to tell her.

'Alice is in Italy.'

Chapter Nineteen

'*Qalbi*, fetch her some more water.' Maria's calm voice issued instructions to Ċensa as she put her arm round Kitty's shoulders. 'Katherine, dear. I know it's a big shock.'

They had led Kitty into a tiled courtyard garden and sat her at a table shaded by a fig tree.

'What?' Kitty's voice was quiet. 'What do you mean she's in Italy?'

She gazed blankly at the lace tablecloth, dappled by sunlight breaking through the big leaves, unable to take it all in. The breeze cooled her cheeks and the scents of the orange tree and of thyme and oregano wafting in the air calmed her pounding heart.

'She can't be in Italy. She can't be.'

Her mind raced. Of all the dreams, all the nightmares she had had about Alice over so many years, this was not one of them. Sometimes when Kitty was torturing herself with her fears, she pictured her little girl cowering amongst strangers on the Underground, sheltering from the Blitz. Other times she worried Alice had been evacuated, all alone, a luggage parcel at her neck, made to dig up turnips and clean out chickens on a

155

dull farm in the countryside. At best, her favourite dream, the one that was like a blade to her heart but that she still hoped and prayed was true, was picturing her daughter on the lap of a kind rosy-cheeked woman, being read stories by a roaring fire, while a dog slept at their feet.

It had never once crossed her mind that she might be in *Italy*.

Enemy territory.

It couldn't be worse.

Maria and Ċensa fussed around her, bringing her water, until finally Maria sat down and clasped her hands on the table.

Kitty stared at her. 'Why? Why the hell is she there?'

'We believe she's in a safehouse. She's with a Maltese woman who lives there.' Maria's face filled with sympathy. She put her hand on Kitty's. 'In Rome.'

'Rome? My God!' Kitty reared up. 'Is she safe? Please, just tell me that she's safe.'

'As far as we know. We think the Catholic Church network in Italy organised—'

'*As far as we know*? What does that mean?' Kitty's eyes flashed with fear and she glanced round as if Alice might appear at any moment, her mind reeling with confusion. 'No, no. She's with a family in England. I'm sure of it.'

'Katherine, I swear I'm not lying to you. I'm sorry you had to find out like this.' Maria shook her head. 'I told Ronald you had a right to know. I've been trying to find a way to tell you. That's why I came to your house that time, after he . . .' She shut her eyes.

Kitty sat, gazing blankly at the garden wall, a thousand questions whirling in her mind. 'Why is she in Italy?' she whispered.

'*Dille tutto, mamma. Dille la verità*,' Ċensa said.

'Not Italian, Ċensa, let's use English.' Maria nodded. 'But I will tell her everything.' She released a long breath. 'You're right. Alice was placed with an English family, initially.'

'You knew?' Kitty looked up at Maria.

'Ronald and I discussed her many times—'

Kitty's stomach curdled at the idea of Maria and Father discussing her and her child.

'I felt so sad for you back then. When he was here that time, I tried to persuade Ronald to let Alice stay with you. We had a big fight.' Maria's eyes filled as she stared at the tablecloth. 'I loved Ronald and everything he stood for, very much. But I told him. He was wrong about this.' Maria looked away, lost in thought. 'And other things . . .'

'Omm,' Ċensa interrupted, frowning at her.

Kitty stared at Maria in surprise. She had expected a long defence of Father's actions. Maria's frankness disarmed her.

'Yes. He bloody well was wrong,' Kitty said tightly, struggling to control her rage. Dammit. She thumped the table so the cups rattled in their saucers. 'So why's she in Rome now?'

Maria breathed in. Her finger agitated a crumb on the tablecloth as she talked.

'Alice settled well with this English family, but apparently her adopted father was killed, fighting in France, and the mother was dying of stomach cancer. There were no other relatives to take her. The adoption people telegraphed your father asking him what he wanted to do.' She looked at Kitty. 'It was late April last year. Remember? Such a dangerous time. So much was happening. Fears that the Nazis would invade France. And then England . . .'

Kitty nodded, remembering. How, as it had seemed the whole of continental Europe would fall to the Nazis, she would wait in the hall at Old Theatre Street, desperate to read the headlines the second the newspaper arrived; how she and Lydia stayed up late, hanging on every word of the BBC nightly broadcast on the Rediffusion.

'So your father arranged for a WREN to bring Alice to Malta. To keep her safe.' She looked up at Kitty. 'Only they never made it. Italy declared war on Britain and Malta. They were trapped as they travelled through Rome.'

'My God.' Tears sprang into Kitty's eyes. She remembered the torrent of Italian that had come hurtling from the radio the night that Il Duce, Mussolini, had declared war on them last summer, the fast and furious ranting that had seemed to go on for hours.

Maria nodded. 'The WREN was ordered home but never made it back. We fear she may have been shot. She must have been Catholic, as somehow, she arranged for Alice to be cared for by this Maltese woman. Rosa Cassar. Our priest knew her here, years ago. Rosa then wrote to my family in Sicily.'

She went into the house, returned with a creased, plain brown envelope and pulled out the wafer-thin paper of the telegram inside. It was stamped *Received HM PO Valletta, 9th June 1940*.

'My cousin's telegram to me was one of the last out of Italy, before all communication stopped. Here.'

She smoothed it on the lace in front of Kitty.

Overhead the distant sound of bombers droned, but they all ignored it.

Kitty picked it up, her hands shaking.

Ricevuta lettera da Rosa Cassar
Alicia in alloggio sicuro a Roma
Troppo pericoloso continuare il viaggio

Luigi

Tears blurred the typed Italian letters as she tried to translate:
Alicia in Rome safehouse . . . travel too dangerous . . .

Her fingers trembled as she read it again, scouring the paper
for every inch of information. Blood pounded in her temples.
The branches overhead seemed to tilt towards her.

What distress her little girl must have gone through. Must
be going through still. Kitty's heart folded over in her chest.
What was this Maltese woman in Rome like? What kind of
'safehouse' was it? Was anyone else, perhaps Jewish people,
sheltering there? She wracked her brains trying to remember
how bad the bombing raids were over Rome. Did they have
good shelters? Would the Maltese woman keep Alice safe?

And she hadn't known. She hadn't known a thing.

It was like all her worst nightmares about Alice. Awful
things happening to her, and she – Kitty, Alice's own mother –
knowing nothing about it. Powerless to help her.

A tear streaked down her cheek.

'He didn't tell me. He never told me anything.'

'I'm so sorry, Katherine.' Maria patted her hand, her eyes
filled with compassion. 'After Ronald passed, I should have
tried harder to find you. Come to your house again. But your
mother made it clear she wouldn't talk to me. She slammed the
door on me.'

'Poor Omm.' Ċensa squeezed her hand. She looked at Kitty.
'We really wanted you to know about Alice.'

'I always wanted you to know. I told Ronald, I would want to know everything if it was my child.' Maria breathed in. 'It is a terrible thing, losing a child.'

She glanced at Ċensa, who laid her head on Maria's shoulder. Automatically, Maria stroked her hair.

I've never stroked my daughter's hair like that. The distant thought floated dully into Kitty's mind.

A breeze rustled the leaves of the fig tree, fluttering the telegram across the table, so Kitty snatched at it. As she read it again, a terrible thought struck her. One she had to know the answer to immediately.

'What was Father going to do when Alice got here?' Her voice was low, threatening.

Maria pulled away from Ċensa, fiddled with a loose thread on her apron.

'He hadn't decided.' Her voice wobbled. 'He always felt guilty for taking her from you. He couldn't forgive himself for everything he had done—'

'I don't care what he felt.'

'I understand.' Maria breathed in. 'He wanted your child to have a proper family.'

'He was protecting himself, his status in the Navy.' Kitty's voice was harsh. 'And I would have loved her. Isn't that more important?'

'I said this to him.' Maria shook her head. 'A mother's love is more important than anything.'

'So he took my daughter, but had Ċensa with you?' The hypocrisy of it winded her and she sat back, breathing hard.

'He saw how hard it was for me, despite his support. He didn't want that for you.'

'I hate him,' Kitty said dully. 'She's *my* child.'

She pulled her baby's photograph from her pocket and passed it to Maria.

Maria stared at it for a long time. 'She's beautiful, Kitty.' She passed the photograph to Ċensa. 'I'm so sorry.'

It was so long since anyone had acknowledged her pain. A tear slid down Kitty's cheek. It was a few moments before she could speak.

'I will find her. I will get her back.'

Maria crossed herself. 'God willing.'

They sat as the sun went down and the shadows grew longer across the courtyard. A bird warbled, the breeze cooling as the afternoon faded.

Ċensa knelt beside her and Kitty felt the warmth of her thin arm reach round her shoulders, the scent of olive oil in her hair.

'Katherine, I know nothing will ever feel right until you find Alice.'

Kitty swallowed. They were being so kind. She looked from Ċensa to Maria. 'Sorry, I was rude earlier. Please, call me Kitty.'

'Kitty, maybe there is a small blessing here.' Ċensa smiled up at her and Kitty gazed, mesmerised, into those brown eyes that shone with innocence and at that little gap between her teeth, so like her own. 'We both have a sister now. Maybe we can start getting to know each other.'

Kitty shook her head. It was all too late now.

'It's not too late,' said Ċensa, as if she could read her mind. She smiled at Kitty. 'The oranges are ripe. Would you like to pick some?'

And she took Kitty's hand and led her into the sunlight.

* * *

The sun was setting as Kitty left that evening. Thin clouds streaked with apricot and rose cast a golden glow on the low stone walls as she cycled through the narrow lanes. The roads were quiet, just the occasional soldier rattling by in an army jeep and a farmer with horse and cart laden with freshly dug fennel and onions. Her feet turned rhythmically on the pedals; the wind lifted her hair and cooled her as she cycled. As the miles passed, she thought about Alice, trapped behind enemy lines in Rome.

Her only link with her was Maria's family in Sicily. A woman she barely knew existed a few weeks ago now held her heart, her daughter, in her hands and she was tied to them for as long as the war lasted.

Kitty was still furious with Father, but for the first time she had seen a glimpse of him as a person in his own right, outside of being her parent. For the first time she began to grasp that the coldness she had grown up with was not her fault, but his own. His lies. His betrayal. What was it Maria had said? That he couldn't forgive himself. At least Kitty understood it now.

But seeing the warmth and affection between Maria and Censa had shown her how different it might have felt to have been forged in a loving family, how this sense of lack, this ache in her chest that was always there, might never have been moulded. How she longed to be part of the kind of warmth and support that their little family offered. And Maria was so kind, so motherly, in a way she had never experienced, so understanding about Alice. A lump filled her throat. It was what she had always longed for.

She was so deep in thought, just the peaceful creak and click of the pedals and the puff of her soft breaths in the evening stillness, that she didn't hear the air raid siren in the far distance. As she rounded the next bend, she heard the faint drone of an aircraft engine. She slowed down and coasted, the distant spires and domes of Valletta bathed in golden light. She glanced up at the sky, now deep orange and lilac, but couldn't see anything and cycled on.

Moments later, the air was cracked by the scream of a plane throttling high in the sky right above her.

A large shadow swooped over her, a dark flash over the ground.

A Messerschmitt 109 – she recognised the engine's roar. She slammed on her brakes. She skidded in a pothole, the back wheel juddered round and she was thrown forward, the handlebars rammed into her ribs. Winded, she fought for breath. As she glanced up, the aircraft reached the tip of its climb. Her heart thumped.

The plane banked round and dived towards her. Its engines screamed as it roared down at her, straight as an arrow.

She froze.

It was coming straight for her. *It was coming straight for her.*

The plane grew bigger; the scream of its dive, the smell of fuel, the cockpit glinting.

She threw down the bike, leapt into the ditch by the side of the road. The plane was right overhead. She could see the pilot's teeth bared, the billow of his yellow cravat. Flames flared from the wings; the *rat-a-tat* of machine gun fire.

He was trying to kill her. *He was trying to kill her.*

She screamed, covered her head with her hands, grit pricking her knees and elbows.

Spitting bullets whistled and cracked, hammered like

hailstones on the road around her, as if trying to stitch her to the ground.

Sharp clangs as a stream of bullets hit the metal bike frame, the whirr as the wheel spun round.

Dust bounced up all around, making her choke.

Then the firing stopped, the roar of the engine climbing away. She huddled, shaking, the smell of cordite in her hair, the metallic taste of blood in her mouth where she'd bitten her tongue, her back wet with sweat.

Slowly the engine died away.

After a few minutes, the distant low monotone of the all-clear sounded.

Moving cautiously, she sat up. Her heart pounded as if it would break her sore ribs, her breaths heaved. She shivered, staring into the sky. The beautiful sunset had faded, the underside of the clouds turning from violet to indigo, and all she could think about was the ugliness of war.

'Come on, Kitty. Pull yourself together.'

Hearing her voice brought her back to herself and she scrambled to her feet. Her blue dress was ripped, covered in mud, her legs as unsteady as those of a baby learning to walk. Bullet cartridges littered the road. She reached for the handlebars and pulled up the bicycle. The frame was bent, a bullet hole through the saddle, a tyre flat. She would have to wheel it back.

He had tried to kill her. That bloody Nazi pilot had tried to kill her.

She could have died. *She could have died.*

It took over an hour to wheel the bike back to Valletta and it was dark when she arrived home. But one thought kept pulsing in her mind. In war, life was short. You had to grab what life you could while you still had the chance.

She deserved a shot at happiness. She was going to embrace this new little family. She was going to give herself a chance at the kind of love she had never really had before.

And they would help her find Alice.

Chapter Twenty

Kitty was still shaken from the attack as she hurried into Fighter Command the next morning. She longed to share her news about finding Maria with Bill and hoped she'd see him today. But the streets of Valletta were strangely quiet and as she walked up Merchants Street, her ears caught the snatched notes of an accordion playing 'Roll Out the Barrel', coming from the Upper Barrakka Gardens.

It could only mean one thing.

She hurried into the gardens, bursting with spring flowers, through the colonnades to the battery. A small crowd had gathered, craning over the railings, cheering and waving handkerchiefs. She stared across Grand Harbour, mesmerised at what she saw.

For the first time in ages, the sapphire water was obscured by a sea of gunmetal grey, turrets and bridges glinting in the low sun. She counted them. Four merchant ships, four destroyers and a cruiser. Other ships from the Mediterranean Fleet were steaming back out of the harbour mouth, having safely escorted the supply convoy to their destination, including the battleships *Barham*, *Valiant* and *Warspite*, which Father had been so proud of. Her heart swelled at the sight of them. Ships meant supplies.

But it also meant air raids. And she was so tired today.

She tried to push thoughts of Alice and the Stuka attack away as she stowed her bag under the plotting table. It would be a busy shift.

Ash, accompanied today by a rear-admiral Kitty vaguely remembered from drinks parties at Old Theatre Street, leant over the balcony in his shirtsleeves, cigarette in hand, his eyes gleaming with delight over his moustache as he explained how the convoy, with all its much-needed supplies, had slipped in from Alexandria under cover of darkness.

'It's taken the protection of the Fleet, as well as our fighter planes, to get them here in one piece,' he said, staring down at D Watch. 'As you know, the battle of supply is the key to the contest here in the Mediterranean. Whoever keeps supplies arriving, can keep fighting. So the Luftwaffe are not going to be happy they've made it here.'

Rita caught Kitty's eye and smiled behind her wire glasses.

'About time we had a spot of good news,' she whispered, her dark curls bouncing. 'Give our boys a boost.'

Kitty smiled, knowing she was thinking about her boyfriend, the fighter pilot in 249 Squadron. They'd met last year at a dance at the Vernon Club for servicemen and Kitty knew how crazy Rita was about him, as she couldn't stop talking about the man.

'Nat says they've been desperate for fuel for weeks.'

'And ammo,' Kitty nodded, remembering what Bill had said.

Above them, Ash was still talking. '. . . and bombing raids are intensifying every day, but we're determined to protect this convoy, especially while the ships are unloaded. We will fight back with every defence at our disposal.'

A few cheers and 'Hear, hear!'s echoed round the room.

'So, stand by everyone. It's going to be a busy morning.'

'Positions please.' Irene looked round at them, her usually resolute face pale and pinched above her peach blouse, her brow, for once, creased with worry. 'Courage, ladies.'

Crikey, if anyone knew about courage it was Irene. Her house had been bombed last week, and she was sleeping in the Old Railway Tunnel shelter. Her sons, both in the Royal Malta Artillery, were stationed at gun emplacements dotted round Grand Harbour.

Kitty shivered as she put her headset on. The ships were sitting ducks. It was going to be hell out there today.

Tension built as the minutes ticked by. No one talked. Ash drummed his pen on the railing of the Shelf and smoked cigarette after cigarette. Just the ticking of the clock and the low hum of the underground ventilation broke the silence. At Ta'Qali the Hurricane pilots were already sitting in their cockpits waiting for the order to scramble.

They all waited.

Kitty leant against the table, every nerve in her body taut. Rita twisted her Claddagh ring round and round on her finger. Everyone strained to hear the first ring of the phone from the Filter Room, the first crackle over the tannoy, the first instruction in their headphones.

It didn't take long for the enemy to appear.

Kitty heard the first position in her headset. She marked up the plot and called it to the senior controller over her microphone.

'Twenty-five Junkers 87s incoming, heading south-east. Angels twelve.' She pushed the plot onto the table.

Next to her the other women of D Watch began calling plots and marking them with wooden triangles on the table, as waves of enemy bombers and fighter planes started appearing, all heading towards Malta.

'Nineteen, no, twenty Messerschmitt 109s accompanying Hostile bombers,' called Rita. 'Heading south-east. Angels fifteen.'

A total of forty-five enemy aircraft. Kitty adjusted her headphones and braced herself, glad Bill wouldn't be involved. She hoped the ships had finished unloading their supplies.

'Scramble Pinto Squadron.' Ash pressed the receiver to his ear and leant over the table, frowning at the map. 'Break into two formations, please. Pinto Red Squadron head up to seventeen Angels. Pinto Blue, to twelve Angels.'

He needed the Hurricane fighters to break into two formations – one to tackle the Messerschmitt fighters, and one to fire at the bombers and stop them unleashing their deadly loads.

'Guns engage!' The guns officer's clipped voice down the telephone ordered all gun emplacements round Grand Harbour to fire, creating a screen of metal shrapnel and smoke over the ships to blind the enemy bombers and make them miss.

'Hostiles twenty miles from target,' called Kitty, marking the enemy bombers as they approached the coast of Malta. She inched their plot forward across the table, towards the spot marking Valletta. 'Hostiles now ten miles from target.'

The air was filled with the calls of the plotters as they moved their marks forward, all converging together, until the map square covering Grand Harbour was filled with clusters of arrow blocks.

Kitty caught Rita's eye. Her face was strained as she looked up at Kitty and mouthed, 'Good luck!' Kitty wasn't sure if she meant it for her, or for Nat, or for all of them.

Douggie, leader of Pinto Red Squadron, yelled over the roar of his engine, his voice crackling over the tannoy.

'Watch out! Bandits at two o'clock. Bloody swarms of them!'

The strafe of bullets, the throttling acceleration of the engine, the whine loud as the plane banked round in the sky.

'Tally ho! Engage!'

'Tally ho! Give 'em hell!' Ash called back.

A faint tremor shook the table; the wooden blocks rattled on the map. They all knew what that meant. Above them, right now, Stukas were dive-bombing the ships.

The hairs on the back of Kitty's neck stood on end as she recalled the wailing scream of the Stuka siren attacking her yesterday, the paralysing fear the sound had made her feel. She glanced at Irene, knowing she must be thinking of her sons out there, exposed but for a few sandbags, loading a Bofors gun, pointing at a sky full of smoke, but her face was unreadable.

Their Hurricanes were up there now, chasing enemy fighters, firing rounds of bullets, ducking and diving in the sky, desperate to shoot as many of the aircraft down as they could, desperate to stop them dropping their bombs, desperate to protect the ships below.

Kitty pressed her headset against her ears, straining to not miss a single aircraft position.

There were two waves of attacks that morning, each lasting over an hour. Kitty and D Watch grew hot, their voices sore from calling plots, trying to avoid bumping into each other as they received aircraft positions through their headphones from the Filter Room. Worse were the calls of 'Pinto Red Two's going down, no parachute' or 'Pinto Blue Four's bought it', or 'Plot faded'.

As the shift ended and A Watch arrived, Ash stood in the gallery, running his hand through his hair, talking loudly into the phone to Ta'Qali.

'So that's nine Stukas shot down? And four more damaged? Good show. Bloody good show.'

The rear-admiral was also on the phone, checking the damage to the ships.

'The bridge of the *City of Lincolnshire* has been destroyed? Damn.' He frowned and rubbed his forehead, the gold brocade on his cuffs glinting under the light. 'And an incendiary fire in the hold of SS *Perthshire*. . .'

Rita pulled on her cardigan, her exhausted eyes shining with relief in her wan face. They had lost two Hurricanes, but Pinto Red Six, her Nat, had landed safely back at Ta'Qali.

'Thank God,' she muttered as Kitty put her arm round her and hugged her.

As the adrenaline ebbed away, Kitty's head throbbed. She bent to pick up her bag as Irene, for once her posture sagging with fatigue, thanked them all for their hard work. Kitty glanced at her. Irene was white with strain, her lips pinched as she struggled to button her jacket, a vein throbbing at her temple.

'Are you alright? You must be so worried about your boys.'

A shadow passed across Irene's face and she nodded tightly. 'They'll have done their best.'

Kitty squeezed her arm, and they walked out of the plotting room together into the warren of corridors. The casualty list wouldn't be out for a few hours. Adela would be out there now, tending to the wounded, and Kitty sent up a prayer that she was alright. Her throat felt thick as she thought about the destruction up above them.

As they turned a corner, voices floated down the corridor from a small office ahead of them.

'I don't like the look of this build-up of German troops on the Greek border . . .'

Kitty's heart sank. Now what was going on?

'We spotted a lot of Junkers 87s,' another voice replied. 'They're moving them to the airfields close by. See here. And here.'

The familiar voice was deep like the purr of an engine. Kitty's heart leapt.

Bill.

She could think of nothing better than seeing him and speeded up towards the door.

He and another RAF officer were examining reconnaissance photographs over a metal desk in the small office, a single bulb giving the green walls a sickly look. Bill had his back to the door, one flying boot up on one of the wooden chairs, his flying jacket thrown over its back.

'Bill?'

Bill swung round, wooden ruler aloft in his good hand.

'Kitty!' His eyes softened and his face broke into his usual lopsided smile. 'I hoped I'd see you.'

Irene's gaze flitted from Bill to Kitty and warmth flickered briefly in her eyes. 'Ah yes, I forgot you two know each other.' She glanced at the photographs, her brow creasing. 'Trouble brewing?'

Bill nodded. 'A build-up of German troops. We think they're planning to invade Greece.'

'Oh no,' Kitty breathed.

Irene blanched. 'My God. We'll be surrounded.' The vein in her throat ticked and her hand fluttered to her head. 'Let's hope they don't succeed.' She turned to Kitty. 'I have to go. I'll see you tomorrow.'

As she walked off down the corridor, Kitty smiled at Bill.

'How are you?' His eyes danced with delight.

'I'm so pleased to see you.' She was surprised to find herself choked up and flooded with an unexpected warmth at the sight of him, a feeling like coming home. Water beaded in her eyes. The last two days had been too much.

Bill glanced at her, his steel-blue eyes concerned, and then turned to the officer. 'I think we've finished, haven't we?' The officer nodded and left the room.

Bill smiled at her and without thinking, she fell into his arms, feeling safe against his firm body.

'That's a welcome I wasn't expecting.' He kissed her and pulled away, pushing the door shut to give them some privacy. 'Are you alright? Those raids must have been tough.'

Kitty shook her head. 'It's not that. Although it's been a hell of a day.' She was suddenly aware of her blouse sticking to her back, the sweat in her armpits, her hair limp and clinging to her skull.

'So how it did go? Meeting Maria? What about Willow End?'

'Willow End?' She had to tear her mind back to yesterday, the conversation about the house. 'She's letting us keep it.'

'Good show, that's great news!' He reached out and squeezed her hand. 'Thank goodness. I'm so thrilled for you.'

'Yes, it's a huge relief.'

She could see his surprise at her muted enthusiasm and added, 'But it was strange, meeting her. Turns out I have a half-sister. Censa.'

'Bloody hell!' His eyes widened and he sat down on the edge of the desk. 'A half-sister? Christ. That's a bit of a shock for you.' He shook his head disapprovingly. 'I'm astonished. So the vice-admiral didn't only have an affair, he led a double life?' His voice rose. 'Had another family? That's ruddy disgraceful.'

Kitty stared at him, knowing he was reassessing his view of Father, re-evaluating him, judging him to be a lesser man.

But it hit her then, like a stone shattering glass. Her blood ran cold.

She longed to tell him, to scream from the rooftops, *I have an illegitimate baby and she's trapped in Rome, please help me.* The relief of just talking about her, sharing her true self, would be such a balm.

But if she told him about Alice, would he rethink his view of her too?

Chapter Twenty-One

'Why didn't you bloody tell me?' Kitty stood, her hands on her hips, her voice raised. 'I can't believe you already knew about her. Christ. After all this time.'

The dainty sandwiches on the silver tea-stand seemed to curl under the scorch of her anger.

'Why did you have to interfere?' Lydia stopped wrapping a teacup and slumped back in the armchair, her face defeated. 'Why did you have to go and damn well find her?'

Kitty shook her head. It was a week later and she'd come home from Fighter Command to find the drawing room empty bar a few bits of furniture and Lydia packing, surrounded by piles of newspaper and a stack of her favourite china tea-service. The BBC News from London on the Rediffusion proudly announced a big victory by the Mediterranean Fleet over the Italian Regia Marina, at a place called Matapan, near Italy. Ash had already briefed them on the battle and much as Kitty wanted to hear more about the good news, she snapped the radio off.

'So you knew who that letter was from,' she said, her voice accusing.

'I guessed it was her.' Lydia pulled out the handkerchief tucked under her wristwatch strap and dabbed at her face. 'But I've never wanted to know anything about her. And I certainly didn't want you to. I'd rather have given up Willow End than know anything about *that woman*.'

'Well, she said we can keep Willow End. She doesn't want it.'

Kitty dropped into an armchair and put her head in her hands. She'd seen Maria and Ċensa a couple of times over the last week and every time she'd come home, she'd been wracked with guilt, wondering how on earth to broach it all with Lydia. How not to hurt her any further, how to soften the blow so it didn't destroy her completely. Kitty had been so worried about worsening Lydia's heart condition.

'I can't believe you didn't tell me.'

'And what good would that have done?' Lydia raised her chin. 'You're my child.'

'I'm not a child any more.'

Lydia gazed at her coolly. 'When you have a child of your own, you will understand.'

Kitty's breath caught in her throat.

The barb wounded her like a knife in the heart. Christ, how could she say that? How could Lydia not know how much pain Kitty was still in at the loss of her child? She didn't bloody deserve to know where Alice was, or anything about her.

'How long have you known?'

Lydia broke eye contact. Fingered the pearls at her neck. 'Since he came back from the Great War.'

'Christ.' Kitty closed her eyes and sank back in her chair.

'All he ever wanted was to keep coming back to Malta. All those postings – months at a time. I knew it wasn't just because it was the headquarters of the Mediterranean Fleet. I'm not a fool.' Lydia reached for the tiny bell on the table and rang it.

Cecilia, their Maltese maid, appeared in the doorway, straightening her apron.

'The bread's sliced too thickly again. Please make some more.'

'Ma'am.' Cecilia bobbed her head, picked the plate of sandwiches off the stand and left the room.

'For God's sake! The sandwiches are fine.'

'These things matter, Katherine. We have standards.'

Kitty clenched her jaw, wanting to shove the whole stand to the floor, scones and all. She fought to keep her anger under control.

'So why did you stay?' Kitty remembered the pain when she had found out about Dexter with his wife.

Lydia stared out of the arched window overlooking the courtyard. Palm leaves rustled in the breeze.

'We do our duty, Kitty. Make the best of things.' Lydia looked back at her, her eyes glittering and hard. 'You see, I could still be the best Navy wife in other ways.'

Kitty nodded, remembering how she had organised endless charity dinners and ladies' teas, even the big garden party to mark Edward VIII becoming king. A lump like a stone formed in her throat as she recognised how those events had just been a way for Lydia to cover her pain, to hide how unloved she felt.

'I'm sorry,' she said.

'You were so like him. Determined. Strong. Wanting your own way. Look at you, running off to London to be a photographer.' She glanced at Kitty. 'Do you remember how you told me you weren't going to become — what was it? "A dowdy cat-loving spinster with thick legs being given hot water bottles for birthdays."' She laughed a bitter laugh. 'I envied you, actually. Being able to escape.'

Kitty swallowed.

Cecilia reappeared with a fresh plate of neatly cut sandwiches, which they both ignored.

'So why did you come to Malta this time?'

Mother's head whipped up. 'You disgraced us. We had no choice but to get you away. What else were you going to do?' She waved a dismissive hand. 'Who would want you after that?'

Her words hung in the silence.

Bitter tears stung the back of Kitty's eyes.

'And maybe, after so many years, I hoped things would be different.' Lydia's eyes glistened. 'Perhaps a fresh start for all of us . . .' A tear shivered on her lower lid, before running down her cheek. She unfolded the handkerchief and wiped it away.

'I'm sorry. I just wish I'd known . . .'

'Well, we can have our fresh start now, can't we?' Lydia gestured to the packing cases.

'What do you mean?'

'The Germans are about to invade Greece, Rommel's charging across North Africa. Thank God, Admiral Cunningham's promised to evacuate us and Nora, his wife – you know, that small woman, likes a jaunty hat – on the first aeroplane out to Gibraltar. Meanwhile, we're to move to a little hotel in Gozo. Far less bombing there.'

Kitty stared at her. 'I told you. I'm staying.'

'What?' Lydia's head shot up. 'Why? For that awkward little pilot?'

'No.' Kitty gritted her teeth. 'For Fighter Command. To help defend Malta. Protect the people.'

And for Alice . . . She wouldn't say her name in front of Lydia, wouldn't let her despoil her baby's name again.

Lydia's expression was charged with neutrality. 'Suit yourself. You always did.' She took a sip of tea. 'You know, you're more like your father than you realise.'

Kitty sat on her bed, surrounded by fiercely yanked-open drawers and piles of aggressively folded dresses and cardigans. She'd already swept all her books off her shelves and was now piling them into stacks and choosing her favourites to put into her suitcase. God, Lydia was infuriating. That she had known the whole time and never said a word.

But as Kitty packed she thought about what Lydia had said, revisiting the weft and weave of the tapestry of her life through this new prism. Christ, no wonder Lydia had been so cold. She too felt unloved. How much damage Father had caused in both their lives. As she calmed down, she knelt on the floor and pulled out a small cardboard box, tied with pink ribbon, from where it had been pushed away from prying eyes deep under her bed.

She put it on the counterpane and placed her hand lightly on the lid. A few specks of dust felt gritty under her fingertips, and she gently brushed them aside.

Her most precious possession. It was a while since she had opened it. She loosened the ribbon, lifted the lid.

She pushed aside layers of tissue and stroked the pale yellow cotton blanket that lay underneath. She lifted it gently and held it to her nostrils. It still smelt of Alice, that baby milk smell, the scent of talcum powder and Johnson's baby oil. Tears beaded in her eyes. She reached into her pocket and pulled out the leather folder. There her daughter was, wrapped in this very blanket, her little fist clenched next to her cheek. Kitty felt in the box and pulled out the tiny cotton bracelet, the tag reading *Alice Campbell*, and caressed it. She remembered the warmth of the tiny hand inside it, Alice's fingertips like seed pearls.

Then the treasured tiny brown envelope, sealed with more ribbon. She slipped it open, peered inside. Soft curls of golden hair. She touched them with her fingers, imagined stroking Alice's warm soft head.

She breathed deeply, taking herself back to that day, at the maternity home, the sterile green walls, the blanket tucked too tight over her legs, a week after Alice's arrival. It had been a difficult delivery, Alice jaundiced at birth, the doctor afraid to separate them. She'd cradled her beautiful baby in her arms, kissed the soles of her tiny pink feet, her weight warm against Kitty's swollen stomach. Kitty lost in a haze, unable to tear her eyes away from her baby's unfocused violet eyes and dark lashes, unable to stop smelling the milky sweetness of her soft skin, unable to stop stroking her fuzz of downy hair. The sense of belonging as Alice's mouth had rooted for her and Kitty had held her to her breast, as if each minute would last for ever, and their bond could never be broken.

And then they had come.

Father's presence looming over her like an evil shadow in his dark suit, his voice echoing, as he introduced the woman in a brown tweed coat, her hair in tight steel coils, her face sharp, her eyes hard. The kind glance of the nurse as she folded the corner of the empty bed across the room.

'Come on, Katherine. You know what we agreed.' Father's voice reverberating across the void.

And Father's words had chilled her because it *was* what they had agreed, but back then she hadn't held Alice. She hadn't had her suckle at her nipple, hadn't looked into the velvet eyes that promised so much future together, hadn't felt her little pink fingers catch in her hair.

Her arms tightening round her baby. The slow seep of her tears. 'No,' she had cried, pushing them away. 'No. You can't take her.'

Father's Commander voice, booming an order, reverberating in the distance as if it were a thousand miles away. 'Don't make a fuss.'

'Now, now, let's not make a scene.' The woman's voice like ice.

And the veined hands like cold claws had reached down and pulled at the warm, soft bundle on her chest. The grip of Father's fingers like iron as he prised her hands from her baby's body. The wave of dizziness washing through her as she tried to push herself from the pillow to fight. Alice's screams filling the room.

Then her warm weight was lifted, cold air rushed in and her baby was gone, just a bundle of blanket, a shock of golden hair as she disappeared out of the door. And all Kitty could do was beg, beseech, wail for them to bring her back.

And later, exhausted and limp with crying, the ache of her delivery throbbing between her legs, the iron smell of blood as she shifted on the sheets. The blackness rising and the emptiness that went on and on for ever.

She picked up the photograph of her father that he had left her in his will, the one she had taken when she was just thirteen, and hurled it across the room, where it shattered against the heavy walnut chest of drawers.

Chapter Twenty-Two

Lydia left the next day. That afternoon after Kitty's early shift, Bill knocked at the front door, grinning proudly as he gestured at the jeep outside.

'Frank helped me "borrow" her. Ask no questions,' he tapped the side of his nose as he stepped through the door, 'especially with that much petrol in her tank.'

He came in, taking off his cap, and stopped abruptly. He stared open-mouthed round the hall at the pillars, the chandelier, the dark oil portraits.

'Some gaff.' He ducked his head in the dining room and released a long whistle. 'Is this what Willow End's like?'

Kitty laughed. 'No, it's far cosier than this.'

'But not quite like living in a flat over the shop.' He eyed her, watching for her reaction.

Goodness, he was worrying about his background again. She didn't give a damn about all that nonsense. Kitty took his hand.

'Come on, shop boy. Let's get me moved out of here. It's far too echoey and empty now.'

They headed upstairs to her room and Kitty sat on her bed to empty her bedside drawer. She was suddenly viscerally aware, with a tingle that spread low in her stomach, of the physicality of Bill's body in the intimacy of her bedroom, his eyes seeing her most private space, his hands on her childhood things. They had never been alone somewhere so private before. She glanced at him. Did he feel it too?

If he did, he showed little sign, chatting away and helping her pack the last of her things, shoving books into boxes, and carrying them down the long flight of stairs. She got on with packing her suitcase.

When they finished, he picked up a small canvas bag he had brought with him, pulled out a brown leather case and offered it to her.

'Here, I got this for you. Thought it was about time you had one.'

She took the case, her heart thudding as she pulled out a Rolleiflex. She breathed in sharply.

'How on earth did you get this?' She cradled the camera as tenderly as a newborn kitten. 'It's beautiful.'

She ran her fingers over the die-cast zinc shell, stroked the black leather casing and peered down the viewing hood. It was like reuniting with an old friend, just the feel of it charging her with a kaleidoscope of happy memories. She glanced up at him, smiling.

'It's got rapid lever advance too. Oh, Bill. It's just marvellous. It's just like my old one at home.'

'Took me a while to find a good one. Not to mention a few cases of whisky.'

'And a roll of 120 too?' There was wonder in her voice as she tipped out the roll of film and unclipped the back of the camera. 'You do know there's a war on?'

Just the smell of it calmed her. Slipping the film into the back, pulling it to the top and winding it on made the hairs rise on the back of her neck. It had been so long since she'd last done this. As she held it in both hands, peering over the top to set the focus and aperture, a wave of longing to take a photograph washed through her.

He smiled, enjoying her delight. 'It's a thank you. For saving the day with that four ships print. Thought you might like to start taking a few of your own. Keep a record of this mad world we're living in.'

She stared into his kind steel-blue eyes, her heart squeezing in her chest. The space between them filled with stillness, as if time stopped for a moment. How had he guessed? He had known, even before she realised herself, just how much she itched to start taking photographs again.

It was as if he really saw her.

'Oh, Bill, that's the loveliest, most thoughtful thing anyone has ever given me.' She leant in to kiss him.

He gazed into her eyes and ran a gentle finger down her cheek. He reached for her and kissed her deeply. She kissed him back, her body exploding with heat and desire at his touch, savouring the smell of his warm skin, the soft touch of his scarred lips, the strength of his arms pulling her close. And with a passion she hadn't felt for years, she pushed him down onto the bed, driven by an urgent need to know the whole of him, right now.

Later, as the sun sank, streaking the clouds with gold and apricot, they drove to Adela's flat, rattling and bouncing over the flagstone streets in the laden jeep. Kitty nursed the camera on her lap and couldn't help smiling at Bill while he shifted gears, his eyes fixed on the road as he swerved round the rubble, the soldiers digging shelters and clearing masonry from the streets.

As the jeep slowed to let an army truck full of troops go by, she caught a glimpse down a steep side street that led to the sea. Two women chatted on stools, baskets of laundry at their feet, scrubbing at soapy washtubs outside what must have been the ruins of their homes. Washing flapped from lines strung overhead, children played among the piles of stone around them. Evening sun sparkled on the soapsuds. Suddenly the women threw their heads back and laughed.

She held her breath.

For the first time in so long a familiar feeling surged through her, the driving need to capture the moment, the quiet intensity of focus. She snatched the camera out of its case, framed the scene, eyes narrowing as she checked focus and aperture. It was the way the soft gold light shone like a halo round one woman's headscarf just so, the merriment in the other's wrinkled face as she threw back her head and laughed – it made her long to capture this very female moment of resilience, of motherly fortitude, of life going on amidst the destruction.

She clicked the shutter.

It was as if she had been brought back to life again.

They pulled up outside the Vincenti Buildings in Floriana. Bill screeched to a stop and hooted the horn.

'*Chérie*, come on up.' Adela leant out of the sixth-floor kitchen window and waved. The jaunty jazz swing of the Glenn Miller Orchestra floated in the background.

An ear-splitting whistle followed, along with a ginger head

poking out of the window, a tea towel on his shoulder.

'Be right down, mate,' Frank yelled to Bill, who gave him a thumbs up, before he leapt out and pulled a box from the back of the jeep.

A thrill of excitement ran though Kitty. A new beginning. Surely that would bring some luck of its own . . .

While Bill and Frank climbed up and down the six flights of stairs with her suitcases and boxes, Adela helped Kitty make up the narrow bed. Her room was small, one wall dominated by a tall window that looked over the street, the rest of the wall space taken up with a chest of drawers, a fan-shaped mirror over it, and a couple of shelves over her bed.

Kitty much preferred the flat's homely, untidy chaos – the familiar posters of Josephine Baker in the living room, the temperamental primer stove in the tiny galley kitchen, the sink that only spat water in the bathroom when it felt like it. It reminded her of the flat in Bloomsbury and for the first time in a long time, she felt at home. She pushed Alice's memory box under the bed and put the camera in the drawer of her bedside table.

'*Chérie*, I am so excited to have you move in with me.' Adela came in, waving a lamp with a rose-pleated silk shade. '*Voila*, for your bedside table.'

'Thank you.' Kitty took it. 'The final touch.' She sat down on the bed and surveyed the room, smiling at Adela. 'I love it already.'

'So when are you seeing Maria again?'

'Friday. I'm really looking forward to seeing them both. They're so sweet.' Kitty patted the bed beside her. 'But sit down and tell me how the nursing's going.'

'Ah, good news.' Adela lolled on the end of the bed. 'I finish my diploma next week. Then we start the driving.' Her big brown eyes twinkled as she flashed Kitty a wide smile. 'I can't wait. I'll be given my own ambulance. Radiators, tyres and oil check instruction on day one. I will be on cloud nine. But I have even better news.' She sat bolt upright.

'What?'

'I met those two Free French pilots, at The Star. Jacques *et* Pierre.'

'What did they say? Did they have news?' Kitty stared at her, agog to know.

Adela crossed her legs under her.

'Jacques, he is tall with the broad shoulders and dark hair, Pierre, he is ten years younger, just a boy really, but *mon Dieu*!' She looked at Kitty earnestly. 'When they were in Tunisia, they stole a German seaplane so they could escape. They flew straight here, to join the Allied forces. But as they came in over the Malta coast, Jacques said he was terrified they would be shot down. So they kept signalling "F-R-A-N-C-E" in Morse code with their lights. They were fired at as they came over Grand Harbour, but luckily Ta'Qali realised and let them land. Can you imagine?'

'Wow.' Kitty nodded. 'So brave.'

'*Vraiment.*' She grabbed Kitty's arm, her eyes shining. 'But the best part is, Jacques said they met a Black soldier in a bar in Tunis.'

'Really?'

'Apparently, they got talking and this soldier said he wanted to escape too, but he was going to try his luck across the desert. Try and join the Free French Army. And I believe . . .' Adela clutched at her, 'that was Louis.'

'Because?' Kitty furrowed her brow, trying to follow Adela's excited gabbled story.

'He said he worked in a *boulangerie* in Paris. And what's more,' Adela's eyes beamed into hers, 'he said if they ever made it to Malta they should look up his sister, as she was a singer in a bar here.' She released Kitty's wrist. 'That's too many coincidences, *n'est-ce pas*? It must be him. It must be.' She rocked, hugging her knees to her chest. 'He's alive. Louis is alive.'

Kitty laughed, delighted for her, and pulled her into a hug. 'That's incredible, Adela. I'm so happy for you.'

'I just know it's him. I just know it!'

Adela pulled away and sprang to her feet, singing 'Happy Days Are Here Again'. Caught up in her infectious joy, Kitty leapt to her feet and the two women twirled round the room together.

'It's my evening off! Let's go dancing!' Adela bubbled with excitement. 'We can all go to the ERA Club and celebrate.'

The dance hall was full of servicemen and women, the buzz of chatter, the clink of glasses loud in the high-ceilinged room. The smell of alcohol, perfume and the hot sweat of people who'd done a difficult day's work hung in the air. Thick fugs of cigarette smoke swirled over tête-à-têtes at small tables, while the four-piece band played on a small platform. A few couples danced, women swirling in evening dresses, men shiny in full dress uniforms, all polished shoes, gold stripes and gilt buttons. The room was hot and stuffy with the blackout curtains tightly drawn despite the mild late-March evening. Bill held her in his arms as he twirled her round the room. Various officers approached her for a turn, but she had torn up her dance card, wanting only to dance with Bill.

From the corner of her eye, as they rounded the long ballroom, Kitty glimpsed Adela, shimmering in her silver lamé. While Frank fetched drinks at the bar, she was talking animatedly to three louche airmen in silk cravats, who leant in sipping gins, spellbound as they hung on her every word.

As they danced a foxtrot, Bill's kind eyes remained fixed on hers, his scarred hand gently clasping her at the waist, his other hand holding her own. Their bodies swayed together, and electric sparks flew through her as the firm muscles of his body pressed against hers. He nuzzled his chin against her neck and pulled her tighter towards him. Her insides seemed to melt with desire for him all over again.

'Kitty Campbell, I think I'm falling for you,' he whispered, his breath hot against her cheek.

'Bill,' she breathed. Her heart banged so hard against her ribs she was sure he must feel it. 'I'm falling for you too.'

But an irritating voice thrummed in her head as she laid it against his chest.

So why wasn't she telling him about Alice, then?

Chapter Twenty-Three

'Smile! Say cheese!'

Kitty peered down the viewfinder of the Rolleiflex cradled in her hands. Maria and Ċensa smiled back at her, smoothing their hair and straightening their skirts, giggling like schoolgirls in the little courtyard garden. Behind them, the evening sun came out and dappled the wall through the heavy boughs of the fig tree. Kitty clicked the shutter, enjoying the beautiful moment. Who knew if there would be any more in this terrible war?

A grey cloud passed across the sinking sun, extinguishing the golden rays. Kitty adjusted the focus to allow for the shadow and shivered, still jittery after the journey there.

The atmosphere on the bus had been tense. All day the news that Germany had invaded Greece had been relentless. Newspaper headlines were emblazoned on the stands; even the Rediffusion, as she got ready, broadcast breathless reports of the Nazis' rapid progress through the country, despite the help of the British defending the Greeks.

The Axis ring around Malta was tightening. Would every country in the Mediterranean fall to the Germans?

Everyone on the bus had sat in silence, old men in straw hats reading the paper, mothers with creased brows shushing children. As they rattled through the narrow village streets of Hamrun and Qormi the unspoken question hung in everyone's mind. Would they be next? The fear of invasion was everywhere. Fresh posters pasted on billboards warned to watch out for enemy parachutists dressed as British officers, curfew had been brought forward to 9.30 p.m., and all the city gates were ordered to be shut overnight.

Kitty glanced down at the viewfinder, as Ċensa babbled about how it was years since she had had her photograph taken and Maria said how blessed she was to have one of them together. It seemed fitting that, after so many years, one of her first photographs should be of the two of them. The new beginning that she prayed would end one day in her being reunited with Alice.

She set the shutter and adjusted the focus, settling into the familiarity of the movements, muscles responding, eyes narrowing as they had so many times before.

'One more, just to be sure it's sharp.'

'I can't keep smiling,' Ċensa said through a clenched grin.

'Hurry, the stew will burn,' said Maria.

She was doing her best to be patient, but Kitty sensed a tension about Maria today. It must be the threat of invasion. Everyone was on edge.

'There.' Kitty clicked the shutter. 'My new little family.'

Ċensa smiled wistfully. 'If only we could all be in it—'

Kitty was surprised to see Maria flash Ċensa a warning glance.

'It's alright, Maria. I wish Alice was here too.' Kitty smiled at them both. 'I'm pleased Ċensa's thinking about her. I love talking about her with you.'

'Good,' nodded Maria, composing herself, 'and Kitty, you should be in it as well. I'd love one of you with us.'

Kitty held out her hand as the first fat drops of rain splashed the dry soil, turning it the colour of a cup of strong tea.

'We'll do it another time.' She glanced at the supper table laid in the garden. 'I suppose we'd better eat indoors now.'

'We can still eat out here,' Maria said hopefully, but as she spoke the clouds opened and more raindrops spattered on their heads. She frowned. 'Alright. If we must, we'll go inside.'

Thunder growled and rain pattered on the windows as they ate. Kitty ignored it, enjoying the warmth of a tumbler of wine, her shoulders dropping, embracing the sensation of feeling part of this little family. Maria had cooked *stuffat tal-fenek*, rabbit stew, and the aromatic scents of frying onions, bubbling red wine and tomato filled the air, making her mouth water. Kitty was pleased to contribute a small goat's cheese she'd found in Mrs Macgil's grocery round the corner from the flat.

For the first time in a while, she stopped thinking about the war, focused on Ċensa's shining innocent eyes as she told her about her day, Maria's warm manner as she offered more stew. They were drinking mint tea, fresh from the garden, and Ċensa was explaining about her job at the Telephone Exchange when the ceiling above their heads creaked loudly.

Kitty jumped. She glanced up at the wooden beams, her nerves suddenly thrumming with tension.

'What's that?'

Maria's glass rattled as she put it back on the table. 'It's just the house, settling in the rain.' But she glanced upwards, frowning.

Ċensa continued. 'So military telephone calls only, and only for two minutes—'

A heavy thud sounded above, as if someone had dropped something weighty.

Kitty stiffened. 'Someone's up there.'

Maria exchanged glances with Ċensa.

'No, *ħanini*. Relax. It's just a shutter slamming.'

But there was something about the nervous look in Maria's eye that made the hairs on the back of Kitty's neck rise.

'There hasn't been a bomb explosion near the house, has there? I heard of a house in Pietà that suffered such bad cracks after a bomb exploded next door, it fell down two days later . . .' Kitty got to her feet. 'I'll go and check.'

Maria put a restraining hand on her arm. 'No, Kitty, please. Don't worry.'

The creak of a floorboard echoed down the stairs.

Kitty stiffened, her eyes widening.

'Is it an intruder?' she whispered.

'No,' Maria and Ċensa called in unison. Maria went pale. 'Just leave it.'

But in a swift move Kitty tiptoed to the bottom of the stairs. She turned to Maria and Ċensa, her finger to her lips.

A rustle on the landing; a shadow fell across the wall at the top of the stairs.

Goosebumps prickled all over Kitty's body. A million thoughts pounded like hammers on a wire. Had parachutists dropped this afternoon? Was this the invasion? Why hadn't there been an alert? Kitty looked round wildly for something to defend herself with, and picked up a heavy ceramic bowl from the dresser.

'No, Kitty.' Maria clapped her hands to her cheeks. 'Put that down. There's no need—'

'Who's there?' Kitty called up the stairs. 'Come down. Right now.'

The bowl trembled in her hands as she lifted it higher, ready to strike. She held her breath.

Footsteps creaked on the landing.

Kitty's heart pounded.

Socked feet appeared on the top step, then patched grey trousers, until a young man in a checked flannel shirt and knitted cardigan appeared, his hands up. He was tall, with a head of dark curly hair, wearing thick-rimmed glasses. He spoke in Italian.

'Don't hurt me. I'm unarmed.'

Somehow, despite his height and the fact he was in the house, he didn't look threatening. In fact, there was something oddly familiar about him.

Kitty lowered the bowl and shot a look at Maria, whose shoulders slumped. She looked resigned, defeated. Censa shut her eyes.

Did they *know* him?

'Who the hell are you?' Kitty said, her chin raised, her voice defiant.

Maria wrung her apron.

'It's Stefano.' She smiled anxiously at Kitty. 'Your half-brother.'

The words hung in the air. The moment stretched for what seemed like an eternity, *half-brother* reverberating in her head. Kitty blinked, unable to believe her ears.

'What?'

She dumped the heavy bowl back on the dresser. Shaking, she looked from the young man to Maria and back again. This didn't make sense. She already had a half-sister. No one had said anything about a half-brother.

'Half-brother? What half-brother?'

Maria went over to the man and put her arm round him, her face shining with love. 'My dear boy. Home at last. Stefano, please, meet Kitty.'

He pushed his glasses up his nose and smiled at Kitty.

Kitty stared at them. 'W-what do you mean?'

'He's your father's son.' Maria spread her hands apologetically, her face timid. 'He's been away a long time.'

'You didn't tell me,' Kitty whispered. 'You didn't say anything.'

Maria's face dropped. 'I'm sorry—'

'So, you're Caterina,' Stefano interrupted with a warm shy smile, 'how lovely to meet you. I never thought I would.'

Kitty took a sharp breath, disarmed by this pleasant boy. She looked wildly round the room, her heart beating so fast she thought it would burst out of her chest. Christ, how many more of them were there? Why hadn't Maria told her about him? She leant back against the dresser, her mind spinning.

'Stefano, couldn't you keep quiet?' Maria took him by the arm, her voice lowered to a hiss. 'Not even for a short while? You've done it now.'

What the hell did she mean? Was Maria hiding him? No wonder she'd been on edge all evening.

They talked in Italian, their voices rising and falling and talking so fast that Kitty couldn't quite follow. Stefano kept gesticulating, his voice loud, argumentative, his face red. She scrutinised him, as she gripped the dresser edge. Father was there in the strong square line of his chin, in his big nose, the slope of his broad shoulders and his height. But there the resemblance ended. He was thin, gangly, his brown eyes lined with long dark lashes, blurred behind the thick round glasses, and he had Maria's full lips. There was something else too, despite his height – he seemed gentler, softer, didn't carry the same air of authority Father had.

So Father had a son. An illegitimate son. Bile churned in her stomach. She shut her eyes. It was too much. The deceit of it all.

'Why have you lied?' she burst out. 'Why didn't you tell me about him?'

There was a long silence.

Maria crumpled against a chair, unable to meet Kitty's eyes.

'I'm sorry you had to find out like this.'

'You never even mentioned him. I trusted you.' Kitty's voice shook with bewilderment. 'Why are you hiding him? Why on earth would you keep him a secret? Jesus, Maria, how many more children did Father have with you?' She slammed her hand down on the dresser and the sting in her palm brought tears to her eyes.

She looked around for her handbag. She just wanted to leave, get out of this house of lies, deceit and false hopes.

Maria sank into an armchair, her head in her hands. Ċensa was silent, her eyes flitting from Kitty to Maria and back to Stefano.

'Are there other . . .' Kitty choked, 'children?'

Maria winced. She shook her head, her face pale. A blue vein throbbed in her throat by the chain of her silver cross. She closed her eyes a moment.

'No. There is just Stefano and Ċensa,' she said eventually. 'You don't understand. I couldn't tell you.'

Kitty lifted her chin. 'Why on earth not?'

Maria shook her head as if she was in a trance.

'I would have understood,' Kitty said, her voice breaking. Tears pricked at the back of her eyes. Dammit, she was going to cry. 'I care about you both.'

'I'm so sorry.' Maria didn't meet Kitty's eyes. 'It would have been better if you'd never found out.'

Kitty stared at her. 'Why?'

Stefano shifted by the bannister and looked Kitty in the eyes.

'Because I've just come from Sicily.'

Half an hour later, Ċensa had made tea and they were sitting in the living room trying to explain it all to her.

'It was the disgrace, you see,' said Maria, her cheeks flushed, smoothing a thread off her apron, 'having a son who'd gone to Fascist Italy. And Ronald a vice-admiral in the Royal Navy. He wouldn't permit us to talk about him. Ever.'

'Why did you go?' Kitty glanced at Stefano, suspicion in her eyes.

'It was before war broke out. I went to my cousin Luigi's farm. We always spent our summer holidays there.'

Ċensa nodded, smiling. 'We both love it there.'

'It's a quiet village on the south coast. I love working with the vines.' His voice was soft, with a sing-song lilt, his melodic Italian accent strong. He felt for the silver St Christopher at his neck. 'But I went last April—'

'When he ran away,' Ċensa cut in.

Maria frowned at Ċensa as if to hush her, but Kitty's mind

was whirring too much to pick up on it.

'And war broke out. I was trapped there,' he continued. 'I hid from the authorities for a while, but eventually I was forced to join a *battaglione*. All young men were. But I didn't want to fight my own people. That's why I had to get away.'

'But how did you even get here?' Kitty blinked at him. 'I mean, nothing's getting into Grand Harbour, barely even the convoys we desperately need.'

How on earth had he got here when the Mediterranean Fleet couldn't manage it? This didn't make any sense.

He glanced away, momentarily embarrassed. 'I was brought on a small fishing boat. Dropped in a cave near Għajn Tuffieħa.'

Kitty narrowed her eyes. 'But why weren't you spotted? What about the mines?'

'Mines?' He looked startled.

'They're all round the island.'

'I didn't know.' He released a low whistle and ran his hands through his unruly hair. 'The fisherman knew the route well, from before the war. And it was a moonless night.'

'But why have you come over now?'

He breathed out. 'I've tried several times to escape. Once I was caught and thrown in prison.' He shuddered. 'I had to make up some story about going on a fishing expedition. Because I was young, they let me go. But it's been hard.' He squeezed Maria's hand and smiled round at them all, his white teeth flashing against his olive skin. 'But now I am here, with Omm.'

'So when did you get here?' Kitty asked, still trying to grasp the facts.

'Two nights ago.' He pushed the thick glasses up his nose and grimaced. 'The sea was rough.'

'He gets very seasick, don't you, *mio caro ragazzo*.' Maria rubbed his arm fondly.

'But he missed us so much.' Ċensa came over and wrapped her arms round his neck. 'It's been nearly a year now.'

'Too long.' Maria ruffled his thick curly hair fondly. 'He wanted to see his *omm* and sister. Be back among us Maltese again.'

'It's true.' He flashed her a smile of lopsided teeth. 'Omm, I've missed your almond *qubbajt*.'

But Kitty's mind was still reeling. 'But surely you can't just leave Italy like that?'

He looked at her steadily, through his long eyelashes. They rested on his cheeks like moths and for a moment Kitty could see the little boy he had been. He wasn't much older now, just out of boyhood, maybe nineteen or twenty, and there was an intensity to him that glowed in his dark brown eyes.

'You know, we share the same father, *mia cara Caterina*, but I wonder if you can understand what it is to be Maltese. I love my country, the people, the villages, the way of life. I missed it so much. And I can't stand to see it being bombed to pieces a moment longer.'

'But it's the Italians who are bombing us.'

'Exactly.' He threw her a boyish smile. 'Not all of us think that is the best way to win this war.' He looked at her, his big round eyes earnest behind the glasses. 'I wanted to come back to help stop the bombing of our beautiful island before they destroy it for ever. I hate what they're doing to Malta.' He waved a carefree hand round the room. 'And now here I am.'

Kitty smiled. His joy at being back was infectious. It was odd sitting here with him, so familiar and yet different. He was like a much warmer, more charming version of Father. Her hackles were raised, her suspicions humming, but he seemed sweet, genuine. It was hard not to believe him.

Kitty looked at Maria, shaking her head as she tried to understand. 'So why are you hiding him, then?'

'I didn't want to tell you because of your job.' Maria spread her hands across the lace tablecloth. 'And right now, people are scared. Suspicious, jumpy. See how you are.'

Kitty nodded. It was true.

'Every day we're warned about parachutists landing, threats of invasion. It sounds extraordinary, doesn't it, that he has come from Sicily?' Maria looked at her steadily. 'People will think, how can this be? We don't want anyone getting the wrong idea, thinking he's an Italian soldier, especially in such times.' She patted Stefano's arm. 'No, it's best for now if he stays here quietly, rests a few days. Then we can see . . .'

'Yes.' Ċensa smoothed a curl behind his ear. 'We want to keep you safe now we have you back.'

Kitty sat back. It all seemed so odd, so strange, but as she looked round the table at the three faces staring at her, smiling, revelling in their joy at being together again, they simply looked like a happy family reunited after a long trip away. For a moment she felt on the back foot, disorientated, out of step with reality, as if she had leapt back in time to a place where the war was no longer on. Maybe they were right, just to be delighted he was back and safe. And yet . . .

'What about you?' Stefano smiled at her. 'Omm says you work for the RAF? That must be exciting, no? What a lot you must know about what's going on.'

'Oh, I just work in admin there,' she said, using the handy

phrase Irene had suggested to bat away awkward questions. 'Nothing very exciting.'

His gaze lingered on her a second and he rapped the table, breaking into a big smile.

'I have something for you.'

'Ah yes, fetch it, *qalbi*. This is good news. I'm glad we can share it with you now.' Maria smiled happily at Kitty.

He got up and hurried upstairs, the floorboards creaking above their heads as he went into one of the bedrooms. He returned, waving a small brown envelope.

'It arrived at the farm, several weeks ago. Luigi, my cousin, said I should bring it for Papa. He said he would want to know.'

'Oh my goodness. You didn't know Father was dead?' interjected Kitty. 'I'm so sorry.'

Stefano raised his chin and gazed at her. 'Don't be. I'm not.'

Kitty saw the coolness in his eyes. So he felt anger towards Father too. She wasn't surprised but wondered why.

'Stefano, hush.' Water sprang into Maria's eyes and she took his hand. 'How can you say such things about your father?'

'What did he ever do for me?' he said resentfully.

'Please.' Maria dropped his hand. 'Don't talk about him like that.'

There was a moment's uneasy silence.

'Anyway, now, you are here.' Stefano smiled at Kitty, his eyes dancing. 'So it's yours. I never thought I would give it to *you*.'

He handed Kitty the envelope. She stared at it a moment and then it hit her. The postmark was from Rome.

Her breath caught. Her hand shook as she opened it.

A small square photograph fell onto the table. She picked it up.

Her heart stilled in her chest.

She knew immediately. Five years old, the same big wide eyes, the same soft fan of thick eyelashes, the rosebud mouth, the point of her little chin. The little girl stared back at her, smiling, her hair in ribboned pigtails, dressed in a pinafore and little boots.

On the back someone had written in black looping ink, *Alicia, February 1941.*

'Alice,' she whispered. She stared at the photograph, trembling in her hand.

Tears beaded in her eyes; her heart pounded, swollen with love.

It was like a mirage, a dream, seeing the daughter she had only ever seen as a baby. She had imagined her for so long, pictured her so many times as a toddler, a little girl. And now here she was. Made real and grown older, before her very eyes. A photograph taken only two months ago. Alive, safe and being looked after by someone who cared enough about her to send a photograph.

A tear spilt down her cheek. She looked up at Stefano, feeling she would do anything to thank this young man. He had brought her the only thing she really wanted in the world.

'Thank you,' she whispered. 'Thank you so much.'

'Rosa Cassar must have sent it. To show she was still safe,' Maria smiled.

Kitty stared at the picture, stroking Alice's face, touching her pinafore, longing to tie those ribbons in her plaits.

A thought struck her and she looked up. 'Was there a letter with the photograph?'

Stefano blinked at her. Was she imagining it, or did he seem to hesitate a moment?

'No, no letter.' His eyes slid away from hers.

Maria leant forward to see the picture.

'She's a beautiful little girl. It's a miracle this photograph has made it all the way to you here.' She crossed herself and kissed the little silver filigree crucifix at her neck. 'We are both mothers. Now you know your baby is safe, maybe you can help me keep mine safe too.'

She put a hand on Kitty's arm and looked her in the eyes.

'Please, I beg you. Don't tell anyone Stefano is here. Please. Promise me you won't tell anyone.'

Kitty blinked at her, overwhelmed with emotion. 'I promise.'

Back at the flat later that evening, she made herself a stiff gin and flopped into the chair overlooking Grand Harbour. The hulking dark outlines of HMS *Sheffield* and half a dozen other ships lay silvered in the moonlight. In the distance, searchlights danced over the ink-black sea.

She stared for hours at the photograph of Alice, her sweet smile, her dancing eyes fanned with beautiful lashes, drinking her in, imprinting her on her heart. She couldn't wait to show it to Adela, but she was out. She would understand how much this meant to her.

And Bill . . .

How she longed to tell him.

Keeping her secret was an actual ache inside the deepest part of her, constantly bubbling up, bursting at its stopper, longing to explode. She needed him to know who she really was. To accept her for who she really was.

But then a thought hit her. If she told him, she would have to explain how she'd got the photograph, and she had promised

Maria she wouldn't tell anyone about Stefano. She breathed out, tapping her fingertips on the glass. Why did it all have to be so complicated?

It felt strange, wrong almost, having to keep Stefano secret, but she supposed she could see the logic of what Maria was saying and Kitty didn't want to let her down, not when they'd all been so kind to her.

She lay the photograph in her lap and sipped her drink, the ice clinking in the silence. She couldn't believe her luck that Stefano had brought it. She would be grateful to him for ever. It was odd, though, how he had arrived, strange he'd been able to land – but then he seemed so genuine, so pleased to be home. And his loyalties clearly lay with Malta . . .

The clatter of heavy footsteps coming up the stairs broke into her thoughts. A knock at the door. Her eyes widened as she glanced at her watch. Who could it be this late?

Another knock.

'Kitty? It's me, Bill.'

Her heart leapt at the sound of his gravelly deep voice through the door.

Before she had really decided what to do, she shoved the photograph under a magazine on the coffee table and ran to open the door. Bill stood in his flying jacket, holding his goggles, his leather motorbike helmet strap dangling under his chin, a big smile on his face. She fell into his arms.

'Bill! What are you doing here?'

'I wanted to see you.' He kissed her and pulled away, yanking the helmet off his head. 'Look, I haven't got long, got to get back to Luqa. Big mission tomorrow. I'll be busy for a few days actually. So how was it seeing Maria and Ċensa again?'

'Good. Lovely, but . . .' She broke off, thinking of the photograph. Of Stefano.

'Good.' He broke into his big lopsided smile and the scar tissue pulled his cheek taut. 'Thank goodness. I'm thrilled you're happy.'

'Bill . . .' She hesitated.

He kissed the tip of her nose. 'Yes, my darling?'

How she wanted to tell him. But could she? Her promise to Maria weighed heavily on her heart. One mother to another. Stefano's safety wasn't her secret to reveal. Her brain whirred as she weighed it all up. But after all she had been through, she was acutely aware of the fragility of life, of the damage lies could do to a relationship. Like a breeze turning on a summer evening, she suddenly wanted Bill to know her whole self, her whole truth. She cleared her throat.

'There's something I need to tell you.'

'What?' His eyes fixed on hers – wide, honest, caring.

She opened her mouth to speak but out of nowhere, Lydia's words reverberated in her mind.

Who would want you after that?

She hesitated, turned away, her heart pounding.

'It's, erm, it's nothing,' she stuttered.

'Tell me.'

'Erm.' She glanced back at him, her mind spinning. She grasped at the flimsiest of straws. 'Maria said the lawyer has accepted her wishes.'

His puzzled eyes stared into hers, and she could see he knew that wasn't what she'd intended to say. Understanding flashed in his eyes, a shadow descended like a shutter closing, and he dropped his gaze. He knew she'd made a choice not to tell him something. He knew, somehow, that in that moment he'd lost. Been shut out.

Her heart lurched. It had all gone wrong, that wasn't what she had meant to do. Confusion prickled up her back.

He glanced at his watch. 'Look, can we catch up properly tomorrow night?' His voice was curt. 'I just didn't want to spend tomorrow flying over Italy, worrying about you.'

'Italy?' Fear snatched at her. Please God, not Rome.

'A convoy we're keeping an eye on, near the coast. I dare say the Luftwaffe will give us their usual welcome.' He pulled on his helmet. 'Sorry, I've got to go.'

'Bill, I-I . . .'

But he gave her a hasty kiss goodbye and was gone.

Kitty stood for a long time by the window, staring as the dark water rippled in the moonlight. Then she went to her bedroom, pulled out the memory box and tucked the photograph of her little girl inside.

Chapter Twenty-Four

'Five plus Bandits, heading south.'

Kitty's headphones crackled into life again. She marked up the wooden block and pushed the Hostile aircrafts plot across the table on the map grid. Looked like they were heading to bomb Ta'Qali airfield.

'Five Me 109s approaching, bearing south at Angels eighteen,' Kitty called into her mic.

'Scramble Pinto Squadron.' Ash stood in the smoke-hazed gallery and peered at the map, dropping ash from the stub pinched between his thumb and forefinger, over the balcony edge. 'Get the chaps up, pronto. Don't want them shot up before they're even airborne.'

Ash's number two, Ops B – Archie; Kitty had met him at the ERA Club – barked his order down the phone to the airfield.

She pictured the pilots, waiting in full kit in deckchairs by their planes, frantically climbing into their cockpits. Thank goodness it wasn't 69 Squadron. Bill was still out, his flight listed on the board, and she hoped he was safe. She swallowed, painfully aware of what a mess she had made of telling him about Alice last night. How she had hurt him.

She had barely slept, worrying. When the air raid siren went off at 2 a.m., she had stumbled downstairs in her dressing gown. On the stairs, she'd passed Mrs Buhagiar, her hair in curlers, as she chivvied old Mr Buhagiar, stiff and slow on his walking stick. She'd helped them down, even though inside Kitty was screaming to get down to the shelter as fast as she could, her heart pumping with fear at the memory of that Messerschmitt attack.

Her stomach clenched, thinking of the Messerschmitts Bill was probably facing alone right now out on reconnaissance. She glanced at the board. His call sign showed he was still somewhere off the Italian coast.

'Pinto Squadron airborne,' Rita called.

Kitty pulled her attention back to the table as aircraft positions came into her headset.

'Bandits descending to fifteen Angels, closing on target,' she called into her mic. She pushed the wooden block marking the enemy plot another inch forward, towards the square containing the airfield. 'Bandits now at twelve thousand feet.'

'Pinto Red Squadron, climb to fourteen Angels,' Ash ordered down the telephone. 'Get above the Hostiles.'

Rita inched Pinto Red Squadron's plot forward, and it was just a matter of minutes until Rita's plot met Kitty's Hostiles in the same square.

'Bandits at target,' called Kitty.

'Pinto Red One here. We're onto them,' shouted Jim, today's squadron leader, cheerfully, his radio crackling over the speaker.

'Good luck, Jimmy. Over,' Ash called and took a deep drag on his cigarette.

'Tally ho! Tally ho!' The radio crackled and buzzed, loud

with engine noise, the rattle of guns firing, the crack of bullets on metal, before the radio cut out.

She and Rita exchanged anxious glances. Kitty gripped her cue tight, listening, waiting.

It had been a long day. Three raids – the first, bombers headed for the gun battery at Sliema; and then, more swarming over the seaplane base at Kalafrana. So far, their chaps had shot down two enemy planes.

Suddenly the speaker buzzed into life.

'Behind you, Pinto Red Three,' yelled Jim. 'Bandit coming out of the sun!'

More guns firing, the scream of an engine's throttle as it pulled up.

Up on the Shelf, Ash's fingers tapped the balustrade.

'Spotted him,' shouted Pinto Red Three, over the strafe of a stream of bullets. The crackle of the R/T for a few more seconds. 'Got him. Bandit on fire, going into the drink,' yelled the pilot. 'They're turning away. Turning away.'

'Nice work, Pinto Red Three. OK, Squadron, return to base. Over.'

Thank God, the skirmish had been short. Kitty pushed her plot across the map, moving the Bandits back across the Malta coast until the 'Raiders passed' was called.

But the tannoy burst back into life. 'Stallion Blue Two calling. Over.'

Bill.

Her head whipped up. Was he alright?

'Copped a spot of flak over the convoy. Over,' he shouted over the engine noise. 'Right engine shot to pieces.'

Kitty gasped, her guts dropping faster than a Stuka dive.

Ash sprang to his feet. 'Bad luck, old boy. Over.'

'Think the undercarriage might be jammed. It's going to be a sticky landing.'

Kitty's heart thumped against her ribcage. No. Not Bill. He had to get back.

Ash rubbed his forehead. 'Keep her nice and steady, old boy. We're on standby for you. Over.'

'I'll do his plot,' Kitty said loudly, exchanging glances with Irene. She gripped her rod. She would plot him back, will him back with every fibre of her being, every bloody inch of the way.

Irene nodded. 'Bring him home, Kitty.'

Kitty gritted her teeth, straightened her shoulders. Bill had to make it. He had to.

Ash gave the order for Fire and Ambulance to be put on standby at Luqa and the runway cleared.

But an engine down? The undercarriage jammed too? It wouldn't be an easy landing.

Kitty's blood pulsed in her ears. She placed his wooden marker on the table as carefully as if it were his plane, her armpits wet with sweat, and adjusted her headphones, not wanting to miss a word from the Filter Room.

'Stallion Blue Two approaching. Bearing south-east at four thousand feet,' she called into her mic.

Up in the plane, high above them, rattling and shaking with engine noise, Frank would be doing the same, plotting from the tiny navigation table just behind Bill, bringing them back.

The cue trembled in her hand. Come on, Bill. He could do this.

'Stallion Blue Two approaching N for Nuts at Angels two.' Kitty inched the plot forward on the map.

The minutes ticked by, everyone silent. Irene's lips moved in prayer. Just the suck and crackle of Ash's cigarette, the swish and click of the wood of Kitty's block as she pushed it forward with every new position she received from the Filter Room.

A cheer as Bill made it back over Malta.

'Stallion Blue Two descending to one thousand feet,' Kitty called into her mic. 'Coming in over Valletta now.'

'Roger that. Hold her steady,' Ash said down the R/T. His fingers gripped the edge of the balcony.

'Lowering landing gear,' Bill shouted over the roar of his single engine.

His familiar deep voice rang out loud in her ears as if he were right beside her. She pictured his eyes steely with concentration, his mouth pursed, hands firm on the controls. A creaking whine rang out.

'Undercarriage not responding. Repeat, undercarriage not coming down.' Bill's voice, calm, steady.

'Try again, Bingo,' Ash called urgently.

Bang! A screaming judder as something mechanical strained.

'It's not coming down.' Bill's voice, tense now. 'Stand by, we're coming in.'

Kitty's stomach clenched. No, no. How the hell would he land? She forced herself to take a deep breath. Focus. She had to focus.

'Approaching at eight hundred feet,' Kitty called, fighting to keep her voice steady, concentrating hard on the Filter Room voice in her headphones. 'Stallion Blue Two now at five hundred feet.'

'Watch out. It's going to be a bit of a belly flop!' yelled Bill.

He was nearly there. So nearly on land.

Surely he could do this. He had to do this.

'Stallion Blue Two approaching Luqa,' Kitty called into her mic. Her fingers gripped her rod. Please make it, Bill, she prayed. Please land safely.

'Prepare for landing,' Bill shouted. 'Stand by, stand by.'

There was an almighty bang as the plane hit the ground. The crunch of twisting metal, the screech of brakes, a rattling almighty roar as it tore along the runway . . . and the radio cut out.

The breath squeezed out of Kitty's body.

A deep hush flowed across the room like fog blanketing a harbour.

Up on the balcony the suck and crackle of a cigarette. The shift of feet round the table. A nervous cough.

'Come in, Bingo. Do you read me, Bingo?' Ash called urgently down the telephone.

Kitty pressed her headphones to her head, straining for any sound. Say something, Bill. Just say something.

Time slowed and stretched, just the ticking of the clock.

There was no reply.

Chapter Twenty-Five

It was half an hour before any news came through, then Ash took a call and beckoned Irene over.

Kitty's heart leapt into her mouth. She was just about keeping herself together, forcing herself to concentrate on the Filter Room's voice in her headphones, pushing plots across the table, calling positions, going through the motions. But she shivered, her armpits slick with sweat, and she had to clench her teeth together to stop them chattering.

She couldn't let herself take her eyes off the table. A kind look, a sympathetic murmur, would undo her completely. But she knew her duty, knew what she'd signed up for. She was expected to be professional, focus on the plots, no matter what. After all, Irene's boy had been shot and was in hospital, but Irene was still here doing her duty.

This was war.

But as Irene took her aside, the thoughts she had worked so hard to keep under control, had been trying not to torture herself with, flooded into her mind. Was Bill dead? Was he bleeding, injured, or worse – she took a sharp breath in – had he been burnt again?

'It's Bingo,' Irene said, her eyes shining with sympathy. 'He's been taken to hospital at Imtarfa. I'm so sorry.'

Kitty could hardly breathe. 'Is he alright?'

Irene shook her head. 'We don't have any details, except that the navigator and gunnery officer escaped unhurt.'

'Really?' Kitty's heart lifted. 'Perhaps the crash wasn't too bad, then?'

'Let's hope not,' Irene smiled kindly. She glanced at her watch. 'Look, you know I can't let you leave the shift early, and visiting hours will be over when you do. But you're off tomorrow. Best just go up there and see . . .'

The next morning Kitty was up early, desperate to catch the first bus. Adela had been out last night, so she hadn't been able to ask her if she had heard anything more about the accident from Frank.

Kitty only remembered it was Easter as she looked round the crowded seats at women and children in Sunday best and hats, chattering excitedly, carrying baskets filled with *figolli* biscuits. Kitty sat oblivious, clenching her fists, willing the bus to go faster.

When the air raid siren wailed, Kitty gritted her teeth. Christ, not now. Would they never get there?

The driver swerved over to the nearest slit-trench and braked hard, making everyone cry out as they lurched forward. Eyes wide, faces pale, they all jumped down from the bus, baskets and hats dropped as they ran to crouch in the trench. In the distance, the hum of bombers grew louder.

A little girl, separated from her mother, stood in the middle of the road crying, 'Omm, Omm!' Her mother, clutching a wailing baby, screamed her name, but the little girl didn't move, crying harder. Kitty jumped out of the trench, ran over to her and scooped her up in her arms. She held her tight and ran back to the trench, telling her she was safe now, it was alright. The little girl's hot wriggling body clung to her, the sweet smell of figs on her fingers, her soft wet cheek pressed to Kitty's.

As the bombers thundered overhead, Kitty shut her eyes, her heart thumping as she curled round the whimpering child. Christ, was this war to take everything from her? For a moment, she imagined holding her own little girl. Was this what it would feel like? The fierce animal urge to protect her, keep her safe, no matter the cost to herself, overwhelmed her. As Kitty clung tighter to the little girl, like a precious talisman, she sent up a prayer to God that if she kept this little girl safe, he would help Rosa Cassar keep Alice safe too.

And as the engines screamed, a clarity came as bright as a morning dewdrop on a petal. She was lucky, proud, to be Alice's mother. She didn't want to have to hide her daughter, or her true self, any longer.

She had nearly lost her chance to be honest with Bill. She wouldn't take that risk again. She would damn well tell Bill about Alice, as soon as she could.

As soon as it was over, they boarded the bus, a silent, subdued group now as they approached the sprawling 90 British General Hospital on the top of the hill at Imtarfa. Kitty craned her neck up at the imposing stone building towering above them, its rows of tall windows, classical columns and balustrades stretching away. Bill was in there somewhere.

She prayed he was alright.

They turned into the long driveway, buzzing with ambulances and stretcher-bearers carrying bandaged soldiers. Nurses scurried between the rows of Red Cross tents erected on the front lawns of the hospital. As soon as they stopped, Kitty hurried up the steps to the double doors and went inside.

She was sent up two flights of stairs into a long airy ward, lined with rows of starched white beds filled with freshly combed and buttoned men in pyjamas. The room smelt of floor polish, antiseptic and the sweat of men's bodies, but sunlight poured through the tall open windows so that the polished floor gleamed, giving it a sparkling air of cleanliness.

Kitty followed Matron, her starched apron crackling, glancing round at the men as she led her to Bill.

He was sitting up in bed doing a crossword puzzle, a fresh bandage wrapped over the scarred side of his head. His tired eyes lit up as he saw her.

'Flying Officer Hamilton, you are incorrigible. I told you to lie down,' Matron tutted. She turned to Kitty. 'You may have one hour.' Her feet squeaked as she pulled the curtain round them and walked away.

'Kitty, my darling. You've come.'

'Thank God, you're alright.' Kitty stared at him, relief flowing through her veins. 'I thought you were—'

'Lord no, I'm right as rain. Apart from the fact that the damn clues are dancing all over the page.' He put down the crossword, wincing under the bandage as he tried to smile. 'It's wonderful to see you.'

Kitty bent and kissed him, warmth running through her at the soft brush of his lips against hers. He was alive. He was fine. Thank God. But his voice wavered despite his cheery words and water shimmered in those familiar blue-grey eyes. He looked pale, drained, the skin of his scar angry and tight.

'Of course I was going to come and see you, after that landing you terrified us all with.'

She sat down on the metal chair by his bed, his flying jacket slung on the back, his RAF cap and a glass of water on the metal table beside it. She took his scarred hand in hers. 'I've been worried sick about you.'

'I wondered if you were in the Ops Room.' His face softened. 'Hope I didn't scare you.'

She nodded, her lips pressed together, unable to reply as the memory of the crash, the sound of screaming, tearing metal, made tears spring into her eyes.

'Kitty, I never want to upset you. You being here,' his Adam's apple bobbed in his throat and his eyes filled again, 'means the world to me.'

His eyes met hers and her heart seemed to skip a beat.

He stroked the back of her hand with his scarred thumb. 'God, you're beautiful.'

'I'm just glad you're alright. You are alright, aren't you?'

'I'm fine.' He smiled ruefully and dropped back against his pillow. 'They say I banged my head as we hit the ground.' He put a trembling hand gingerly to the bandage on his head. 'Must have passed out after we landed, so now they're making all this fuss about me having concussion. Grounded to bed-duty for twenty-four hours. 'Course, I'm right as rain now that I've seen you, my darling.'

Those steel-blue kind eyes looked deep into hers.

'Oh, Bill.' She squeezed his hand. He interlaced her fingers with his and her insides melted.

He leant over to his jacket pocket beside the bed, rifled in it, wincing as he moved, and pulled out his lucky bullet.

'Worked like a charm again.' He held it out to her, his face earnest. 'I want you to have it. To keep you safe.'

She shook her head, water brimming in her eyes.

'Oh, Bill, that's the sweetest thing anyone has ever offered me,' she closed his fingers back over the bullet, 'but I can't take it. It's your lucky bullet. I want it to keep you safe. Really.'

She leant over and kissed him gently. A cough from the man in the next bed made them jump apart. Bill glanced at her ruefully.

'So how are you?'

Her hand went to her own pocket, touching the photograph of Alice. Her pulse speeded up. So much to tell him. But Bill's wan face, his exhausted eyes and the brisk sound of the nurse's voice beyond the curtains made her stop. Maybe this wasn't the best time or place to tell him. Maybe it was too much, right now.

'There's so much I need to tell you, but—'

The wail of the air raid siren echoed through the ward.

From behind the curtain, she heard Matron scurry forward, clapping her hands together. 'Anyone who can walk, go down to the shelter. Those who can't, you'll be perfectly safe here with the nurses.'

'Shall we stay?' Bill raised his eyebrow at Kitty. 'They won't bomb a Red Cross hospital. Not even the Germans would do that.'

The ack-ack guns boomed and the heavy drone of bombers in the distance made Kitty's eyes widen. It sounded like a lot of planes. She pulled back the curtain round Bill's bed and ran to a window. Malta stretched away beneath her, dominated by the ancient walls of Mdina, to her left the beehive dome of Mosta and below her Ta'Qali airport. Villages lay dotted across the island where bombs were exploding, grey smoke rising.

But it was the sky that caught her attention. Row after row of bombers were heading in a straight line towards them, drifts of black bombs falling from them like confetti. They whistled and exploded, *boom, boom, boom*, palls of black smoke rising where they hit the ground.

'They're heading straight for us!' Kitty shouted. She rushed to help Bill out of bed.

'I can get up, I'm fine.' But as he stood, he reeled and nearly fell back against the bed. He smiled apologetically. 'Just a tad dizzy.'

Kitty held him round the waist, pulled his arm across her shoulder and stepped with him towards the door. Around them patients were being helped from their beds, but some couldn't move, with plaster casts on their legs or bodies. Nurses busied themselves, tucking in blankets and murmuring soothing words.

Christ, the nurses couldn't leave some of the patients. Had to stay with them during raids. How terrifying. She gazed at them with awe.

But the whistling of bombs and crash of explosions were getting louder, rattling windows, jolting the brown medicine bottles on the nurses' trolley.

'They're getting nearer. Hurry,' Kitty shouted as they limped through the ward, Bill's weight heavy against her. 'Quick! Let's get to the shelter.'

The crash of explosions was deafening now, the *boom, boom,*

boom of each one coming faster. She was going to bloody well get him down those stairs if it killed her.

'Hurry!' She pulled him, almost dragging him, her shoulder aching with the effort.

Bill staggered as if he were drunk. He glanced round.

'Bloody hell! They are bombing the hospital!' He tried to pull away from her. 'Leave me. Just go! Get to the shelter.'

But she gripped him tighter round the waist and heaved him forward. He tried to help her, taking uneven steps, and they made it out onto the landing. Kitty glanced out of the tall window and an arrow formation of silver planes roared towards them, bombs falling from their undersides.

'Get down!' she screamed.

She pulled Bill down and threw herself on top of him, her hands over her head.

A whistle overhead, its high-pitched whine echoing like a banshee in the stairwell, and she braced herself. A deafening bang, and then a blast of pressure blew them against the wall; the ear-splitting shatter of glass, the crash of masonry exploding. Dust poured on their hair and backs, the smell of cordite and black smoke choking the air.

Kitty lay stunned.

The bombers passed overhead, until they gradually, slowly, faded away.

Chapter Twenty-Six

Once the all-clear sounded, she helped Bill, now even more pale and exhausted, back to bed, where he soon fell asleep. For an hour or two, she busied herself around the ward, assisting the nurses settling other patients, shaking out blankets, fetching water and sweeping up glass that had shattered across the linoleum. From outside came the clang of ambulances, the crash of falling masonry and the shouts of soldiers and firemen fighting blazes all over the site.

'Thank you, Miss . . . ?' Matron said as Kitty gazed about her, wondering what else she could do to help.

'Campbell. Kitty Campbell.'

'You've been a great help, but we can manage now. I'm sure you have things to do. We'll take care of Flying Officer Hamilton. I expect he'll recover quickly.'

Kitty nodded gratefully, took a last glance at Bill, still sleeping, and hurried downstairs. As she walked into reception, a group of nurses, patients on crutches and ambulance staff shushed her. They were crowded round the Rediffusion speaker, frowning, listening intently to the latest news, as it solemnly announced that this Easter Sunday had been one of the worst days of bombing the island had endured.

'*. . . There have been three hundred bomb strikes in civilian areas and many villages badly hit, including Rabat, Attard, St Julian's . . .*'

Kitty's heart thudded. Villages had been hit too? Her mouth went dry. What about Żebbuġ? Had Żebbuġ been bombed?

'*. . . and telephone lines are down across the island. Twenty-eight bombs hit the 90 British General Hospital, one a direct hit on the isolation wing . . .*'

People gasped in shock and turned to each other. Exclamations of 'Twenty-eight bombs!', 'Bastards!', and 'How could they?' filled the wood-panelled hall.

But Kitty was already banging her way out through the front doors.

Maria!

Suppose their house had been hit? She had to get to them, immediately.

Her palms were clammy as she ran down the steps and looked wildly about her, wondering if she could hitch a lift somehow. But there was just chaos.

Black smoke billowed across the hospital grounds and the smell of cordite was pungent in the air. Soldiers shouted orders, siren bells clanged as ambulances pulled up in long lines, doctors called instructions as stretchers were hastily carried into Casualty. Makeshift triage tents were being set up, broken glass was being swept up and water gushed as firemen hosed into an operating theatre.

On a reflex, she reached into her bag and pulled out her camera, quickly photographing the destruction, the courage and resilience of staff as they cleared up.

As she clicked the shutter, an ambulance pulled up beside her, large red crosses in white circles painted on its side, its engine throaty as it throbbed on the drive.

'Kitty! Kitty!' A cheery arm waved from the driver's window and a smiling face leant out.

'Adela? Oh my goodness! It's you!' Kitty could have cried with relief at the sight of her. 'Look at you.' She snapped a photograph of Adela in her peaked cap and uniform behind the large metal wheel.

'What are you doing here?' Adela's eyes widened. 'Are you hurt?'

'No, it's Bill. He was brought in after that crash landing.'

'I know, it sounded so frightening. Is he alright? Frank said he'd been brought here.'

'Just concussion. They say he should be fine.'

'Thank God.' Adela glanced up at the row of shattered windows. 'I can't believe those Nazi bastards hit the hospital.'

'It was terrifying.'

'Where are you going now?' Adela gestured to the passenger side. 'Do you want a lift?'

'I'd love one. Would that be alright?'

'*Bien sûr*. Ruby won't mind. We've just dropped off our casualty, we're heading back to Valletta to collect more.'

'Can you drop me in Żebbuġ on your way?'

'There again?' Adela raised an eyebrow and looked at her. 'Of course. Hop in.'

Kitty climbed up into the ambulance, and Adela pulled on the huge gearstick and revved the engine. Adela glanced through the small doorway into the back at the assistant sitting on a bench behind her, called 'Hold tight,' and they roared off.

She looked tiny behind the enormous heavy wheel and had to use all her strength to turn it as they swung down the drive and out onto the road.

'How's it going?' asked Kitty, watching in awe this side to Adela she hadn't seen before. But then nothing should surprise her about Adela. Under that glamorous exterior lay a strong and capable woman.

Adela patted the dashboard and flashed Kitty a smile. 'So long as I check the radiator and tyres every morning, we seem to get along just fine.'

Kitty laughed, relaxing as they rattled along the winding lanes.

'So Żebbuġ again? No wonder I never see you.' Adela glanced sideways at Kitty. 'You're spending a lot of time with Maria and Ċensa these days.'

'Well, why not? They're my family now.' She glanced at Adela. Was she jealous?

'They're not your family,' Adela said, an edge to her voice. 'You don't know anything about them. Not really.'

'I do,' Kitty bridled, but heat flooded her face as she remembered how she had found out about Stefano. She stared out of the window. 'Well, I'm getting to know them . . .'

'Just be careful, *chérie*,' Adela said gently, casting Kitty another long sideways glance. 'I don't want you to get hurt.'

Kitty looked resolutely out of the windscreen ahead, her jaw set, refusing to catch Adela's eye. How dare Adela judge her? She had no idea how it felt to find this new family. Especially one that could help her find her daughter.

There was a long silence. As they bounced along, a circular beer mat jiggled from the rear-view mirror, obscuring some of her view.

'What's that?' Kitty shouted over the growl of the noisy engine, wanting to make peace.

Adela glanced at her, a wide smile brightening her face, as she heaved on the gearstick and slowed to a junction. 'Jacques brought it to the club last night. You know? The Free French pilot who met Louis?'

'A beer mat?'

Adela raised her eyebrows, her eyes dancing as she drove. 'Take a look at it.'

Kitty turned it round. On the back was a small sketch of what looked like a shop, a striped awning over a window of baguettes, and the name *Boulangerie Lavigne* emblazoned on the top. The words *À bientôt* and a kiss were scrawled next to it.

Kitty stared at it, puzzled for a moment. She breathed out as the penny dropped. 'Oh my word. It's your family's bakery.'

Adela threw her a dazzling grin.

'Louis gave it to him in Tunis. Said if he ever met me in Malta, to pass it on.'

Kitty sat back in her seat. 'That's incredible, Adela.'

'So it *was* him Jacques met. Louis is alive. I'm so happy.'

'Oh darling, that's wonderful.' Kitty rubbed her arm, longing to hug her but anxious not to disturb her driving. 'I'm so happy for you.'

They were approaching Żebbuġ, the colourful balconied houses looking relatively unscathed, thank goodness. Adela turned into the church square and pulled up under an olive tree.

'I know he's alive, Kitty. He's alive. It's the best Easter present ever,' Adela smiled. 'Now I understand how much you must want to find Alice.'

* * *

Kitty was surprised to see Maria, in the pristine white of her nurse's uniform, medical bag in hand, hurrying up the road towards her, Ċensa close behind.

'Maria, Ċensa,' she called, 'are you alright?'

'Kitty! You're safe! Thank the Blessed Virgin.' Maria dropped her bag and wrapped her arms round Kitty. 'We were worried about you.'

'I was worried about you too. That's why I've come.'

Ċensa caught up and they hugged, but Maria's eyes widened as she looked Kitty up and down.

'Are you alright? You're not hurt?'

Kitty glanced at her skirt, covered in dust, and brushed smears of grey ash off her pink blouse.

'I was at Imtarfa. Seeing Bill.'

'My God! We heard it was bad there,' said Ċensa, exchanging glances with Maria.

'Is Bill alright too?'

'Concussed after a bad landing. He should be fine.'

'Good, good. Look I'm sorry, I have to go.' Maria shook her head. 'We heard about the bombing at Attard. I'm going to see if I can help.'

Ċensa smiled apologetically. 'And I have to get to the Telephone Exchange—'

'Go, go.'

Maria picked up her medical bag. 'Sorry to miss you this time,' she gestured to the house, lowering her voice, 'but he's home. The key's under the geranium pot. And there's some stew left on the stove.' She hugged Kitty again, murmuring, 'I'm so glad you're safe,' and then they turned and hurried down the street.

Kitty found the key and let herself in, calling a quiet hello. Stefano was sitting at the table and he jumped up, startled, like a baby giraffe, too tall in the small room. Behind him the table was laid with dirty plates, a dish of *figolli* half eaten on the table, the sweet-smelling almond filling oozing out of the biscuits. A vase of white Easter lilies and blue irises stood on the mantelpiece.

'Caterina. What a surprise.'

He had heavy shadows under his eyes, his clothes crumpled, as if he'd been asleep most of the day, yet he looked more tired than when she'd last seen him. Kitty told him she had just come from Imtarfa, how pleased she was they were all safe.

'*Sì, sì*, we got off lightly, I think, but it sounded like the fires of hell had fallen. We could hear it here. Even the windows were rattling.'

'It was terrifying.'

Stefano ran a hand through his hair and yawned. 'Do you want some stew?'

'Please,' Kitty said, suddenly realising how hungry she was. She cleared the table as Stefano warmed the stew, thinking this would be a good opportunity to get to know him better, find out more about him.

They sat down, Stefano chewing a *figolla* while Kitty ate. The silence of the house throbbed in her ears after the noise of the bombing.

'Thank you so much for that photograph.' Kitty put her hand on his arm. 'It means so much to me.'

'I can see how much she means to you.' He flashed her his warm crooked-tooth smile. 'It must have been sad for you. I was just a boy, but we used to hear Omm and Father talk about your baby. I'm sure you wish you knew more about her.'

'Of course. I would do anything to know more about her.'

A glint ignited in his dark brown eyes. 'Really?'

'I mean, it's terrible not to know how she is. I worry all the time.' Kitty finished her stew and sat back, her stomach warm and full. She gestured at her empty plate. 'Is she getting enough to eat, is she being well looked after, is she safe?' Kitty pressed her lips together, trying to hold back her tears. 'Is she . . .' her voice cracked, 'happy?'

'I'm so sorry.' Stefano shifted in his seat.

Kitty looked at him. 'I know you said there was no letter with that photograph, but was any other letter, apart from that first one, ever sent to your cousins?'

He shook his head, his eyes fixed on her behind the thick glasses. 'War's dangerous,' he shrugged. 'People are careful what they say in letters.'

'I know. But were there ever any others?'

'Not that I knew about,' he said carefully. He looked down at his plate. 'If there had been, Luigi would have wanted me to bring them here.'

Kitty nodded, disappointment trickling through her veins.

'Sorry,' he added.

He was sweet, but he didn't understand. He didn't comprehend the bitter loss she felt, the grief that ate at her every day. How could he? He was just a young lad, really.

They went out into the garden, warm sunshine slanting over the wall onto the fresh leaves of the orange tree. He picked up a trowel and started pulling up weeds. Kitty sat at the table beside him, now covered in fresh green seedling pots, and watched him work, his fingers nimble in the soil.

'So, Ċensa said you ran away to Italy. Before the war. Why was that?' It was a question that had been nagging at her.

He looked up at her with an expression that said, *You know why.*

'Father.'

'Why?' Her voice was gentle. 'What did he do?'

'He never liked me for who I really am,' Stefano burst out. He threw down the trowel and stood up.

'I know how that feels.'

'You and me both, eh?' Stefano glanced at her and pointed to a young almond tree, froths of pale pink flowers blossoming in the corner. 'I planted that when I was twelve. He told me to stop wasting my time. Play some proper sports.'

'Oh, Stefano.'

He shook his head. 'We used to hear so much about you when we were growing up. You taking your first photographs, going off to the big lights of London, setting up your own studio. It was like you were the most important child . . . I hated you sometimes.'

'I would have probably felt the same if I'd known about you.'

'Oh, we had a few good times. My favourite days were in the holidays, when he took me out fishing in a little boat at Fisherman's Cove.' Stefano took off his glasses and rubbed the lenses on his shirt. 'But he couldn't accept me. At school, I loved poetry and acting. He made me play cricket and football. At home we spoke Maltese, but we had to speak English when he was here. Everything British, you know?' He put his glasses back on. 'He made me join the Royal Malta Artillery to "give me some backbone".'

She shook her head. 'I'm sorry.'

He shrugged. 'I refused. Anything to rebel.' He looked at her, pulling the sleeves of his knitted cardigan over his fingers.

'What made you leave?'

His eye challenged hers, hesitating. 'I met someone. In the church choir. We'd leave messages for each other, under the hymn books at the back of the church. Where and when to meet, you know?'

Kitty nodded encouragingly.

Stefano picked up a thyme seedling in a terracotta pot, pulled at its leaves.

'The last time Father saw me was here. He caught me . . .' he blinked at her, cheeks flushing, daring her to judge him, 'in bed. With a boy. That was why I ran away to Sicily.'

He knelt and put the seedling in the hole, patting the soil round it.

'I'm so sorry.'

So that was why Stefano had fled to Italy. To escape Father. She understood all too well the kind of hurt, the anger that grew when people were ashamed of you, when they tried to take something away from you. An unease about him, a tightness that had been building in her, ebbed away.

'Look at the two of us. Our lives ruined by the same man, eh?' He smiled up at her bitterly.

She blinked at him, startled. Stefano was so resentful. Was she like that? Did she want to stay feeling that stuck with her anger too?

'But enough of all that.' He pushed his glasses up his nose. 'What do you think the British will do to get revenge for all this bombing?'

Kitty shrugged. 'We'll fight back. Like we always do.'

'But there must be some plan? A big attack to strike a blow against the enemy?' He stared at her. 'An attack against an Italian airfield or something?'

'You know I can't say.' She patted his arm.

She smiled at Stefano, feeling sorry for him. For all his outward charm, he seemed an unhappy, intense young man, but his questions were making her feel uneasy. She got up to go.

'I'd better get home. Thank you for the stew. And send my love to Maria and Censa.'

Chapter Twenty-Seven

'But *chérie*, the bombings are getting worse. There are more every day.' Adela, her eyes full of anxiety, leant against the bathroom door.

It was later that night and Kitty was at home, rubbing Pond's Cold Cream on her face in the mirror over the sink, her hair up in a towel. It had been a hell of a day and she was starting a string of night shifts tomorrow, so she wanted to get to bed and get as much sleep as she could. In the background the swing of the Glenn Miller Orchestra played on the Rediffusion in the living room, the cheerful melody irritating, jarring with Adela's apprehensive mood.

'And there are so many air raids at night now.' Adela's voice quavered. Water welled in her eyes. 'It's frightening.'

'I know, it's hideous, darling.' Kitty put the pot down, her face blurring in the condensation on the mirror as she glanced at Adela.

She was dressed in crimson satin ready for her set at The Star, but above its shimmer, she looked tired, shadows smudged under her eyes, despite her heavy make-up.

Kitty's heart tugged and she pulled her into a hug. 'Maybe

you should skip the club tonight? Have a quiet night in with me?'

Adela shook her head. 'The only time I feel like myself is when I'm singing.'

She sank onto the edge of the bath, an ambulance apron dripping from a line above. Her scarlet nails tapped the edge of the enamel, her brown eyes fretful.

'And the bombing's not just aimed at Grand Harbour or the airfields any more. It's everyone. Ordinary people, children, babies even.' Adela's voice broke. She shook her head. 'And the wounded. So many, day after day . . .'

Kitty glanced at the large rust-brown stain in the middle of Adela's apron, which even Adela's diligent scrubbing couldn't remove. What awful sights she must see. Especially on a day like today. A chill ran through her.

'I'm sorry, sweetie.'

'And I meant to tell you. Yesterday evening, we were called to the gun emplacement up at Sliema.' Adela's eyes filled with tears. 'A parachute bomb. All five men dead. Blown apart.'

'Adela, no . . .'

A tear dripped on the floor tile. For a moment Adela couldn't speak. 'I picked up Sergeant Cortis. Carmela's father.'

'Oh my God.' Kitty breathed in sharply. 'No. No.' She sank onto the side of the bath beside Adela. 'Not Carmela's father.'

An image flashed in her mind. Mrs Cortis in her kitchen, Carmela on her lap. Her throat constricted. Poor little Carmela. What an ocean of grief that poor family were facing. She would go and see them, check they were alright.

'They're getting closer, I can feel it.' Adela's quiet voice broke into her thoughts. 'Please, tell me. What are they saying at

Fighter Command?' She swallowed. 'Will the Germans invade us?'

Kitty hesitated a moment too long. She longed to reassure her, but what could she say? 'We won't let them.' Her voice sounded falsely cheery, and she cursed herself for not being more convincing. 'The Luftwaffe are throwing everything they've got at us and no one is showing any signs of surrendering.'

Adela stared at her. 'The Greeks are. Look how quickly the Germans have got to Athens. They're flying their ugly swastika over *l'Acropole*. They say it will be Crete next. Then what?'

Their eyes met.

Kitty knew what Adela was thinking. How scared she was. They'd seen it on the newsreel at The Regent. Occupation across Europe, Nazi troops forcing people into ghettoes, cruel retaliations against villagers in Greece and France. And they had all heard rumours about the work-camps for the Jews.

'You should see how much is going on behind the scenes. How hard people are fighting, planning missions, doing their utmost to defend us. We shot down ten enemy planes in that raid last week.'

'Right, right.' Adela patted her hand. 'Sorry, *ma chérie*. There's no point in this gloomy talk.' She stood up and sprayed herself with Guerlain. 'I must go.'

'Can you take a night off soon? You must be exhausted.' Kitty followed Adela into the living room, raising her voice as 'In the Mood' reached its trumpeted crescendo. Adela strapped on her shoes and as the applause sounded at the end of the programme, did a twirl and a mock bow.

'You know the show must go on.' She flashed Kitty a faint smile.

Kitty smiled back. 'Well, bombings or not, you look lovely, darling. The boys at the club are in for a real treat tonight.'

Their eyes met. They were both putting on a brave face for each other. How else could they get through days like this?

'Must dash.' Adela grabbed her bag off the coffee table, blew a kiss and breezed out of the door.

Churchill came on the radio, his voice broadcasting over the crackling BBC airwaves all the way from the House of Commons. It seemed a million miles away and Kitty stood up to switch it off.

'. . . *the loss of our position in the Mediterranean and of Malta, would be among the heaviest blows we could sustain.*'

At the mention of Malta, she stopped, her fingers on the dial.

His voice continued, steady, slow and supremely confident.

'*We are determined to fight for them, with all the resources of the British Empire . . .*'

Kitty swallowed.

'*And we have every reason to believe that we shall be successful.*'

She turned off the radio and walked into her bedroom, praying he was right.

Chapter Twenty-Eight

It was over a fortnight later when Kitty hurried into Valletta to meet Bill. With buses running so infrequently he'd offered to take her to Mġarr where the Cortis family now lived with relatives.

As she walked up Kingsway, she was struck by the damage everywhere, so many shells of buildings – the city law courts, a cinema, even the belfry towers of St John's Co-Cathedral. Rubble lay piled up everywhere and dust wafted in the wind. She paused, taking photographs of the women queuing for food rations, trying to hold their families together, of the damaged homes in familiar streets.

What with her night shifts and Bill being sent away on a mission for a few days, she hadn't seen him since the bombing at the hospital. Her heart lifted at the thought of seeing him again. They'd communicated by notes and she knew he was better and flying once more. One of his scrawled notes in her pigeonhole said he wanted to take her out to dinner to *thank her for saving his life*, but the reason she wanted to see him was to finally tell him.

Her secret had been burning inside her like a stone left in the sun.

As she walked past the opera house, miraculously still intact, she held her face up to the early May sunshine, enjoying the warmth on her skin. Working nights had been a shock to her system and although Rita had told her that sometimes on a quiet night between raids they could occasionally get a few minutes' shut-eye, stretched out under the plotting table, this week there'd been no chance.

Adela was right. The bombings were getting more frequent and more devastating, every night.

'How has she been?' Kitty's arms wrapped round Carmela who sat in her lap, her violet eyes wide, sucking her thumb. Adela had stitched a cuddly rabbit from an old brown shawl and now Carmela clung to it.

Mrs Cortis shook her head as she arranged the red campions and white oxeye daisies Kitty had picked at the road's edge on the way over.

'She doesn't fully understand. Not yet.' Mrs Cortis crossed herself.

Kitty nodded and stared at the framed photograph of Mrs Cortis's uniformed husband that sat on the lace tablecloth of the kitchen table, a candle burning in front of it. He looked young in the photograph.

Kitty glanced at Bill across the room, busy showing Carmela's young cousin in a quiet voice how his pocket compass worked. He had been so kind to the Cortis family, had even brought them a small gift of his own, a bar of soap wrapped in newspaper that had made even sad Mrs Cortis's eyes light up.

'We're so very sorry.'

Mrs Cortis nodded as she sat down, her face pale and

dignified over the print apron covering her black dress, just the quiver of her lip giving away her feelings. Her sister, who looked identical, bustled about in the kitchen bringing them hot tea in glasses.

Kitty stroked Carmela's hair, kissing her baby-pink cheek. Mrs Cortis glanced at her husband's photograph, rubbed a thumb over the frame.

'He was a sergeant, you know. This was taken when Victor joined up a few years ago.' She sighed. 'I don't have a more recent one of him.'

Kitty sat up, a thought striking her.

'Mrs Cortis, would you like me to take a photograph of you and Carmela? I have my camera here.'

Tears sprang to Mrs Cortis's eyes. 'You could do that?' A tear seeped down her cheek. 'Carmela, wouldn't that be wonderful? To have a picture of you for always?'

The little girl's face lit up. Kitty got out her camera and made it into a game as she took pictures of them both.

She, of all mothers, knew how important a photograph of your only child could be.

Afterwards they roared back to Valletta, stopping to let Kitty pop into the flat to change into her emerald-green strappy dress. For the first time there was no Lydia to criticise, just Bill whispering 'You look beautiful,' as he took her hand and led her back downstairs. They walked to The Monico in Zachary Street, the atmosphere in the busy restaurant a million miles away from the sorrow of the Cortis's house, and ordered from the rationed menu.

Around them, the chatter of diners in evening frocks and

dress uniform hummed, laughter rang out and the rattle of ice cubes in cocktail shakers brought them back to normal life. The lamps shone brightly, sparkling on the silverware, and waiters in bow-ties scurried back and forth with silver-salvered domes balanced on the flat of their hands.

Bill's scar looked less taut tonight, his face relaxed as he ate his octopus in onion sauce. Kitty's palms were clammy as she sipped her gin. Now she was here and ready to tell him, her mouth was dry and she couldn't seem to find the right moment.

'I wanted to thank you so much for the other day.' Bill took her hand across the white tablecloth. 'You saved my life.'

'Hardly. We didn't even make it to the shelter.'

His eyes locked on hers. They were filled with such adoration, such passion, she could have drowned in them.

'But you cared enough to try. And you threw yourself over me to protect me. You know, you really are the most remarkable woman, Kitty.'

Heat rose in her cheeks at his intensity. 'I just did what anyone—'

'And you're a natural with that little girl. Such a tragedy for her. She probably won't remember her father.'

Kitty's throat tightened. Like her own little girl wouldn't remember her.

Bill's face softened as he saw her eyes fill. 'Carmela seems to really love you.'

Kitty looked down at her baked macaroni. Her whole body had tingled when Bill's eyes had been on her at Carmela's house, but now under their gaze, her stomach churned.

Now. Now was the moment. Her heart speeded up under the V-neckline of her dress.

'You're so caring and motherly with her.' He squeezed Kitty's hand.

'I care about her so much. More than you can know.'

Her voice came out strident, too loud. She pulled her hand away and shifted on her chair. Do it. Just tell him. A shadow passed across his face and he gazed at her expectantly. She could see in his eyes that he knew the mood between them had shifted.

She cleared her throat. 'There's something I need to tell you, Bill.'

'That doesn't sound good.'

'No, please. But . . . it's something you may not like.'

'I'm sure I'll understand.' He gestured to his scarred face and smiled gently. 'You know, I've loved you enough to let you touch my imperfections.' He stared at her. 'When are you going to let me touch yours?'

All the breath squeezed out of her body.

It was that feeling again. That he saw her. Saw her pain. Her heart stopped hammering, her shoulders dropped, the stress flooding out of her body like water through an opened dam.

'I had a baby,' she said simply, 'in 1936.'

He blinked, for a moment not taking it in.

'A daughter.'

'My God.' He sat back. His Adam's apple worked as he digested what she had said, then his eyes flooded with compassion. 'I wasn't expecting that. Oh, Kitty.'

Now she had started she couldn't stop, wanted him to know everything, the whole of her.

'I wasn't married. He, the father, didn't want to know.' It was as if her throat was full of cotton wool.

'How hard that must have been for you.' He reached across the table and took her hand.

Her eyes brimmed and she fought to swallow down the tears. He wasn't judging her.

He waited, his eyes calm and steady, her hand in his, until she was ready to speak.

'A little girl. My little girl.' She hesitated. It was a precious gift to say her name out loud, only given to those who deserved to hear it. 'Her name's Alice.'

'A beautiful name.' He stared at her, curiously. 'So where is she?'

Her throat closed and she looked down at her plate. How could she say the words? How could she admit what she'd done?

Wordlessly, she pulled out the photograph from her pocket and passed it to him.

He stared at her baby's face for a long while.

'She's beautiful.'

A memory flashed – the green sterile walls, the warmth of Alice's tiny body against her, cold fingers tugging her away, Father's booming voice. *We agreed, Kitty . . .*

'She was taken away. To live with an adopted family. But they couldn't keep her.' She let the words sink into the buzz of chatter.

'Oh my God. I'm so sorry.' He came round the table, knelt beside her and pulled her close. 'I'm so sorry.'

'Now she's in Rome. In hiding.' Her voice broke. Tears came then, a slow seep.

He pulled her close and held her tight.

It was late as they walked back to the flat. Valletta was deathly quiet. The streetlights were out, the houses blacked out. No one was about. Their footsteps rang out on the stone as they walked side by side up South Street. In the distance a dog barked. An ARP warden stepped forward from a shelter door and shouted at them to get a move on, curfew was starting.

Bill's words still rang in her ears. She had told him who she really was, and he had accepted it. Accepted her. Said how he was glad she trusted him enough to tell him. How he was so sorry for the pain she had suffered. How brave he thought she was.

'So you don't mind I wasn't married?'

'God, no,' he laughed. 'You may not believe it, but I've been no saint myself. In fact, I was with a woman in Birmingham for several years. Everyone wanted us to get married, but it wasn't right.' He breathed out. 'I broke it off when the RAF finally accepted me.'

He glanced at her as they walked. 'If there's one thing my accident has taught me, it's the importance of accepting yourself for who you are.'

Kitty smiled in the darkness. 'Well, Bill Hamilton, it turns out you can be quite deep when you want to be.'

They turned into Kingsway and in the pitch dark of the street, Kitty's ankle twisted on a lump of bomb rubble. She lost her balance and flailed, arms windmilling in the air. Bill's arm shot out, steadying her, holding her upright.

'It's alright, I've got you,' he murmured in her ear, his voice low and tender.

She sank against his body, his fingers firm at her waist. She breathed in the scent of his warm skin and her stomach somersaulted. Arm in arm, they walked carefully on to Floriana until they reached the doorway of her silent building, shrouded in darkness, every window shuttered.

'Thank you again for telling me about Alice.' They stopped and he tucked a curl behind her ear. 'I'm honoured that you did. You're a very brave woman, Katherine Campbell.'

But she wasn't. She wasn't, she thought dully. The guilt she'd carried like a sack full of boulders welled up in her. She hadn't had to go along with Father's plan. She could have fought harder to keep Alice. She could see that now. After all, Maria had managed with Censa and Stefano. If she had wanted to find a way, surely she could have found one?

'The really brave thing would have been to keep her.'

Bill wrapped his arms round her. 'Shhh, don't say that.' He kissed her lips. 'Don't torture yourself. You did what was best at the time. It's all any of us can do.'

The moon came out from behind a cloud and silver glinted on the tip of his nose, the jut of his chin.

'You know, guilt is a terrible thing.' He pulled away, hesitating, as if wondering whether to tell her something. His feet shifted on the steps.

'That night, when we bailed out? I got Mackie out, but I didn't tell you. I left Logie behind.' His voice cracked. 'I can still hear him screaming in the gun turret behind me . . .'

'Oh, Bill.'

'I should have gone back, helped him escape. But the fire—'

'Don't, Bill. Shhh.' In the moonlight, water glittered in his eyes. She cupped his scarred cheek. 'Darling, you've suffered enough.'

'He was still alive,' he choked, 'and I abandoned him. I abandoned him.'

She wrapped her arms round him and held him tight, and

they stood pressed together as if they would never be parted.

Eventually Kitty opened the door, took his hand and led him upstairs.

She lay in the dim lamplight of her bedroom, the curtains drawn tight to keep the blackout, her cheek on his warm bare chest, her knee hooked over his leg, the two of them pressed together in the tangle of sheets on the narrow bed.

Her fingers caressed the tender scarred skin that ran down the right side of his body. Before, he hadn't wanted her to see the scars, had stripped off quickly, turning away from her, before getting into bed. She'd been surprised to find the long imprint of the fire right down his body, had kissed his wounds, wishing she could kiss all his pain and guilt away. How much he had suffered, and so alone. Like her.

Maybe he was right. Maybe they had both done the best they could at the time.

This time their lovemaking was slow, tender, gentle, their passion both an exploration and an acceptance, a forgiveness of each other, and of themselves.

He took her hand, laced his fingers through hers.

'I love you so much, Kitty.'

She had never thought she would hear those words again. Hadn't believed she deserved to hear them, ever again.

She knew, now, what a gift they were.

His grey-blue eyes stared into hers, filled with trust and love, and something inside her seemed to shift as she whispered back, 'I love you.'

Chapter Twenty-Nine

A couple of weeks later, Kitty finished her night shift in the Ops Room and headed down the long gloomy corridor. A *thump, thump, clap; thump, thump, clap* sound echoed from a room up ahead and she wondered what on earth it was. It grew louder as she approached the Briefing Room.

The door was ajar and she glanced in. Ash perched on a desk, bouncing a tennis ball one-handed against the wall, cigarette pinched between his other thumb and forefinger, as he gazed at some reconnaissance photographs pinned to the board.

Something big was definitely up.

A message had come into the Ops Room about twenty minutes ago; there had been a few whispered conversations up on the Shelf and then Ash had stridden out frowning, and disappeared, even though there was a battle with Junkers 88s underway. Tension had surged round the room. She had exchanged uneasy glances with Rita, until Irene had told them to concentrate on the planes they were plotting.

Now Ash was here, his usually composed face flushed and stormy. She was about to glide past, when she heard another sound: a voice, arguing.

Bill. A spark lit inside her.

As if he could feel her presence, Ash turned and frowned. 'What is it?'

'Nothing. See you tomorrow.' She walked further down the corridor away from the doorway, but Bill came barrelling out, still in his sheepskin flying jacket and trousers. Worry filled his eyes.

'The Germans have invaded Crete,' he said tersely. 'Thousands of parachutists. Overwhelming numbers. Bitter fighting.'

Her mouth went dry. 'Oh God.' They would be next. Everywhere else in the Med nearby had fallen to the Germans now. Goosebumps prickled all over her body.

'We're evacuating all British troops from Crete.' Bill glanced at his watch. 'The governor's addressing the island in about ten minutes.'

Kitty nodded.

He stared at her, his eyes filled with concern. 'Are you OK? I've been worried about you.'

'It's the night shifts. I barely sleep,' she muttered, longing to take his hand, touch his face, but knowing she couldn't. Not here.

'I miss you when I'm not with you,' he said hoarsely. 'A lot.'

'I miss you too.'

'I'm heading out to the Italian coast to check where some troopships are headed.' He frowned, glancing round to check no one was in earshot. 'Look, we're placing booby traps at the airfields. They're saying German parachutists could dress in British uniforms. There are rumours they landed in Crete dressed as nuns. Please, take care.' He squeezed her hand and disappeared back into the Briefing Room.

When she got to the entrance hall, a small crowd of officers, plotters and clerks were gathered round the Rediffusion speaker, stiff and subdued, listening to the governor's announcement. She exchanged glances with Irene.

'Not only will we never give up Malta, but we have no intention of allowing it to be taken from us, whether by the Germans or the Italians . . .'

Governor Dobbie was in full flow, despite the static of the speaker.

'It is possible that the hardest times are now at our very doors,' he continued. *'We have to brace ourselves for the great and supreme effort which perhaps will be required of us . . .'*

'We'll never give in to the Nazi bastards!' someone cried out. 'We'll fight them, each and every one of us.'

Fists punched the air, voices cried, 'Hear, hear.'

Kitty cheered too. Of course they would never give up Malta. They would fight to keep their island free, even if they were the last ones in the Mediterranean standing against the Germans. They had to keep Britain afloat to win the war.

Kitty raised her knuckles and knocked again. Silence from the other side of the door. Of course, they were out. And she couldn't call out to Stefano. Dammit.

She had cycled out of Valletta, the winding lanes unusually busy with troops and trucks so she was left swerving and waiting in ditches for them to pass. Out in the countryside, she surprised herself by struggling to take the right turnings, shocked they had started painting out the road signs. She'd had to stop and ask the way from a soldier, stripped to the waist as he brandished a dripping paintbrush, and he'd said it was to confuse enemy parachutists. Goosebumps prickled up her back.

Now standing outside Maria's door, the sun hot on her back from the late May sunshine, she was sweaty, thirsty and desperate to talk to Maria. If the Germans invaded, they couldn't find that telegram. It had Rosa Cassar's name on it, mentioned a safehouse. She had to get Maria to destroy it.

The thud of heavy feet hurrying down the stairs echoed.

'It's me, Kitty,' she called, relieved.

The door opened a crack and Stefano peered round. He glanced up and down the street.

'Quick, come in.' He opened the door and she stepped inside.

'Is Maria in——?'

Italian voices burbled from the wireless in the kitchen.

Kitty froze.

What on earth? A woman's voice shrieking, '*Non vincerete mai la guerra.*' *You can never win the war. Surrender now before you are invaded.*

The hairs rose on the back of her neck.

Stefano stiffened for a moment, before disappearing into the kitchen and switching off the radio.

'What the hell's that?' Kitty's voice was wary.

Stefano shrugged, but a red flush crept up his neck. 'Nothing. I like to listen to Rome Radio sometimes.'

'But it's full of propaganda.'

'I like the music programmes and comedy shows.' Stefano pulled his cardigan sleeves over his fists, his eyes watchful. 'We grew up with them.'

'Right.'

'You listen to your English programmes on the BBC, don't you? It's the same thing.' He smiled. 'Would you like some water?'

'Please.' Kitty rolled her shoulders. He was right. She was overreacting. Too jumpy.

Stefano handed her the glass. He looked as tired as before, his eyes stained in shadow, olive skin wan, stubble dark on his chin.

'Neither of them are here. Omm's doing a scabies clinic for the kids over in Rabat, Ċensa's at work.'

'Are you still staying . . . in?' She was going to say 'staying hidden', but it sounded too dramatic. He was just Stefano, back home, after all.

'Yes,' Stefano shrugged.

'Aren't you sick of it? Couldn't you tell friends you're here?'

He rubbed his chin. 'I'm not sure that would be wise right now.'

'Yes, you're right.' Kitty sank into a chair. 'That's why I've come. I need to speak to Maria. She needs to destroy that telegram with Rosa's name in it. We can't leave the name of someone helping us lying around for the Germans to find.'

'Really?' He frowned. 'I don't know where she keeps it. But do you think that's necessary?'

'I hope not.' She looked at him. 'But the raids are never-ending. We're still losing too many pilots, and we desperately need more Hurricanes.'

'Are more coming?' He sat down opposite her.

'Maybe. There's a convoy—' She stopped herself just in time. Ash had said a major convoy of Hurricanes were on board HMS *Arkwright* and HMS *Furious*, sailing from Gibraltar, due to be escorted to Malta tomorrow. She looked at Stefano. 'Maybe.'

'What does that mean?'

'It means *maybe*,' she said, her cheeks flushing. Of course she shouldn't say anything, even if he was family.

'But there are six new Hurricanes at Ta'Qali?'

'Yes, but . . .' She frowned at him. How on earth did he know that? Had it been reported in the *Times of Malta*? She wracked her brain trying to remember. But there seemed to have been a shift in the atmosphere of the room. An unease sprang up between them.

Stefano's eyes drilled into hers. 'You said there's a convoy. Is it heading from Alexandria?'

She looked away. 'You know I can't tell you.' Why did he ask her these questions when he knew she couldn't answer them?

He crossed his legs, picked at a thread on his trousers and smiled at her. Was it just in her head, or did his smile not seem to reach his eyes?

'You must be worried about your little girl.'

'All the time.' Relax, Kitty, he's just trying to be nice. Interested. It was sweet of him to talk about her. Not many people did.

'I was thinking about what you said. About finding out more about her. I have contacts in the church in Sicily. They know about the safehouses. Maybe I could find out more information about her.'

Her heart lurched. 'Oh, I'd love that,' she burst out. She blinked as she stopped and considered what he'd said. 'But how on earth could you do that?'

His eyes narrowed behind his thick round glasses. 'I could try and find a way. *Maybe*.' He raised an eyebrow and she laughed.

'No, but seriously, how?'

'I know people.' He took off his glasses and rubbed them on his flannel shirt. 'Like you do.'

'What? In Italy, you mean?'

'I could find out some helpful information, details . . .' He looked at her. 'We could help each other out.' A crooked smile. 'A swap maybe.'

She blinked at him, too astonished to reply.

'What do you mean?'

'Think about it.' He gazed at her. 'It could work for us both.'

'What?'

He was joking, wasn't he? She laughed nervously and looked at him.

He stared back, his face unreadable.

A cold tide of understanding pulsed through her veins. She put down her glass, her hand shaking.

What was he saying? Was he suggesting what she thought he was? Surely Stefano wasn't actually asking for information from Fighter Command? Her mind reeled as a thousand questions crowded in. Surely that wasn't what he meant. But how could he get in touch with anyone in Italy? Did he have some sort of transmitter or wireless, or did he know someone who did? And if he could find out that kind of information about Alice, who on earth was he in touch with?

Christ.

'What were you doing in Sicily? Before you left?' Her voice shook. It had always bothered her about his story.

He gave her a guarded look. 'I told you. I was working on Luigi's farm. And then they made me join up. But I only did a few weeks' training. Drills, marches, weapons training, before I escaped.'

'Right.' Kitty stared at him.

There was something disingenuous about him, about the way the look in his eyes didn't match his half-smile, the way the boyish act seemed to have been dropped. It filled her with unease. Her mind spun. Christ. Maybe he hadn't just come back because he loved Malta.

So what on earth was he doing here?

Her stomach churned.

Now she thought about it, she didn't really know much about him. How he spent his days. And why was he always so tired? She was filled with the sudden need to go upstairs and look in his room, see if there were any clues as to what he was doing every day, why he was really here.

'Yes, right. Well, I'm still worried about that telegram.' She tried to conjure a convincing smile. 'I'll just nip upstairs and see if I can find it anywhere.'

He nodded, his gaze impassive.

She went up to Maria's room and pretended to look under the bed on either side of the room. She made a show of scraping a chair and noisily opening a drawer or two before tiptoeing next door to the small room Stefano used. The door was ajar and she pushed it open, praying it wouldn't squeak. There was just a single bed, a shelf under the window lined with books and an old wooden train, a chest of drawers with a poetry book on top.

From downstairs came the clink of cutlery. Stefano must be stacking plates in the kitchen. She slid open a drawer or two and felt inside. All filled with shirts and underthings. Another of those knitted cardigans he was so fond of. His boots stood beside the drawers and she picked one up. The toes and soles were covered in red-brown mud and grass. She frowned. There was no grass here in Maria's courtyard. Had he been out? But when?

She knelt down, but there was a clatter from the kitchen. She froze. When the noise stopped, she peered under the bed. There was a battered leather suitcase. Her heart thudded. Could there be a wireless set in it? Christ. Was he in contact with a *battaglione* in Italy?

She eased out the suitcase as quietly as she could across the floorboards, praying none would creak. Her palms were clammy as she clicked the clasps and opened it. It was full of old *Boy's Own* comics, a tangled Slinky and a moth-eared teddy in a knitted waistcoat. She scrabbled through it, the blood in her ears pounding, sweat pooling under her arms. There must be something here. Surely.

She sat back, her heart thudding in her ears. There was nothing suspicious. Nothing at all.

'What are you doing?'

Kitty jumped so hard, her head hit the back of the chair behind her. Stefano glared at her furiously from the doorway, arms folded across his chest.

'How dare you go through my things.' His eyes burnt with fury.

'I-I . . .' Heat rose up her face and she struggled to her feet.

'Leave my stuff alone.' He snatched a comic from her hand. 'How dare you go through my stuff. And after I offered to help you.' He slammed the suitcase lid shut. 'So my own sister doesn't trust me? God, and I'm only trying to protect you all. What is it with this family? You're just like Father.'

'Sorry, I'm sorry,' she mumbled. She couldn't meet his eyes.

'I don't know what the hell you think you're looking for, but there's nothing to find.'

'I'm sorry, Stefano.' She moved towards the door. 'I've got to go.'

He didn't step aside and his tall frame towered over her, his hand on the door jamb blocking her way. The air was tense. For a split second she thought he was going to stop her leaving, but after a moment, he stepped aside.

She ran downstairs and flew out of the door.

Fool, fool, fool. Her mind raged as she pumped the pedals as hard as she could. Her breath burnt in her lungs and her leg muscles ached as she reached the fields at the edge of the village. She braked to a stop, climbed off the bike and leant against the low stone wall, panting.

She felt ridiculous. She'd let her fears, her suspicions, her jumpiness run away with her and now she'd really offended Stefano. Dammit. There had been nothing in his room. He was just a boy, returned home. She trusted Maria and Ċensa, and they genuinely thought he was home because he had escaped. Because he was loyal to Malta. She knew that much was true. She'd seen the conviction in his eyes when he said it. He was just a frustrated young man trying to show off, make himself seem big.

But he had been suggesting he could get information from Italy, hadn't he? But how? How could he possibly be in touch with anyone in Italy? But then, someone had brought him here, by boat. She had always thought it strange. Could he really be communicating with Italy? She breathed in. He'd been listening to Rome Radio, for God's sake. He'd trained in an Italian *battaglione*. Where did his loyalties really lie?

She knew what he had said. *I could find out some information . . . we could help each other out . . . a swap maybe.* Was he really suggesting something worse? Something much worse? She groaned and covered her face with her hands.

And those boots . . . he had definitely been somewhere, although he said he wasn't leaving the house. Was he going out? Maybe at night? Did Maria and Ċensa know? And grass. She knew one place where there was lots of grass in Malta. An airfield.

But what was she to do? She had no proof of anything. He could deny what he'd said to her, say she'd misunderstood. And maybe she had. She hoped she had. Perhaps the best thing to do would be to talk to Maria, see if she knew anything more.

She picked up the bicycle and headed across the dusty green island to Rabat, the spires and domes of Valletta in the distance, a topaz sea shimmering beyond, her thoughts churning.

Chapter Thirty

Kitty hurried to the square in Rabat and looked around. The bakery was open and an old man in a stained flannel waistcoat sat outside with a cup of coffee, wedged next to the figs and aubergines stacked up by the grocer's.

'*Skużani sinjur, fejn hi l-iskola?*' she asked him.

He pointed to the street on the right-hand corner and muttered a few words.

The shouts and laughter of children in the playground guided her to the school, a small two-storey stone building, not much bigger than a house. She pushed her way through the gate into a small walled courtyard. Scruffily dressed children kicked a rag ball, while a group of girls with long plaits played hopscotch. In the far corner, under the wide shade of a leafy fig tree, Maria, in a white nurse's dress and apron, sat on a stool, examining a small boy's fingers. A teacher beside her was shouting at a line of children, corralling them into an orderly queue.

'Well done, Victor. They look perfect,' Maria was saying. Her kind eyes crinkled at the little boy as she patted his hands. 'No need for cream.'

The boy mumbled '*Grazzi*,' and the next little boy in too-long shorts took his place on the stool.

Kitty walked over to them and Maria's face lit up as she saw her. 'Kitty. Are you alright? What are you doing here?'

'Everything's fine.' Kitty smiled reassuringly at the little boy. 'Sorry to interrupt. I just need to speak to you, when you've finished.'

Maria smiled up at her. 'Give me a few minutes. I won't be long.'

'Of course.'

Kitty went and waited by the school gates in the warm sunshine. She stared at the little girls, chatting as they hopped over the numbered squares. Her eye followed one, aged about six, with light brown hair and a blue pinafore, giggling as she called out the numbers.

What was Alice doing now? Was she able to play like this in Rome? Tears pricked at Kitty's eyes.

As the teacher blew the whistle, the children streamed back into school and the playground fell quiet. Maria packed up her medical bag and came over, the wings of her nurse's cap fluttering in the breeze. She hugged Kitty.

'What is it, *hanini*?' Maria's eyes filled with concern. 'You look worried.'

'They've invaded Crete. The telegram . . .'

Maria's eyes widened and she glanced round, checking no one was in earshot. 'Come.'

She propelled Kitty towards a small church, further down the street. The wooden door creaked as she pushed it open and they entered the cool dark interior. The church was empty, silent, not much more than a chapel, just an ornately painted altar at the end lit by the flames flickering from two tall silver candlestands. The resinous smell of incense hung heavy in the air. Maria led Kitty into the back row of the wooden pews, and Kitty waited while she bowed her head and made the sign of the cross.

'The telegram,' Kitty blurted out. 'We need to destroy it.'

Maria clapped her hand to her mouth. 'The safehouse,' her eyes widened, 'and Rosa's name. It could endanger them.'

'If the Nazis find it . . .'

'Those Fascist bastards. Yes, yes, of course. I'll go straight home and burn it.' Maria patted Kitty's hand. 'Don't you worry.'

'Thank you—'

Maria's mouth set in a determined line. 'We mustn't bring trouble to those who are helping us. We'll keep them both safe, God willing.'

'Thank you, I knew you'd understand.'

Kitty straightened the hymn book on the narrow wooden shelf in front of her. Now she was here, she didn't know how to start. How could she accuse Stefano to Maria's face? 'And there's something else I wanted to ask you,' she cleared her throat, 'about Stefano.'

Maria smiled. 'What do you want to know about my dear boy?'

'Have you told anyone about him yet?'

'No.' Maria looked at her, puzzled. 'Especially now . . .'

'Is he going out at all?'

'Of course not.' The crease deepened on Maria's forehead under her cap. She rubbed Kitty's arm. 'Why are you asking, *hanini*?'

Kitty glanced away, wondering how to put forward her suspicions so they wouldn't upset her.

'It's just that I popped upstairs to try and find the telegram and I-I happened to see his boots. They were muddy. Grassy. I think he's going out.'

'No, he isn't.' Maria shook her head and removed her hand from Kitty's arm. 'They were probably muddy from when he arrived, or from the garden—'

'But he's always so tired in the day.'

Maria opened her hands. 'He's a young man. He's frustrated being stuck at home.' She stared at Kitty, concern flashing in her eyes. 'Why are you asking all these questions about him?'

Kitty rubbed a splinter in the wood of the pew in front. *I could find out some information . . . we could help each other out . . . a swap maybe.* She took a deep breath. 'Could he be going out at night?'

'I've told you he's not!' Irritation flared in Maria's eyes. 'I'd hear him. Why on earth would you think he's doing that?'

Kitty swallowed. 'He said he could get information for me. About Alice.'

'What?' Maria looked puzzled. 'I don't know what he means. Maybe he thought we could ask here.' She gestured around her. 'The Church have a powerful network across the Catholic world, and we've known some priests a very long time. I expect he was just trying to help you.'

'Right.' Kitty pushed her hands into her pockets, wondering if she should say any more. But she had to know. She had to. 'He said he would ask someone in Sicily. But that set me wondering. I mean, how could he find out from someone in Sicily, from here?'

'Of course he can't,' Maria said sharply. She folded her hands on her medical bag. 'What are you saying?'

Kitty ground her toe on the marble floor. 'He said he could get information about Alice. As a swap. For information from me. From Fighter Command.'

There was a moment of silence.

'*Per la Madonna*! How can you say this!' Maria's eyes burnt with indignation. 'He's just a boy. He's bored.' She shrugged. 'He was probably trying to play the big guy who knows everything. Showing off. You know what men are like. You must have misunderstood.'

'Maybe. But—'

'He's your half-brother, Kitty.' Maria's eyes flashed. 'Don't be ridiculous. What exactly are you accusing him of?'

'I'm not accusing him. I just . . .' Kitty's stomach somersaulted. This wasn't going at all how had she meant it to.

Maria looked wounded. She shook her head. 'We welcome you into our family. Offer you love, affection – and you suspect him? What? Because of a pair of muddy boots? I thought you cared about us.'

'I do care about you,' Kitty said, desperately. This wasn't coming out right. For a moment Kitty felt ridiculous for ever imagining Stefano had a wireless or had ever said anything suspicious. Maria was right, he was just a boy with a lively imagination and too much time on his hands. What had he said? That he was trying to protect them all? And after all, Maria would never lie in church.

Kitty put her hand on Maria's. 'I'm not accusing him, Maria. I—'

'Stefano is a good boy and he loves his country. I'm surprised

I have to tell you that.' She pushed Kitty's hand away, hurt shining in her eyes. 'I trusted you, *ḥanini*.'

'You *can* trust me. Please, Maria—'

'I hope so.' Maria frowned, concern in her voice. 'He is my boy, you know. I care about him like you care about your little girl.' She lifted the small watch pinned to her chest. 'I have to go.' Her face closed down and she pushed past Kitty to get out of the pew.

'Maria, I didn't mean—'

'There are more children in Attard needing medical attention.' Her voice was cold. 'Excuse me.'

Kitty sat in the pew, her head in her hands as Maria's footsteps clipped over the marble and the heavy door clunked shut.

Adela was right. There was a lot she didn't really know about this family.

Chapter Thirty-One

The next evening, Kitty waited for Bill at the ERA Club, tapping her finger on her glass. She was still feeling bruised by the horrible conversation with Maria and was doing her best to shake off the unease, the dark shadow it had left over her. For a moment she considered telling Bill about Stefano, but then he would be left in the same awful churn of uncertainty as she was. Anyway, she had promised Maria she wouldn't tell anyone about him, and after all, it wasn't like she had any real evidence.

She glanced at the clock by the bar. Bill was usually pretty punctual, but he was late. Unease was beginning to prickle up her spine, as she worried that something had happened to him, when he hurried in, pulling his cap off his head. He glanced around the busy diners at the white-clothed tables, searching for her, then saluted a senior officer and hurried over.

'Sorry, sorry.' He leant over and kissed her. 'Got stuck at the airfield in a debrief.' He threw his cap on the table. 'What are you having?'

'Another G&T, please.'

He signalled for two more drinks to the barman and sat down, smoothing back his hair.

He looked drained, tired, poor love, the skin of his scar taut and red, his eyebrowless eye drooping and bloodshot. He released a long breath. 'What a day.'

'Oh God. We're not being—'

'Invaded? No.' He shook his head and flexed his scarred hand to stretch it out. 'No, just hours of flying. We've been searching for this enemy convoy all day. A big one. The usual Luftwaffe flak as we photographed it.' He smiled wryly, but as his lip tightened, he flinched.

'Are you alright?'

'I'm fine,' he said, but the fingers of his good hand drummed on the table. 'There's also one of our own convoys on its way to us and we need to get it here in one piece.'

'I heard.'

'And we're just so low on aviation fuel, ammunition . . .'

'And food,' said Kitty, pushing the unappealing menu over to him. Rationing had been tightened again.

'Quite.'

The waiter arrived with their drinks on a silver tray, but as he served them, he caught sight of Bill's face. Shock flashed in the waiter's eyes; he jolted and knocked over one of the tonic bottles.

'Sorry, sorry, sir,' he flustered, embarrassed, dabbing at the wet tablecloth with a tea towel.

'Just leave it, man.' Bill's eyes glittered with fury. 'Drop of tonic doesn't bloody matter.' But his face burnt and he pushed his hair so it flopped over his forehead.

Kitty's insides contracted. Oh God, poor darling Bill. How awful for him. He had enough on his plate without this.

The waiter left them and Kitty squeezed his hand. 'Ignore him, darling. He's an idiot.'

Bill couldn't meet her eyes and carried on speaking, trying to pretend nothing had happened, but his leg jigged under the table.

'Now Jerry are in Crete, it's going to be even harder for us to get supplies through. The Germans have got bases across the whole bloody Mediterranean, so they can bomb our convoys and send their own wherever they need them.' He shook his head. 'It's like time's running out.'

'I know.' Kitty clasped her glass even tighter.

'So . . .' He leant forward and lowered his voice, even though the big room was noisy with the chatter of servicemen, the clink of glasses. His tone was full of bravado, but his eyes were shadowed with unease. 'We're going to run more attacks on their bloody convoys.'

'Oh, Bill.'

Her stomach flipped over like a fish. She knew what that meant. More reconnaissance missions on his own, photographing ships protected by dozens of enemy fighters and anti-aircraft guns. And he was already exhausted. Tense. Look at him.

'We're planning more missions. Things are going to get busy, so I'm not sure how much I'm going to see you over the next few weeks.'

Don't go, she wanted to scream. *Don't do it.* She had seen too many aircraft shot down recently, heard 'Going down, no parachute' or 'Plot faded' called in the Ops Room too many times. She suddenly wanted nothing more than to lay her head down, shut her eyes and just for a moment, pretend it wasn't all happening.

'We'll see each other when we can. And I'll be there, darling. Tracking you on the ground.'

He smiled tightly. 'I like to think you're down there, keeping an eye on me.'

'The worst thing is when I have to go off duty and you're not back yet,' she added primly. 'That's not much fun.'

'Getting attached? I like that too. Very much.'

Kitty looked away. Getting attached? She supposed she was . . . but she was keeping yet another secret from him. Her insides turned to liquid.

'Kitty, I love you so much.'

Their eyes met. She caressed his face with her fingertips. 'Oh Bill, darling. It's so lovely to see you properly again.'

He took her hand. 'Darling, we may not have much time—'

'Don't say that. Please don't say that.' She didn't want to think about it. Couldn't think about it.

'Kitty, I'm in love with you. I know we haven't known each other long, but I just want us to be together as much as we can, while we can. Who knows how long we've got—'

'Don't.' She shut her eyes. A shiver ran through her.

'I love you, Kitty.' His earnest blue-grey eyes stared into hers. He reached into his jacket pocket and pulled out a small, battered leather box, his scarred fingers fumbling with the lid. A gold band nestled in the yellowing silk, a tiny diamond on the top.

'Kitty Campbell, will you marry me?'

All the air squeezed out of her.

'It's Grandmother's . . . but if you don't like it, we can choose another.'

'Bill, it's beautiful but . . .'

'Please. Just say you'll marry me.'

'Oh, darling.' Her heart thumped like a racehorse after the Grand National. 'I-I wasn't expecting this . . .'

Was this really happening? The sound of chatter faded, the crowd in the room went out of focus. A thousand thoughts whirled in her mind. It was too soon; she wasn't ready for this. Not yet. She didn't know if she could trust her new family and now here was Bill asking him to put all his trust in her, and she was still keeping secrets from him, for God's sake. She hadn't considered it, hadn't thought whether she could let herself go, let herself rely on him, need him. Someone who could hurt her, destroy her and then abandon her, as everyone else she had loved had already done . . .

She shrank back in her seat.

'Bill, darling. It's just so soon.' She didn't want to hurt him, of course she didn't. 'I love you, I do, but . . .'

He sat back. Disappointment and betrayal replaced love in his eyes.

'I see.' His mouth set, his face hardened.

'Bill, I love you—'

'But not enough.'

He snapped the ring box shut and laughed hollowly.

'You know, all my life I've not felt good enough. Not good enough to get to university, not good enough to join the RAF and not even bloody good enough to be admitted to an officer's club, until I came here. And now I'm bloody ugly too.' His eyes burnt at her as he stuffed the ring box back in

266

his pocket. 'But I didn't think you'd think I wasn't good enough either.'

He jumped to his feet and jammed his cap on his head, yanking it down so the peak covered his scar.

'Bill, of course I don't think—'

'Don't you?' He glared at her.

Then he turned and strode away.

Chapter Thirty-Two

The air raid siren wailed yet again as she hurried into work, and she dodged into the nearest shelter on the street for the third time. She'd tried to sleep again this afternoon, a blanket over her head, but the argument with Bill still replayed in her mind, over and over, like a tormenting loop. She hadn't seen him since.

But the air raids were incessant and the final straw this afternoon had been a huge bomb explosion a couple of streets away, one that had blown out the windows in their apartment, despite the sticky tape that they had criss-crossed over them. So many buildings had lost the glass in their windows now, and by the time she'd swept up the worst of the shards and stuck the blackout blinds down to keep the breeze out, she'd given up and gone down to the shelter. There she'd tossed and turned, trying to sleep under her blanket in a corner, people coming and going, chattering around her, children kicking stones down the aisles between bunk beds.

Now as she hurried into her night shift, she had to dodge from street to street, shelter to shelter, clutching her tin hat on her head, flinching if a string of bombs landed too close, her fingers in her ears as the anti-aircraft guns up on the ramparts round Grand Harbour boomed back against the bombers. Once she was stopped by a Malta Defence guard and had to flash her Fighter Command ID pass before he'd let her through. But Irene had made it very clear that they were never to be late, air raid or not.

But, thought Kitty, as she hauled herself out of the shelter and back onto the pavement in Britannia Street, no one had any idea back then just how many attacks there would be.

She arrived at Fighter Command, lost in thought, Bill's words *but not enough* echoing in her mind as she strode through the corridors. It was the sound of Bill's actual voice that cut across her consciousness.

She stopped in her tracks.

She was outside Ash's office. The two men had their backs to her, staring at yet more reconnaissance photographs of a convoy at sea. Bill must have hotfooted them over from Luqa. She stood, fixed to the spot, longing to talk to him, to put her arms round him, to make everything better between them.

'So this was about 2 p.m. today,' Bill was saying, pointing a ruler at one of the pictures, 'about thirty miles south of Taranto. Possibly two troopships, and four destroyers. We circled further afield, found two cruisers eight miles off to starboard—'

'You're right,' Ash said, 'we should strike while the iron is hot. Attack before they get any further.'

As if he could feel her gaze on the back of his neck, Bill glanced round.

He stared at her for a moment, deep sadness in his eyes. Then he threw her a resigned half-smile and turned back to Ash.

It was as if he had closed a door. Shut her out.

She leant back against the wall, heart thumping, willing him to turn again, so she could tell him that she loved him, but they carried on talking, their backs to her. Footsteps approached down the corridor and she jolted back to herself, smoothed her dress and walked away.

The Operations Room was thick with tension and the fug of too many tired bodies. Irene looked pinched and tense. One of her sons, Giovanni, was due to be operated on at the hospital at Imtarfa.

Kitty was surprised to see Ash still there up in the gallery, despite the raids that had gone on all day. He looked pale, dark pouches under his eyes. Even his moustache seemed to droop. His fingers pinched round the stub of a cigarette, smoke hanging like fog above the officers on the Shelf, but there was an undercurrent of tension, a sense of suspense. It was as if they all knew they were fighting for their lives.

Kitty jumped when the phone rang, announcing the first raid of the shift at 20.54.

'Twenty Bandits, seventeen thousand feet, bearing south,' came the call in her headphones from the Filter Room.

Kitty repeated the message back into her mic to the controllers up on the Shelf, as she marked the plot and pushed it forward.

'Twenty Me 109s now approaching N for Nuts,' she updated, as new positions came through her headphones.

'249 Squadron, scramble, scramble.' Ash leant over the Shelf, watching the raiders' approach on the table below.

He snatched up the radio telephone to Ta'Qali and barked

a series of instructions. The gunnery officer ordered the anti-aircraft guns to open fire.

Twenty fighters. Plus a dozen bombers being plotted by Rita. Another big attack. They were in for a long night. Kitty adjusted her headphones, bracing her shoulders, ears straining for instructions.

'Raiders party dividing now. Twenty Hostiles remaining at seventeen thousand feet, bearing south; twelve Hostiles heading down to Angels twelve,' she called into her mic.

The enemy planes were remaining high to distract the anti-aircraft guns, while the second wave would split off and come flying in lower to lay mines and drop bombs. Kitty knew their tactics now. She divided the plot, creating another one, and pushed them into position. More aircraft positions were relayed to her and the others on D Watch, as Ash, realising the severity of the attack, scrambled even more Hurricanes to intercept.

'Bandit second wave descending. Now at eight thousand feet.'

Lillian's calm voice from the Filter Room sounded in Kitty's ears and she moved the plot marking those aircraft closer to Valletta, calling out each change in position to the Operations Room. The Luftwaffe were making no bones about it. Just indiscriminately bombing civilians.

'Hold your positions, Pinto Red Squadron. Looks like Grand Harbour and Valletta are the target. Keep your eyes open,' called Ash down the R/T phone.

'Roger. Red Leader here. I've got 'em.'

'They're coming in now. Stand by, stand by.'

'Roger that.' A crackle and then a shout. 'Christ, bloody swarms of them. Tally ho, tally ho!'

Firing sounded, the rumble of engines, the scream as a plane flung itself into a dive.

Ash put his hand over the receiver and turned to his Ops, his expression grave. 'Is everything up?'

Ops nodded. 'The lot.'

Across the room, Irene caught Kitty's eye. They were throwing everything they had at the Germans. Every last fighter plane on the island.

But was it enough?

All night, their positions flowed into Kitty's headphones thick and fast, a constant stream of voices, calm but urgent, a litany of aircraft types, heights and positions that left Kitty's pulse racing and sweat blooming under her arms. Her head ached and she struggled to concentrate; the numbers, heights and positions began to jumble in her head as she moved the plots, her voice hoarse from calling out the position changes.

The others on D Watch did the same, and they struggled to stay out of each other's way as they leant over the table moving the plots, repeating back their positions so Ash and the other officers up on the Shelf could direct the pilots through the attack.

'Ten Macchi fighters, twelve thousand feet, vector 225,' came Lillian's call in her ears.

Macchis? Italian fighters too. They hadn't had this many Italian aircraft attack for weeks.

Kitty's stomach squeezed as she placed their plot on the table and called it out. Even more Italian planes were coming over now. What was going on?

An uneasy feeling gripped her spine as she leant over the

table, pushing the rod to move her plots. Could this have anything to do with Stefano? She shook herself. She mustn't be absurd. He was just a troubled, confused boy. He couldn't be part of this. But the idea sparked inside her, like a glowing ember.

Occasionally the R/T burst into life over the speaker, with the sounds of firing, engines roaring, the scream as a plane went into a dive, a pilot excitedly shouting. 'Pinto Red Fourteen. Hit a Junkers 87! He's on fire. Headed for the drink!'

Or a voice yelling, 'Behind you, Pinto Red Eight! He's on your tail.'

Or 'Look up, Red Nine. Three o'clock.'

The attacks went on and on, the aircraft coming round to make multiple raids until Kitty and the others on D Watch struggled to move the plots fast enough across the squares. How many bombs must they be dropping?

It was nearly two hours later when the all-clear was given at 23.54. Just as Kitty leant back against the table to take a breath, another wave of enemy SM.79 Italian bombers were spotted coming over St Thomas Bay.

More Italian planes.

That unease tugged again about Stefano. Surely this was just a coincidence. But that ember glowed brighter inside her, taking hold until it burnt hot. Nausea rolled in her stomach.

'They're heading for Luqa,' Ash called and picked up the phone. 'Sorry, Mack. Scramble, scramble 249 Squadron again.'

The Italian planes circled over the airfield dropping bombs and Kitty thought back to the dreadful raid she'd been caught in with Bill, all those weeks ago, a lifetime ago. She sent up a prayer that Bill was somewhere safe. Was he thinking of her too? Tears pricked. She shook them away. She couldn't think about that now.

The phones rang throughout the night; in one update, a squadron leader notified the Operations Room that two Macchis and three Me 109s had been shot down, and loud cheers filled the room. But a Hurricane had been shot down over the sea, two minesweepers in Grand Harbour had been sunk, and HMS *Encounter* was damaged. An inflammable store in the dockyards had taken a direct hit and a huge fire was burning out of control.

As the raid ended, Rita glanced at Kitty.

'Are you alright? You don't look too well.'

'I'm fine,' Kitty said. Her head ached, her back hurt and she was sick with worry. 'Just didn't sleep too well today.'

'I know that feeling.' Rita raised an eyebrow. Her face was drawn. 'The night from hell. Again.'

Kitty smiled weakly. Crikey, she'd better pull herself together.

But at 01.55 came an alert from a watch station to the west of the island. 'Parachutists at large, everyone. Warning! Parachutists reported on the west of the island.'

Ash glanced at the army and guns officers. 'Better get every man you've got on red alert. This is it.'

The army officer grabbed the R/T. 'Get the invasion alert siren on standby. And get me Malta Defence.'

The officer in charge of guns bellowed down the telephone for more information, numbers, locations. Tense murmurs ran round the Ops Room.

Was this the invasion beginning? Was that why so many Italian planes had come today, as well as German?

The room fell silent. Ice pitted in Kitty's stomach. Her hand trembled on her cue. Were Italian troops also being used as parachutists? Christ, was this what Stefano was here for? That ember had caught fire now, fanning roaring flames inside her. Had he helped them in some way? Nausea rose up her throat and flashes darted across her eyes. The plotting table seemed to come up at her and she gripped it for support, blinking hard. Surely he could not be part of this.

Could he?

The plotters exchanged scared, hollow-eyed glances, gripping their cues. Ash jabbed out his cigarette, frowning at the plotting table, as if he had missed something. The uneasy silence seemed to stretch.

Minutes later, the tannoy crackled into life.

'Stand down, stand down. False alarm.' The 'parachutists' turned out to be a pilot who had bailed out of a shot-down Heinkel, who had been reported by two watch stations.

Relieved chatter hummed around the room and Kitty sank against the table, breathing hard. She glanced at Irene, hoping no one had noticed how she was feeling. Up on the balcony, the controllers ignored cooling cups of tea.

Kitty shivered, her shoulders tight, her insides turning to liquid as Theresa, the young Maltese woman in the Filter Room, announced the approach of another fifteen enemy aircraft. Her hands shook as she picked up her rod to mark it.

Chapter Thirty-Three

Something was wrong. Very wrong. Kitty could see it in the eyes of the new shift as she made her way the next morning through the gloomy tunnels back to reception. Plotters, civilian women in dusty stained clothes, RAF officers and army officers one by one passed her, and everyone had the same glazed haunted look, deep shadows under their eyes, exhausted from a long night in the shelters, shoulders hunched as if they could not withstand another blow.

A senior naval officer hurried past her, black soot smudged on his face and gold epaulettes, a smell of cordite on his uniform.

Kitty stopped him, 'Sir, excuse me please. I've been on all night. How bad was it?'

His gaze looked right through her. 'Dozens of bombs hit Valletta, Pietà Creek, Floriana, Sliema. And more at St Thomas Bay. Lots of casualties and houses damaged. We don't know numbers yet.'

Kitty's stomach clenched.

'Thank you,' she whispered as he hurried away.

She leant against the wall for a moment, taking deep breaths. Floriana. Adela. She had to get home.

* * *

She burst out of the doors, blinking in the glare of the bright morning sunshine. Palls of thick choking dust blew up, making her eyes sting. Coughing, she scrambled, her lace-up shoes crunching over broken glass, as she hurried past the Auberge de Castille, heading for the Porta Reale. Black columns of smoke rose over the buildings and the clang of ambulance bells, the shouts of soldiers and the wails of an old woman filled the air. A battalion of soldiers, new by the looks of it, marched past her, entering the city in combat shorts, rifles on their shoulders. Her camera jolted against her hip in her bag, but she didn't stop to take pictures.

Her dress stuck to her back, her chest was tight and she pressed her handkerchief to her nose to breathe through the dust. A stream of water from a blown-up main gushed down the steps of a side street, and she trod carefully, taking care not the slip on the sludge of wet ashes. As she passed another building, she saw three floors of the front balcony concertinaed together, a woman's leg poking out from the midst of stones and timber beams, just the lace hem of her nightdress showing on her thigh.

Kitty turned away and vomited into the gutter.

But as she reached what she thought was the Vincenti Buildings, confusion flooded her. This wasn't their street, was it? Two houses down, sunlight flooded the road through a gash in the line of the tall buildings, dust motes blizzarding in the rays. She glanced back at the name high on the building on the corner. It was the Vincenti Buildings.

But it was unrecognisable.

Two apartment buildings, each six floors high, had disappeared completely, replaced by a mountain of stone blocks and girders. A fire still raged in one of the heaps and firemen hosed water onto it. Acrid smoke coiled into the sky. Outside stood a crowd of people shrouded in dust, an ambulance with its back doors open and Red Cross workers leaning over a stretcher on the ground.

Kitty stopped, every hair standing on end. No, no. No. It couldn't be their flat. It had to be a mistake.

She blinked, waiting for the pall of smoke to clear. The remaining buildings either side looked strangely tall and blank-eyed, all the windows blown out. An undamaged box of red geraniums nodded in the breeze on the fourth-floor balcony.

Their building had been hit. Their apartment.

Cold gripped her spine.

'Adela! Adela!' she screamed. She sprinted towards the group of people.

A figure in a tattered dressing gown covered with dirt detached herself and ran towards her.

'Kitty!' she cried. 'Kitty, you're safe.'

At the sound of her voice, the woman's ghostly face coalesced from a blur of grey dust to reveal Adela's warm eyes, Adela's strong features. They ran to each other and held each other tight.

'I thought I'd lost you,' Kitty sobbed. She wiped Adela's ash-stained face tenderly, pushed a dark curl off her face. 'I didn't think you'd made it to a shelter.'

They squeezed each other tight, until a thought struck Kitty and she pulled away, suddenly filled with apprehension. 'Did everyone get out?'

'Mr and Mrs Buhagiar were in the shelter with us, and Mrs Macgil with her three, and the Gatt family, and the Callejas had already left for her cousins. So yes, all accounted for.'

'Thank God.'

Adela pulled her over to the crowd standing in front of the ruins of their building, and pointed up to the top.

'Look.'

The floor of Adela's bedroom slanted downwards towards them. Three walls had been blown away, but the fourth remained. Clinging to it was a torn poster of Josephine Baker, and underneath the little gate-legged table with Adela's sewing machine on top. Beside it, a small pile of turquoise fabric fluttered in the breeze, the dress Adela had been cutting out last weekend. The old standing-lamp, its pink pleated shade now grey with dust, stood intact against the wall and her chest of drawers, one drawer blown open, revealed a froth of silk underwear. It looked like a badly arranged stage set.

'Look. My sewing machine. It's survived!' She pulled Kitty's arm. 'I've got to get it.'

'But it's not safe.'

'I'll be alright.'

Kitty smiled at the hope shining in Adela's eyes. 'Come on, then. I'll give you a hand. I know how precious that machine is to you.'

But she glanced away, so Adela wouldn't see the tears beading in her eyes. Could her own most precious possession be saved? Her memory box. Alice's blanket. The curls of golden hair. The beautiful new photograph of her little girl. Where were they? Were they still salvageable?

Her eyes flicked back and forth across the tall mound, but all she could see was a heap of stone rubble.

'Oh, Kitty, that's awful of me.' Adela clapped a hand to her mouth. 'I'm sure we'll find something of yours. Let's see if we can spot anything.'

A loud hoot sounded and an army lorry turned into the road, raising even more clouds of dust as it screeched to a halt beside the crowd. A group of soldiers jumped down and unloaded ladders, wooden planks, scaffolding and tools. Adela stared at them.

'I'll see if I can borrow a ladder.'

Minutes later they were carefully adjusting the ladder up against the rubble mound, checking how stable it was. They extended the ladder, two neighbours holding each side, and Adela started to climb. There was a rumble as some masonry shifted, a rattle of small stones and grit falling. Adela stopped. Everyone watched, holding their breath.

'Easy, there,' called Kitty, holding the bottom of the ladder. 'Wait a second.'

Slowly, carefully, Adela climbed to the top and pressed the tiled floor cautiously. It remained stable, so she carefully heaved herself up into a crouch. A creak echoed and she paused, stock-still, until it stopped.

'Stay there. Let me come up.' Kitty climbed the rungs, trying not to look down, as Adela lowered herself to her hands and knees and inched across the floor. 'Adela, be careful. Go slowly.'

The crowd watching from below held their breath.

As Adela crawled forward, Kitty reached the top and glanced to the side where her room would have been. Everything looked completely crushed, buried in a mangle of stone. She swallowed. She couldn't think about that now.

When Adela reached the little table, she knelt up. The

wooden boards creaked again and grit poured off the edge of the floor, like water off a roof edge.

Kitty choked, dust floating into her nostrils and eyes.

'Wait for it to settle.'

Below, heads tilted upwards. The crowd stopped talking. All eyes focused on Adela as she reached for her sewing machine and gingerly lifted it off the table.

A groaning, shifting noise of creaking wood and cascading stones echoed.

Adela froze.

A sharp intake of breath from the spectators.

'Stop!' Kitty said, her voice quiet. 'Don't move.'

When the noise stopped, Adela cradled the machine like a baby, grabbed the moiré fabric off the table beside it and reversed slowly back on her knees.

Kitty stood, feet braced against the sides of the ladder, an arm stretched out, to take the machine. She didn't dare make a sound or movement as Adela inched her way gingerly back.

Their eyes met.

'Thank you,' Adela whispered. She beamed as she passed Kitty the machine.

Kitty gripped the ladder with one hand and took the arched gold-etched machine in the other, like a handle. It was heavy as she took its full weight, making her own body lean awkwardly to one side. She breathed heavily, sweat damp under her arms as she tried not to wobble. For a moment, she struggled to find her balance. When she was steady, she pushed the toe of her shoe down, feeling cautiously for each rung as she started back down the ladder.

As she made it to the bottom, Mrs Buhagiar took the

machine and set it on the ground. The crowd cheered again. Adela climbed back onto the ladder and all eyes turned up to her. She hurried back down, picked up the sewing machine and lifted it like a trophy. Everyone cheered.

'We did it,' she cried, grabbing Kitty's hand and raising it, so people clapped, delighted to witness a joyful moment amongst all the destruction. As Adela took her bows, ever the showgirl, Kitty wandered away.

She stood apart, eyes narrowed, scouring the rubble, determined to find the memory box. She walked a little further along, guessing where her bedroom window would have been. The bathroom taps still clung to the pink tiles on one wall and just beside them, crushed under a mass of stone, she could see the flutter of a scrap of blue cotton that looked like her favourite dress.

She'd left it hanging over the bath to dry. She swallowed, trying desperately not to cry.

Where was her bed? She just needed to find her bed. You never knew, maybe the metal frame of it could have protected the box. Shielded it from being crushed. Her eyes roved along the stone blocks, searching.

A few yards away, peeking out from a row of limestone boulders, was a twist of white iron bedframe, poking out at an angle from a stack of blocks. Her bed. There was her bed.

Her heart leapt. She stepped closer, her eyes narrowed, running over the area near the frame. But the ruins were as tight-packed as a stone wall. The wind blew, and a tiny scrap of something yellow lifted and flapped against the stones that crushed it. She took a sharp breath in, stepping even closer, eyes screwed tight, until the wind blew again. A tiny strip of singed yellow waffle blanket fluttered out of the masonry, like a flag in surrender.

Her heart thudded. Alice's blanket. *Alice's blanket.*

And somewhere, crushed underneath that mound of rocks, was the envelope with her little girl's most precious curl of hair and her new photograph. The last pieces of her that she possessed.

Her knees crumpled and she sank to the pavement, her shoulders slumped, her face covered with her hands as exhaustion washed through her.

She had lost everything that mattered most in the world to her. Her possessions, her home, Maria, Bill. And now the last link to her daughter.

She sat, for a moment, as unmoving as the stone that had taken everything.

But then she looked round. Anger flared inside her at the smoking ruins, the shattered buildings, the broken shutters swaying in the breeze. How dare the Fascist bastards damage her country like this. How dare they kill and injure people.

Fight fired up in her and the embers of suspicion that had been flickering in her gut throughout the night blazed again.

A bicycle leant against a low wall nearby and an idea came into her head.

There was one thing she could do.

That she had to do.

She didn't have to sit here dwelling on the damage and destruction around her. She could sort this out, right now, once and for all.

Almost before she knew what she was doing, she grabbed the bike and rode off down the street.

Chapter Thirty-Four

An hour later, Kitty stood outside Maria's house, waiting until an old woman with a basket walked through the shaft of sunlight at the end of the street, before she fumbled under the geranium pot and fished out the key. She opened the door and stepped inside. The house was warm and hushed, dust motes floating in the sunlight streaming in from the still courtyard, the smell of thyme and fried onion still hanging in the air from yesterday's dinner.

'Maria,' she called, although she was sure Maria would be out. She shut the door behind her. 'Stefano?' She glanced into the living room. Empty. She checked the kitchen. Empty and the back door shut, the courtyard empty.

Silence thrummed in her ears.

'Stefano? Are you here?' she called up the stairs.

No answer.

He could be asleep perhaps. Her stomach tightened.

Or maybe he wasn't here.

She went upstairs. The landing was gloomy, no sunshine pouring in here. A chill ran through her. His bedroom door was closed.

'Stefano,' she called, her voice sharp.

No reply.

She listened. No sounds of breathing. Her heart speeded up.

She knocked.

Silence.

She opened his door and stepped inside. The room was empty, his bed neatly made, the poetry book stacked on his desk.

But his boots were gone.

She stepped back onto the landing, pushed Maria's and Censa's doors open. Both empty.

She stood in the doorway of his room, tapping the door frame. He wasn't here. The hairs rose on the back of her neck. He wasn't bloody here. She knew it. She'd damn well known he wouldn't be.

He *was* going out. And in broad daylight too. But where the hell was he going?

She rifled round his room, opening drawers, pulling out the suitcase under his bed and searching it. Still nothing out of the ordinary. She stood, frowning round the room. What was she missing? There had to be some clue here, something that would tell her what he was up to . . .

A thud downstairs. The front door pushed open. Heavy footsteps.

Stefano.

Kitty breathed in sharply.

Quick as a flash, she moved out of his room and onto the landing. She listened, her pulse throbbing in her ears. His footsteps moved into the kitchen and as quietly as she could, she tiptoed downstairs. She stopped in the kitchen doorway.

'You've been out.' Her voice was accusing.

Stefano jumped, dropped a cup on the counter so the rim chipped. He turned round, panic flashing across his face.

'*Merda*! Kitty. What the hell are you doing here?'

She ignored his question. 'Where have you been, Stefano?'

He swallowed, his Adam's apple bobbing up and down. 'You frightened the life out of me.'

'Where have you been?'

His eyes darted sideways behind his glasses, as if searching for an escape.

'I-I was just going to buy some . . . bread.' His voice petered out. He folded his arms across his chest.

'Where is it, then?' Her voice was icy.

He glanced foolishly at the empty bread basket.

'Don't lie. You've been out. I knew you were. I told Maria—'

'Leave her out of this,' he growled.

Kitty laughed hollowly. 'Bit late to worry about that now. Where were you, Stefano?'

'None of your damn business.' His eyes flared. 'I don't have to explain myself to you.'

'Yes, you do, when we're all keeping your very existence here secret. What are you up to? Are you spying?'

He flinched at the word.

'Don't be ridiculous.'

'You were asking for "information". And you've been out when you promised Maria you'd stay in.'

'I told you, I only wanted to know so I could protect my family.' He turned and stared out of the kitchen window, his face filled with panic. A struggle seemed to be going on in his thoughts. 'I-I was . . .'

'Visiting airfields, is that it? Counting aircraft?'

He froze imperceptibly. There was a pause.

'It's not . . . it's not what you think.' He seemed to be deciding something and turned to her, his face softening. He rubbed his chin. '*La mia Caterina.* I've been visiting someone. My old . . . friend. The one I told you about.' He flushed red. 'I didn't want Omm to know.'

'What?'

'I had to see him.'

His old boyfriend? Kitty blinked at him, her heart thudding. That wasn't what she'd expected to hear at all.

'I-I . . . love him.'

'Really?' Kitty stepped back, as startled as if she'd been slapped. 'So you haven't been visiting airfields . . .' Heat burnt in her cheeks. 'But the grass,' she said, feebly.

'We meet outside the village,' he lowered his eyes.

Silence hung between them. She suddenly felt foolish about her suspicions, her wild ideas. She was too jumpy, too mistrustful. She was tired, confused, hadn't slept in hours. Her imagination had spiralled after a long and tiring night. As Maria said, he was her half-brother, for God's sake. And yet . . .

'Where do you meet?'

Panic flashed in his eyes again. 'Erm, a farmer's field.'

'Right.'

'Please. Don't tell Omm.'

A heavy tension filled the air, as dark as the smoke hanging over Valletta, and suddenly Kitty couldn't wait to get out of there.

'Sorry, sorry.' Her palms were wet and she wiped them on her skirt.

'Don't worry, Caterina.' An insincere laugh. 'I forgive you.'

But his voice sent a shiver through her.

'I must get back.' Kitty turned to go.

He walked her to the front door and opened it for her.

But as she glanced up at him, did she imagine it, or was there sheer relief shining in his eyes?

She cycled back to Floriana, going over and over what Stefano had said, a burning feeling in her chest. On the face of it, his explanation was entirely plausible . . . so why did she feel so on edge? Acid lapped at her throat, her skin prickled, her senses ringing, and she was not sure if she believed him. It was as if her gut couldn't accept the facts he was saying and she hadn't yet figured out why.

She propped the bicycle back against the wall, hoping the owner hadn't missed it. A braking lorry screeched and she glanced round.

An RAF truck jolted to a stop in the middle of the road and a flying officer jumped down. For a moment her heart lurched. Was that Bill?

But she glimpsed his ginger hair under his cap. Frank. He glanced round, searching for Adela, then spotted her and ran, enfolding her in his embrace.

Kitty stood, watching, waiting. Hoping Bill might appear.

More airmen in boilersuits climbed out, pulling up the truck's tarpaulin, unloading shovels, tools and buckets.

But Bill wasn't with them.

Her shoulders slumped, her heart aching as she turned away.

'Kitty, Kitty!'

Adela had detached herself from the crowd, an army blanket over her shoulders, and was hurrying towards her.

'*Chérie*, where have you been all this time?' She put her arm round her. 'You look exhausted. And you're shaking. Come, sit in the truck, have some tea.'

A crowd still milled round the building, where soldiers handed out tin mugs of tea, while others had made a tidy roadway through the fallen masonry. Someone had managed to salvage a few things: Mrs Buhagiar nursed a dented saucepan as tenderly as if it were a newborn baby, and Mr Buhagiar sat on an ornate wooden stool, two of its carved legs rather blackened. Adela's sewing machine now stood on the gate-leg table on the street, with the pile of clothes and the lampstand beside it, although the silk lampshade now had a scorch mark.

Adela led her to the truck and Kitty hopped up to sit on the tailgate. Adela wrapped the army blanket round her shoulders, Kitty shivering despite the early summer heat, and an ARP warden appeared with a steaming mug and thrust it into her hand.

'*Sinjura, tidher eżawrita. Ħu dan.* Miss, you look tired. Take this.'

'I'm fine, really.' Kitty took the cup gratefully. The sweetened hot liquid ran through her empty insides, bringing her to life.

'You don't look it.' Adela eyed her. 'I'm sorry, Kitty. I tried to find something of yours, but just look at it.' Adela waved at the mound of rubble. 'But the good news is, Mr Formosa here,' Adela smiled at the ARP warden, 'says there's an apartment empty round the corner.' She lowered her voice and whispered in Kitty's ear, 'Bargain rent, no one else wants it.' And in a louder voice for Mr Formosa's benefit, Adela added, 'but it will be *très pratique* for us to get to work.'

'That's great, Adela.' Kitty squeezed her hand, barely able to keep her eyes open. She yawned. Christ, she was exhausted. 'Thank you. I hadn't even thought where we might go. All I want to do is sleep.'

Chapter Thirty-Five

Soft golden light cracked from the edges of the blackout curtains, a gentle warm breeze playing across Kitty's cheek when she woke. She blinked, momentarily disorientated.

Gosh, was it evening already?

Something prickly and musty-smelling tickled her nostrils and she scrabbled at her cheek, pushing it away. The army blanket. Adela must have laid it on her, earlier. She felt nauseous and for a moment wondered if she was going to be sick.

What time was it? Was Adela still here?

She lay for a second, blinking in the fading light.

They had walked to the new apartment on the second floor, their feet sticking to the linoleum, and had glanced round the dusty living room, furnished with a wooden settee, a single chair and a side table. Kitty had taken the small room at the back of the flat, laid down on the mattress and fallen fast asleep. No wonder she felt sick. She hadn't eaten all last night or today.

Outside on the road came the roar of a motorbike, getting louder until it stopped close by. A door banged and footsteps echoed up the marble stairs, out in the hall of the building. From the living room, she heard the chatter of Adela and Frank's voices. She really ought to get up. She pushed the blanket off her legs, rubbed her eyes.

A firm rap at the front door, someone on the landing, the squeak of hinges and Frank's voice.

'Bingo! Come on in, old chap. Glad you found us.'

Kitty's heart jumped in her chest. She sat bolt upright in bed. Bill.

He had come.

A few minutes later, she opened the living room door, frantically smoothing down her hair. Three heads swivelled as they stared up at her.

'Hello, Bill.'

They were sitting in the bare room, lit by the scorched standing-lamp in the corner, the blackouts bowing like sails in the sunset breeze through the glassless windows. Someone had hauled the gate-legged table and Singer machine up to the flat and they sat against the wall in pride of place. The folded square of turquoise moiré sat on top, a trophy waiting to be sewn.

'Kitty.'

Bill's face brightened and he leapt to his feet. He stepped towards her as if to kiss her and then remembering, stopped awkwardly. He ran his hand through his hair. The ringed indentation of his leather goggles was white and bloodless in the skin of his scar, his face smudged with black dust.

'Thank God, you're alright.'

Kitty was suddenly hideously aware that she was still in the crumpled sage-green dress from her night shift and her armpits were sticky. She smoothed her collar as she sat down.

'*Chérie*, you're awake at last.' Adela glanced at Frank. 'Frank, we need to visit the services supplies for some blankets and pots, *oui*?'

He looked momentarily puzzled, then caught on and jumped to his feet. Adela ushered him out, saying they'd be back in an hour. Kitty stared at their retreating backs, grateful they had left her alone to talk to Bill.

Bill fidgeted with the goggles in his hands. Dirt was rimed round his fingernails, oil and dust on his battledress.

'Bill, I—' she started.

'Heard Floriana took a pasting last night.' He leapt in, talking quickly, as if warding off what she might say. 'Just wanted to check you were alright.'

Tension hung between them like a thundercloud. There was so much she wanted to say, so much she needed to tell him . . .

She stared into his eyes. 'I'm so sorry, Bill, I—'

'Please, don't apologise.' He broke eye contact, held his hand up. 'Not necessary. Sorry I couldn't get here sooner. Lot of bombs dropped on the airfield, a lot of clearing up to do.' He twisted the battered leather strap in his hands.

Kitty nodded. He was being so formal. Holding her at a distance. The tightness in the room stretched.

'Bill, I need to talk to you. I've longed to talk to you. I want to explain—'

'We're doing a big mission,' he burst out. He looked on edge, the scarring taut across his cheek, pulling his eyelid down further than usual. 'A major attack, working with the Navy. You'll hear about it soon enough.' He cleared his throat, still not meeting her eye. 'I'll be bombing an enemy troop convoy.'

'Bombing? But you're photo reconnaissance!'

'They need to use us as bombers.' He shook his head. 'There's not enough of the Blenheim bombers, we've lost too many. So our Marylands have been asked to join the attack.'

'Join the attack? My God.' Ice ran down her spine and she sank into a chair.

'We'll be going in to bomb before the Blenheims,' Bill looked away, 'to draw fire away from them.'

'Like a decoy, you mean?' Her skin rose in goosebumps.

'We'll be the first wave. Getting in low over the ships so we attract enemy fire,' he swallowed, 'so the Blenheims can bomb from a higher altitude.'

'Bill, no.'

She reached out to take his hand, but he moved it behind him. Pain knifed in her chest. He was being so cold, the way he was talking, melting the closeness, the intimacy between them.

He stared out of the window, the sky beyond streaked with gold and pink clouds. 'We're only going to get one go at this. It's a steep angle, and we've got to get in close.'

'Get in close? What do you mean?'

'We'll be practising the angle of attack on the ships at the cliffs of Filfla. We'll have to dive in as low as we can at the base of them, as if that were the convoy, drop our bombs, then pull up sharply. Got to get the moment we pull up just right.' He gestured a steep dive-bomb and sharp pull-up with his hand. 'Not that Marylands are made for dive-bombing.' He threw her a weak smile.

Kitty's throat closed. It was dangerous. Too dangerous. She longed to touch him, to pull him close, but he was already standing up, adjusting his goggles.

'Righto. I just wanted to say cheerio.'

He smiled, a sad twist of his lips that didn't reach his eyes, and stepped towards the door.

She jumped to her feet. 'Wait, I didn't mean what I said—'

'I've got to get back.'

Their eyes met across the room, his full of anguish, hers begging him to stay.

'Bill, please. We need to talk.' She wanted to tell him how much she loved him, that she hadn't meant it the way it had come out the other day. That she needed more time, there was so much going on . . . and God, how she longed to tell him everything about Stefano, longed to ask him for his advice. 'Let me explain—'

'I think everything's been said,' he replied, pulling the goggles onto his forehead. He stopped at the door and his fingers drummed a quick beat on the frame.

'Bill, wait. I love you—'

'I shouldn't have come.'

And he was gone, the door shutting behind him, his footsteps loud down the stone stairs.

She wrenched open the flat door, leant over the stairwell.

'Bill!'

But the building door slammed shut. Outside came the loud throttle of his motorbike as he kickstarted the engine. She sank to the floor, rested her head against the bannister, as he roared away into the dusk. She realised then, with a chill that made her teeth chatter.

He didn't think he was going to survive the mission.

He had come to say goodbye.

Chapter Thirty-Six

She sat, trembling, as the evening faded into night, until thirst forced her into the narrow kitchen. There was just a one-ring Primus stove, a small oven on uneven legs and a table pressed against the wall with two wooden chairs. A watercolour of St Paul's Bay hung at an angle from a nail on the wall, the only splash of colour in the dingy room. Who had painted that? What had happened to the people who had lived here before?

She turned on the tap and air choked out of it, followed by a spurt of dirty water, speckled with black dust and debris. The water pipes had been hit. She looked in the curtained cupboard under the sink and found an old terracotta jug. That would have to do.

Outside there was an eerie silence. No one was about, it was past curfew. She shouldn't be out, but she needed to drink. She walked down the dark street, feeling a step ahead with the toe of her shoe, mindful of the rubble all over the streets. The metal handle of the water pump glinted in the near-full moon that appeared behind the clouds.

The handle creaked as she pumped, her arm aching with the effort. She splashed a little water on her shoes and bent to wipe it off – they were her only pair now – and as she straightened up, a footstep scraped on the limestone behind her.

She glanced round, assuming a neighbour wanted water, and glimpsed the shape of a tall figure. There was a rustle, her head was pulled back and something was yanked over her face. She was blinded.

She dropped the jug. Her hands flew to her throat. Something coarse tightened round her neck. She cried out, but her voice was muffled. Bristled cord bit into her throat and she choked.

Someone gripped her arms, hands like iron bands digging into her flesh. Voices muttered; the scuffling of feet as she was pulled.

She kicked out, her feet striking air, fighting, writhing, gasping for breath as she was dragged backward. The heels of her shoes caught in the cobbles, and she stumbled. She was going to fall, she was going to fall.

She tried to scream, but hessian filled her mouth and she couldn't breathe, she couldn't breathe, she couldn't breathe—

She was slammed back against a wall so hard she bit her tongue.

Pain seared through her skull and shooting lights dizzied her. The iron taste of blood filled her mouth.

Her mind careened in free-fall. Had the invasion happened? Had she been caught by parachutists? What would they do to her? Her heart pounded so hard she thought it would break her ribs.

Whispers, scuffling, the scrape of heavy boots, and the sack was yanked off her head. Stars fired across her vision as she blinked in the darkness.

'G-get off me!' she cried, kicking out.

'Shhh, keep it down.'

Wait, did she recognise that voice?

'Stefano?' Her tongue flopped in her mouth like a wet flannel.

'Be quiet.'

'It *is* you!' Relief flooded her.

The moon came out from behind a cloud and for a moment glinted on the rim of his glasses, the white of his eye, the jut of his nose as he stared at her.

'Sorry about that, Caterina.'

'W-what? Wh-what's this all about?' She couldn't stop trembling.

The gleam of a pointed blade and a second, stocky man, a cap low over his face, pushed her back against the wall.

'Hey, stop it,' she gasped. Her shoulder blade throbbed with pain as he held her. 'What the hell are you doing?'

Where even were they? Would anyone help if she screamed? Kitty glanced left and right, but darkness stretched in both directions. It looked like a narrow alley, between the tall buildings. She wrestled, trying to break free, but the second man kept his meaty grip on her, pinning her to the stone.

'Get off!' Sweat trickled down her back. 'Let me go.'

'Only if you keep quiet.' But Stefano muttered a few words in Italian to the other man and he released her.

'What the hell, Stefano?' Kitty rubbed her aching shoulder. 'What are you doing?'

Stefano sighed. 'I didn't want it to be like this. But you've given me no choice.' He ran a hand through his unruly hair. 'You shouldn't have come snooping about today.'

She breathed out, dread dropping like a stone in her stomach.

Oh God, it was true. It was all bloody true. He had been out. He had been out spying.

'You lied to me!'

'Why did you have to be so nosey, eh? So suspicious?'

'You bastard! I trusted you. I believed your lies. How could you?'

'Have you told anyone about me?' He leant closer. The smell of garlic and stale cigarettes hit her nostrils.

'No.'

God, how she wished she had. How could she have been so blind? Kitty looked wildly up and down the alley again. No one knew she was here. Stay calm. Keep him talking, reassure him. 'Look, earlier, I just wanted to talk to you. There's no need for this.'

'You know, I thought it was my lucky day when I heard you worked at Fighter Command.' The whites of Stefano's eyes glinted as he stared at her. 'It could have worked for both of us. I tried to ask you nicely. Gave you that photograph of your daughter. Tried to show you how we could work together.'

A chill ran through her veins.

'I knew it. I knew I was right.'

'All I wanted was a small piece of information—'

'I would never tell you military secrets. I would never betray my country!'

He shook his head and she could see his smile flash in the moonlight. 'No one's talking about betrayal. I just wanted a few details—'

'Christ, Stefano, why? Why are you doing this? I thought you loved Malta. But you're betraying it.'

'I'm not. I'm helping Malta.' He breathed out heavily,

pushing his glasses up his nose. 'You don't get it, do you? You British. This isn't your country. It's ours. We've lost ourselves, lost our heritage, under British rule. And look how Malta's paying the price for your war. I don't want to see her being bombed to pieces any more. The Italians are Latins like us. If we work with them, we can stop all this destruction.'

Kitty let out a hollow laugh. 'But the Maltese don't want the Fascists to win. Maria certainly doesn't. She'll be devastated you're doing this.'

'She doesn't understand either,' he sighed. 'Omm's gone *loco* waiting all these years for her British admiral to leave his wife. She needs to understand what's best for them. And so do you.'

She stiffened. 'You haven't hurt them, have you?'

'Don't be ridiculous. They're my family.'

'*Forza*!' The stocky man spoke angrily in Italian. His knife gleamed in the moonlight as he pushed her back against the wall and pressed the sharp tip to her neck.

She froze as it cut her skin. Blood trickled down inside her collar and she gritted her teeth.

'I won't help you.'

Stefano shook his head. 'Caterina, I never wanted it to come to this.' There was a rustling noise as he rifled in his pocket. 'You may not want to help me, but you might want to help Alicia.'

Kitty went cold. 'What do you mean?'

He gestured to the other man to let her go and she stumbled forward, feeling her neck. Blood oozed, sticky under her hand.

'I lied that day when I said there wasn't a letter with her photograph.'

Kitty's heart stopped.

He held up an envelope. The white paper shone in the moonlight as he waved it in front of her.

'What?' Tears sprang into her eyes. How could he have lied? How could he be so cruel? 'How could you?'

'It has news of her. What she likes to eat, play, how she spends her time. Kids' stuff,' he shrugged.

She dropped back against the wall, breathing fast. It was as if he had reached into her chest and twisted her heart with his fist. The yearning that came over her was a pain she had never experienced.

It was a moment before she could think straight.

'How do I know it's genuine? Let me see.' She grabbed for the letter, but Stefano snatched it out of her reach.

'I'm not a fool,' Stefano smiled. His fingers fumbled inside the envelope. 'And there's this. It also came with the photograph.'

A curl of golden hair glimmered in the moonlight.

Alice's hair. It was long and silky, the hair of an older child. Her child. She had to touch it, feel it between her fingers, needed to touch it as a drowning woman needs air.

'Please.' Her voice was quiet. 'Let me have it.'

'You want it, eh?' There was relief in Stefano's voice. 'You can have it when you've told me what I need to know.'

'Give it to me.' She lunged for the lock of hair, but he snatched it out of her grasp.

'*Zitta, stronza!*' The other man grabbed her arms, twisted them behind her in one meaty hand. She kicked at him, but he dodged away.

'How dare you, Stefano. How can you do this to me.'

'I want to give it you, I do. But time's running out. And I'm getting a lot of pressure from Italy.' He ran his hand through his hair. 'You were right,' he said with a small laugh, 'I've been watching the airfields. Over a dozen Hurricanes delivered yesterday. Defences being reinforced. Troops moved across the island. And there's a full moon coming. Is it that night? Something's going on. Something big. I need to know what.'

She breathed in. The big mission Bill had talked about. Stefano knew about it? She lifted her chin.

'I don't know what you're talking about.'

'You can find out, though.' He smiled a crooked smile and dropped the curl back in the envelope. 'I want to know the target and when the operation is planned. Timings. How many bombers, how many fighters.'

There was a moment's silence.

'Please, Stefano, don't do this. Don't make me do this—'

'I wasn't lying when I said I have contacts in Italy. My network through my *battaglione* is wide.' He folded the envelope and slipped it back in his jacket pocket. 'I have Alice's address, you see, on this letter.'

Her stomach somersaulted. What the hell? He had Alice's *address*? He knew where she was? Her heart pounded against her ribs. She had to get that letter, she had to . . .

He peered into her face and the whites of his eyes glistened. 'And if, at any time, you double-cross me in any way, I will send a wireless message saying exactly where a British child is being hidden in Trastevere in Rome.'

She froze. Ice coiled round her insides. Stefano could report Alice's location to the Fascists? What kind of monster was he?

Her mind reeled, picturing Alice being arrested, torn screaming from the apron strings of the woman who was looking after her, dragged off by hard-faced soldiers in jackboots, taken to a prison camp . . .

'You bastard. She's your niece, for Christ's sake.'

'Keep your voice down,' he hissed, glancing up the alley. 'Look, you can keep her safe. Be a good mother. Find out about this mission. Target, date, time, plan. It's just one small thing in this war – you can do this, no? For your daughter?'

Kitty could only blink at the ground, silenced at the horror of what he was asking.

'I want the details tomorrow night.'

Her head whipped up. 'I can't do that. I can't find out so fast.' Panic rose, tightening her throat.

'I need it tomorrow.'

'No, I need more time. Give me more time.'

Stefano breathed in. A muttered discussion with the other man in Italian, something about radioing into base, changing times . . .

Stefano turned to her. 'Two days. Here, thirty minutes after curfew. Oh, and don't bother going home to find me. I'm at our hideout.'

He nodded at the other man, who released her wrists. The world went black as the sack was pulled over her head and their footsteps disappeared down the alley.

She waited a few minutes, straining to catch any sound, wondering if they had really gone. In the distance a bomber droned.

Eventually she reached up and pulled the hood off. She blinked in the dark, letting her eyes adjust. Her palms were wet and she wiped them on her skirt. Bile rose in her throat and she vomited. She leant against the wall, shivering, taking deep gulps of air until her breathing slowed.

The moon came out from behind a cloud and a faint wisp of something gold glinted on the stone.

She snatched up the strands of hair, cradled them in her palm. Alice.

At least she had a wisp of her back once more.

Chapter Thirty-Seven

Adela crouched over a big tea-chest in the living room, her squeals of delight echoing in the hall as Kitty returned to the flat.

'Look what we've got, *chérie*,' Adela called out to her. 'Frank brought this back from the services mission. He's lugged it upstairs for us. Isn't he a darling?'

Kitty walked into the living room, her fingers still gripped over her palm cradling the precious strands of Alice's hair. Bedding, towels, saucepans and a smattering of crockery cascaded all over the floor.

'A whole new set of things! And new clothes too!' Adela twirled round, a cotton dress held up in front of her. 'So much more flattering than my ambulance overalls!' She glanced at Kitty. '*Mon Dieu!*' Adela stopped in her tracks and lowered the pink cotton flower-sprigged dress. 'You look like you've seen a ghost.'

Kitty dropped into a chair. 'I was fetching water.'

She winced, remembering the jug, smashed on the ground by the water pump.

'What are those marks on your neck?' Adela crouched down

at her side. She held Kitty's chin, moved her face from side to side. 'And your wrist?' she gasped. '*Mon Dieu*, both your wrists. They're covered in red marks.'

Her clear brown eyes looked into Kitty's, full of apprehension as she pulled out her handkerchief and rubbed Kitty's face. 'What's happened to you, *chérie*?'

Kitty's eyes brimmed. She shook her head, opened her palm to show Adela.

'I found a lock of Alice's hair.' Her voice was dull.

Adela's face filled with astonishment. 'Did you search the ruins?' She sat back on her heels. 'When I think of you alone, scrambling around there in the dark. You could have been killed.'

Kitty blinked. Adela thought she'd found her things, her memory box. Maybe it was better that way. She couldn't tell her what had really happened.

'Now, we must keep the treasure safe. *Attends*.'

Adela got up and went into her bedroom, and Kitty could hear the drawer being pulled open and slid shut again. She returned to the sitting room carrying a small pink silk pouch.

'Kitty, I know how much this means to you. Put Alice's keepsake in here.'

She slid the silk pouch under her pillow that night. Adela was so kind. Kitty longed to be able to confide everything to her, but that would just entangle Adela in it too. No, Kitty couldn't tell her. No one could know anything about this. No one.

Kitty lay staring up at the ceiling late into the night, turning it all over in her head. What was she going to do?

She'd been a fool to trust him. How could she not have seen him for what he really was? But he'd seemed such a sweet boy, shy, scared, glad to be home. How he had deceived them all. She wondered if Maria knew yet, if she had any idea why he had run off. She needed to contact them, check if Maria and Ċensa were alright.

But for him to threaten to report her little girl's safehouse to the Fascists . . . The blood ran cold in her veins. She would do everything in her power to protect her child. She had to keep her safe. She had to.

But how could she stop him?

She had no idea where he was hiding out. And if she reported him, it might take them time to find him, and if she didn't meet him when he'd said, he'd tell the Italian Fascists where her daughter was being hidden . . .

She breathed out, her pulse too fast, teeth chattering in the quiet of the room.

She had to find out where he was. If Maria or Ċensa knew, the authorities could arrest him, before he could give Alice away.

But suppose they didn't know? Her stomach filled with acid. The alternative – helping him – was unthinkable. She thought back to taking the Oath of Secrecy that first day at Fighter Command.

How she had thought nothing, ever, would make her betray her country. Her people.

She curled into a ball and groaned, remembering the anxiety etched on Bill's face earlier that evening. All those pilots, soldiers, sailors fighting to save lives, their homes, their freedom. Fighting for their very survival.

She could never betray them.

How could she choose between her daughter and her country?

Kitty kicked off the sheet, eyes wide open in the darkness. The night was too warm, too stuffy with the blackouts over the window. She got up and pulled at the edge, so a slight breeze blew through the crack, cooling her damp skin. She rested her cheek against the window frame. Outside the harbour was dark, silent. Beams of yellow searchlights weaved across the dark sky.

It was an impossible choice. The weight of it all was like a boulder crushing her.

There had to be a way out, there had to be . . .

The air raid siren's high-pitched wail rang out. The creak of Adela's door. Her voice on the landing.

'Kitty? Are you coming?' Adela's torch shining on her.

'Go, Adela. I'll be there in a second.'

Adela's footsteps pattered along the linoleum, echoed away down the stairs, but Kitty sat unmoving.

Let them do their worst.

Chapter Thirty-Eight

'Kitty! What are you doing here?'

Irene looked up from the *Times of Malta* she was reading. 'Jolly bad luck about your flat.' She put the paper down and gestured Kitty to take a seat.

They were in Irene's tiny office, her desk arranged as neatly as her appearance, with the pen-pot on a lace doily, pencil sharp and lined up neatly beside a leather-bound notebook. Irene's hair was slicked into a tidy bun, the wide lapels of her ivory blouse pressed, her face powdered, which made Kitty suddenly aware of how dishevelled and unkempt she looked.

She'd woken that morning feeling sick, the memory of the terrible choice she had to make returning to her like a dark cloud. She'd gone out for water from the pump to wash in, her feet crunching in the shards from the broken jug, and had stood pumping, filling a saucepan, feeling nervous, jumpy, glancing over her shoulder wondering if Stefano was still watching her. What he wanted her to do sat writhing inside her, like a poisonous snake.

She smoothed her crumpled skirt, trying to pull herself together.

'Have you found anywhere yet?' Irene smiled kindly. 'You know you can have two days off while you get sorted.'

'We've found somewhere. It's basic but honestly, I'd rather be at work than sitting in an empty flat.'

Irene nodded, her face sympathetic. Kitty knew Irene had moved out of the Old Railway Tunnel shelter and in with relatives. They were all in the same boat these days.

'How's your son?' she said, remembering to ask.

Irene breathed out. 'Giovanni's recovering, slowly.' She looked away, her eyes filling. 'He's lost a leg.'

'Irene, I'm so sorry.' That poor boy. Kitty reached across the desk and squeezed her hand.

'We all have our crosses to bear.' Irene cleared her throat and placed her hands together on the desk as if folding the matter away. 'Now, sure you're ready to start work?'

'Absolutely.' Kitty forced herself to sound bright, hoping she seemed convincing, normal.

'Good. We're planning a big mission. Operation Intercept. Join the briefing this afternoon.'

Kitty's stomach clenched. This was it. The mission Bill was talking about. The one Stefano had seen preparations for.

'Everything depends on it.' Irene gestured to the headline on the newspaper that screamed MALTA: THE MASTERKEY TO THE BRITISH EMPIRE in big letters. 'Churchill's warned we're hanging by a thread against the enemy in the Mediterranean.'

Kitty nodded. She had heard some of his speech from London on the Rediffusion as she arrived in reception, and had stopped for a moment to listen. If Malta fell, they were all lost.

Christ. And she'd been asked to betray this mission?

No, no, no. She dug her nails into her palms. What the hell was she going to do?

'We're throwing everything at this one. Biggest operation we've ever done.' Irene tapped her pencil on her notebook. 'For the first time, the RAF are working closely with the Navy, warships, submarines, the Fleet Air Arm, the lot.'

'Gosh,' Kitty said, picturing for a moment how busy the plotting table would be.

Irene raised an eyebrow. 'And between you and me, Ash has requested D Watch for the mission.'

'That's marvellous.'

'Yes, a credit to our team. And as you're one of our best plotters, I want you there.'

'Thank you.'

'Just one thing.' Irene gazed at her shrewdly. 'Bingo Hamilton is scheduled on the mission. I know some of the girls would find that difficult if . . . Well, are you going to be alright with that?'

Kitty knew what Irene was thinking. How the pilots didn't always make it back. She swallowed.

'You can rely on me.' God, how she wished she had sorted things out between her and Bill last night. How she wished she'd told him about Stefano . . .

'Good.'

Kitty glanced at the telephone on her desk and cleared her throat. 'Just one more thing. Might I make a short telephone call? I want to, erm, let someone know about the new flat.'

Irene threw her a quizzical look. 'I'll allow it this one time. But you know the rules. Two minutes.'

Irene pushed the telephone across the desk, got up and left

the room. Kitty picked up the receiver, waited for the exchange and gave Maria's number. Her chest tightened as the line clicked through.

Please be in. Please, she thought. She had to know where Stefano was. She had to.

But the phone just rang and rang.

'The enemy convoy is taking thousands of German soldiers to Rommel in North Africa. It's a big convoy – four liners, five merchant ships, as well as two destroyers and a battlecruiser.' Ash rapped the reconnaissance photographs with his stick.

'Intelligence reports have reached London that it will be leaving Naples, heading for Tripoli. We have to stop it.'

He looked round the Briefing Room, full of aircrew, naval officers and Maltese staff. He stood shoulder to shoulder at the head of the room with all the big guns – a cluster of senior officers from the RAF, the Navy, the Fleet Air Arm and an unusually young-looking major, sporting a monocle, from the Allied Intelligence Corps. Kitty had never seen him before. She was also surprised to see Admiral Cunningham, Commander-in-Chief of the Fleet, recognising him from Father's drinks parties.

Their caps, a row of brocade and gold insignia, stood on the table in front of them.

'The fall of Crete has taught us a lot of lessons about how to defend ourselves,' Ash continued. 'Now the War Office in London have sent orders to our governor. We have to stop the Germans taking Egypt. If they do, the door to the Empire is wide open to them.'

Kitty's chest tightened and she balled her fists. Why did it have to be the most important mission they'd ever run that

Stefano was asking her to betray. What on earth was she going to do?

'And the situation has never been more serious. We must stop this enemy convoy reaching Tripoli. At all costs.'

A murmur ran round the room.

'I emphasise again,' said Ash. 'At. All. Costs.'

They all knew what that meant.

Everyone in the smoke-filled room fell silent, the air thick with tension, fuggy with the heat of too many bodies crushed together.

Nausea swirled in her stomach, panic reaching up through her insides and gripping her heart. If only Bill were here. She glanced wildly round the room. But she couldn't see the back of his head among the officers lined up in front of her.

Everyone was staring at the briefing board, a mosaic of maps, reconnaissance photographs and string tied to pins showing squadron routes in and out of the target. She knew many of the officers from nights out with Bill, pilots from 69 Squadron and from 249 Squadron, although she didn't know the naval officers or flying officers from 830 Squadron of the Royal Fleet Air Arm. The whole of D Watch was there, along with some of her women colleagues from the Filter Room, Radar and Wireless Intercept. So where was Bill?

Ash continued, jabbing at the large photograph of the ships, tiny marks on the grainy photos taken from over 16,000 feet up.

'Reconnaissance reports show the convoy consists of these four: *Esperia, Marco Polo, Oceania* and *Neptunia.*'

He pointed them out one by one, his finger and thumb pinched round a cigarette, waving it so the inch of ash threatened to flake off and singe the pictures.

'We can't allow these troop reinforcements to get through to Rommel. As you know, he already has our troops pushed right back to Egypt, and holds Tobruk under siege.'

The other commanders nodded in agreement.

'So, in a combined air and sea operation, submarines HMS *Urge*, *Unbeaten* and *Upholder* will be sent to intercept the convoy as they reach south of Messina, followed by RAF Blenheim low-level torpedo bombers.' Ash looked round the room. 'However, in view of the high number of recent Blenheim losses, 69 Squadron will also help with the attack.'

Murmurs of surprise rustled round the room.

It was just as Bill had said. Kitty shifted on her metal chair, unease creeping through her.

'Reconnaissance Marylands from 69 Squadron are being re-equipped to carry bombs and will go in first to distract the convoy, so the second strike-force of thirteen Swordfishes of 830 Squadron can come in with torpedoes, before the main attack by the Blenheims.'

'Excuse me, sir.' A hand waved at the back.

'Yes?'

'Are the Marylands really up to it? They haven't been used for bombing for years.'

Ash eyed the young pilot, a cheeky-looking fellow with a green silk cravat at his neck, and slowly tapped his cigarette out in the upturned Nazi shell case that served as an ashtray.

'You've heard about the accident this morning, Macintosh?'

Kitty stiffened. What accident?

A buzz broke out around the room.

They'd already had an accident at Filfla? This was what Bill had feared, she knew it. What had he said? *The planes weren't really cut out for dive-bombing*. Her heart thudded. She imagined plunging down, down, your stomach rising in your throat, the roar in your ears deafening, the cliffs vast, filling your windscreen, and in a split-second, before it was too late, you had to drop your bombs, then pull up, the engine screaming, praying you hadn't left it too late . . .

Ash hushed the room.

'One of the aircraft sustained some damage during dive-bombing practice this morning at Filfla, the rocky outcrop just south of Malta. Just a hatch off. Nothing to worry about. Macintosh, I'd spend more of your time worrying about that anti-aircraft flak Jerry'll be warming up for us.

'Now, I've asked D Watch to run the Operations Room – thank you, Irene.' He nodded at her standing against the wall to the side, and Kitty caught her eye.

'And we need a slick and well-run operation on the night.'

Ash continued the briefing, the pilots clarifying flying heights, route directions, expected timings. Behind Kitty, the door opened and a draught of fresh air blew in. She glanced round. One of the girls from the Filter Room peered in, scanning the room. Her eyes lighted on Kitty, and she beckoned to her. Kitty got up, as heads swivelled round to see what all the disturbance was.

'You're wanted on the blower,' the woman whispered. 'The Telephone Exchange. Said it's urgent.'

Her insides dropped. Was it about Bill? Had he been in the accident after all?

She picked up the receiver in the Filter Room.

'Hello? Katherine Campbell speaking.'

'Kitty.' A woman's voice. 'Is that you?'

Kitty breathed out. Ċensa! Thank God.

'Ċensa, are you alright?'

'We've been so worried about you. We heard about the terrible bombing in Floriana. Then Erminia told me someone had asked for our number this morning and I knew it must be you.'

'I'm fine. Listen, Ċensa, do you know where Stefano is?'

'No.'

'Look, he threatened me . . .'

'What?' A gasping sob.

'Ċensa, he's spying—'

'He's gone.' She broke down, sobbing. 'We don't know where he is. He left yesterday. Taken all his clothes, everything with him.'

Kitty's stomach dropped into her shoes. 'Are you both alright?'

A sniff. 'Omm's distraught.'

'Have you any idea where he's gone? Anywhere at all?'

'No.' The line crackled badly.

'Think, please, Ċensa.' Kitty's ears strained for the answer over the hiss on the line. 'What about that boy, that friend of his?'

'Lorenzo? He was called up ages ago.' Ċensa sounded puzzled.

Of course. Of course Stefano had been lying about that. But she had to find out where he was. She had to. Then she could report it and the whole terrible choice would go away. 'Think, Ċensa. Is there anyone else he'd go to? Anywhere he'd feel safe?'

'I don't know. Nowhere I can think of.'

Christ, he couldn't just have vanished into thin air. Where the hell could he be?

'Please, don't turn him in. It would break Omm's heart. Please. If he contacts you again, do what he wants.'

'Ċensa, please think. Where could he be?'

She gripped the Bakelite as if she could squeeze the answer out of it, every inch of her willing Ċensa to say where he might be, release her from this terrible decision she had to make . . .

But the line went dead, just the long hum of disconnection echoing in her ear.

'Ah, we wondered where you'd got to.'

Irene hurried over as Kitty walked into the Operations Room. 'It's been a busy afternoon.' Irene nodded at the plotting table, covered in marked-up red, yellow and blue blocks, the other plotters busy pushing them across the big map. 'You alright to help out for the rest of the shift?'

Kitty nodded and picked up a headset, her mind still in a daze. She smiled absent-mindedly at Rita, who was frowning at something she was hearing through her headphones.

'Stallion Blue Two at twelve thousand feet, vector 265.' Bill's voice came over the speaker.

Kitty startled.

'Bill's out?' she asked Irene. 'I thought he was practising at Filfla.'

Irene shook her head. 'They're tracking the convoy.' She glanced up at Ash, on the Shelf. 'They want regular reconnaissance checks on its position. Bingo's the best there is.'

'I'll plot him home.' Kitty reached for a block and placed it ready on the table, glad for a moment to push the whole horrible decision aside. The sound of his voice made warmth bloom deep inside her, her body unconsciously responding to him, linking them together. She was glad she was here to watch over him. She would will him back, bring him home.

She listened for his aircraft position in her headphones. 'Stallion Blue Two at Angels eight, approaching N for Nuts,' she called.

'Roger Stallion Blue Two, glad you're back,' Ash said into the radio telephone, sitting back in his chair on the Shelf, smoke curling round his head. 'Convoy still on target, I trust?'

'Still on course. Fierce barrage from the welcoming committee, though. Betty'll need a bit of a patch-up,' Bill called over the roar of his engine.

At least he was not far from home now. For the first time that day, the knot in her stomach uncoiled a little, soothed again at the sound of his calm, confident voice.

'Roger that. Nice work, thank you, Bingo. You can come home now,' Ash called. 'Luqa, stand by for incoming friendly.'

Irene smiled reassuringly. He was over Maltese waters, only a few minutes away from home now. Kitty breathed out, inched his plot forward.

'Stallion Blue Two descending to Angels seven.'

Rita's alarmed eyes flitted to Kitty's as she received instructions on her headphones.

'Bandits approaching, Bandits approaching at ten thousand feet, heading south,' Rita called, placing a new block on the table. 'Two Me 109s approaching.'

Fear pricked at Kitty. Her heart speeded up. Two enemy fighters? Christ.

Ash frowned, leaning over the balcony, focusing on the plotting table.

'Watch out, Stallion Blue Two. Two Bandits behind you.'

'Roger, copy that.' Bill's voice sounded urgent, louder, and as he pushed forward the throttle the engine noise rose in a crescendo to a high-pitched roar.

Lillian's voice came over Kitty's headphones from the Filter Room, giving her his position.

'Stallion Blue Two now at ten thousand feet.'

She pushed his plot forward an inch into the next grid square, over the coast of Malta. Her throat closed as Rita pushed the Hostiles into the same grid square as Bill.

'Climb, Bingo, to twelve thousand feet. Get on top of them,' Ash called. He turned to the guns officer at his side. 'And get every bloody AA gun you've got blazing.'

'Affirmative, over.' Bill's engine whined as he forced more power out of it.

'Stallion Blue Two climbing to Angels twelve,' Kitty called, pushing his plot forward.

Ash glanced at Irene, shaking his head. 'Damn. There's no one left I can send up.'

Kitty shut her eyes, the hairs rising on the back of her neck. He had to get above them. He had to. But he would have his work cut out in his slow Maryland. The Messerschmitts were much faster, could run rings round them. He'd be wringing every knot out of his aircraft, glancing frantically out of the cockpit to see if the Me 109s were in sight yet. And the plane was damaged.

She gripped the edge of the table, steadying herself against it. And Frank just behind him in the aircraft would be trying to get his machine gun lined up, desperate to get a shot at them.

Every muscle in her body clenched as she waited for the next radar position to be reported from the Filter Room, so she could push his plot another inch closer to Luqa.

'Stallion Blue Two over St Paul's Bay,' Kitty called, pushing his plot forward. He was so close to landing.

But the Me 109s were dangerously close behind him. Rita lifted anguished eyes to Kitty and pushed the enemy plot right next to Bill's.

'Eyes open, Bingo,' Ash called. 'Bandits at six o'clock.'

'Spotted them,' Bill cried. 'Tally ho!' The staccato of their machine guns, the throttling whine of the engine. The radio cut out.

No one spoke.

Up on the Shelf, Ash sucked at his cigarette. Ops stood motionless, frowning at the table, the phone clamped to his ear. Kitty's headphones crackled as the Filter Room passed on a radar direction finding report that Bill's plane had descended.

'Stallion Blue Two at four thousand feet,' she called into her mic, adjusting the plot height and position, her blouse sticking to her back, the rush of blood in her ears loud. He must be coming down to gain more speed. 'Descending to two thousand feet.'

He was nearing Luqa now. So close. Just keep him safe, she prayed, please keep him safe. The chant ran in her head on a loop as she plotted him down, the Me 109s in pursuit.

Total silence fell. Ash blew out a long stream of smoke.

He was fighting for his life. Kitty couldn't breathe.

Seconds felt like hours.

Then the words she never wanted to hear in her headphones.

'Plot on Stallion Blue Two faded.'

'Plot on Stallion Blue Two faded.' Mechanically, Kitty

repeated the words into her mic, as if her voice hadn't caught up with her head.

Faded.

Gone. Shot down.

As the words sank in, a strangled noise caught in her throat. Her rod dropped from her fingers and hit the table, the sound cracking round the room like a bullet. She leant against the table, desperate to hear further messages in her headphones. A sighting of Bill, a glimpse of a blip on radar, a call on the R/T.

Across the table, Rita moved the plots of the two Me 109s as they turned and retreated back across the sea to Sicily.

But there were no further plots on Stallion Blue Two.

Chapter Thirty-Nine

'They may have bailed out at the last minute.' Ash tapped his V for Victory cigarette and eyed her carefully through a wreath of smoke. 'They may be picked up. Bingo's bailed out before, hasn't he?'

Irene, sitting beside her, nodded. 'And a Hurricane pilot was rescued, remember two or three weeks ago, just off the coast near Dingli.' She put her hand on Kitty's. 'Let's give it a few hours, shall we?'

Kitty nodded, picked at a loose thread on her skirt. The shift had ended in a blur after she'd removed Bill's plot from the table. She'd felt numb. Rigid. Gone through the motions mechanically, as she was expected to do, remained professional, stayed calm, calling aircraft positions, marking plots, pushing them across the table as if she could keep going for ever.

Irene had kept glancing at her across the room and at one point, she'd seen her exchange anxious looks with Ash. The only time she thought she might lose it was when Rita, pushing a plot near hers, squeezed her arm and whispered, 'I'm so sorry,' in her ear. Tears burnt at the back of her eyes, but she had blinked them down.

Frank would have gone down too. It would break Adela's heart. A tear squeezed out then. She wanted to be the one to tell her.

After the shift ended, Ash and Irene had asked her for a quick word and led her to his office. Numb to the core she nodded politely, unable to focus on what they were saying, their words swimming in her ears, her eyes fixed on the poster behind them that urged them to take care; who knew who was listening; walls have ears. Her cup of tea stood cooling, untouched, in front of her.

'We just don't know yet, Campbell. But the Kalafrana seaplane boys'll be out looking, you can be sure of that. And we bloody well need his crew for Operation Intercept.' He looked at her and jabbed his cigarette out in the saucer. 'So buck up.' He threw her a quick smile and got to his feet.

'You'll be the first to hear if there's any news.' Irene smiled reassuringly, and patted Kitty's hand again. 'I'm sorry, Kitty. It's awful waiting.'

'Thank you,' whispered Kitty, as they both left the room.

It seemed odd, unworldly, that it was still day when she emerged from the tunnels, blinking in the sunlight of the summer evening. Kitty gulped at the fresh air, feeling like she couldn't breathe, crushed by the weight of it all. It was as if a lifetime had passed since she set foot inside that morning, not just a day. Nausea still fizzed in her stomach and she needed to sit for a moment. Rest.

Think what to do.

She walked to the Upper Barrakka Gardens, the eucalyptus trees throwing long evening shadows over the paths, and passed under the colonnades of arches. She leant over the wrought iron railing overlooking Grand Harbour, relishing the warm breeze against her cheeks. Far below, the water glittered like diamonds in the golden light and two frigates moored in the docks looked as if halos glowed around them. The sight soothed her. She sat down on a bench and watched a *dgħajsa* being rowed across the water, the ripples from the narrow boat flowing in an ever-widening bronzed triangle behind.

She realised then just how much she wanted to spend the rest of her life with Bill. She had felt unlovable for so long, had been so surprised to find love again, that she had fought against it, not trusted it, when it was right there in front of her.

And she should have talked to him about Stefano. God, how she longed to have his advice with this soul-wrenching decision she faced. Time was ticking by and she still had no idea what to do. Panic rose in her throat like acid as her thoughts drifted to Stefano. She swallowed it down. *Think about Bill*, she told herself.

Darling Bill.

All the kind things he had done for her over the last few weeks. How he kept showing how much he cared. How he accepted Alice. She may not have known him long, but war had a way of collapsing time, intensifying feelings, making small things count for so much more. She should have let him go off knowing they would be together, that he meant as much to her as she did to him.

She should have said yes.

As dusk fell, Kitty leant against the wall, her mouth dry as sawdust, a strange nausea tossing in her stomach, waiting by the back door of The Star for Adela. She could hear the top notes of the saxophone, the bass of drums, the buzz of cheers and shouts from the servicemen inside – happy people, snatching a joyful evening in the midst of war. They seemed a world apart right now.

Strait Street was busy with sailors, soldiers, airmen, spilling out of bars and cafés, arm in arm, singing, chattering as shadows deepened over the long flight of steps up the hill. Some gave her curious glances as they passed by and Kitty shrank back into the doorway, dreading Adela's arrival, wondering how on earth she was going to tell her about Frank, hating with every inch of her being that she would have to be the one to hurt her.

Wild clapping erupted inside, more cheers and hoots. A few minutes later, the clip of high heels on the other side of the door. Adela's voice.

'Oh, Gianni, stop complaining. You know I'll always do an encore.'

A muffled reply, then Adela calling, '*Au revoir, chérie. À demain.*'

Adela burst out of the door, her battered handbag swinging on her arm, her eyes heavily shadowed in thick stage make-up, hair glossy with oil under the stage door lamp. She stopped in her tracks when she saw Kitty's face.

'*Mon Dieu*, what is it?' She clapped a hand to her mouth. 'Don't tell me we've been bombed again?'

Kitty swallowed, ground the toe of her shoe into the pavement and shook her head miserably.

'Come, let's walk.'

She hooked her arm in Adela's and they set off, Kitty leading them down a quiet street, her throat tight.

'Why have you come to meet me?' Adela glanced at her. 'What's going on? You're making me nervous.'

'I wasn't sure if you'd be coming straight home tonight. I need to talk to you.'

'Now you're really scaring me.' She stopped and gripped Kitty's arm, her eyes flashing in the dusk. 'Is it Frank?'

'My darling, I'm so sorry . . .'

'What's happened? Is he alright?'

'Oh my sweet, they were on reconnaissance—'

'Frank wasn't.' Adela shook her head. 'He's sick. Malta Belly.'

Kitty's breath caught. 'Really?'

'Confined to barracks.'

'Are you sure?'

Moonlight glinted on the whites of Adela's wide eyes. 'Yes. He couldn't meet me today.'

'Thank God.' Kitty fell back against the wall, light-headed with relief. 'Thank God.'

'Why?' Adela frowned, perplexed. 'What's happened?'

'It's, it's . . . Bill. They were shot down this afternoon. Just off the coast.'

Adela gasped. She stood stock-still, taking it in, then reached for Kitty, her face full of compassion. Kitty's shoulders heaved as she sobbed on her shoulder and Adela let her cry, holding her close, murmuring, 'I'm so sorry, *chérie*, I'm so sorry.'

After a while, Kitty pulled away, dashing at her face with the back of her hand.

'Sorry.'

'Don't be.' From her handbag, Adela pulled out a handkerchief and gave it to her.

Kitty wiped her eyes and they sat side by side on a doorway

step. The moon came out and silvered the steps rising up the street like a line of piano keys.

'Might they be picked up?'

Kitty shrugged. 'Maybe,' her voice was flat, 'but it's been hours.'

'There's still a chance. I would keep hoping if it was Frank.'

There was a moment's silence.

'The worst thing is, I wasn't honest with him.' Kitty wiped her nose and glanced at Adela. 'And I haven't been honest with you.'

Adela gazed at her, bewilderment shining in her eyes. 'What do you mean?'

'You were right about not knowing everything about my new family. Turns out I have a half-brother.'

'What?' Adela's eyes widened.

'And I've just found out. He's a spy.'

'What? Seriously? How do you know?'

Kitty scrumpled the handkerchief into a tight ball. 'He's blackmailing me.'

'Oh, *mon Dieu*.' Adela stared at her.

'To give him secrets about this big mission we're planning.'

'What?' Outrage, alarm, flashed across Adela's face. 'You can't do that. Have you reported him?'

Kitty shook her head. 'I can't.' Tears seeped down her cheeks.

'Why not? Kitty, you have to.'

'He knows where Alice is.' Kitty's voice was dull.

Adela gasped.

'He says he'll report where she is to the Italian Fascists if I don't give him the information he wants.'

Adela stared at Kitty for a long moment, her hands on her

cheeks, as the implications of what that meant sank in. '*Ma pauvre.*' She put her arm round Kitty, pressed her temple to Kitty's. 'That's a terrible choice to make.'

They sat for a moment, pressed together in the darkness. The street was still, just the shouts and singing from drunk servicemen carousing nearby. From Grand Harbour came the distant throb of a ship's engine entering port.

Kitty told Adela the whole story about Stefano's arrival, her suspicions and how he'd attacked her in the alley. It was such a relief to tell someone. To say it out loud, to share the load, the impossible weight that was crushing her. Kitty rolled her shoulders, feeling the pressure lift as she talked. 'But I can't see a way out,' she finished.

Adela released a long breath. 'You know you have to report him.'

'Don't you think I want to do the right thing?' Kitty snapped. 'But he'll report Alice's safehouse to the Blackshirts if I don't do as he says. I don't know what the hell to do.'

'Surely he wouldn't turn in a child?'

'He will. He's desperate. He was in the Italian Army, for God's sake. He has a wireless . . . and he's been lying to us for weeks. Think how you'd feel if it was Louis.'

Adela looked up, chastened. 'You're right. I'm sorry. I would fight like a tiger to save him.'

'Exactly.'

'*Sacrebleu.*' Adela pulled out a cigarette and lit up. 'Bastard.' She breathed out a stream of smoke as if she could blow him away.

'Of course I can't betray my country,' Kitty pulled at the corner of linen in her hand, 'I just don't know what to do. I've no idea where he's hiding. If I report him and they can't find him and I don't show up at the meeting, he'll radio her location in.' She dashed at a tear. 'The army won't care about her . . . and I'll never get that letter with her address.'

'And Maria doesn't know where he is?'

'No.'

'*Merde.*' Adela tapped her ash away, thinking.

Up the street a door opened, and a rectangle of yellow light flashed across the limestone; the roar of chatter and laughter, a soldier's drunken chorus of 'Knees Up, Mother Brown' fading in the night air.

'But hold on.' Adela turned to her abruptly. 'You do know where he is going to be. In two nights' time.'

'So? How does that help?' Kitty nodded, not following.

'Think about it.' Adela dropped the cigarette and ground it out with the toe of her court shoe. 'If you report him, they can help you. You can go and meet him as he's said, but have some soldiers with you.'

'That won't work. He'll see them, run off and report her.'

'You're not thinking straight! Not if they hide. They're soldiers. They'll know how to do surveillance or something.'

'Oh my God, you're right!' Kitty sat bolt upright, as if a bucket of cold water had been thrown over her.

She'd been so shocked, confused and worried since she'd been attacked, it was as if she'd been in a fog. But suddenly, she could see a way out. 'I could lead the soldiers straight to him!'

'*Exactement.*' Adela nodded, her eyes shining with excitement.

'They can arrest him, he'll have no time to radio in and Alice would be safe.'

Her heart lifted. She was sitting, thinking it through, checking the plan from every angle, making sure Alice would be kept safe, when another thought struck her and she turned to Adela.

'We could even set a trap.' She clapped a hand to her mouth, dizzy at the possibilities. 'Give him false information, so he passes it to the enemy. Then surprise him with an arrest.' She threw her arms round Adela. 'Oh, thank you. You're a genius, Adela. I've been struggling to see a way to do the right thing. Thank you so much.'

As she hurried away up the street, a feeling of relief filled her as she realised that, for the first time, she could actually do something to keep her little girl safe.

Chapter Forty

The streets were dark as she hurried back to Fighter Command. Although it was late, she was relieved to find Ash still in his small office, tie loose, a cigarette pinched between finger and thumb of one hand, his head resting on the other, wearily going through papers. She knocked on the door and he looked up, surprised.

'Campbell. I thought your shift had finished?'

'I need to speak to you. It's important.' She shut the door behind her.

His eyes widened, but he gestured for her to sit down.

'You're wondering if there's any news of Bingo.'

'Have you heard anything?'

Ash cleared his throat. 'Not yet. But I haven't had word that they've called off the search.'

She pressed her lips together, feeling tears prick again. Her hands twisted in her lap.

'Don't give up hope.' Ash's voice was gruff, kindly. He smoothed his moustache. 'It's summer and we've had chaps in the water a few hours before. He's a resourceful sort of bloke.'

She nodded, trying to swallow back the tears. She cleared her throat.

'Actually, I have some important information I need to tell you.'

'Really?' He raised an eyebrow and leant back in his chair. 'About what?'

She took a deep breath. 'There's a spy on the island. He's trying to find out about Operation Intercept. We have to stop him.'

She told him how she had been threatened the previous night in an alley by two men, how she knew who her attacker was; but sitting opposite Ash, his scrutinising eyes on hers, she couldn't bring herself to tell him about Alice. Couldn't bear to delve into her past, reveal that much of her heart, her soul, to him in this dingy, smoke-filled underground office. And even if she did, he'd never understand. He was a man. As she talked on, his eyebrows rose higher up his forehead and his face filled with astonishment and concern. He didn't take a single drag of his cigarette.

'Good God. That must have been pretty frightening.' He tapped the drooping ash away, frowning, his expression puzzled as he digested all she'd said. 'So he's your half-brother? But I thought you were Vice-Admiral Campbell's daughter?'

'Since my father died, I have found out certain unpalatable truths about his past.' Kitty worked to keep her voice steady. 'A secret family. I have a half-sister and half-brother.'

'Good Lord.' Ash looked away, momentarily embarrassed. He pulled at his moustache. 'But why has this Montebello character threatened you now?'

'I was getting suspicious. The questions he was asking me . . .

I finally confronted him. He denied everything, of course. But it must have rattled him. That's why he attacked me last night.'

'What did he want to know?'

'He'd realised a big mission was being planned and wanted more details. Said he had noticed troop movements, the arrival of more Hurricanes, things like that. I think he's been going out at night, spying on the airfields.'

'Bloody hell. Right under our noses?' Ash sprang forward, jotting in his notebook. 'Well, we can do something about security right now. Make sure we're protecting the location of the fuel and ammo dumps, keep them hidden from prying eyes.' He looked up and narrowed his eyes at her. 'Did he say what target he suspected?'

Kitty shut her eyes for a moment, thinking back to that night in the alley. 'No. He wanted to know times, dates, numbers of aircraft, that kind of thing. Said he was being pressurised for information from Italy.'

'Did he now.' Ash's eyes were as sharp as flint arrows. He stubbed the cigarette out and picked up one of the darts that sat to the side of his desk, fidgeting with the fletching as he digested what she'd said. She'd only noticed the Nazi swastika that he kept on the back of his door as a dartboard when she shut the door earlier.

'Christ. This is all we need.' Ash rubbed his forehead. 'When did you suspect him?'

'Just a few days ago. But I had no proof, no evidence, until last night.'

'When did he want to meet you again?'

'Tomorrow night. Just before curfew. Same alley.' Kitty sat up in her chair, her gaze fixed on Ash's face. 'Look, I've been thinking. We can set a trap. I can go to the meeting, give him false information about Operation Intercept, throw him off the scent. Then soldiers can follow him back to his hideaway until we're sure he's radioed the wrong information to Italy.'

Ash eyed her admiringly. 'That's a damn good idea.' He pulled another Victory cigarette out of his pack and lit it. 'But could you pull it off?'

Kitty tried to hide the wave of irritation that ran through her, remembering Irene's words that first day. *Men expect us women to let them down.*

'Of course. We could completely throw him off the scent of the real target.'

'Yes. Not a bad idea at all.' He eyed her, drumming his fingers on the desk. 'I need to speak to the chaps in Allied Intelligence, see what they know . . . So how long do you think he's been spying?' There was a crackle as the tip of his cigarette glowed.

Kitty swallowed. She knew how bad this sounded. 'I don't know. But he arrived in Malta two months ago.'

'He *arrived* here. Two months ago?' His eyes widened and he sat forward. 'Good God, Campbell! You mean he doesn't live here?'

She shook her head. 'He'd been in Sicily. He was trapped there when war broke out.'

'Sicily!'

'He said he escaped by fishing boat,' she ploughed on. 'He said he loves Malta – he wanted to come back to help protect her—'

'And you believed that?' A red flush crept up his neck and cheeks.

'I had no reason not to.'

Ash cleared his throat and a deep crease formed on his forehead. His chair creaked as he leant forward and fixed his eyes on her. 'His landing in a small boat at night from Sicily didn't alert you that he might be a problem? When we are all on full alert for spies? Did it not occur to you to report him?'

She shook her head. 'I believed him.' Her voice was quiet. 'He's family. Father's son. His mother begged me not to tell anyone.'

Even as she said the words out loud, she realised how naïve, how stupid they sounded. Her face filled with heat.

'Fresh from Italy? At the least, didn't it cross your mind that he might have information we would have been interested in?' He gazed at her in disbelief. 'And all this time you've worked here, hearing top-secret information—'

'I never talk about my work outside here. Ever,' said Kitty, stung.

'And you've just attended one of the most top-secret briefings about one of the most important operations we've ever run.' He slammed his hand hard down on the desk. 'Do you realise how bad that looks?'

A wave of anger rolled through her and she stiffened. 'I told you.' Her voice was loud, indignant. She stared Ash in the eyes. 'Last night, he dragged me down an alley and threatened me with a knife. That was the first time I knew for sure he was spying.'

'And you didn't report it sooner?' He glanced at his watch. 'It's nearly twenty-four hours since he attacked you.' His eyes were steely. 'Why the delay? He could have been up to anything since then.'

'I'm telling you now. I'd just been bombed. I was shocked.'

Her heart thudded. She should tell him about Alice. The terrible choice. About the leverage Stefano had over her, so he would understand, but anger throbbed through her. She was trying to bloody help.

'Look, this is ridiculous. You know me. I've worked here for months. Surely you must see I was in a difficult position with my new family.'

'It all looks very suspicious,' he narrowed his eyes at her, 'and I'm left feeling unsure where your loyalties really lie. I need to investigate further. Find out more about this Stefano Montebello and his associates. And in any case, if he's following you, we need to keep you safe. You're our only lead to him.'

He reached for the telephone, started to dial and glanced across at her.

'It's probably best if you spend the night in our custody rooms here, while we carry out further investigations.'

'What?' Kitty blinked at him. 'You're arresting me?' Her voice was incredulous. After all she had told him. 'You can't do that.'

'The security of Malta is the most important thing here. I hope you understand that, Campbell.'

A few minutes later, two burly military policemen appeared in the doorway and Ash gestured at her. 'Take her down to the cells.'

'Wait, no. This is ridiculous. You can't do this.'

Kitty looked up at the two burly officers, both sweating in their uniforms, truncheons swinging from their belts, puffing from hurrying down the corridor. She was more used to seeing them in Strait Street, manhandling drunken soldiers after a night in the clubs.

The officers glanced at her, momentarily surprised to see a woman was the troublemaker, then stepped to each side of her and in one smooth movement hooked their arms under hers and pulled her to her feet.

'Stop,' she pleaded with Ash. 'I'm telling you the truth. We need to make a plan for tomorrow.'

But the officers almost lifted her towards the door.

Ash came round the desk and looked her in the eye.

'If what you say is true, you've nothing to be afraid of. But we need to investigate all this.' He nodded to the military police officers. 'Take her downstairs.'

The soldiers' boots hammered on the long stone corridors as they went down several flights of stairs and turned left and right along different passages. The air grew dank the further down they went. She hadn't known there were so many floors below the Operations Room.

They arrived at a metal door marked *Cell 4*. One of the officers fished in his pocket and pulled out a bunch of keys on a long chain. The door screeched in the echoing silence as he unlocked it and pushed her forward through the gloomy doorway.

She fell against the far wall. The room was bare: stone walls, a metal bucket and a small wooden pallet like a wide shelf, a pile of thin military blankets folded at one end. The air was thick and stale, fetid in her nostrils, making her feel nauseous again. A single light bulb swung from the ceiling, emitting a slight buzz. She'd had no idea these cells were even here. Who on earth had been put here before her?

'Alright?'

The officer stood by the metal door, about to shut it, his gaze filled with a mixture of curiosity and reluctance about locking up a civilian woman.

She stepped forward. Bile rose in her throat and she worked hard to swallow it down. Her heart raced. He was going to lock her in this tiny space.

'Wait. Please.'

He hesitated, holding the door a few inches ajar. 'What is it, miss?'

'How long will I be here?'

He shrugged. 'Dunno, miss. That's up to them upstairs.' He looked her in the eye. 'Sorry. But orders is orders.'

And he swung the door so it thudded shut, a loud clang reverberating off the walls of the narrow cell. The key clunked in the lock and their footsteps retreated down the corridor and faded away.

The sudden thick silence throbbed in her ears.

She slumped on the bench. Anger rose up that Ash didn't believe her, when she was telling the truth. All she'd wanted was to plan how they could capture Stefano and not give him any chance to radio Italy and give Alice's whereabouts away. She had taken a huge risk in deciding to tell him. And now it had all gone wrong.

She kicked the bucket and it flew across the tiny space, clattering against the wall, rolling backward and forward with a grind of metal until it stilled. She'd just put her face in her hands when a thought struck her, making her freeze as if an ice cube were sliding down her neck.

Suppose Ash thought he could just take soldiers to the alley and arrest Stefano tomorrow night, without her?

Her heart thudded. Stefano was smart. He would spot the soldiers, leave, radio Italy and give away Alice's location to the Nazis . . .

No, no, no.

She rocked herself, shivering with fear. She had to be involved in that arrest. She had to be the bait. She had to keep Stefano thinking they were working with him until the moment they arrested him. And they could use Stefano to their advantage, didn't Ash see that? Give him false information, get him to tell the Italians the wrong target for Operation Intercept, and then follow him so they could arrest him before he had a chance to betray Alice.

Her fingers felt for the photograph folder in her pocket. She should have told Ash about Alice. How Stefano was using her little girl to blackmail her into giving him what he wanted. Then Ash would have understood. She needed another chance to persuade Ash of her plan to trap Stefano. Time was running out. She had to make that meeting tomorrow night. She had to.

She hammered at the door, shouting and shouting, until her voice went hoarse and her throat ached.

But no one bloody came.

Chapter Forty-One

Minutes seemed to pass like hours as she sat in the gloom of the tiny cell. The bulb buzzed in a high monotone that set her teeth on edge. Shivering, she pulled up a blanket and huddled against the wall.

Above all else, there was still no news of Bill. Was he still alive? Bile burst up her throat again and she rushed for the bucket and vomited. She knelt, gripping the bucket, and retched again, strings of saliva hanging from her lips, until her throat was sore and her insides hollowed out.

When the urge to be sick passed, she sat back exhausted, wiping her mouth. Why was she vomiting so much? She had eaten little in the last twenty-four hours and yet she felt so nauseous. But then she'd felt nauseous a lot lately . . .

A faint fluttering in her stomach, like the brush of butterfly wingtips, tickled her insides, low in her pelvis. She breathed in sharply. She knew that feeling. Remembered it from all those years ago, when she was carrying Alice.

Was she pregnant again?

She sat up, her body tingling with excitement. No wonder her breasts were feeling swollen and tender. She tried to remember her last period, trying to tick the weeks off on her fingers, but for so long now she had been preoccupied with Maria and Stefano, distracted with work and Bill, and they muddled in her mind.

She thought back to that first time, the passion and desire, the many nights since of tenderness and joy. She hugged her stomach, smiling, filled with elation at the miracle growing inside her.

Whatever happened, she still had a part of him, she still had his baby to love and cherish. How blessed she was. Darling Bill. How thrilled he would be if he knew. Happiness welled up, a warmth spreading inside her.

She knew then.

She was stronger now. She would cherish this baby, bring up this child alone this time, even if Bill didn't come back. She would find a way, for Bill's sake and for hers, no matter what the challenges.

But first she had to save her other child.

The rap of footsteps approaching in the corridor woke her.

Her head throbbed; her eyes felt heavy, her tongue furred as a wet flannel. The footsteps stopped outside her cell door.

She glanced at her watch, blinking, disorientated. Eight o'clock. It must be morning.

Voices, the scrape of metal, the clank of keys against the lock. The door creaked open and the guard came in.

Kitty drew herself up, fighting the morning sickness that threatened to overwhelm her.

'I need to see the air officer commanding. Right away.'

Minutes later, she was back in Ash's office sipping a steaming cup of tea and eating toast. Kitty took it as a good sign that she appeared to no longer need a police guard, but there was still a fluttering feeling in her stomach. She forced down the plain bread, hoping it would settle it.

Footsteps sounded outside, down the corridor. Ash was coming. Kitty stiffened.

'Kitty?'

Her head whipped round. She took a sharp breath.

'Bill?'

It was him. He was alive.

She jumped up and ran to him. 'Thank God. Oh Bill, it's you!'

But the eye on the good side of his face was red and swollen like a squashed plum. A bandage, now bloodstained, had been wrapped round his head. A deep cut slashed his chin. He broke into a crooked smile and she flung herself into his arms. His face sought hers and covered every inch with kisses, murmuring her name over and over. Kitty pressed herself against him, drinking in the warmth of his firm chest, the strength of his arms around her, the distinctive tang of salty seawater, never wanting to let him go.

'That's quite a welcome.' His bloodshot eyes shone. 'Not quite what I imagined as I bobbed about in the Med.'

'They found you,' she whispered. 'No one told me.'

She shivered and dropped into the chair next to Ash's desk, staring up at him. He was dressed in borrowed clothes, a knitted sweater that was too big and baggy trousers.

'Seems I'm becoming quite the old hand at swimming my way out of trouble,' he smiled, squatting down beside her. His face looked pallid with exhaustion. 'We were in the water about four hours. Have to say, it may be summer, but that sea is bloody freezing.'

Her heart squeezed.

'My God, look at you.' She took his scarred hand and gently interlaced her fingers with his. 'And the others?'

'All picked up, safe and sound.' He smiled. 'Frank was off sick, lucky bugger, but Tubby and Jim got picked up with me, although Tubby's got a bullet in his shoulder,' he grimaced. 'He's at Imtarfa having an op.'

Kitty's eyes filled with relief. 'You're really here,' she whispered. 'Bill, I'm so sorry. I was trying to tell you, the other evening when you came to say goodbye. I wanted to—'

'No, Kitty, it's my fault. I shouldn't have reacted like that. I was too proud, too insecure when I stormed out that day.' He shook his head. 'I had a lot of time to think when I was in the drink. About you, and me.' He looked her in the eyes. 'How much I wanted to survive just to tell you one more time how much I love you. That your love is the greatest gift I could ever receive. How I knew you did love me, but I was throwing away our chance of happiness together out of my own foolish pride. It doesn't matter if you don't want to marry me, if I can just be with you.'

'But I do want to marry you, I do. I want to be with you. When I thought I'd lost you . . .' She choked.

'Oh, Kitty.'

He pulled her close and kissed her, their lips soft and warm, melding together.

Bill pulled away. 'Anyway, what about you? What's all this nonsense about you and a spy?'

She shut her eyes, wishing she'd told him weeks ago. 'He's my half-brother.'

'Your half-brother? What half-brother?'

'I should have told you about him.' She sighed. 'But right

now, we've got to stop him. He says if I don't do as he says, he'll tell contacts in his *battaglione* where Alice is hidden.'

'You know where Alice is?' His eyes filled with confusion. 'What on earth's happened?'

She poured out the whole story, how she hadn't wanted to hurt Maria, had believed Stefano had escaped from Sicily. How when she started having doubts about him, she hadn't wanted to make Bill complicit in the secret. How she hadn't fully realised what Stefano wanted until he'd threatened her in the alley, blackmailing her with Alice's life. How she hadn't known what to do.

As she talked, Bill paced the small office, his battered face frowning.

'I don't understand,' Bill said, his hands behind his back. 'Ash is a sensible sort of bloke. Why wouldn't he believe you? He may not agree with you knowing about this Stefano chap for quite as long as you have, but surely he can see what you're suggesting is a good way forward? We get Stefano, you ensure Alice's safety . . . what's the problem?'

'I didn't tell him about Alice.' Kitty's voice was quiet. 'He doesn't understand the hold Stefano has over me. I couldn't bear to tell him . . .'

'Oh, my love.' He picked up her hands, kissed her fingertips.

'So it doesn't make sense to him, why I would keep it secret.'

'Keep what a secret?' Ash barrelled through the doorway, Irene close behind him. He frowned. 'Don't tell me there's more I need to know?'

Half an hour later, Irene was crammed in beside her and Bill on hastily found chairs round Ash's desk, along with General

Roberts from the British Army, a solid stocky man she'd seen at various briefings and whom Ash just called Hugh; and a young officer, Major Johnny Vernon, from the Allied Intelligence Corps, whom she'd only seen at the Intercept briefing before.

In fact, before that she'd never seen anyone from the Allied Intelligence Corps – their door, marked *Entry only to authorised personnel*, was always kept firmly shut. She glanced at him, her interest spiked. He was a determined-faced chap with a swallow's wing of black oiled hair. He kept earnestly pushing in his monocle, his eyes opening in surprise as Kitty finished explaining about her little girl.

'Good Lord,' he said. 'It's all a bit improper.'

'Hmm. It is rather irregular.' Ash frowned disapprovingly at Kitty. 'But it does make more sense now. I suppose I can see why it took you nearly twenty-four hours to report his attack.' He tapped his cigarette, so that an inch of white ash fell into the shell cartridge. 'Montebello put you in a tricky position—'

'An impossible position for a mother,' Irene interrupted, smiling reassuringly at Kitty. 'Goodness, I don't know what I'd have done in your shoes.'

Ash cleared his throat and glanced at Major Vernon, who held up a thick military intelligence folder, stamped *Top Secret* in large red letters across the front. 'Anyway, turns out Johnny here has quite the file on Montebello. Certainly backs up what you're saying about him.'

Kitty could see Stefano's name upside down in the top right-hand corner. Major Vernon opened it and flicked through some of the pages inside.

'Seems you're right about him.' Major Vernon's voice was

plummy and clipped. He pushed his monocle in and glanced up at her. 'Did you know Stefano Montebello joined Malta's pro-Italian Nationalist Party, when he was sixteen?'

'The Nationalist Party?' Kitty startled.

'They didn't want Malta to be under British rule any more. They had some sway back then.'

Kitty nodded. 'It was all in the papers when we first arrived here.'

She remembered how angry Father had been about the Nationalists, how he would thump the dining table at how misguided they were and ask why they didn't recognise all that Britain was doing for them. Little had she known how personal Father's rages about the Nationalists had been. His own son was one.

'When war was declared, everyone in the party was rounded up,' said the major. 'Montebello was arrested with several others, including their leader, Enrico Mizzi. They're interned here.'

'Except it seems Montebello was released from prison,' Ash sucked at his cigarette and a ribbon of smoke drifted across the papers, 'on special orders from Vice-Admiral Campbell, who offered to guarantee his security. A few months later, Montebello disappeared.'

'Christ,' Kitty breathed out. 'That's when he ran away to Italy.'

It was all making sense now. How mortified Father must have been. Why he'd forbidden them all to talk about Stefano. Why Maria wanted his return kept secret.

'Now, if I understand the situation correctly,' Ash said, 'this Montebello character still has some dangerous leverage over the life of your daughter.'

'Exactly. I'm extremely concerned to think of the danger

she's in. It's bad enough that she's in Rome at all.' Kitty's throat closed as the image of her little girl playing with her plaits flashed in her mind. She put the cup down in its saucer. 'So I've thought long and hard about what could be the best plan.'

They all nodded expectantly.

'I'll go to the rendezvous tonight. I can give Stefano false details about the operation. We should keep it to the same time, so the timings work on the night, but we can give him a false target, false numbers of aircraft involved and so on.'

'Won't he be expecting that? Think I'd be jolly suspicious of someone betraying her country quite so easily.' Ash frowned.

Irene and Kitty exchanged irritated glances.

'It's not "easily", Ash.' Irene said. 'He knows how much she cares about her daughter.'

'He brought me her photograph,' Kitty said. 'He also has a letter from Rosa, the woman who runs the safehouse, that he knows I'm desperate to have.'

'I'm sure he'll believe Kitty,' Irene continued smoothly, 'he'll be convinced she's trying to save her child. He knows what we Maltese mothers are like.'

'Right.' Kitty nodded, grateful for Irene's support. 'Now, what we don't know is where he's hiding out, or where his wireless is. Nor do we know what time he radios back to Italy—'

'She's right, you know,' Major Vernon interrupted her, surprise in his voice.

Kitty caught Irene's eye.

'Wireless operators do usually follow a set pattern and timing,' the major continued thoughtfully, 'so we'll need to follow him back to his hideout, watch his routine and let him send the signal back. Nor do we have a clear idea of how many others are involved. Miss Campbell's right. We probably shouldn't arrest him until Intercept begins. If at any time things don't seem absolutely shipshape to his receivers in Sicily, they might guess it's a trap.'

Kitty nodded. 'It's got to seem like a completely normal day. We can't give the game away.'

'And of course, we'll have troops providing backup at all times,' said General Roberts.

Ash twiddled a dart in his fingers, his eyes gleaming. 'This could be a marvellous opportunity. We could completely distract them with false information. Get them to move troops, aircraft, to the wrong places. It could change the course of the war in the Mediterranean.'

'It could certainly help us.' Bill's eyes shone. 'We could tell them we're bombing Tripoli, that would get them to move fighter planes and troops there – all in the wrong place. That would give us the advantage of surprise and make the convoy a much easier target for us.'

'Excellent idea.' Ash nodded at Bill. 'Right, leave it with us to plan the details.' He snapped the folder shut. 'Go home and rest, Campbell, you look done in after that night in the er . . .' he coughed, 'downstairs. We'll need you on top form tonight to make this work. Let's meet again at 17.00 hours in the Briefing Room, and we'll run over the final plan of action.'

The morning sun was high in the azure sky as Kitty and Bill emerged from the tunnels and took deep breaths of the salty fresh air.

A seagull drifted overhead and Kitty glanced down the

narrow street to the sparkling sea, waves rippling silver as a frigate chugged by. She held her face up to the sun and wondered where Alice was right now. Was she outside under this same bright sun? The thought warmed her and for the first time in ages, she felt a calmness, a peace, a sense that if this went well tonight, she might finally get to read that letter, find out more about her daughter.

They walked back to Kitty's flat, where she washed away the grime of the cell and fell into bed, revelling in the fact she could stretch out properly and sleep. Bill sat on the bed beside her, and she stroked his bandaged head.

'Won't you join me? You must be exhausted.'

He kissed her. 'Darling Kitty. I have to get back. We're doing practice flying at the cliffs in Filfla all day today.'

'Surely not after yesterday?'

'No one else can fly the Marylands and we're so short of planes, especially now we've just lost mine,' he grimaced. 'Look, it'll all be over in a couple of days. I want to do my best, make sure Intercept is a success.'

He lay down and took her in his arms. They kissed, a long deep kiss that Kitty wished could go on for ever.

Eventually he pulled away. 'I must go,' he whispered, his voice hoarse.

She couldn't bear for him to leave and held him tight in her arms, suddenly wanting to give him the greatest gift that she could. She stared at him as he buttoned his uniform jacket, straightened his cravat, a sudden shimmer of fear running through her as she recalled Dexter's reaction to the same news. She dismissed it. That was then. This was now. Bill was a better, kinder man. She was stronger, braver.

'I have something to tell you.' She sat up in bed and thumped the pillow behind her. She took his bruised hand, interlinked her fingers gently with his and looked him in those swollen eyes. 'I'm not a hundred per cent sure yet, it's early days. I need to see a doctor to confirm things . . .'

He looked at her, his face suddenly filled with hope, his eyes shining with excitement. 'Kitty, darling. Are you saying . . . ?'

She nodded, smiling. 'We're having a baby.'

He let out a whoop, gathering her in his arms, and his eyes filled with tears of joy.

Chapter Forty-Two

The street was silent when she received the signal to step outside that night. She walked towards the alley, her shoes tapping on the stone as she passed the pump. No one was about. Not even the moon was out, instead hidden behind a cloud. She glanced round feeling alone in the darkness, even though she knew armed soldiers were watching her from windows and doorways and from the faked plumbing repair van parked just across the street. Another team huddled behind a heap of blown-up masonry, waiting to follow Stefano when he left.

The alley to her right was like a black mouth ready to swallow her. Kitty hesitated at its corner. She glanced up at the blank, blacked-out windows of the buildings opposite, listening for a tell-tale cough, or sneeze, a murmured instruction.

Nothing but silence.

Goosebumps rose as she remembered last time. The sack constricting her throat, the blade piercing her neck. She shivered, although it was a warm evening, pulled her cardigan across her chest. She could do this. She mentally ran over everything they had covered in the briefing; she had memorised the plan, the fake time and fake location. *Don't embellish. Don't appear to give the information too willingly.* Ash's words rang in her ears.

Her fingers reached for her baby's photograph in her pocket. She could do this.

She stepped forward. A rustle from behind. She whirled round, her heart thumping. A quiet miaow, the scrabble of paws landing on a wall.

Just a cat.

She breathed out, her heart thudding. She took another step forward, touching the walls to feel her way. Darkness swallowed her until she couldn't see the way back to the alley's entrance. She stopped, waited, shifting her feet uneasily.

Maybe he wasn't going to come. Maybe he didn't need her information any more.

A crunch in the dark. She spun round.

'So blood is thicker than water.'

She could hear an edge of relief in his voice.

'Stefano.'

'I'm glad you're here.'

A glint of moonlight on his thick glasses, the smell of garlic and cigarettes on his breath. Beside him she could just make out the bulk of the other man, the glint of the blade in his hand. Her breathing quickened.

'You gave me no choice.'

'Are you alone?' He sounded agitated, jumpy.

'Yes.' Her voice echoed back at her between the walls.

'Do you have the information?'

Kitty's chest tightened. What she wanted to ask was so important to her. 'If I give it to you, will you give me the letter about my daughter?'

'I don't think you're in a position to negotiate.' His voice sounded amused. 'Not if you want her to stay safe.'

Kitty's heart thudded. She must tread carefully. 'Of course I do, but you know how badly I want to know where she is. But if I tell you everything about Intercept, I still won't know where she is, unless you give me the letter.'

He breathed out sharply and she could feel his impatience rising. But she had to know, she had to.

'If what you tell me proves to be correct, you keep her safe. Isn't that enough?' Stefano shifted his feet.

'Please, Stefano. You know how important the letter is to me. How much I need to know about her.' She turned to him, her voice pleading, playing up to the role he had cast her in. 'I'm giving you what you want. That was the deal.' She gripped his arm. 'Isn't it enough for you that I'm betraying my country?'

He shook her hand away. 'OK, OK. If the mission goes ahead as you tell me, I'll make sure you get the letter.'

'How? Do you want to meet again?'

'No.' He hesitated, thinking. 'Maybe the church—'

'*Basta*!' The stocky man muttered to hurry it up in Italian.

Kitty's heart thumped. The church? Which church? What did he mean?

'What? Can't I just meet you?'

'You won't see me again, sis.' He shook his head. 'My boat—'

'Shh, Stefano.' Another shorter figure stepped forward from the blackness, a hat low over their face. 'Be quiet.'

Kitty startled, unable to believe her ears.

'Ċensa?'

Kitty screwed up her eyes, desperate to see the slight figure in the dark. 'Ċensa? Is that you?' Christ, surely she couldn't be involved in all this. 'What the hell are you doing here?'

'I'm with Stefano now.' Ċensa raised her head defiantly, and the point of her chin caught a glimmer of light as the nearly full moon came out from behind a cloud. Her hair was tucked up under a man's straw hat. 'We have to save my country.'

'Oh Ċensa, sweetheart.' Kitty released a long breath. 'You're not saving your country. You're giving it to the Fascists.'

'Our friends. And they'll stop the bombing and bring us peace,' said Ċensa, her voice full of defiance.

'What?' Kitty swallowed, stunned at the naivety of her words.

Kitty's head throbbed. How long had Ċensa been involved in this? Surely Stefano must have dragged her into it, dazzled her with his stories of life in Italy, like a returning prodigal brother. Kitty's fists clenched as a wave of fury swept through her.

'How could you, Stefano. Maria will be devastated. You know she hates the Fascists. What kind of monster are you?' She shoved against him and he stumbled.

The other man growled and stepped forward; a gleam as he raised the knife.

'*Stai zitto.*' *Shut up.*

A stinging blow across her face. A metallic taste filled her mouth, her cheek burning as if pressed to a hotplate. Sparks of light blizzarded in the darkness.

'Just give me the information,' Stefano growled.

Kitty swallowed. Sweat slicked under her arms. She needed to calm down, do what he said, not antagonise them. Focus. She needed them to believe her. Kitty blinked in the darkness, dragging the plan from the corners of her mind.

'It's tomorrow evening.'

'We'll have to move fast,' Stefano grunted in the darkness. 'Target?'

'Tripoli Harbour.'

He whistled quietly. 'You're sure?'

'Yes.'

'Not Trapani?'

'It's Tripoli.'

He put his face close to hers, that smell of garlic and cigarettes again. 'How do I know you're not lying?'

'Why would I lie? My daughter's life is in your hands.'

He grunted, stepped back.

She needed to convince him. 'It's a major attack. They're throwing everything at it. I was at the mission briefing at Fighter Command. It's a big bombing raid, several waves . . .'

'What time?'

'First attack wave is leaving at 19.30. Second at 20.00.'

Words in Italian. Something about a change in tactics, needing to radio in, she couldn't quite hear. The other man gestured at her, asked a question. More rapid talking.

Did they believe her? Her heart pounded. What would she do if they didn't? She must hold her nerve, stay silent. She pressed her lips together.

Stefano turned to her.

'How many squadrons?'

'All of them, including 249 Squadron and 69 Squadron.' They would know that from watching the airfields. She didn't need to mention the Navy's Royal Fleet Air Arm.

'Ships?'

'That's all I know.'

Stefano grunted, hesitating. 'Come on. Are battleships involved? Destroyers? Submarines?'

She swallowed. 'I work at RAF HQ. We're just briefed on aircraft movements.' She fought to keep her voice calm, level. Be convincing. 'I don't know anything about ship movements, now Father's dead.' She wanted to remind him. Make him think of Father. Their shared blood.

Stefano grunted. 'Well, we'll see, won't we? If the attack happens as you say, Alicia will be safe. If you're lying . . . you'll never see her again.'

They turned, their footsteps scraping as they left the alley.

Half an hour later, Kitty was back with Bill and the other officers in the stuffy gloom of the Briefing Room at Fighter Command, where Ash had gathered the team. They pored over a map of Malta spread across the table under the dim light bulb. The whirr of the ventilation seemed louder at night, with fewer people around.

'I'm pretty sure he believed me.' Kitty leant over the map. Stefano's last words still echoed uncomfortably in her mind. *If you're lying . . . you'll never see her again.* 'And the surveillance teams still have him in their sights?'

Ash glanced at Major Johnny Vernon. He pushed his monocle in and nodded. 'They won't lose him.'

'I think he's bamboozled my half-sister Ċensa into joining him. But she's not a spy. She's just a simple village girl.' She looked at the major. 'Please. Go easy on her.'

His eye squeezed his monocle tighter. 'We'll see about that.'

'I think he's got a boat coming to pick him up,' Kitty continued. 'It sounds like he's leaving soon.'

'His cover's blown. If I was him, I'd leave too,' said Bill. His eye was still swollen and purple and the jagged wound across his chin oozed, catching the bulb's light.

'You're right,' said Major Vernon. 'We'll keep a tight track of his movements until we're ready to arrest him.'

'He won't leave in daylight,' said Ash thoughtfully.

'I think he'll leave tomorrow night, straight after the mission, after he's made sure all is as I said. He definitely seems under pressure for this to go well,' said Kitty. 'He mentioned a boat. I think he'll slip away as he arrived, in a small fishing boat.'

They all stared down at the map.

'The question is, where?' said Major Vernon. 'If we knew, we could get a boat in place to intercept it—'

'I think I know where he'll leave from,' said Kitty.

They all stared at her. 'Where?'

She remembered the conversation she'd had with him in the garden, weeks ago, the fond way he'd spoken of the fishing trip with Father. She pointed at the map.

'Here, this cave at Għar ir-Riħ. Fisherman's Cove.'

'I don't think so,' Major Vernon said dismissively. 'Rather too near the seaplane station at Kalafrana, I'd say.'

'Exactly,' said Kitty, looking round at them. 'No one would think of looking there.'

It was after midnight when Kitty and Bill finally walked home, arm in arm, their footsteps echoing in the quiet darkness as they walked towards Kingsway. No one was about except a patrolling ARP warden who checked their passes and told them to keep it down. Kitty glanced at Bill's swollen eye, the bandaged wound on his head. Was it even safe for him to still be flying, after the crash and all the shock?

She squeezed his hand. 'How was it at Filfla today?'

'Fine,' he said, but his voice wavered. 'The Maryland's just not that happy pulling out of such a steep dive, but I'm getting there.' She saw the flash of his teeth as he smiled at her in the darkness. 'At least after your sterling work tonight, those ack-ack guns and Messerschmitts won't be expecting us.'

She smiled, a little surge of triumph swelling her chest. 'I hope you're right. I hope it works and they arm Tripoli to the back teeth. Still, I wish you didn't have to go up tomorrow, darling. You need rest.'

'I wouldn't miss it for the world. The biggest op we've done yet?' They turned towards her apartment. 'But afterwards, Ash has promised me leave. Maybe we could get away to Gozo for a day or two?'

'I'd love that.' She laid her head against his shoulder. Maybe she could visit Lydia too, make her peace with her.

'Kitty Campbell, anyone would think you cared about me.'

She hit him lightly on the chest. 'You know I do.'

'Well, in that case . . .' He stopped and fumbled inside his jacket, pulled out a small round box from a pocket. 'I think we should make this official. I didn't do it properly last time.'

She smiled as he knelt down, happiness surging through her.

'Katherine Campbell, I thought when I was in the water the other day that I would never get the chance to ask you this again. But here I am, the luckiest man alive.' Moonlight caught the earnest sparkle in his eyes. 'Kitty, I love you so much and I can't wait a second longer. Will you make me the happiest man alive by saying you will marry me?'

She wanted to laugh, cry, shout for joy, as she stuttered out her reply. 'Yes, oh yes.'

He rose to his feet, kissed her and grabbed her left hand, gently threading the ring onto her finger.

Her heart fluttered as she gazed down on the diamond band glistening on her outstretched hand, thinking how precarious such happiness was in wartime; how, like life, it could be destroyed in an instant at any moment, and how lucky she was to have this second chance.

'There,' said Bill. 'We're officially engaged.'

He kissed her again, and the astonished ARP warden patrolling across the street slung her bell under her arm and applauded in the darkness.

Chapter Forty-Three

'All set, everyone? Any further questions?' Irene looked at Kitty and the other eight women of D Watch, gathered round the plotting table. 'There's a lot riding on this mission. Let's give them our best show, eh? Keep your nerves steady and concentrate on the detail. Good luck, everyone.'

There was a buzz in the Operations Room that evening, an air of expectation hanging along with the fog of tobacco, a sense of something important happening. Everyone had dressed a little more smartly. Bright lipstick, polished shoes, a jaunty brooch here and there, as if they could sense the importance of the night.

Even Ash up on the Shelf for once looked formal in his buttoned-up jacket, the gold on his cap and buttons glinting in the overhead light, the rows of ribbon-bars under the wings on his chest a testament to his battle years, although of course a cigarette was still pinched between his thumb and forefinger as usual. There were several senior officers from across the services in the gallery with him, including an admiral and General Roberts, and the usual buzz of chatter and banter was restrained today. Major Johnny Vernon nodded down at Kitty and smiled.

'Well done for last night. I knew you'd pull it off,' Irene whispered. She glanced up at the senior officers on the balcony. 'They're still underestimating us.' She rolled her eyes at Kitty.

'And how,' Kitty said, remembering the major's dismissiveness last night. But she was worried. The plan had to go right. They had to arrest Stefano before he realised he'd been lied to.

All day she had watched the skies, anxious to spot any unusual activity. Had the enemy found out they had the wrong information? Were they trying to run a big counter-attack or bomb the aircraft before they could take off? But everything seemed like business as usual, just the standard raids.

The first wave of four Marylands, Stallion Reds, whose role was to find the convoy heading down from Naples and then lead the thirteen Swordfishes of the Fleet Air Arm 830 Squadron to it, took off first, at 19.30 sharp. They got off to a good start, no enemy aircraft in sight, and had a clear run away from Malta, heading in the direction of Tripoli in case Stefano was watching. They then looped round far out to sea to set a new course for just off the toe of Italy, to where the fast-moving convoy had progressed. D Watch were taking a moment's break, lighting cigarettes, making cups of tea and dashing to the lavatory.

Bill's plane was in the second wave, the Stallion Blues, which had taken off a little later. As she placed the plot marking his four Marylands on the table, she couldn't help but think Bill's group were like bait – going in to launch the main attack to distract the enemy fighter planes and anti-aircraft guns from attacking the heavier bombers that were following just after. As the Marylands climbed higher into the evening skies, she pushed their plot over the Malta coast and back out towards Messina.

Ash wished them the best of luck on the R/T. 'Be a sport, Bingo. Get a troopship for us.'

Bill laughed over the drone of his engine. 'Righto, we'll do our best. Great visibility and beautiful sunset up here. We'll be back before you know it. Stallion Blue Two, over and out.'

Radar ran out at thirty miles offshore. They would be in Italian waters by now, heading to the last sighting of the convoy off the Italian coast. Radio contact was forbidden. They didn't want to give away their positions to the enemy. Luckily the weather was good, the day had been hot, the skies clear, and she thought about Bill up there in his cockpit. She prayed his eye was less swollen today, his scarred hand strong enough to pull up the throttle to get him out of that dive.

We'll be back before you know it. He was trying to reassure her. He knew she'd be listening. Waiting.

From the balcony, she heard her name called. She looked up. Ash was holding some black and white photographs and beckoning her upstairs. She hurried up the staircase, nodding at the other senior officers.

'Thought you'd like to know, old girl.' He thrust an aerial photograph of an unfamiliar harbour into her hands. 'Good show last night. Some reconnaissance chaps have been out this morning over Tripoli and these have just arrived. Look, you can see. Here, and here,' he gestured at the photograph, 'they're moving troops – see these dots, they're Nazi trucks – closer to defend the port.'

He pulled out another photograph from the pile on the desk. A wider shot in the desert of an airfield covered in tiny crosses. He pointed at these. 'Best news is these. Flown in this morning. A squadron of Messerschmitt fighters and a few Junkers 88s.' He looked up at her triumphantly, a twinkle in his eye. 'It worked. They think the raid is at Tripoli.'

'So there'll be fewer fighters protecting the convoy?'

'You bet.' He smiled. 'You did it. Montebello passed on the information. And they bought it, hook, line and sinker.'

'Thank God.' She breathed out and gripped the balcony behind her. It was working, the plan was working.

'Good show.'

'Well done, good work.'

Major Vernon and General Roberts smiled at her.

'Any news on Stefano's whereabouts?'

Major Vernon smiled, the monocle lying on his chest.

'You were right about that Fisherman's Cove. He's moved round Malta a fair bit today, checking the airfields and so on, but most recent word is they're holed up in an abandoned hut on the cliff above the cave. We're keeping a close watch on them. Intercepting their wireless communications and so on. We'll go in for the arrest as soon as our chaps get close to target.'

'Right. Just so long as he doesn't realise he's got the wrong target—'

'Don't you worry.' He winked at her. 'I've a team already in position, ready to swoop in on them.'

'Thank you.' Kitty exhaled, relief flooding through her.

'It would actually be helpful if you could come down to the cove, soon as you've finished here, to identify him.'

'Good idea.' Ash shoved the photographs onto the desk behind him. 'Excellent work, Campbell. Because of you, we've got a much better chance of stopping that convoy.'

A few hours later an undercurrent of tension simmered in the Operations Room. The attack must be over and the Marylands were due back any time now. Everyone was silent, listening, waiting for the first radio call to come in. Up on the roof of the Auberge de Castille and around the island, Kitty knew spotters had binoculars trained on the night skies. Kitty couldn't stop checking her watch. She drummed her fingers on the plotting table. What had happened in Italy? Had they sunk any ships?

Up on the Shelf, Ash took a drag at his cigarette, leaning over the balcony to stare at the table. He caught Kitty's eye and nodded.

'Friendly four, Angels fourteen. Approaching vector 230,' Rita suddenly announced into her microphone, delight in her voice. A ripple of relief ran round the room. Kitty stiffened. Please let it be Bill.

But of course it was the first four Marylands of 69 Squadron, the Stallion Reds, that appeared, who had led the Swordfishes to the convoy, picked up by radar as they approached the island. Rita tracked their position and height as they flew closer to home and the whole room cheered. Messages started coming through, phones ringing, as the Filter Room fed the information through to the plotters and to the officers on the Shelf. The air crackled with expectation. Ash jumped to his feet, talking into the phone, his conversation with the aircraft pilot relayed over the tannoy.

'Welcome back, Stallion Red One, Ash here. Any luck out there?'

'We caught them by surprise alright!' There was delight in the pilot's voice over the roar of his engine. 'Landed a few hits on a couple of the liners, before their guns woke up. Over.'

A murmur of relief rippled round the room.

'Pretty fierce barrage once they spotted us, though. But we gave 'em as good back! Over.'

Kitty's fingers tightened on her rod as she exchanged glances with Irene. 'A pretty fierce barrage' – that was what Bill, in the next wave approaching the convoy, would be flying straight into, paving the way for the Blenheims.

Ash sucked at his cigarette, smiling. 'Great news, Stallion Red One. Head into land, soon as you can.'

The plotters moved their wooden blocks marking Stallion Red Section across the table. Inch by inch they pushed them forward until the first wave of Marylands landed at Luqa.

Kitty clamped her headphones securely to her head, straining not to miss a message, longing to hear the voice from the Filter Room giving her a position for Stallion Blue Two and the other Marylands.

'Friendly three, approaching N for Nuts, Angels fifteen, vector south-west.' The voice rang out in her headset.

Kitty froze. Friendly three? There were supposed to be four. The other Marylands Bill had been leading were a group of four. Her heart thudded. Pulling herself together, she repeated the position into her microphone and moved the plot to the Malta coastline.

The minutes ticked by and the plots busied on the table as the skies nearing Malta filled with more returning Swordfishes.

But where was the other Maryland? Fear gripped like iron bands round Kitty's chest as she pushed the plots closer to home.

Ash stared at the table, fingers tapping the desk, absent-mindedly flicking ash off his cigarette. He picked up the radio phone.

'Stallion Blue Two. Do you read me?' Ash called. The room fell silent.

The loudspeaker crackled and buzzed. Everyone seemed to be holding their breath. Kitty's palms were wet as she held the rod.

'Stallion Blue Two, come in please.'

More static. A silence.

Then a loud roar. A voice.

'Stallion Blue Two, hearing you loud and clear.'

It was Bill. His voice filled the room.

All the air seemed to leave Kitty's body. He was alive. Thank God, he was alive.

A loud sigh of relief rippled round.

'Bingo, what luck out there?' Ash cut to the chase.

'Ted's bought it. He took some flak, tail on fire, crashed into the sea. We circled round, but no sign of life.'

'Damn.' Ash breathed out heavily.

A heavy silence fell in the room. Kitty's mouth went dry. She quietly removed the Stallion Blue Three plot from the table and called the 'plot faded'.

More crackle on the tannoy. 'But direct hits on two merchant ships and another merchant vessel burning amidships,' Kitty could hear the triumph in Bill's voice, 'and looks like the whole damn convoy's turning away.'

'Nice work, Bingo, thank you.' Ash punched the air and grinned round the whole room. 'You can come home now.'

The officers on the Shelf rose to their feet like a wave, cheering and clapping. The plotters put down their rods and cheered. Kitty ran forward and hugged Irene, jigging with joy.

They had done it. And Bill was still alive.

Now she just had to make sure Stefano was arrested.

Chapter Forty-Four

The car crunched in complete darkness down the winding gravel road, headlamps blacked out, until the soldier driving brought it to a halt.

'Better walk from here, sir,' he said over his shoulder to Kitty and the major in the back seat. 'Don't want to get too close to the cliff edge.'

Kitty and Major Vernon climbed out. The warm wind caught her hair and whipped it round her face; the tang of salt tasted sharp and she was deafened by the crashing roar of the waves as they pounded the rocks below. They walked in the pitch black, tripping over clumps of spiky shrubs, to the edge of the cliff, the major shouting over the wind to her to be careful. They stood on the cliff edge, the full moon glimmering across the wide bay, highlighting rows of silvered waves that raced across the sea towards them. To her left, round the corner of the cliffs, yellow searchlights criss-crossed high in the night sky.

As her eyes adjusted, she made out the shapes of jeeps and trucks along the clifftop and the outline of a hut. Voices called to one another in the dark. A soldier staggered out of the hut door carrying a heavy box-like suitcase and put it in the back of a jeep. Bet that's the wireless, she thought. My God, how long had Stefano been transmitting messages from here?

'Is that where they've been hiding?' Kitty gestured to the hut.

'Yup, they've been camped out here a while, we reckon – there's bedding, a Primus ring and so on,' said Major Vernon.

'Has he messaged Italy tonight?'

'Last contact was at 18.00 hours.'

Kitty breathed in sharply. 'Do we know what Stefano said?'

'He confirmed the target. And their position for pick-up.'

'Are you sure?' Her voice wobbled with anxiety.

'Ah yes,' the major's monocle caught in the moonlight as he turned to her, 'your daughter. Don't worry, we intercepted the message. No mention of the little girl and there's been no radio contact since. Your daughter's safe.'

'Thank you.' Kitty breathed out, speechless with relief. Her shoulders dropped, her legs turned wobbly and she suddenly felt weak. 'What about the letter? Have you found it?'

'Not so far, but we'll keep searching.'

They hurried across the cliff towards the hut, Kitty's fists clenched at her sides. Might Stefano have hidden the letter there?

She had to find it. She had to.

She went through the open door, where two soldiers were still searching the place with flashlights. The small hut smelt damp. Her feet crunched on the wood floor as she gazed round and her eye caught on a small rickety table, covered with maps and notebooks. She grabbed a notebook and rifled through the pages, then picked up another and another, shaking them to see if an envelope dropped out.

Nothing.

Kitty's gaze fell to a mattress on the floor. She picked up the corner and searched underneath it, lifted the small pillow. Nothing. She shifted aside the canvas camp bed, shook the blanket. She stood up and gazed round. Dammit. There was nowhere else to look. Her mind whirred, wondering where the letter might be. Maybe Stefano still had it on him?

'The letter's not here.'

The major appeared at her side.

'We've done a thorough search of the place. Those notebooks contain rows of figures and numbers, aircraft most likely. Positions of fuel dumps. It's extraordinary to think how long he might have been feeding information to Italy.'

'Christ.' It was worse than she'd thought. How long had he been coming here, spying on them all?

They went back outside and walked to the cliff edge.

'So, turns out there is a rowing boat in the cave below,' the major cleared his throat, 'as you erm, suggested. After that last wireless message our men went down to it. Looks like they planned to row out to a fishing boat. The Navy have sent a ship to locate it.'

As Kitty squinted in the darkness, the head of a soldier emerged along the cliff edge, his helmet silhouetted in the silver light, presumably coming up from a path that went down to the cave below. He was swiftly followed by another figure, then another, their rifles catching in the silver moonlight, until a group appeared on the clifftop.

Had they caught Stefano? Her mouth went dry. Was Censa still with him?

A tall man came into view and the glint of glasses on his face made her heart leap into her mouth. From his height and the slope of his broad shoulders, that had to be him. Her stomach tightened. Thank God. A soldier pushed him down and she realised his hands were tied behind his back. A stocky shorter man was pushed down beside him, and then a short slight figure.

Ċensa.

Dammit, why had she joined in with all this? Kitty's chest tightened.

'Right, here they are.' Major Vernon nodded in approval. 'Could you come and identify our ringleader?'

They walked towards the prisoners sitting on the ground, ringed by soldiers. Stefano looked up.

'You!' his voice rang out in the wind. 'You did this?'

'Kitty! Why are you here?' said Ċensa, startled.

'You betrayed us,' Stefano said, fury in his voice. 'Our own sister gave us away.'

Kitty looked down at him, contempt running through her veins like ice water.

'You gave me no choice. You betrayed us all. And you blackmailed me. You were going to give up my daughter. How could you?' She longed to punch him, kick him, pummel his smug face with her fists.

'I didn't know he'd threatened Alice like that.' Ċensa's voice was sulky. 'I would never have hurt her.'

Kitty crouched down and looked Ċensa in the eye. She shook her head. 'Ċensa, my little sister. Why did you do this? Did you think what it'll do to Maria?'

'I'm sorry if it hurts her.' She stared at Kitty, defiance flashing across her panicked face. 'But she must see I had to help my country.'

Kitty shook her head. 'Oh, Ċensa . . .'

The major stepped in and kicked Stefano's boot. 'So this is Stefano Montebello?'

'It is.' Kitty stood up. She crossed her arms. 'Where's the letter, Stefano?'

He stared up at her. Even in the darkness she could see the rage on his face.

'As if I'd give it to you now.'

'Where is it?' Her voice rose in the night air.

'*Vaffanculo!*' *Fuck off!*

The major gave orders to the waiting soldiers. They pounced on him, roughly searching his pockets, raking through his clothes so that he cried out, even pulling off his boots and shaking them.

There was no letter.

When they'd finished, Stefano released a low laugh.

'You'll never find it,' his eyes flared behind his glasses, 'and you'll never win. We'll defeat you. And then I'll come after you.'

Kitty lunged, grabbed him by his jacket collar and shook him so hard his glasses fell off his face.

'Where is it, Stefano?' she shouted. 'Where have you put the letter?'

He wriggled out of her grip and raised his chin defiantly as the soldiers cocked their guns.

'I've destroyed it.'

Kitty drew herself up, her heart banging in her chest, and slapped him round his smug face.

'Liar!' Anger boiled through her and she kicked out at his foot. 'You're lying. All you do is lie. To all of us. And I don't believe you.' The blood pulsed in her ears. 'I will find it, you bastard. We've searched the hut. And I'll search everywhere else until I bloody find it.'

He didn't reply. Just pressed his lips together and gazed out to sea.

Chapter Forty-Five

The next morning, Kitty was back on duty at 8 a.m. At Morning Prayers, Ash, looking ten years younger and grinning from the previous day's successes, was perched on the desk at the front, and for once, instead of smoking, bounced a tennis ball from hand to hand. The feeling of celebration as he looked round the men and women gathered in the Briefing Room was palpable. For the first time in ages, people were smiling and there was a relaxed feel to the place.

'We heard late last night. The War Office in London has sent its congratulations to us all. Operation Intercept has been a great success. We've hit the Axis supply lines between Italy and North Africa badly and bought us some breathing time to equip our own troops.'

Cheering and clapping broke out around the room, and Ash waited for it to die down before continuing.

'Early reconnaissance shows that two ships were hit in the attack, one merchant ship was left burning amidships, and the convoy has been forced to turn round and limp back to the port at Taranto in Italy. This has stopped, at least for now, the arrival of yet more German troops in North Africa.' He cleared his throat. 'I am also pleased to announce that, along with our colleagues in Allied Intelligence, we have caught a spy. He, along with his accomplices, is in custody and will be dealt with by the courts.'

Astonished murmuring rippled round the room.

His eye fell on Kitty.

'We owe a great vote of thanks to one person who has helped us stop this appalling haemorrhage of information that could have been so damaging for us. I'd like to thank Miss Katherine Campbell for her help in bringing him to justice.'

All heads in the room swivelled to stare at her and Kitty shifted in her seat.

'You did a great job for us yesterday, Campbell. I've discussed it with Irene and we're pleased to announce that we'd like to appoint you Captain of C Watch. I know you'll do a sterling job.'

'Thank you.' Kitty smiled back at him. 'I'd like that very much.'

It was a few days later and the sun was still hot in the sky as Kitty cycled into the main square in Żebbuġ, after her shift had ended. An old woman in a faldetta hurried by, a small loaf under her arm, and a man pulled a small cart piled high with white figs and apricots.

She wandered into the shade and propped her bike up against the trunk of a pink flowering oleander tree, and a wave of sadness filled her, thinking of all the happy times she had spent here. She glanced in the direction of Maria's street, hoping that one day, she might be able to visit her again. If Maria could ever understand. Ever forgive her.

Guilt crushed her heart, heavy as a stone. But Stefano, in making his choice of who to support in this war, had left her no choice.

Now he and Ċensa were in prison, waiting to be tried by a British war tribunal. Judging by the newspaper billboards, Malta was up in arms at the spy who'd betrayed them.

A warm breeze blew and she pressed her sun hat to her head to stop it lifting off. Her stomach fluttered and she put her hand to her waistband. It felt tight, uncomfortable, her tummy expanding every day now. She would have to let out her dresses.

She shaded her eyes, the stone of the baroque church dazzling in the hot June sun, its creamy bell tower and cross bright against the cobalt-blue sky. She hoped, prayed, her hunch was right. After all, it was her last chance. It had taken her a while to figure out what he might have meant when he said *Maybe the church*. Maybe *our* church, he had meant. Where he had met his young lover.

The stones of the square shimmered as she walked, heat baking through her sandals. She went up the steps inside, blinking as her eyes adjusted to the gloom. The air was cool, thick with the cloying scents of incense. She gazed around at the soaring red and gold pillars and the decorated arches of the vaulted ceiling. Beyond the rows of wooden pews, a woman knelt in prayer by the ornate gold altar, where small white candles burnt. She made the sign of the cross, rose to her feet and turned to head down the aisle towards Kitty.

Maria.

Kitty froze, rooted to the spot.

The two women eyed each other for a second, before Maria looked away. She looked thin and exhausted and a deep well of sorrow filled her red eyes. Poor Maria. She had been through so much. Kitty's chest tightened.

As she drew near to Kitty, Maria stopped. She was trembling and Kitty longed to reach out to her, to touch her, to pull her into a hug. But Maria didn't look at Kitty, wouldn't look at her. Kept her eyes fixed ahead, her lips pursed.

A chill ran through Kitty's veins.

'I'm so sorry,' Kitty whispered.

Silence pressed back at her.

Maria put her hand to the silver cross at her neck, staring distantly down the aisle towards the doors.

'I wish he'd never come back,' she said quietly.

She moved forward, still not looking at Kitty, her footsteps echoing on the stone until the door creaked and banged shut behind her.

Kitty stood shivering in the silence. She glanced round the church. How much this church had been part of Maria's life.

Of Stefano's life.

She thought of him as a choirboy, playing in the vestry; the years of family masses, the secret meetings with his first love. How he had rebelled. Angry as she was at him, a ripple of sympathy ran through her. So much damage Father had done to them both.

But that was all in the past. Now she was here to think about the future.

Flickering candlelight threw glinting diamonds across the sheen of the wooden pews, as her eyes slid round to the tall pile of hymn books stacked on one of the shelves near the back of the church. Stefano's words echoed in her ears. *We'd leave messages for each other, under the hymn books at the back of the church. Where and when to meet, you know?* She breathed in and her heart banged painfully against her ribs. Suppose she was wrong? Suppose the letter wasn't there?

She had no idea where else to look. This was it.

Hope surged through her and she hurried to the shelf, glancing round to check there was no one else in the church. A hush pressed back at her.

She picked up the old leather-bound books, their musty papery smell strong in her nostrils. Dust motes danced in the jewelled light as she moved them aside.

Was it here?

Working fast, she moved the books until she was down to the last few. She picked up one, then another, leafing through them, checking inside their covers. Nothing.

Her palms were clammy as she got to the last two books. She picked up the one on top and shook it. Nothing fell out. Nothing stuck out underneath the book below.

Her pulse galloped. Maybe he'd been telling the truth. Maybe he had destroyed it. Her stomach plummeted at the thought.

She reached out to pick up the last book and as her fingers touched the cover, she shut her eyes, unable to bear the pain of lifting it and seeing nothing there. Her fast shallow breaths echoed in her ears.

She picked up the book. Slowly she opened her eyes.

Forced herself to look at the shelf.

A plain brown envelope lay there.

Her hands trembled as she picked it up. She turned it over. There was no name on it.

She stepped to a nearby chair and dropped into it.

He had come back. He had left her the letter. Some tie of blood, or loyalty, or shared family experience meant he hadn't broken his word. Like her, he'd been desperate to do what he thought was the right thing. For a second, she felt their connection of kinship, the shared experience of their father that had brought them both to this moment.

Her fingers shook so much she could barely tear the envelope open.

She pulled out the thin paper, tightly written with a looping hand in blue ink, scarcely able to focus. The letter was in Italian and dated *18th February 1941*.

Via della Paglia, Roma was written in the left corner.

Dear Signor and Signora Montebello,

I write to you with news of Alicia to reassure you she is well. Such a beautiful, kind little girl, she is becoming quite the light in my life. She sits beside me now, running her chubby fingers through the flour as we make rigatoni on our balcony, although she prefers sweet things. I regret how much she must stay indoors, but she loves to draw and play with our dog, Biscotti. She looks forward to the day she sees you.

Tears sprang into her eyes. It was a while before Kitty could read on.

I will not write again, I fear the post is becoming less reliable.

Yours, R.

Kitty read the letter over and over, puzzling at its contents.

Of course. Alice wouldn't speak Italian. She wouldn't be allowed outside in case she gave herself away. And the woman had taken a risk in writing at all. That's what she meant when she said the post was 'less reliable'. Letters were probably read and censored by the Fascist Italian government.

She put the letter in her lap, lost in thought. Signora Rosa sounded kind. Warm. Thank God.

As she picked up the envelope, a small drawing fell out.

A simple child's figure of a little girl with two yellow bunches and a blue dress, playing with a brown dog.

Kitty's eyes blurred.

Her little girl had drawn this with her own dear hands. Her daughter.

A tear dropped down her cheek.

Alice was safe. And she was happy.

She had found her.

She had found her at last.

Epilogue

Rome, July 1944

Kitty sat under the awning sipping coffee across from the church in Piazza di Sant'Egidio, watching, waiting. Morning sunshine shafted over the terracotta rooftops into the square, turning the dark cobbles a soft grey, warming the ochre and apricot walls of the houses, and brightening the pink flowers of the bougainvillea growing up the walls.

The square was quiet, just an old man smoking in the shade of a pomegranate tree, an old woman hurrying with her basket to join the bread queue round the corner, so unlike the rest of Rome that bustled with the sea of khaki, jeeps and Vickers machine guns of the Allied Eighth Army. Not to mention the crowds of displaced refugees.

Rome had only been liberated a month ago. Bill had wanted her to wait before she came, until the Allies had pushed further north to Florence. It was true Nazi troops were still not that far away and last night, as she'd lain in her bed in her pensione, she'd heard distant gunfire echoing in the hills. But Kitty had been adamant. The Allies were advancing in France after D-Day, the Germans were in retreat across Europe, and she couldn't wait another minute to find her.

She had waited far too many years already.

She pulled Rosa's letter out of her bag.

She couldn't believe she was finally here, that this day that she had dreamt of for so long might finally come. Her stomach fizzed with a mix of excitement and apprehension. She had grown used to the empty ache that had filled her insides, to all the years of yearning and hope, of grief and sadness and disappointment.

She stared at the little drawing Alice had done of herself. It seemed unreal, unworldly, that at last she might finally hear Alice's childish laugh, stare into Alice's beautiful eyes, that she might put her arms round Alice and hold her tight. She swallowed, trying to steady her galloping thoughts.

But the letter had been sent three years ago. Who knew what might have happened since, especially as Rome had been under German occupation.

Ash had pulled endless strings to secure her a special permit to travel, and Bill had flown her to Naples. At the station, it had been a sobering reminder to see that the trains were still in Reichsbahn livery, marked with destinations like Köln or München. As the train rattled north through the countryside, she'd passed burnt-out Sherman tanks by the roadsides and lines of sticks with a Tommy's helmet on top; the unmarked graves of Allied soldiers who had died fighting.

Bill had wanted to come with her, but aside from his wounded leg, still not right after he'd been shot in the Battle of Sicily last year, she had wanted to come alone, even though the exhibition of her photographs, *The Women's War*, was opening at the Palazzo de La Salle in Valletta shortly. Adela was being a complete brick and had offered to help Bill look after Peter by day, before her evening set at The Star. Kitty smiled, thinking about her darling little boy, wondering what he was doing right now. Peter's blue-grey eyes were the spit of Bill's, and he was just as mad on planes as his dad too.

She had arrived yesterday evening, marvelling to see Rome more or less intact. It was nowhere near as damaged as Malta, although the bombing at home had finally stopped last year, after the Allies had launched the successful invasion of Sicily and started the pushback to recapture Italy. Kitty had walked round the Colosseum, vast and eerie in the moonlight, so different to how it had seemed on her journey to Malta all those years ago.

This morning she had hurried to Trastevere, and by asking locals who weren't fooled by her accented Italian and seemed delighted to chat to someone British, hugging her and thanking her for their liberation, quickly found the church that gave the piazza its name. Her skin had goosebumped as she found the Via della Paglia. It was a narrow street off the square, lined on either side by tall buildings in ochre, geranium pots on the doorsteps, washing strung between the buildings. She had gazed up, the sun hot on her face, ears straining for a child's laugh or shout, but all she'd heard was the coo of pigeons behind her in the square. The closed green shutters gave away nothing about their occupants.

Her heart banged against her ribs like a drum.

Alice lived here. Somewhere down this street. But where? There was no building number in the letter.

She had written to Rosa Cassar as soon as the Allies had captured Rome in June, but who knew in these chaotic times if the letter had ever got here.

So she watched, waited.

A young girl crossed the square wheeling a bicycle. Too young. An old woman in a headscarf went into the church carrying a mop and bucket. Too old.

She had just finished the coffee and resolved to work her way down the street knocking on doors, when a woman with dark hair, in her forties, dressed in a faded green shirt dress, hurried into the square. She carried a basket heavy with shopping. At her side trotted a brown dog.

Kitty stiffened.

Our dog, Biscotti, Rosa had written. Kitty glanced at the crayoned drawing, although she didn't need to, could see the picture with her eyes closed. The brown dog.

Her heart thudded. She left a few lire on the table and followed the woman as she disappeared down the alley, watching to see which doorway she went through. Kitty followed her and tried the door. It gave way to the shadowy gloom of a dark courtyard, a curve of stone stairs leading to her right. Above came the echo of a door shutting. Excited barking, distant voices.

She hurried up the stairs, sweat blooming on her back. Was she really about to see her little girl? She hesitated, her hand trembling on the bannister.

To have come so far, to have waited so long.

She knocked at the door. Footsteps, then the woman with the dark hair opened it, peering suspiciously through the crack. Behind her, a volley of furious yapping.

'Rosa?'

She had a kind face, intelligent shrewd eyes ringed by dark shadows, but her cheeks looked pinched, her collarbones protruding under her thin dress.

'*Sì. Chi lo chiede?*' *Who's asking?*

She was wary, and no wonder after a year of Nazi occupation. And who else might she still have hiding in her home?

'I'm so sorry to just turn up like this . . .' Kitty replied in Italian, her voice tailing away.

'Oh,' Rosa exclaimed, her hands flying to her mouth, her eyes widening. 'Are you . . . ?'

Kitty had prepared a whole speech in Italian, an explanation, an apology, but the words she had longed to say for so long burst out.

'I'm Alice's mother.'

Rosa's hand froze on the door; she looked stunned for a moment. Then her face flooded with relief.

'*Dio mio!*' She opened the door and stepped aside, gesturing Kitty in. 'Please, come in.' Her English was as crisp as if she were reading the news on the BBC. 'I got your letter. I had no idea you would come so soon.'

As Kitty stepped through into the large airy room, the dog barked even more loudly from somewhere in the flat and Rosa called to it to be quiet.

It was Kitty's turn to be surprised. 'You speak English?'

Rosa nodded. 'My husband was British, although I was born in Malta. He worked for Thomas Cook Travel Agency. We got trapped here when war broke out.'

Kitty's stomach was somersaulting as fast as it had in the Maryland flying over here, as she was ushered into a bright sitting room. Sunlight poured in from the shutters ajar over the small balcony.

Rosa bustled off to make tea and Kitty crumpled onto the small settee, her legs turning to jelly.

Alice lived here.

Her heart lurched, as on the table by the window she saw a set of crayons and a crocheted small bear.

Alice had actually touched these things. Kitty's pulse pounded in her ears. Alice was here. She was really here.

Rosa bustled back into the room with the tea-tray. 'I replied to your letter, but I didn't think you would be able to get here for months.'

Kitty shook her head. 'It hadn't arrived yet. But how is she?'

'Well. Happy.' Rosa smiled broadly. 'Loves drawing. She's out with my eldest daughter. Such a lovely little girl. I told her all about you. She's very excited, as you can imagine.'

Kitty could hardly breathe. Alice knew about her? It was more than she could have hoped for.

'I've always talked to her about her family, hoping someone would come one day to find her,' Rosa continued, sitting in the chair opposite.

'How can I ever thank you?' Kitty stared at Rosa. Such a brave woman. She had done so much for Alice and for goodness knew how many other people. 'You've saved her life. I will never be able to thank you enough.'

Rosa smiled and gestured her thanks away, but a tired look washed across her face, a look that spoke volumes of the fear of arrest she must have endured, of the knock at the door at night, the summons to Gestapo HQ.

'Many people passed through this apartment over the last two years . . .' she threw a small smile at Kitty, 'but Alice has always been my favourite.'

Tears welled in Kitty's eyes. 'Thank you, Rosa, so much. I know it won't be easy for her, for any of us, but—'

The front door banged open and Biscotti barked again, scratching at the kitchen door as running feet echoed in the hall. A little girl in a blue dress dashed into the living room, her honey plaits flying.

Alice.

Right here, in front of her.

The world seemed to stop. Time held its breath. The air stilled and went quiet. The barking, the sounds from the street outside faded away.

How long had Kitty dreamt of this moment. How long had she searched for her, how many times had she thought she would never find her, that she was lost to her for ever.

Kitty drank in this first precious sight of her, Alice's cheeks rosy from the sun, her warm hazel eyes shining, her honey hair straggling out of two plaits, one green ribbon trailing over her shoulder. So grown-up at eight, and yet so familiar. Kitty could still see the baby in her, the frizz of curly hair at her hairline, the fan of dark lashes on her cheek, her sweet rosebud lips.

'Can Biscotti have that bone now, Aunt Rosa?' Alice stopped in her tracks, startled to see Kitty. 'Oh. Are more people coming to stay?' She turned to Kitty with a shy smile that showed the gap between her two front teeth. 'Hello.'

Kitty's breath stopped in her chest. In that moment, her insides shifted and resettled, the ache deep inside her vanishing as the pieces of her cracked heart came together again.

'Alice. This is the lady I told you about, who might come one day.' Rosa's voice was choked with tears.

Kitty knelt down in front of Alice and smiled into those wide hazel-brown eyes, so like her own. Love surged through her.

Alice gazed back at her, her eyes puzzled, innocent, open. 'Are you my real mother?'

'Yes, Alice, my darling girl. I am.' Kitty opened her arms. 'And I'm overjoyed to have found you at last. I love you so much. I always have.'

Alice hesitated a moment, looking back at Kitty, her eyes widening in wonder and hope. Her eyes darted to Rosa, who nodded at her, then back to Kitty. Then the little girl ran to her and threw her thin arms round her neck. Her soft cheek pressed next to Kitty's and her warm sweet breath fluttered in Kitty's ear. And all Kitty wanted to do was pull her close, hold her little body tight and never let go.

A Note from the Author

The first time I set foot in the Plotting Room at RAF Fighter Control in Valletta, a shiver ran through me. As the museum guide described how the women of Lascaris used to plot aircraft battles and missions during the long Siege of Malta, I just knew I had to write about these unsung heroes. It was their daily work, under terrible conditions, being bombed, shot at and starved, that played such a pivotal role in shaping the course of the war in the Mediterranean.

But while many millions of women contributed to the war effort worldwide, what made these Maltese and British women unusual was that they were not part of the military. They were civilians, local women trusted with a crucial role that in Britain and other theatres of war was undertaken by WAAFs. I wanted to give some insight into just how extraordinary that was.

The War HQ Tunnels, the combined headquarters for Britain's three fighting services between August 1940 and May 1943, and the Lascaris War Rooms, are today restored and run by *Fondazzjoni Wirt Artna*, the Malta Heritage Trust. It is an extraordinary site, everything preserved as it was in World War II, a dream of a place to visit if you love history and imagining past lives, as I do. You feel the gloom, the closeness of the walls, the fuggy staleness of the air, imagine the fear and tension as bombs rained down above. I would highly recommend a visit if you are lucky enough to go to Malta.

This place is also a testament to the courage and determination of people who never flinched, fighting for years against the odds, a fortitude that led to the Allies ultimately winning the war. Cut off from the world by the Luftwaffe and the Regia Aeronautica, with warships and mines surrounding the island and being attacked day and night, they were entirely besieged. No wonder Malta was awarded the George Cross for bravery in 1942.

I also wanted to explore the dilemma women faced at that time – how to be strong, to make a difference, to make their own choices, especially in a time of war, with the gender and traditional constraints of the period. The more I read about the unusual role these women had, the more I wanted to capture a sense of what life must have been like for them as they struggled every day into the Operations Room. Nowhere else in the world suffered such intense and continuous bombing at that time. Many more bombs were dropped on Malta than were dropped on London or on Coventry. Over 1,500 civilians were killed, thousands more injured, and more than 75 per cent of homes and buildings on the island were destroyed.

As I researched, the idea for Kitty's story grew in my mind. The discovery of *Malta: War Diary*, an online daily record of attacks, air raids and missions was incredibly exciting, as was researching the archive of the *Times of Malta* for 1941. This not only made war headlines real but brought 1941 Valletta to life with its adverts for dinner dances and cinema showings, as did listening to the voices of those who served there, thanks to the Imperial War Museum Collections. I read many accounts and stories of people who lived on the island at that time, and have drawn on this research to create the backdrop and events for Kitty's story. I am particularly indebted to James Holland's brilliant book, *Fortress Malta*, Paul McDonald's *Ladies of Lascaris*, for the account of forces entertainer and plotter Christina Ratcliffe, BEM, and reconnaissance pilot Wing Commander Adrian Warburton, DSO, DFC, as well as Frederick Galea's *Carve Malta on My Heart*, Michael Galea's *Malta: Diary of a War, 1940–1945*, Diana Mackintosh and Douglas Thompson's *Spitfire Girl*, and Virginia Nicholson's beautiful book, *Singled Out*.

But of course, while real events and people inspired this book, it is above all a work of fiction. While I have tried to stay true to historical events and facts as much as possible, such as the *Illustrious* blitz that saw Germany come into the war with Malta, Luqa airfield suffering its first major attack on 26th February 1941 and the bombing of the 90 British General Hospital at Imtarfa on Easter Sunday, some details and events have been altered or imagined to suit the needs of the story. I based the Number 8 Operations Room at Lascaris from February 1941, for example, even though it only opened there in May 1941, as it seemed unnecessary for the story to include the move from its original location at RAF HQ in Scots Street.

The major attack Kitty is blackmailed about is suggested by an attack on a troopship convoy carried out at the end of June 1941. Stefano is very loosely based on a real Maltese spy, Borg Pisani, who landed from Sicily in May 1942 to report back to Italy on the island's morale and defence capabilities. He was swiftly arrested and hanged for treason in November that year. And Rosa Cassar and her safehouse in Rome were inspired by Henrietta 'Chetta' Chevalier, BEM, a Maltese woman who was credited with helping more than 4,000 people to safety. She is buried at the Santa Maria Addolorata Cemetery in Paola, Malta. A memorial garden has been planted in her honour at the Malta Aviation Museum.

Finally, the official language of Malta is of course Maltese, but the British forces at that time tended to use British street names and to pronounce Maltese words or names as they would have sounded in English. For the sake of historical authenticity, I have done the same in this book. I hope Maltese readers can forgive me.

Acknowledgements

I owe so many people heartfelt thanks for their continuing belief, encouragement and confidence in me.

First to my agent, Clare Coombes, whose sound editorial judgement has helped me develop this book beyond measure. And for introducing me to the supportive group of fellow writers at Liverpool Literary Agency. Our WhatsApp group is nothing if not entertaining!

To Lesley Crooks at the wonderful Allison & Busby for her enthusiasm about the book and whose thoughtful questions have helped to improve it. Huge thanks to Susie Dunlop and all the team for their nimble and efficient approach at launching *Wings Over Valletta*, especially to Emma Hawes for gently introducing me to the production schedule and Sara Magness for her attention to detail on the copy-edit. I'm immensely grateful to Christina Griffiths for the beautiful cover and to Daniel Scott and Amber Jupp for their sales, marketing and publicity efforts behind the scenes.

I would also like to thank Robert Navarro for kindly giving up his time to help with the Maltese language – any mistakes that remain are my own.

Back where it all began, when I had an itch to write but no idea how to go about it. Huge thanks to Adrienne Dines, novelist and writing teacher extraordinaire, whose workshop I walked into many years ago and who has so inspired me. Huge thanks to all the Byfleet Writers, Andrew Lunn, Janet Fludder, Ella Zubeidi, Wendy Lane, Mo McDonnel, Christine Dawood, Sally Blackmore and the late Sheila Fairmainer – our workshops never fail to surprise and amuse.

Special thanks to the excellent Bridport Novel Award for longlisting my work. Your faith in my chapters gave me the confidence and validation to carry on when doubt loomed. A huge thank you also to the writers and courses that have helped me learn how to write and edit a novel over the years. Nikesh Shukla at Faber Academy, Anna Davis at Curtis Brown and of course, the craft and industry advice treasure chest that is Jericho Writers.

Massive thanks to my Faber group – Jackie Ballard, Eric Burger, Katie Kuppens-Britton, Vivien Lambe, Maryam Namazie, Meera Tailor and George Wigzell – excellent writers all. I am so lucky to have found you. From the first day we got together, I have been able to trust you to critique my work, with brilliance and kindness. I literally could not have done this without you. You are geniuses all and deserve every bit of the success that I am sure is coming your way.

Thank you to my lovely Book Group, Cathy, Linda, Valerie, Dom, Jo, Elspeth, Karen and Diana for sharing my passion to read, for the many cheery evenings over the years and the enlightening, if speedy, discussions on the books. Nothing like getting straight to the heart of what makes a story work!

Thank you to all my lovely, dear friends who through the

years have shared parenting, toddlers, teenagers and empty nests and all the while kept up a steady flow of walks, joyful meals and lots of cake. In particular my Parkside pals, Lisa, Catherine, Debra, Mary, Susanne, Jackie, Sam and Chris. Thanks also to Lesley for trying to teach me about gardening while we talk books, to Mariana for keeping up the FaceTime chats no matter where she is in the world, and to all my friends who keep reminding me to stop already and have fun: Jackie, Anne, Suzy, Kate, Caroline, Sarah, you know who you are. Very special thanks to my best friend Sara Russell who has always been there, with her strong confidence I would get there eventually, holding me up with shining positivity as I slid into the sloughs of despond or wittered about plot points that weren't working.

Especial thanks to Mum and Dad, who always told me I should write a book, and every few years kept asking me if I was doing it yet. To Liesl and Kevin for all the shared memories.

And finally, to Olivia and William, who have put up with a distracted mother for years, but whose loving support and encouragement never fails. I love you more than I can ever say and I am so proud of the mature, kind and clever adults you have become.

And of course, first and last to Jonathan. My rock, my light, my everything, always.

After reading History at Oxford University, TRACY COOK produced and directed documentary series for the BBC. She moved into freelance journalism and PR, but her lifelong dream has always been to write. After graduating from the Faber Academy Writing a Novel course, she was longlisted for the Bridport Novel Prize in 2021. *Wings Over Valletta* is her first published novel. She lives in Surrey with her husband.

@tracycookwriter